EVERYBODY KNOWS

What readers are saying:

'All I can say is WOW. So well cr[...] a crime novel can get.'

'An achingly painful read, but brilliantly constructed and beautifully written.'

'A page-turner until the end.'

'I couldn't stop reading. The plot twists, characters and ending are all spellbinding.'

'What a wild crazy ride this story takes you on.'

'Dark and spectacular . . . I couldn't stop reading this.'

'Fantastic. Character development, great dialogue and fast-paced action makes this a must-read.'

Further praise for *Everybody Knows*:

'A pure hit of neo-noir. It is dark, violent, bold.' Harlan Coben

'The best mystery novel I've read in years . . . terrifying and exhilarating.' James Patterson

'Searing, timely . . . *Everybody Knows* pulls back Hollywood's velvet curtain, exposing the sordid machinations on which the industry runs and the seamy complicity which keeps it humming.' Megan Abbott

'Brilliant . . . combining the brutality of James Ellroy with the poetic sensibility of Raymond Chandler, Harper takes the reader on a searing journey into LA's underworld where truth and righteousness have become irrelevant and only power has currency. This neo-noir is a must read.'
Publisher's Weekly

'Glittering and gritty in the mode of James Ellroy's *LA Confidential*, this is [a] perfectly provocative read . . . this tale delivers the punch and pleasure of a big-screen epic.'
Oprah Daily

'A bonafide page-turner [which] pings with one-liners and scenes worthy of Raymond Chandler and Nathanael West.'
Wall Street Journal

'Fans of neo-noir will find a lot to like here, as Harper displays an encyclopedic knowledge of pop culture and Hollywood history as he spins a tale that isn't just ripped from the headlines—it's probably predicting them.'
BookPage

ALSO BY JORDAN HARPER

The Last King of California
She Rides Shotgun
Love and Other Wounds: Stories

JORDAN HARPER

EVERYBODY KNOWS

faber

First published in the UK in 2023
by Faber & Faber Ltd
The Bindery, 51 Hatton Garden
London ECIN 8HN

First published in the USA in 2023
by Mulholland Books / Little, Brown and Company
Hachette Book Group
1290 Avenue of the Americas, New York, NY 10104, USA

Typeset by Typo•glyphix, Burton-on-Trent DE14 3HE
Printed and bound by CPI Group (UK) Ltd, Croydon CRO 4YY

A CIP record for this book
is available from the British Library

ISBN 978–0–571–38245–3

2 4 6 8 10 9 7 5 3 1

For Megan

I have lived in the monster and I know its entrails.

—José Martí

PART ONE

This Brutal Phantasmagoria

Chapter One

MAE

The Chateau Marmont

Los Angeles burns.

Some sicko is torching homeless camps. Tonight they hit a tent city in Los Feliz near the 5. The fire spread to Griffith Park. The smoke makes the sunset unbelievable. The particles in the air slash the light, shift it red. They make the sky a neon wound.

Mae waits outside the secret entrance to the Chateau Marmont. She watches Saturday-night tourists wander Sunset Boulevard, their eyes bloodshot from the smoke. They cough and trade looks. They never thought the Sunset Strip would smell like a campfire.

Mae moves around the sidewalk like a boxer before the fight. Her face is sharp and bookish, framed in a Lulu bob. She wears a vintage floral jumpsuit. She's got eyes like a wolf on the hunt—she hides them behind chunky oversized glasses. Nobody ever sees her coming.

She shifts her weight from foot to foot—these heels weren't made for legwork. She put them on for a first date she canceled twenty minutes ago when she got the text from Dan. No big loss—the date was with a stand-up comedian she met on Bumble. Comedians on a date tend to treat a woman like a test audience, or like their shrink, or they think you're a chucklefucker and they don't even have to try.

Dan's text had read HANNAH CHATEAU ASAP followed by the number for Hannah Heard's new assistant. Dan's text was cryptic per usual. The rules say *keep as much as possible UNSAID*.

The Chateau Marmont: the hippest no-tell hotel in the world. This shabby-chic Gothic castle slouching against the base of the Hollywood Hills. The way to the hotel proper is up a small winding road to Mae's left. This secret entrance on Sunset leads straight to the grotto where the private cottages are. The unmarked door built into the white-brick wall is made of green cloth—someone could slash it easily and go marauding among the rich and famous. But no one ever does.

Chateau jobs tend to be messy. They tend to be drama. They tend to be a fucking blast. Hannah Heard increases the odds of all three exponentially.

The green-cloth door swings open. The girl on the other side is early twenties. She's got blue hair and an Alaska Thunderfuck T-shirt worn as a dress—her vibe is manic pixie e-girl. Her eyes are wide like a rabbit in a trap. Mae pegs her as having a milk-brief life in the Industry. It's not that the girl feels fear—it's that she lets it show.

The rules say *wear your mask tight*.

"I'm Hannah's assistant. Shira." She swallows her voice before it can make it all the way out of her mouth. The sort of on-its-face weakness that makes Mae chew the inside of her cheek. "You're the publicist?"

"Something like that. Take me to her."

*

4

In the grotto everything is Xanax soft. The hooting of the Strip fades away. Even the smoke stench from the wildfires is blotted somehow. Everything rustles dreamlike, all bougainvillea and bamboo and art deco stained glass. On each side of the grotto sit six little cottages. There is a brick lagoon at the center of it, still and tranquil, full of water lilies and mossy stones.

One thing breaks the dream: The concrete Buddha at the foot of the lagoon is spilled on his side. The fall decapitated him. His severed head smiles up at the sky. Mae figures it must have just happened. The Chateau is pretty good about hiding bodies.

Shira sees Mae looking at the toppled god.

She says, "She had a long flight."

The girl knows how to say things without saying them. Maybe she'll make it here after all.

Hannah's cottage smells like an industrial dump site—the ammonia bite of whatever they've been smoking makes Mae's eyes tear up. She turns to the assistant before she can close the door behind them.

"Leave it open."

"The smell—"

"Nobody cares."

The cottage's front room is beyond trashed. Clothes in piles tumbling out of Gucci luggage, this mix of couture and sweatpants. Room service trays and empty bottles crowd every surface. A plate of fries jellied in ketchup. Kombucha bottles turned into ashtrays. A tray of Dom Pérignon and Cool Ranch Doritos. On the table a baggie of something yellow-white like chunks of bone sits next to a well-used glass pipe. Mae looks down—she's kicking rock-hard dog turds. It must have taken weeks to do this damage—but the assistant said Hannah just flew in. Hannah's running a tab when she's not even in town—and the cottages go for a grand a night.

Two men and a woman slouch on the vintage couch like throw pillows. Lifestyle and face fillers have turned them into triplets. Mae knows the type: remoras, fish that eat the trash off the body of a shark. They take in Mae with blank fishy eyes.

Mochi, a yappy little dog, white and fluffy when groomed but now grayish and dreaded, yaps in from the kitchen, a shrill little herald announcing the entrance of the one and only Hannah Heard.

You know her face. Even with her hoodie pulled up and the oversized sunglasses, you know it. The knowing floats in the air like wildfire smoke. Even if you didn't watch all six of her seasons on *As If!* or her tween-crap movies, you know her. Maybe you even know how she used to be marked for greatness. How she had wit, she had timing, she had heart. You saw her thirst-trap *Vanity Fair* cover the month she turned eighteen. In the past few years you saw the lost roles and the flops, or you saw the tabloid shit—the stuff Mae and Dan couldn't kill—as she spiraled into some sort of slow-motion car crash of the soul.

Red-wine stains on her orange Celine hoodie—another thousand dollars down the drain. But it's the sunglasses that Mae's thinking about. Hannah is wearing too-big sunglasses in a dark room. The job is under those glasses.

Hannah's voice comes out chopped and screwed: "Hey, bitch. You look absolutely gorge."

"You mean like big and empty?"

Hannah doesn't get it. They fake-kiss hello. The sweat coming out of Hannah has a paint-thinner tang. Her body is pumping out toxins any way it can. The hug turns heavy, Hannah leaning into her, begging Mae to take her weight. Mae holds her up the best she can.

"You have Narcan?" Mae asks Shira over Hannah's shoulder. The assistant nods like *yeah*. Hannah pushes her way out of the hug.

"Fuck all the way off. Nobody fucks with fent anymore. Not since Brad."

Brad Cherry in Mae's head—a beautiful dead boy spread across a California king mattress. Mae's first corpse. Mae forgot Hannah had done *As If!* with Brad back when they were kids, before the rot set in for both of them. She blinks the sight of the dead boy from her mind.

"This is Mae," Hannah says to the triplets. "She's a goddamn killer."

"Hannah," Mae says, pitching her voice just right—threaded with care and compassion, enough to comfort Hannah but not so much that she'd feel the condescension. The rules say *handle the client*. "Why don't you take off your sunglasses and tell me why I'm here?"

Hannah takes off her glasses. Her left eye is purple and swollen like a split plum.

Mae keeps the mask on tight. Her face doesn't flicker. The rules say *keep it to yourself*. She turns to Shira again.

"What's her call time?"

"Makeup at four a.m."

"Shit."

According to the Story—the one cooked up by Hannah's team—Hannah's been rehabbing her life these past six months. The publicists set up redemption-arc interviews with friendlies at the big glossies. They tipped off paps to snap candids of her buying organic juices and vegan wraps at Erewhon. The Story worked. Tomorrow she starts filming on an Oscar-bait indie drama. It's not the lead, but it's a good part. If all goes well, the Story can enter its second act: Pop Actress Proves She's Got Chops.

Her eye fucks up everything.

The movie people will go apeshit when they see Hannah's eye. They can maybe film around her or fix her eye in post. CGI makeovers are boilerplate for the big stars—contractually obligated digital eye lifts and virtual Botox. But Hannah isn't big like that. If Hannah's eye fucks up her first day, if they see it as a symptom of being terminally fucked-up, the producers will shitcan her and bring in whatever next-year's-model actress they sure as hell already have in the wings.

Mae knows that in the Industry, if a man falls off a cliff, maybe he can climb back up—people will even stick their hands over the side to yank him to safety. But once a woman falls, she's fallen for good. If she's clinging to the edge, folk might stomp on her fingers just for the love of the game. Hannah loses this movie and she drops into the void. The rules say *protect the client—even from themselves.*

The job is *keep Hannah's gig safe.*

"Where's Tonya?" Hannah's manager.

"Turning tricks on Santa Monica for all I know," Hannah says. "Bitch won't call me back."

"Jonathan?" Her lawyer.

"Incommunicado."

"What about Enrique?" Her features agent.

"He said call you guys."

That *plop-plop-plop* you hear is the sound of rats hitting water. Hannah's team has made their call about which way this will go. They're not going to try explaining her eye to the producers. They're throwing it to the black-bag team. And Dan threw it to her.

"Hannah, I need to know what happened." Mae nods toward the bedroom hallway like *let's talk in there.* Hannah shakes her head, dismisses the triplets on the couch with a wave.

"What, the walking dead over there? They're absolutely wrecked anyway. I bet we sound like Charlie Brown's teacher to them."

"Okay, then. So thrill me."

Hannah tells Mae the story in chunks and sprays. She leaves big pieces UNSAID. Mae can stitch it together.

The whisper network calls it yachting. Women get flown overseas to party on boats with rich men—rich as in numbers so big the human brain wasn't built to understand them. The yachts circuit the globe, chasing bikini weather, staying in international waters: 24/7/365/all the way around the world. The women are the party favors. They used to fly wannabe actresses out of Burbank by the planeload. Rumor is now most of the women are flown in from Eastern

9

Europe—it's cheaper. Rumor is now flights from LA are more selective. Rumor is now it's famous faces only, flown out in private jets for six figures a night. It looks like the rumors are true.

Mae knows the rumors are always true. Even the false ones.

Hannah's trip went like this: a private car to the Santa Monica airport to a private jet to someplace in France to another private hangar, no customs—she didn't even bring her passport. From that hangar, a fifty-foot walk to a helicopter. Her feet touched French soil for a minute tops. The helicopter took her into international waters. It landed on a support boat—a hundred-foot cruiser that trailed a mega-yacht, carrying helicopters and water scooters and other toys. The support craft housed security, staff, and girls who didn't make the cut. An antique wood-bodied tender shuttled her over to the three-story mega-yacht, where the client was waiting. There were ten girls already on board. But Hannah was the prize.

She doesn't say how she got the gig, who set it up, who put it in motion. She tells parts of it—the worst parts—in a baby-doll singsong delivered to Mochi. She laughs it off like *no big deal*. Maybe she even thinks she means it.

Inside Mae all these things kick up—the horror of it, but also the thrill, the thrill of inside knowledge of this secret world. To see the world the way it really is.

It is sickening.

It is electrifying.

"He thought he was slick. He tried to film me . . . like, during. So I threw his phone out the window or whatever."

"Porthole," Shira says. Hannah's eyes fall on her and the girl shrinks down. Mae can see their whole relationship in that one beat—the late-night calls, the endless errands and picky food orders, the browbeatings and insults and weird moments of love. Not many jobs are as demanding or as intimate as Hollywood assistant—and all of them pay better.

"Porthole. Anyhow, I gifted the asshole's phone to the dolphins. So . . . " Hannah touches her eye. She stops talking as some memory washes over her. Tears gloss her good eye. She chews the air, makes a face like it tastes bad. For a second it all threatens to become too real. Then Hannah swallows whatever is trying to get out and the moment passes. She smiles that megawatt smile, the one that bought her ticket to the show.

"Is he a name?" Mae asks. A possible added level of difficulty.

"Not here, anyway."

"Where, then?"

"I don't know. One of those countries where it's okay for hairy old fat guys to walk around in a banana hammock."

Hannah reaches into the center pocket of her hoodie, pulls out a drawstring bag. She dumps it out. A fistful of loose diamonds shines crazy-beautiful in her palm.

"I guess he felt bad about it," she says, but not like she means it. "These are, like, reparations. How much are they worth?"

"I have no idea. Maybe ask your manager?"

Hannah shakes her head *nuh-uh*. "Then she'll want commission." She shoves the loose diamonds back in her hoodie pocket. "Probably more than I'm making from this movie anyway."

She makes a noise like someone carrying something very heavy. She looks up and talks to the ceiling.

"Fucking Eric. Look what you've done to me."

"Speedo guy's name was Eric?"

"Not him," Hannah says. "Forget it. You don't fucking get it."

Mae's brain coughs up a name—Eric Algar, creator/showrunner of *As If!* The man who discovered Hannah and most of the other teen stars in town. Rumors painted him as a major-league creeper. One of a hundred Mae could name if she really sat down and thought about it.

Like her friend Sarah says:

Nobody talks.

But everybody whispers.

They stand there in the silent aftermath of Hannah's story. Mae clacks her nails on her cell phone. Mochi *yip-yip-yip*s in Hannah's arms. Mae takes a deep breath like the internet says to. She focuses on the job. The monster on the boat will be untouched by all this, that's a given—that's just how the game is played.

"I need fresh air," she says. "When I come back, I'll be smart."

Outside the grotto is golden-hour gorgeous. Mae can hear muffled sex grunts from the cottage on the left. It just adds to the luxe vibe. The headless Buddha is gone. She knew it would be. They can cover up a dead god as quick as anything else.

Mae weighs her options. The rest of Hannah's team have clearly marked her as already dead. Mae could walk right now and the only person who'd be pissed is Hannah. And if Mae walks, in two days Hannah won't matter enough to worry about.

She walks through the grotto and up the stairs to the pool. A photo shoot at the water's edge is grabbing the golden-hour light. The man at its center is so pretty you can feel the pressure of it against your eyeballs when you look at him. People hold cameras, reflective pads to bounce light. Mae looks at a young girl standing there with a plastic bottle of liquid food for the model. When you first start in the business, sometimes your job could be done by an inanimate object, and they want you to know it.

The thought summons ghosts of bad jobs past. It kicks up anger. Mae decides to use it. She decides to save Hannah's ass just to show them she can do it. Pleasure pulses at the center of her brain. Angry joy is her favorite kind. It makes her feel alive.

She turns the job over in her head. She reviews the first principles of a cover-up that Dan taught her.

Don't worry about the truth. It's not that the truth isn't important. It just doesn't matter.

A lie that is never believed by anyone can still have power—if it gives people permission to do what they want to do anyway.

Have a bloody glove—*the objective correlative, the one real thing you can point to that makes the lies feel solid.*

Give them horror or give them heartstrings. Nothing else sticks.

It comes to her all at once.

She walks back to the cottage. She doesn't even look at the triplets. She pitches her voice to Hannah like *this is an order.*

"Jump in the shower, bitch. We're going to make a movie."

The first time you're in the room with a star—not just a famous person, but a *star*—you get it instantly. You cannot take your eyes off them. And under all the sludge and pain, Hannah can still shine.

When they are done shooting in the bedroom—when Hannah nails every line and beat Mae has scripted for her—Mae heads into the main room. The triplets haven't moved. One of the men has slumped into unconsciousness, a string of drool hanging from his mouth. Mae waves to Shira like *come here.*

"She's uploading the video to Instagram. If she's got something that will make her sleep, give it to her. She can still get six hours. Get these three out of here. Have them all sign nondisclosure agreements before they leave."

"How am I supposed to do that?"

Mae grabs her purse from the counter. "Here. I always carry blank ones."

Mae decides to stay close until the video hits. She walks past the pool—it's night now and the photo shoot is done. She walks past Bungalow 3, where John Belushi OD'd. She walks down the steps where Jim Morrison cracked his head open in a drunken fall. She crosses the driveway where

Helmut Newton lost control of his Cadillac and rammed a wall and died. The ghosts just add to the luxe vibes.

She enters the hotel, goes up the stairs to the lobby. Gary Oldman passes her in a big Quaker hat. She goes to the hostess stand. All the hostesses wear the same shade of rust. They are all the same brand of gorgeous. Mae name-drops Hannah. She sees the holy terror in the hostess's eyes. It works—there's a spot open in the tiny corner bar. She orders a cocktail—something with yuzu and mescal that tastes like delicious leather. Dakota Johnson passes her in a giant faux-fur coat. There's some floral scent pumped into the air. Sam Rockwell and Walton Goggins sit at a crowded table behind her. Grimes on the stereo—this ingenue voice singing the word *violence* over and over again. She steals glances at the famous faces stealing glances at her—trying to figure out if she's someone. She likes feeling like a mystery. Being Schrödinger's big shot. She lets the hotel's magic calm her down. She doesn't think about men on yachts doing whatever they please.

Her phone buzzes in her purse. Dan. No cell phones allowed in the bar. She drops a twenty and a five on the bar. She answers her phone on the move. Dan doesn't bother with hellos.

"Her fucking dog?" Pure joy in his voice.

"Give them horror or give them heartstrings. Nothing else sticks. Somebody told me that once."

He laughs.

"So I guess she uploaded it?" she asks.

The video runs about two minutes. Hannah holds Mochi, her sunglasses on, telling a funny story about the

15

little dog needing to take her anxiety medicine—how she hates it, how she always squirms. The story climaxes with a wiggling Mochi headbutting Hannah. Hannah takes off her glasses at just the right moment—the black eye plays like a punch line. She lets Mochi lick her face—all is forgiven. The video plays perfect. Hashtag mochi the bruiser. Hashtag viral as hell.

"The studio already retweeted the video," he says. "They know a hit when they see it."

"So she's still in the picture?" Mae stops in the hotel vestibule.

"Cameras start rolling at six a.m. They'll fix her eye in post. Her manager called me. Said kudos to you. Said you steered the ship past the rocks."

The manager didn't say that. That was how Dan talked. She knows him well. She knows he won't ask what the real story is, not over the phone.

"Think she'll make it to the end of the shoot?"

"Imagine me giving a shit," he says. He laughs. There's something off about his tone. It makes Mae nervous. They have learned to read each other. Mae knows this conversation could have waited until Monday. She knows it is a pretext for something else. She knows small talk is done, and he's ready to pivot to his real reason for calling.

"Got plans after work on Monday?" he asks.

"Barre class maybe."

"Come have a drink with me." Something in the tone raises gooseflesh on her arms.

Dan is her favorite boss she's ever had. He's never yelled at her or made her feel stupid or thrown things at her.

And he's never hit on her.

"A drink?" she says like she's never heard of them, a pure conversational punt while she scrambles inside.

"The Polo Lounge," he says. "I'm buying. But keep it QT, okay?"

Bad vibes on top of bad vibes. The Polo Lounge, inside the Beverly Hills Hotel. Drinks at a hotel bar. California king beds an elevator ride away.

"Any reason?"

"I just want to share my grand vision for a brighter future. Namely, yours." She knows how good he is at lying, at wearing a mask. That she can feel it slipping, even over the phone—it fucks with her. She wants to lie, pretend to remember fake plans. She can't do it. He'll know it's a lie, the same way she knows he's lying now. It will piss him off. The rules say *handle your boss the same way you handle a client.*

"Book it," she says. The rest of the conversation passes in a blur. Her brain scrambles with possibilities. When it ends she makes her way down the hotel driveway to the valet stand. She gives her ticket to a waiting valet. He's wearing a tuxedo shirt and a full sweat. He sprints. She waits.

A Maybach stops in front of the valet stand. The man who climbs from the back seat is old, great-grandpa old, from the veins on his hand and the spider-wisp of his hair. His frail chest is the color of fish belly under his black silk shirt. A woman a quarter his age climbs out with him—an assistant, not a girlfriend, Mae can tell by the clothes. But he grasps her forearm in just the wrong way, and Mae sees the reaction—the girl is good, she keeps the shiver to her eyes. She watches them head up to the hotel. She wonders about doctors—when they look at someone, can they even see the person anymore? Or do they just see the meat, the guts and veins and tumors? Because when Mae looks at people, all she sees are secrets.

Chapter Two

CHRIS

Mid-Wilshire

The Brit's apartment looks like a picture from a catalog but it stinks like sour laundry. Glass jars full of marbles, antique toys placed just so—all this useless bullshit. Framed posters everywhere, chintzy cheesy slogans in big bold type: LIVE LAUGH REPEAT. MAKE YOUR OWN MAGIC. PERSPIRATION LEADS TO INSPIRATION. Ring lights and tripods everywhere. The Brit's whole world is just a set.

Chris stands in the middle of it all, a clear intruder in this world. He's forty-one. He's huge in a way that used to say *offensive lineman*—these days he's trending toward ogre. He's in a 3XL tracksuit. His hair is uncombed; his skin is pale under a patchy beard.

He is a fist on someone else's arm.

He surveys the apartment as he shuts the door behind him. A couple of turntables and a mixer on a stand. The kitchen area of the open floor plan is crammed with cardboard boxes—muscle supplements, herbal testosterone boosters, sugar-free energy drinks. Sponcon. The Brit posts pictures of himself with this shit for money.

The front door is cheap and hollow—in his cop days Chris would have kicked it open in one try. Instead he

19

jammed his way in using a credit card. Here's what being an ex-cop teaches you: There's all these invisible walls that keep everybody in line. And if you refuse to see them, they just aren't there anymore. Once you walk through the walls, they never come back up again.

He checks his phone. Patrick texted him ten minutes ago letting him know that the Brit had left the bar in Little Tokyo. Chris figures he's got another ten minutes before the Brit makes it home. He tosses the apartment to kill time. He searches it the way they taught him in the academy—marking a grid in his mind, working top to bottom. Cop habits die hard.

He finds a salad of pills in a sandwich baggie. He finds an 8-ball of fish-scale cocaine hidden in the couch. He finds a mirror frosted with coke residue. He finds sex toys and coconut oil in the nightstand—and a rubber pussy in the sock drawer. He finds a stack of hundred-dollar bills in a suit pocket in the closet. He pockets the cash, the coke, and the pills.

Cop habits die hard.

He finishes the search. He sits on the couch. He takes out his phone and then puts it away again. He stands up. His bad knee crackles like walkie static.

He hears steps in the hallway. He hears a key drunkenly scraping the lock.

The door opens. In walks this skinny little Brit with cocaine eyes—he's quasi-famous in a way that means nothing to Chris. He sees Chris. He freezes. Chris can see himself reflected in the kid's eyes. This troll of a man standing in his apartment.

"The fuck are you, mate?" He tries to brazen it out—his voice doesn't play along. His face flushes in a way that tells Chris he is a bleeder.

Chris puts off his *don't-run-don't-yell* vibes. The Brit doesn't do anything at all. His fight-or-flight system is all jammed up.

"Now," Chris says, "let me tell you where you fucked up."

Chris moves toward the Brit. The kid doesn't run. He's smart enough to know there's no place to run to. That it will be worse if he does. Chris moves past him and shuts the door.

"You fucked up the same way you all fuck up. You got greedy."

"You're the one fucking up, mate. Like maybe you're as stupid as you look. Do you know who I am?"

"Yes. Maybe you could have kept selling dirt to the gossip sites forever. But you got greedy."

The Brit has a lot of D-level famous friends—reality show and Instagram influencer division. He's been selling secrets on the down low—selling them to whoever is buying. TMZ and Truth or Dare and what's left of the print tabloids.

Last month the Brit sold a story about B-list actor Patrick DePaulo burning a hole in his septum with coke. Truth or Dare ran it: PATRICK DEPAULO'S COCAINE NOSE JOB. Maybe it seemed routine to the Brit. Maybe he didn't know how bad he was fucking up. Maybe the Brit never got around to asking Patrick what his dad did for a living. Maybe he thought Patrick could afford a Bugatti and a never-ending cocaine buffet off of sporadic sitcom guest spots. Patrick's daddy, Leonard, owns BlackGuard, LA's biggest private security firm—surveillance, countersurveillance, protection, and so many other UNSAID services.

BlackGuard subcontracted the job, per usual. Patrick's daddy didn't want to use his firm directly when it came to family business. They needed a layer of plausible deniability if the job goes bad. So BlackGuard reached out to Stephen Acker. Acker is a lawyer and another arm of what Chris thinks of as the Beast. Acker reached out to Chris, per usual. Chris is Patrick's favorite fist.

"You didn't do your homework about who you were selling out."

Something connects in the Brit's head. This gleam Chris can't quite read in his eyes.

"This is because of Patrick, isn't it?"

So the Brit does know who Patrick's daddy is. That means he knew what he was doing. It means whether he knows it on the surface or not, maybe the Brit wanted this to happen. He wanted to go down.

"How we caught you is," Chris tells the Brit now, "we flushed the toilet."

"Flushed the fucking toilet?" The Brit sits down on the couch.

"We fed all of Patrick's *friends* a different piece of fake dirt. Then we waited to see which turd would come out the pipe. That story Patrick DePaulo told you about Alana Dupree using in rehab? The one you sold to Truth or Dare two days ago? You were the only person Patrick told that bullshit story to. That's how we knew you were the rat."

The Brit slumps forward, cradles his face in his hands. Behind the fear in his eyes, there's still this weird gleam.

"Flushed the fucking toilet."

"It's an old trick," Chris says. "But it's a good one."

Chris should know—it's the one they used to catch him.

The Brit jams his hand between the couch cushions—he's feeling for his coke stash. Chris winks at him, pats his pocket where the 8-ball rides. The Brit fish-flops backward.

"A petty fucking thief too, aren't you? So I sold a fucking story. So what? Everybody runs off at the mouth, why not get paid for it?"

The way he says it makes Chris think of Mae Pruett. What was her line? *Nobody talks, but everybody whispers.* He pushes her to the back of his mind—that was a long time ago.

"His daddy has soldiers and killers and you're who he sent, huh? A member of the fucking goon squad?"

Chris knows it for sure now. Something inside the Brit set his life up for this moment to occur.

Chris has seen the type before.

"I'm going to hurt you now."

"Not my face, huh, mate? I got to film tomorrow."

Chris nods. He would have left his face alone anyway. Nobody wants to stop the show. Chris moves to the Brit. He picks him up off the couch. He holds him by the shoulders. He knees him in the guts. The Brit pukes air—Chris keeps him on his feet. He lets the Brit catch his breath. His face a mask of pain, that weird gleam in his eyes. Chris knees him again. This time he lets him drop. Chris kneels slow—his bad knee creaks. Chris gets to work. He doesn't feel anything while he hurts the Brit. He's not sure the Brit does either.

Chapter Three

MAE

The West Hollywood Hills/Sixth Street

Mae doesn't want to go home just yet—she's got all this stuff burning inside her. She also has a smoke-induced headache. She turns right out of the Chateau. She crosses the line into the city of West Hollywood. All these party bars and hotels crowd the Strip. The buildings and sky are festooned with billboards for TV shows and movies. Everything is a sequel or a reboot or an adaptation. Everything is an echo of something else. It's like her friend Sarah says about the Industry: Somebody somewhere catches lightning in a bottle—and all over town people run out and they buy bottles.

She takes a right off Sunset, straight up into the Hills. Sixty seconds later she's in a different world. Winding roads, impossible houses. Houses that look like kings' cottages, Bauhaus white boxes, houses that hang from cliffs like suicides. Numbers float in her head. Five point three million. Seven point two million. Four point seven million.

She drives in the hills, deep and high. She opens her moonroof, lets in some air. That firewood scent floats in. She rises toward the top of the hills. Los Angeles sits gleaming below her. Up through the moonroof the sky is flat and black—light pollution kills it. Under the dead sky the city glows. Like the city reached up into the night and stole the stars for itself.

Twenty years ago. There's this twelve-year-old girl sitting on a bed in Monett, Missouri. Her eyes are big and green. Her name is Amanda Mae Pruett. She hates it here. She wants to be anywhere else.

Dad takes her shooting sometimes. Guns scare her and thrill her. How they erupt with pure power. She sits on the bed and smells gunpowder on her hands. Her ears ring with the ghosts of gunshots—even with ear protection the noise is intense. She picks up a .22 shell on her desk. How the brass shines. How it carries this potential in it. This power to explode.

I am a bullet, she decides. *And I'm going to build a gun that will shoot me out of here.*

I am a bullet.

She came to LA about a decade ago, fresh out of Duke. She'd spent her four years there shaping herself into something new. She stripped down this girl named Mandy Mae Pruett, this girl from the Ozarks who made out with wild boys with mean eyes and big trucks. She burned the shit-kicker twang from her voice. She sliced off her first name. She took on being called by her middle name the way she took on harsh bangs and cat-eye makeup and skinny emo boyfriends. She sewed new parts onto her to see what would fit.

Her first Industry job was as PA on a single-cam sitcom. The women on the show had a special place, a closet behind the craft services table. "What's it for?" she'd asked the second AD who showed it to her. "It's where we go to cry," the second AD had answered. Mae had laughed at that, thinking how some women were so weak. How some women gave the rest of them a bad name. Until the day number-one-on-the-call-sheet yelled at her for eight minutes straight because she'd got his breakfast order wrong. She got him a new breakfast. Then she'd found her way to the special place. Afterward, she built new walls inside herself.

She moved on. She worked as an assistant for an agent at a Big Four agency—she dodged staplers and ass pats. She learned how to dig her nails into her palms just so while getting screamed at—turning the rage back on herself.

She told herself *I am a bullet*. And she was one, more and more.

She moved on. She landed an entry-level job at a PR firm. She took to it. She worked under a woman with a cigarette-scarred voice who hated Mae for reasons Mae only dimly understood. The woman liked to put Mae into close contact with very bad men. The woman got this gleam in her eyes, knowing she was sending Mae into all these viper pits. Mae thought about how some people had bad things done to them, and they just couldn't wait to push that pain onto someone else. She learned to write press releases, learned how to glad-hand reporters, learned how much of our lives is just stories we tell one another, or ourselves.

Dan cold-called her one day. He worked for Mitnick & Associates—LA's preeminent crisis management firm. He took her to coffee. He pitched her just right: *Black-bag PR is a rush. We don't get the good news out—we keep the bad news in. It's like James Bond, Hollywood sleaze edition. You'll go places nobody else in the world gets to go. You'll know things that nobody else in the world will know. You'll do ugly things for ugly people—but, hey, the pay is commensurate. You'll get a peek behind the curtain. It will scare you. But it will buzz you too.*

She came aboard. She signed nondisclosure and non-disparagement contracts. She took her vow of silence.

Dan taught her well. She started to think she'd found what she was supposed to do. She thrived. At first she didn't know why. One day it came in the form of a weird quick flashback: Mae's family dinner table as a kid, everyone eating in silence, all these crazy UNSAID things. Her dad swallowed his shame. Her mom swallowed her sadness. As a kid Mae learned to read faces and silences. She learned to do things without being told. She learned how to enjoy being angry—and how to use it so it didn't burn her up. She didn't know then that this was training. She didn't know she was being shaped to fight this secret war.

Then came the day, standing over Brad Cherry's body sprawled across a California king, that she learned for sure that her mantra was true. That when she needed to be, she was cold and hard with a center of fire.

I am a bullet.

Mae gets lost off Benedict Canyon. The roads get narrower.

Mae gets lost inside her head. Dan's voice plays in a loop. *Come have a drink with me.*

She's been at Mitnick & Associates for three years now. Three years running, Dan is the best boss she's ever had.

27

He's the first person to see the fight boiling in her and tell her not to hide it—the first person to cry havoc and let her slip. *Take scalps,* he tells her. *Wear an ear necklace.*

And he never hits on her.

Maybe she caught the tone wrong. It doesn't make sense for him to come on to her. Unless it does. Dan fucks around on Jenny—Mae's known that for years. The shame-hunch of his shoulders as he talks on a cell phone at his desk, his back turned to the door, speaking in whispers. The way he guards his phone sometimes when texts come in.

She turns from Benedict Canyon Road to Cielo Drive. The houses are bigger and farther apart. They hide behind huge gates. The numbers in Mae's head get bigger. Ten point two million. Twelve point eight million.

She will not sleep with Dan. The cons list is a mile long. His paunch, the smacking way he eats, the fact that he's married already to a woman Mae knows. The fact that he has kids. The fact that it will hurt her the way it always hurts women in the long run to sleep with their bosses. Most of all, she won't because she doesn't want him like that.

But she does need him as an ally. If this is what she's afraid it is, she'll have to handle him. It makes her exhausted just to think about it.

She hits a dead end. She starts a three-point turn to head back down the hill. Her headlights paint a huge wooden gate built into a stone wall. Something clicks for her. Cielo Drive—the Manson murders. Sharon Tate and her friends died bad right here. Well, both here and not here. They tore down the death house a few years back and built this mansion. It's the same piece of land, but they gave it a new address. They hid the ghosts the best they could. Mae sympathizes. Hiding ghosts is her job too.

Mae opens the door to her place. Mandy runs to her over-joyed. She's the ugliest dog in the world—this pony-keg mix of bulldog and who knows what, just wrinkles and sad eyes and farts. Mae loves her big and loves her fierce.

She'd gotten her last year, after a bad day of doing bad things. One of those days when she had to take off her glasses before looking in the mirror, to make herself blurry, to hide herself from herself.

Mandy had some other name at the shelter, but Mae ignored it. Mae already had a name to spare. She looked at this ugly happy stinky loving girl and she decided to call her Mandy—the first name that Mae had cast aside so many years ago. She gave this sweet innocent thing her childhood name and pampered and loved her and kept her safe.

The rules say *never think too hard about whys*.

Chapter Four

CHRIS

Koreatown

Neon lights the night. A cartoon octopus in a chef's hat winks at Chris from a restaurant sign. A Catholic church advertises Mass in five languages. Chris passes a side-street tent village, doubled in size from last month. Beware the Bum Bomber.

From the Brit's apartment to Koreatown, thirty minutes of bad traffic. Chris was born and raised in Simi Valley—SoCal suburban Copland. Chris moved to Koreatown after he got tossed from the sheriff's department. Chris likes living someplace where he is an outsider. It feels honest to him.

He rolls down the window—grilled-meat smells float on the air. KBBQ, halal kebab joints, an al pastor street vendor. Chris is caught in a weird traffic snarl. A K-pop boy band is getting towed in a fifties convertible with a camera on the hood. They lip-sync to bass-heavy playback. A teenage girl on the sidewalk sees them. She Beatlemania-shrieks. Chris rolls up the window, toggles on some music. Nipsey Hussle—one of LA's newest ghosts.

Pain shoots up Chris's left arm. A sudden fist in his chest. *Not a heart attack,* he tells himself.

He chews baby aspirin dry. The bile-sour taste fills his mouth. The fist in his chest relaxes. The first time he had chest pains he went to the ER. He spent three hours in the waiting room next to a moaning woman with a leaky colostomy bag. Now he doesn't bother. It's never a heart attack—until it is.

The music dies—a call coming in over Bluetooth. Acker.

"Tell me everything," Acker says. He doesn't mean it. Acker doesn't want anything said out loud.

"We're happy," Chris says.

"Of course we are, baby. You're the best." Acker is so up front with his bullshit it almost counts as honesty. "Black-Guard wants you to come in on Monday. Standard debrief."

"Yeah, sure."

"This is good for you," Acker says. "A solid like this for the big man's son."

Chris clicks off. Horns in cacophony bring his mind back to the road. The truck towing the boy band is stuck—a man wearing nothing but newspapers and street grime stands in the middle of Wilshire. His eyes burn with holy truth. He's delivering some sort of sermon. Maybe it's the word of God—the horns drown it all out anyway.

His apartment is in Koreatown just south of Wilshire. It's in a grand old building that must have really been something once. The building has an old neon sign proclaiming it the ambassador. The apartments are big with hardwood floors and old limestone walls.

Chris's place is messy in that way that lets you know nobody else has been here in a very long time. He hides the cash he took from the Brit—he eyeballs it at about three grand. He hides the coke. He'll pass it along to Patrick DePaulo to curry favor next time he sees him. Chris won't mess with coke, not anymore. Coke was for the old days, the warrior-king days.

He eats pork katsu curry from a strip mall nearby. It's delicious and he barely tastes it at all. He watches old sitcoms. He has curry burps. He tries to find a name for what he is feeling, and when that doesn't work, he tries to feel nothing at all. He picks through the pills he stole from the Brit. He IDs a Demerol. He pops it. It kicks in quick. He settles back in his chair, drifts into some sort of warm half world. He cues up another sitcom. He looks at the scraped and torn knuckles. He flexes his hands—the pain pops from the joints in a distant way. The scene with the Brit already feeling like it happened to somebody else—or maybe to no one at all.

He remembers the homeless preacher and his crazy eyes. His mouth moving with holy scripture. Chris tries to imagine what God would say to him. But when he tries to think of the words all he can hear is car horns.

Chapter Five

MAE

Brentwood

Mae hits the door to the office complex braced for an ice-water plunge. Cyrus—the Mitnick of Mitnick & Associates—runs hot. He keeps the air conditioners running at full all the time. He sweats through two shirts a day anyway. Everyone else freezes. The women wear winter coats in their offices. The assistants—the ones who must look good all the time, who are out on display in their cubicles—shove their feet into furred boots and sip coffee and bone broth. They try not to shiver as Cyrus passes.

Mae drops off her stuff in her office before the Monday-morning staff meeting. She takes her regular seat next to Dan at the conference table—this burnished slab of live edge walnut. He gives a distracted *hey there* nod. He flaps his arms to keep warm. He's in a black suit paired with scuffed combat boots. It's his signature look—his nod to his Orange County punk teenage years. He's midforties now, his hair still more black than gray.

She tries to suss out whatever weird vibes she'd caught from him on the phone. He radiates stress. He radiates *no small talk*. His assistant, Tze, comes out of nowhere, drops his usual coffee with oat milk in front of him, retreats to the back of the room with the other assistants. Dan acknowledges her only by sipping the coffee.

The rest of the table does Monday-morning chatter per usual. They talk about the Griffith Park fire. The LAPD confirmed the homeless camp bomber is responsible. Truth or Dare has labeled him the Bum Bomber. One homeless man flash-fried in the initial blast—the second Bum Bomber fatality. The fire is 80 percent contained—something like two hundred acres of parkland scorched.

Hector Restrepo says he spent the weekend with his wife in Santa Barbara.

"I love Santa Barbara," Joss McCook—late thirties, his fade razor-sharp—says. "It's just got this feeling—it's so warm and comfortable."

"Like the tub you crawl into before you slit your wrists," Mae says.

"Cynicism is not an affectation, it is an affliction," Joss says. She sticks out her tongue at him. She peeks over to Dan—he is someplace else completely.

The talk turns to private schools. Every member of the team with children sends them to private schools exclusively—they talk about the schools like organized crime protection rackets shaking them down. It's one of Dan's favorite topics—today he stays focused on his phone.

Cy comes in last per usual. Late fifties, the kind of haircut where it's short but you know it's still a scissors cut, the kind that looks best with the soft white hair of old rich men. He's triathlete-fit, fatless and vascular. He takes his seat at the head of the table.

"I hope everyone had a fulfilling and relaxing weekend,"

Helen Poirer says. She's midfifties, yoga-thin. She's Cyrus's right hand—his knife hand, Dan calls her. She waits for a beat—Dan notices and pockets his cell phone. Helen smiles—her teeth are crazy white. "Let's see what's on everyone's plates this week."

They run through jobs. It's a smear of scandals and solutions.

Helen goes over the DMS Warehouse job—some woman led a walkout in Albany to protest working conditions. Unsafe conditions, workers pissing in jars because they don't have time for bathroom breaks. She's bringing bad PR to the company. The good news is they've dug up something juicy—a restraining order from an ex-boyfriend. She's eminently smearable. Helen's strategy is a Cyrus Mitnick classic: *Find a lead steer.* The rules say *the press are cattle*. You find a big-name journalist, feed the story to them—the rest of the press will follow the lead steer. It's cynical in the extreme—Mae has seen it work a thousand times. Helen's giving the story to the *New York Times*. If they run with it, other journalists will start investigating the woman themselves.

Helen switches gears. Ray Chase—a former cable executive who got fired when he strangled his girlfriend at a Malibu valet stand. Rehabbing bad men is a Helen specialty. Helen's the person who first got reporters to put the word *moment* in the phrase *MeToo moment*. Because moments pass. Chase thinks his moment has. He's ready to come in from the cold. Helen's making calls, looking for a reporter to write up his redemption arc—how he went to India, got a tattoo in Sanskrit, meditated and went vegan. Helen says it may be too soon—so far the reporters have given off *ick-no-thanks* vibes. Chase might need three more months in deep freeze before he's ready for his comeback.

"Tell him this too shall pass," Mitnick says. "Tell him soon enough."

Joss runs through the Pasadena police chief corruption case—twenty-one lawsuits filed against her in her first year in office. Racial slurs and inappropriate comments. He's setting up a TV interview—he's paired her with a stylist to give her a glow-up. He's branding her a no-nonsense girl-boss who is ruffling feathers. He's branding the lawsuits vindictive and sexist.

Cyrus asks Hector about the Crenshaw Revitalization Complex—real estate investors trying to launch a massive five-over-one apartment complex / shopping plaza in the Crenshaw Opportunity Zone—the kind of talk that makes Mae's eyes cross. The deal is hung up with city council—Councilman O'Dwyer holding it in committee. He's facing a progressive in his primary—it's not looking good. Local protestors are trying to make a stink, pushing for more affordable housing and environmental controls. More bad press might kill the deal for good. Billions hang in the balance. So far Hector's convinced the big outlets that it isn't news—but the *LA Times* is getting antsy. Cyrus agrees to call the publisher at the *Times* to buy more time.

Helen turns an eye to Mae: "Can you run Cyrus through the Bishoi case?"

Mae puts on a mask—call this one *the consummate professional*.

"Andre Bishoi—he's the line producer on *DEA Border*

Force. Last month they had a car stunt go wrong; the car went through a barrier and crashed into video village. The on-set writer lost a leg. A crew member leaked to *Deadline* that the crash came on their third sixteen-hour day in a row, the director canceled the safety briefing to make his day, and that our client Bishoi refused to okay expensive safety measures. Basically said the crash was production's fault."

No one asks if those things are true. No one cares. The only job is to disconnect power from responsibility.

"Have you developed a client-protection strategy?" Cyrus asks. Mae waits a beat for Dan to answer—he usually handles questions from Cyrus. This time he stays mum. She plows on.

"We subcontracted BlackGuard Security to run a report on the stunt driver," she says. "They turned up a quashed DUI from about ten years ago. I checked the police report for the on-set accident—the police didn't give the driver a drunk test. I fed it to Steph at *Hollywood Reporter*, pointed out there was no Breathalyzer or blood drawn after the crash. She's going to run with it."

She doesn't say the police didn't do a Breathalyzer because there was no reason to. All that matters is that they can point to the quashed DUI. The rules say *have an objective correlative*.

"The *Greenlight* defense," Cyrus says. Everyone nods. Mae catches a quizzical look from Dan's assistant, Tze. She's too young to know the story—back in the cocaine years, an action movie set disaster, four kid actors killed, the whole production team walked on manslaughter charges. Some stunt coordinator ate the blame.

37

The Beast goes way back.

"Nice work," Cyrus says, knocking Mae from the memory. The meeting moves on—Dan stays stuck in whatever world he's in.

Mae half listens as they move on to some local burrito chain with an E. coli outbreak. She thinks about a food travel show she watched a few nights ago. These rich French people eating these tiny little birds in one bite, bones and all. The rich people put a napkin over their heads before they eat them—the idea is that the napkin stops God from being able to see their sin. *We're a napkin,* she thinks; a weird laughing jag threatens to spill out of her. *We're the little napkin they use to hide themselves as they eat and eat and eat.*

Chapter Six

CHRIS

Calabasas

They hook him to the polygraph straight off.

Yokoyama straps a rubber tube across his chest. Another across his gut—it stretches tighter each time he comes in. The tubes are to measure breathing. A blood pressure cuff on his left arm—they have to swap the first one out for something bigger. It's the right arm—the squeezing doesn't trigger arm-pain heart-attack fantasies.

Yokoyama straps clips to his fingers—conductivity to measure the sweat on his fingertips. Yokoyama is maybe thirty. He split the ATF for the private sector as soon as he had a marketable skill. His hair is an undercut, shaved raw on the sides, floppy orange-blond on top, like the weird kids had back when Chris was in high school. He smiles at Chris's cracked, torn knuckles. He says, "I always got to be careful with your hands."

"If you two are done flirting," Eisner says from his fold-out chair, "I'd like to get this done and processed by lunchtime."

Eisner is ex-FBI—check out his perfect posture, his regulation haircut. Ex-feds never lose the stick up their ass. Everybody at BlackGuard is ex-something. Ex-cop, ex-fed, ex-military. Everybody got trained on the government dime.

The room is perfect white, featureless except for the two-way mirror on one wall. The room is supposed to put off interrogation-room vibes. Maybe it does for someone not in the know. Chris has been in plenty of real interrogation rooms. They're dirtier than this, smaller than this. They smell like spilled coffee and unwashed balls. This place is a cop-show theme park.

Yokoyama finishes up on Chris. He takes a seat behind the polygraph machine. He flips a switch. He nods to Eisner like *go*.

"Please state your name."

"Christopher Peter Tamburro."

"Age?"

"Forty-one."

Everyone in the room knows polygraphs are bullshit. They're pseudoscience—strictly inadmissible in court.

"You are employed as an investigator by attorney Stephen Acker?"

"Yeah."

Polygraph machines don't detect lies—they detect nerves. People *might* get nervous when they lie—so polygraphs *might* flag when someone is lying. BlackGuard uses them anyway—it's a way to get things on the record. Chris knows the trick is in what they ask and what they don't. They get to write the history. And then they get to bury it someplace they can dig it up—if it helps them.

"And how long has he employed you?"

"Seven years."

"And before that?"

Maybe the chest tubes pick up how his breath hitches.

He sees Eisner smirk. Chris imagines the sound of Eisner's nose snapping. He wonders how it looks on the machine.

"Sheriff's department."

Eisner puckers his lips. It's supposed to be a smirk.

"That's the Los Angeles Sheriff's Department?"

"Yes."

"And how long were you with the sheriff's department?"

"About ten years."

"And what were your reasons for leaving the sheriff's department?"

"Don't ride me."

They called it the Firearm Trace Task Force. Sheriff's department's version of CRASH. An anti-gang unit in all but name. The official mandate was to get guns off the streets of the San Fernando Valley—nobody cared how. Chris was a first-round draft pick. He was huge. He was a third-generation cop. He radiated pure danger. He joined the unit. He learned the rules—the ones they said out loud and the ones they didn't. The way to fill out a report so it says what you need it to say. How to skim. Anything above thirty-three grams of cocaine was considered felony weight—nearly every bust they ever made just happened to be thirty-three grams. They skimmed gram thirty-four and above—the system didn't need it. The unit did. They planted it when they needed a bust. They sold it through cutouts— an eighty/twenty split. They snorted it when adrenaline wasn't enough to get through a long night.

It got heavier. It got faster. Cash grabs led to shakedowns. Pretty soon they were skimming guns they stole from gangbangers—everybody in the unit had a holdout piece stashed somewhere—Chris's was this grip-taped .357 he pulled from a Vineland Boy in North Hollywood. Nobody ever said out loud why they were keeping the hot guns— that someday they'd need to drop one by a cooling body. Everybody knew that day would come.

Chris learned to love being feared. His size stood out even among the cops. He wanted to get bigger. He started popping test and trenbolone, stacking on muscle, his body like a zoo animal—he'd look at himself in the mirror, scared and pumped, his muscles shredded and cut, and there was this look in his eyes, this wild thing that wasn't him.

It got heavier. People got hurt. Sometimes it was Chris who hurt them. Maybe once there had been a reason Chris had wanted to be a cop. Now being a cop was the thing that mattered, the end that justified everything.

Chris passed a hundred tests he didn't know were tests at the time. The ones who failed the tests, who snitched to brass or didn't take food on the arm or didn't laugh at the right jokes, that type never lasted. They just disappeared and Chris forgot they had ever been there. The ones who stayed rocketed through the night, kicked down doors, ran red lights with a WHOOP-WHOOP and a *fuck-you-I'm-a-cop*.

If anybody else went home and drank and ate themselves numb, if they had phantom heart attacks and woke up in full sweats, they sure as hell never talked about it. So Chris never talked about it either. He went to the ER sure that all the test and trenbolone and coke were going to pop his heart. They gave him an EKG. They said it was all in his head. The lizard part of his brain wanted him to think he was dying. But Chris didn't know why.

His man Stepanyan in the evidence locker dropped a hint—a pound of coke tagged into evidence. Chris thought it was a solid score—he decided to do it solo. It was the feds flushing the toilet. The feds pulled Chris out of a squad car and threw him in the back of one of their own.

Lots of toilets got flushed. Lots of people went down. The feds built a RICO case against the whole department—the third one this decade. The feds went after the sheriff's department with both hands. They'd been too loud, too out of control. The feds tried to get Chris to flip. He stayed silent. His union rep said hang strong. His friends on the force sent these hollow texts of support—he could read the UNSAID *don't take us down with you.*

Chris got put on paid suspension. He sat around his apartment. The hours stretched; the days flew by.

He moved the grip-taped drop gun from his car to his nightstand. He didn't let himself think about why. His bedroom started to fill with this invisible heaviness. He began to spend more time there.

His union rep said hang strong—and said the jail time would be minimal. He tried to picture life without the badge. This hollow thing. If he wasn't a cop, he was nothing at all.

In the nights he would wake up as if slapped. The pain in his chest pinning him to the bed.

Be a heart attack.

But it never was.

The DA filed charges. The suspension became permanent. They took his badge.

He wasn't a cop anymore. He spent hours walking through LA. Nobody ever looked his way. Like he was already a ghost.

He made the decision about what he was going to do without admitting to himself that he'd made it. And the thing he knows for sure is he would have done it if Stephen Acker hadn't called.

He pitched himself as Jesus come back to save the sinners—namely, a specific sinner named Sergeant Chris Tamburro.

"There won't be jail time," Acker told him. "That's a promise."

"Why not?"

"Because you won't be useful in jail."

"Useful to who?"

"To the kind of people who can make this go away. Do you need more than that?"

Chris thought it over. Not being a cop anymore—but being something.

"What do I need to do?"

"Say yes."

"Yes."

The charges were dropped the next day. Chris took the drop piece out of the nightstand. He threw it into the LA River.

"Can you describe how you came to do investigative work for Patrick DePaulo?"

"I was contacted by Stephen Acker, who told me that I was being subcontracted out. It wasn't the first time."

Chris can't remember if it was him or Mae who came up with the phrase *the Beast*. Mae's firm, BlackGuard, Acker, a web of other lawyers and PR firms and private security consultants. Lawyers and black-bag publicists and security services and investigators—eyes and ears and arms and fists.

"And were you informed why you were being sub-contracted out?"

"A defamatory item appeared on the gossip website Truth or Dare about Patrick DePaulo. It was the latest in a series of defamatory pieces about DePaulo and his friends. He wanted to know which of his so-called friends sold them the story."

He didn't say *the story was true*. He didn't say *cocaine chewed a hole in his septum—that's why he's got a new nose*. You don't drop dirt on the client on record. Especially when it's the founder's son.

"And what did you do to track down the so-called friend?"

"I worked with Patrick DePaulo to develop a list of suspects. We planted different false stories with all of them. Only one story made it out into the wild."

"And who was the person you deemed responsible?"

Chris says the Brit's name. He sees Yokoyama's eyebrow lift—he must watch trash TV.

"What did you do next?"

"I broke into the suspect's apartment. I waited for him to come home. When he did, I extracted a confession from him."

"And then what did you do?"

"I physically assaulted him."

He pops those scabbed knuckles. He watches Eisner swallow. He watches him check Chris's vitals—Chris knows his heart rate is steady.

"Were you ordered by Stephen Acker to assault the suspect?"

"No." It's the truth.

"Were you ordered by Patrick DePaulo to assault the suspect?"

"No." Chris didn't need to be told. That's part of the reason they use him.

Eisner clicks off the recorder. He has what he needs—all responsibility pushed down onto Chris.

Chris doesn't mind—his admission of guilt is built into his fee structure.

From the outside it looks like any other office building. Yokoyama comes out behind him.

Chris stops on the steps down to the parking lot. He looks out at Calabasas—these dried-up rolling hills dotted with the houses of very rich people, the kind who want both big acreage and quick access to the west side. Yokoyama pulls a cigarette—he is one of the last of the LA smokers. Chris feels emptied out, cleaner—it's the lapsed Catholic in him, that post-confession unclenching.

"How'd I do?"

Yokoyama shrugs. They never talk about what happens in the room outside the room. He offers Chris a smoke. Chris takes it—he could use the human moment. Yokoyama lights it for him. The smoke is slick in his mouth. He lets it drift out without taking it in his lungs.

Yokoyama gestures with his smoke toward the hills.

"You ever think, one flick"—he mimes flicking his smoke—"and you could burn down half the state?"

"You the Bum Bomber, Yokoyama?"

Yokoyama keeps his eyes on the hills. Leonard DePaulo—BlackGuard's founder—lives up there somewhere. The office gives him a ten-minute commute—and dooms most of his employees to two hours of traffic every day.

"I was gonna burn stuff up? I wouldn't start with the homeless. They're not the problem." Yokoyama's voice does that thing where you want it to sound like you're joking but you aren't.

Chris lets a little smoke into his lungs. That old queasy buzz is instantaneous.

A black SUV rolls up. The way it parks in the red zone makes Chris think about when he was a cop and he parked wherever he wanted. All four doors swing open at once. Four men climb out. They've got buzz cuts and beards—they radiate ex-military. They wear all black. They walk up like they own the place. They pass Chris and Yokoyama like they're potted plants.

The one in the lead, his hair a white buzz cut, is as big as Chris back when Chris was juicing. Matt Matilla—Chris recognizes him from BlackGuard's YouTube channel. He's ex–Special Forces—he flies cross-country teaching cops how to kill. He runs seminars for feds and cops and wannabes. He brings in major money for BlackGuard. He also works for them—him and his handpicked crew, the Special Operations Department. Rumors float—there's a

47

whole world underneath BlackGuard that Chris has no clue about. Arms of the Beast that Chris has never seen.

"I hear things about those guys," Chris says, hoping to hear more.

"Do you?"

"Yeah." Chris lets it sit. Yokoyama hates the silence. Chris figures he'll break it.

"Here's what I can tell you," Yokoyama says, his voice pitched low. "You know how when you do a job, they have you come in and polygraph you, get it all down on tape?"

"Yeah."

"Well, nobody ever asks me to polygraph them."

Chapter Seven

MAE

Brentwood / Beverly Hills

She manages to stay busy most of the day. She works with her door closed, rolling calls with reporters, mostly just glad-hand chatter to keep them friendly—swapping restaurant recs and non-explosive gossip. She stays clear of Dan—his weird energy makes playing normal too hard.

He leaves at ten minutes to six without a word. She gives him a ten-minute head start.

She drives from Brentwood to Beverly Hills gripping the wheel so tight her knuckles turn white. She runs through alternative scenarios. She knows two things. She cannot lose Dan as an ally. And she will not sleep with him.

She hits bad traffic on Sunset per usual. Commuters mixed with star-map buses, open-air tourists gawking at the house of Ted Danson or whomever.

She fights through traffic, hangs a left toward the great pink pleasure dome of the Beverly Hills Hotel. The valet opens the door—he says something but she can't hear it over the roar of blood in her ears. A couple stands waiting for their own car—the woman has billows of blond hair framing her acid-peel face, her teeth like pearls between Joker-plump lips. Her husband stands like a sack of

49

something wet, puffs of gray hair lifting his shirt, tangling out from the button gaps like prisoners grasping between bars. He looks the age the woman is not allowed to be.

Mae walks through indoor palm trees to the Polo Lounge. She thinks about how much of her life is spent in hotels. She gives Dan's name to the hostess. The hostess leads her back—her dress yawns, flawless skin, a back that will haunt Mae in the gym for months. She leads her to the back of the bar, where it is dark. Dan is shaking the last drops of what looks like whiskey from between the ice cubes in his glass. A ten-minute head start and he's already one drink down. He sees her coming, puts down the glass.

She runs through the jiujitsu of rejecting a man without hurting his pride. Deflection, spin—protect his ego at all costs. Never let the anger show. Never let the disgust show.

"Hey there, shooter," he says. He opens his arms for a hug. This is a moment. If he lingers or squeezes or holds her too close, she'll know.

Your standard LA hug. No squeezing, no cheek-to-cheek, just the hug-as-handshake.

But he holds it longer than he should.

She sits down. She wonders if she should record the conversation. She pushes that aside. They order drinks—Dan orders another Manhattan, she orders a mescal margarita.

They sit in electric silence. She knows he won't start with whatever he has to say until the drinks come. He won't risk an interruption or being overheard. Standard tradecraft in a town where everyone knows everyone.

Her brain conjures waking nightmares. Would he start with a hand on her hand? Confessions of how Jenny had gone frigid? Or maybe he'd say something about marital arrangements, how Jenny *understood*. Maybe he'd dangle all the things he could do for her. Maybe a foot will creep under the table—she locks herself down to kill the shudder.

The drinks come. She takes a long sip—not too long. She needs to nurse it. She needs to stay cool. No matter how her thirst barks at her.

The waitress leaves.

This is the moment.

Dan asks her, "You seeing anybody?"

Shit shit shit.

Lime-juice acid rises at the back of her throat.

She thinks about lying. She knows it's a dumb move. He'll ask questions; she'll have to invent someone. She reminds herself that the goal is to keep this man as an ally. Why do men have to make it so hard?

"I've got Mandy, doesn't that count?"

He smiles—not just at the laugh line. The answer pleased him—it was what he was looking for.

"One dog's enough, huh?" he says. "You still at that place on Sixth Street?"

She nods like *yup*.

"It's a two-bedroom place, right?"

She nods again—on the inside she's totally lost.

He drains his drink. She sees him take the deep breath, steeling himself. Her jaw tight with nerves.

"Dan . . ." she says. She's got her talk ready. Steer the conversation. Keep it professional. Talk about respect. *Handle him.*

It all plays out in slow motion. He reaches into his pocket.

He takes out a plastic card. It has the logo of the hotel. It's a hotel room key card. He places it in the middle of the table. His face doesn't change. He leaves it there.

Shit shit shit shit shit shit shit.

Eyes from other tables glance their way. Knowing smiles on men's faces.

She studies his eyes. She thinks about what's going on. She thinks about everything she knows about Dan. She comes to a surprising conclusion. She takes a leap.

"Dan—why do you want it to look like we're having an affair?"

The moment breaks. He smiles like *atta girl*.

"How do you know I don't want to have one?"

"Because if you were bringing me here to try and bang me, you wouldn't make it look so much like you were bringing me here to try and bang me. You're better at constructing a narrative than this. But here we are, in public, in a hotel bar full of Industry people, and here's the key card right here on the table for anyone to see. You want it to look like we're sleeping together. You're controlling the narrative, just like you taught me. And I want to know why."

"You tell me," he says. She wants to slap the smile off his face. The asshole is having fun with this. His smile transmutes her anxiety to rage. She uses it. She puts together an answer.

"If anybody sees us you want them to think we're having an affair. That means you think maybe people are watching. You're building up a cover story for something else—and if this is the cover story, then I'm guessing it's pretty big and it's pretty bad."

He smiles. Another test passed. Even now she feels the

glow of his approval, even though she's furious, even though she's so tired of needing to prove herself.

"You're good," he says. "You got it in you to be one of the best. I always said so. Ever since Brad Cherry."

That beautiful dead boy appears in her head again—why does he keep bobbing to the surface?

"Then treat me like it."

"Do me a favor," he says. "If you're going to dog me out, smile while you do it. Trust me, we need the illusion."

She plays along, pastes on her smile. "You asshole—you think it's funny. It's not fucking funny, Dan. You can't play around with shit like this."

"You never know who is watching."

"That's paranoid."

"Just because you're paranoid," he sings—a passable Kurt Cobain.

"It matters," she says. "Men don't think it matters but it does. It hurts me to have people think I fuck my boss. It's not a joke."

"You're right," Dan says. "I'm sorry." The bullshit contrition just gooses her anger more. She clenches her glass—she wonders if she's strong enough to shatter it.

He rattles his ice. He studies her—he's waiting for the rage to pass. It pisses her off how well he knows her. He knows her curiosity—her need to be on the inside, to know secrets—will trump her anger eventually. He knows her too well. And just to prove it, just as she feels her jaw unclench, he moves forward:

"How is your sister?" Another question out of left field.

"Fine, I guess." Alicia had stayed in Monett, kept close to

53

Dad. Mae mostly only sees her through social media, where Alicia looks like some cursed portrait of Mae, ten years older instead of the two years younger that she actually is, tired eyes, children hanging off her.

"You got a niece, right?"

"Two."

"Were you around during the pregnancies?"

"Not really. We aren't that close."

"Just wondered if you had much experience with pregnancy. Our surrogate was in Mexico so we only saw her once or twice."

He's all over the place. Boyfriends, guest bedrooms, pregnancy.

"Dan. You're throwing chaff in the air."

"Is that what I'm doing?" he asks.

"You mentioned Brad Cherry—you want to remind me I can handle heavy stuff. You show me that you're setting up a cover story. And now you're talking about kids."

He smiles like *keep going*. She swirls her drink. She puts the pieces together. They don't all fit—but enough do to make her figure it out.

"So where are you trying to lead me?"

"You tell me."

"Jesus. Well, this for sure isn't for the firm, or we'd be there right now. So you've got . . . what, some side hustle?"

He smiles like *keep going*.

"Something heavy."

He smiles like *keep going*.

She doesn't say *something illegal*. She just says, "Dan . . . you're going to be partner someday. Why risk it?"

"Look," he says. "You're good at what you do. You work hard. I appreciate the shit out of you. But here's the truth. If you show up every day, do your job right, show up early, work late, always hit your mark, you'll climb the ladder all the way up to the job of getting coffee for the person who crawled over you to get to the top. Or some kid who was born in a corner office. Somebody's fucking nephew."

"And you have a better way?"

"At the root of every fortune is a crime. You ever hear that?"

"Yeah. I've heard that."

She waits for him to speak again. They sit in the white-noise din of the bar for a long beat.

"So," Mae says. "You're going to build a fortune. Are you going to tell me what the crime is?"

"No."

"You absolute dick."

He laughs.

"Once I let you in, you can't back out. Even hearing what I have to tell you, it's like jumping out of an airplane—once you jump, there's no going back. To know about it is to be inside. No second thoughts. And no phones, texts, nothing. We play this with maximum op sec."

"If this is a joke, I'm going to murder you."

He waves at the waitress.

"No joke, shooter. Here's what I'm going to do. Tomorrow night, same bat time, same bat channel. I'm going to sit at this table, I'm going to order a drink. I'm going to drink it. If you sit down across from me then, I'll tell you everything. If you don't, then this never happened. Life rolls on same as ever."

He smiles at her. He times it so he gets the last word before the waitress gets within hearing range.

"You already do all this dirt," he says. "You might as well do it for yourself for once."

Chapter Eight

CHRIS

Venice

Chris's bad knee screams—he opens the driver's-side door to let it stretch out.

Shit duty. A booty-call footman. Sitting outside a spa on Abbot Kinney waiting for Dave Gifford—the press calls him a promoter, but everyone on the inside knows he's a bagman, cutting side deals with agents and managers, channeling fat bribes to get their A-list clients to cut their quotes. Chris doesn't know if it's legal or not. Or if at a certain level that even means anything.

Chris checks his rearview. Everyone on this slice of Abbot Kinney dresses like a toddler, shorts and big T-shirts, but somehow you know the big dumb T-shirt cost three hundred dollars. Chris looks for people who stick out. He's working counterintelligence—looking for divorce-lawyer investigators sent by Gifford's wife. His wife is paranoid—as the saying goes, just because you're paranoid doesn't mean your husband isn't fucking everything above room temperature. Dave and his wife are playing this game for big stakes. Dave's passed the ten-year mark on his marriage—after ten years, California state law mandates alimony for life. It's never occurred to him to quit fucking around.

Chris cracks the window, tries to catch a smell of the ocean. He tries to do the math—he hasn't seen surf in maybe a year. He takes a deep breath. He can't smell anything but smoke from the woodfire grill down the street. He thinks about Mae anyway—even the ghost of the ocean is enough to kick up memories.

He likes her right away. These big green eyes behind these big glasses. She looks right at him—her eyes don't reflect the dead body lying right in front of them. A lot of people wouldn't handle the fear so well. After all, it is her first corpse.

The bed Brad Cherry lies in is not his own. He's house swapping with an A-lister who is staying in his place in Cobble Hill while he takes her place in Venice. He got into the A-lister's stash. He snorted a fat line of heroin—turns out the A-lister's dope is too rich for Brad's blood. Now he's dead in the A-lister's bed.

Brad was Mae's client. She found the body. She didn't need to be told what to do. She called her bosses. Her bosses called Acker. Acker called him.

That's who Chris is. The person you call while the body cools.

The job is clear. Brad Cherry is dead and that's too bad— but that's no reason to drag the A-lister through the mud. Chris worries he's going to have to explain it to her. He doesn't have to worry. She calls the shots. Chris and Mae clean up the room. They flush the A-lister's stash—Chris keeps enough to plant in Brad's pocket, make it look like he scored some Venice boardwalk smack that he couldn't handle. They leave Brad for the maid to find.

They walk the beach of Venice. Dirty sand and tourists. They go to a bar down the street, watch the TV, wait to see if the cover-up will hold. If the story they've crafted will hang together. While they wait, they talk. They sit in the bar and they come clean with each other. They find something amazing, something scary as hell—they can't hide from each other. It's like they see each other naked long before they take off their clothes. Their whole lives are lies—but they can't lie to each other.

He tells her about the chest pains. He tells her about the drop piece in the nightstand. How close he had come. And that at least he's not dead, but sometimes it feels like his life is just ticking off days until the last one. Suicide on the subscription model.

They walk down to the water's edge. Gray waves in the dark. That feeling when you are drunk and the air is the temperature of your skin and you get how everything is connected in this simple wordless way.

The pulse in his neck when he looks at her. The tingles at the roots of his hair. This feeling it takes him a long time to name.

Alive.

From here they can see the A-lister's house. An ambulance out front.

Her little hand takes his. This jolt in his chest—nothing at all like a heart attack.

He tells her, "It's like I'm in this backward purgatory. Like maybe if I commit enough sins, I'll be able to get free."

She turns to him, her face looking up at his. In her eyes he can see another way.

He kisses her then, hard.

Waves crash in little thunders.

They watch news helicopters swarm over the beach—they kiss while sirens rise in the night.

The dream breaks with an opening door.

"Scare ya?" Gifford's in a post-fuck glow. He climbs in shotgun. He doesn't like the feeling of being driven around—he doesn't want his servants to feel like servants.

Chris drives to an omakase joint in Mar Vista—four hundred bucks per person and you leave hungry, Gifford tells him. He's meeting his wife there. Chris wonders what they talk about, sitting there with their fish flown in from Japan and their lies.

But maybe lies are what you need. That thing that made him and Mae work at first—the way they couldn't hide from each other—that's what killed it in the end. Neither one of them could do what they do and face the truth of it day after day. It came down to a choice: the life or each other. Mae chose the life. Chris said he did too. He knew she knew he was lying.

"Last time I was at this place," Gifford says, "I ate this thing, they call it shirako, and when I was done, I was like, what was that? And they say *it's the male of the cod*. And it took me a beat before I figure I'd just ate a fish's cum sack. For real, his cum sack. I told them usually the one eating the cum isn't the one picking up the check."

Chris makes a sound like laughter. In his head he is driving them both straight into the ocean.

Chapter Nine

MAE

Sixth Street

The real estate agents used to call this strip of Sixth Street Beverly Hills Adjacent—the street ends three blocks west at the Beverly Hills city line. Beverly Hills has lost its luster in the past few years. Now they call Mae's neighborhood Beverly Glen. Mae lives on the bottom floor of a pink 1920s two-story duplex. Crown molding, hardwood beams—old Hollywood glamour. Her landlord wrote some Michael J. Fox comedy back in the day. He used his green envelopes to buy a few properties.

The upstairs apartment belongs to a fortysomething fashion designer with a twenty-five-year-old boyfriend. She's always in Europe on business. He's always entertaining other twentysomethings. Bass lines rumble late into the night. Mae prays for his death on the regular.

She feeds Mandy. She orders Thai food. She pours screwtop rosé. She thinks about what Dan said.

You already do all this dirt. You might as well do it for yourself for once.

She scratches Mandy's belly—Mandy rubs her paw on her nose, Mandy-speak for *more*. Mae gives her more. She takes out her phone. She knows she needs to talk to someone. Someone she can be honest with.

It makes her think of Chris. The way it had been too real. Naked before they ever took off their clothes. Chris had fucked her with the whole of his being, this pure wonder in his eyes at the sight of her that made her feel wanted in a way no one else had ever done. He said what he needed and she gave it to him and she said what she needed and he gave it to her. Waking up in the middle of the night grasping for each other in the dark, fucking again and then eating ice cream in bed, sheets ruined. Fucking until her joy came out in wild laughter.

But then there were the nights when she wanted the lies. Needed them if she wanted to live. She couldn't take being with someone who saw through all the bullshit she needed to make it through this life. They hadn't ended badly. But it had been sad. It had been some sort of admission for her to be given something that good and know it wasn't going to work.

She comes out of the memory with a little jolt—the reverie long enough that her phone has gone to sleep in her hand. She googles the time in Romania—7:30 a.m. Sarah ought to be up. Sarah used to be an actress—a couple of prestige TV parts, you might know her if you saw her. She transitioned to producing at thirty-five—she said her ego couldn't handle the life of a middle-aged actress. Right now she's on-set for some streaming-service show filming in Bucharest.

She can tell Sarah everything. Sarah will be thrilled—it's hot gossip for sure. She'll forbid Mae from going back to meet Dan. She'll tell her she can't get involved in some crazy probably illegal scheme without even knowing what it is. And by telling Sarah, Mae knows, she'll kill the idea. She'll have broken Dan's rule about keeping it quiet. That has to be the smart move. Whatever Dan has cooking has to be majorly illegal. It has to involve double-crossing the Beast.

Call Sarah. Kill the deal.

The phone ring is a strange chirp, passing through some Romanian filter.

"Hey, girl," Sarah says, far away and tinny.

"How's filming?"

"Filming? Oh, we've stopped filming. We've reverted to prep. The network blew up five episodes' worth of scripts. They blew up scripts they already greenlit. The writers' room's been let go for months now. So we had to stop filming. We're burning a hundred K a day keeping cast and crew on ice while the showrunner rewrites everything."

"Well, if it brings the world another green-tinted, joyless prestige drama, it's worth it."

"Ha ha. Joke all you want. The Industry is totally fucked. I don't even know what we're doing. Seventy new shows are debuting this month across all platforms. Seventy. I get up every day and I put out fires and we try to make this show and the really fucked-up thing is, if we didn't? Who would ever know? What would change? Would even the network notice?"

"So what I'm hearing is you're having fun and loving life."

"Everything's on fire and nobody cares. Speaking of, how's LA?"

It's not until she opens her mouth that she realizes she's not going to tell Sarah about Dan.

"Just work stuff," she says. "You follow Hannah Heard on Instagram . . . ?"

She tells Sarah the Hannah story. She gets her laughing. She knows now—she doesn't want to kill the deal. She wants to know Dan's secret. Of course she does. He knows her so well. He left it a mystery on purpose to draw her in. It worked. She's in.

Dan's car isn't in his spot the next day. Mae cruises by his office. Tze tells her he's in meetings over in Burbank most of the day. He's reachable by phone—Tze offers to connect them. Mae waves it off. Dan said *no phones*. Anyway, she doesn't want to talk to him. She just wants to look him in the eyes. For him to look into hers.

She works. She rolls calls. She does everything on auto-pilot. The rest of her brain conjures hypothetical schemes. She figures out the most likely play. She says it out loud like a character in a movie.

"Blackmail."

Blackmail isn't unheard-of in the black-bag world. Shakedowns happen. Too many secrets worth too much money float through people's hands. Too many cell phone videos and scorned employees. Usually the shakedowns happen UNSAID. You triple-charge the client and dare them to ask you why. The bill is saying *here is what the secret is worth.*

Dan had the platforms—he could plant stories anywhere from *Variety* to the *New York Times*. When you spend your time killing stories, you learn how to make them live. If Dan was planning to move into the world of real blackmail, it meant he had proof of something hard and undeniable.

"Mae."

She jolts from her reverie to see Cyrus standing in the doorway. She sits up straight. Nine a.m.—he's already got pit stains.

"Good morning, Cyrus."

"Have you seen Dan yet?"

"Tze says he's in meetings all day. The Burbank thing. Can I help you with anything?"

"We might need to move fast on something for one of his clients. Ward Parker."

"Just don't tell me there's another dead body."

She means it as a joke. Cyrus's face lets her know it's not.

"It's not a body," he says. "In some ways, it's worse."

Ward Parker: Democratic fundraiser in West Hollywood. He plays with big-time money and big-time power. He packages donations for the mayor, the governor, three different congressmen. The entirety of West Hollywood City Hall and half of LA's are in his pocket. Nobody knows where his money came from. Nobody cares.

Everybody knows his hobby is party-and-play. Ward Parker gets off on watching men shoot crank. First came a few close calls, EMTs and friendly doctors sent over to revive a few ODs. Then a death—a man flown in from Florida, meth-fried on a mattress in a West Hollywood Heights apartment. The cops treated it as misadventure. Parker hired Frederick Kim, the Beast's primo defense lawyer. Kim brought in Dan to stop the rumors from reaching print.

Then came the second body. Another man dead on Parker's couch with a needle in his arm. A man with four prostitution busts and three drug busts. Parker brought in the team again. Again the cops played ball. Nobody wrote about it. Everybody whispered. Dan killed a network news investigation. Dan paid a kill fee to keep a story out of Truth or Dare. The *LA Times* went to print—Dan got it watered down into nothing. Of course rumors spread. A few Twitter threads went viral. So what? They burned themselves out. The story didn't breach containment. It didn't really leave Dan's control.

There were whispers of bodies that nobody saw. Whispers that Parker had to bring in a cleanup crew. Whispers about the special ops team over at BlackGuard. Heavy, heavy shit. The most UNSAID shit in the world. Mae thinks about the vanished Buddha at the Chateau Marmont.

"All we have right now is," Cyrus says, "a man walked into the West Hollywood substation with a handcuff on his wrist and needle tracks on his arm. He informed the police that Parker held him against his will, paid him money, and then restrained him, injected him with intravenous drugs against his will. He claims he managed to free himself from his restraints and get out a window. As of right now, the report is unfiled—so it's not public yet. But if they arrest him, the whole team will have its hands full. Obviously, this is Dan's baby—you'll fill him in ASAP?"

"No problem," Mae says. She does it completely on autopilot. The conversation continues. She projects someone who is listening and interacting. Inside she's screaming and laughing all mixed together. Maybe it's a coincidence—Dan's biggest client landing back in the shit right as Dan is planning some huge play.

Or maybe Dan is planning on blackmailing Ward Parker.

It scares her.

But it juices her more.

It's the kind of traffic so bad that the worst part of Mae hopes somebody is dead at the end of it, so at least there is a worthy reason everything is so fucked-up.

She's running late. Hannah walked off the set in front of a *New York Times Magazine* reporter—the Mochi-video goodwill evaporated. Mae spent the afternoon on the phone with the reporter, trying to figure out how he was going to write it up. He wasn't playing ball. She suspected an incoming hit piece. Good news was the story wouldn't run for a month at least. The earth goes around the sun a thousand times a day anymore.

Mae plays fast drums on the steering wheel. She cuts off the podcast on her phone. She cues up Rihanna. She sings, "Bitch better have my money." She plays fast drums. She sits in traffic. It moves ahead in fits and starts. In other cities people honk their horns. LA jams are silent. In LA people know it's useless to yell at the gods.

Mae pounds the horn. She yells at the gods.

The gods answer back *fuck you*—an LASD chopper flies overhead. LA traffic's herald of doom. A chopper means a car chase, a bad crash, a wannabe jumper on a freeway overpass. It means the kind of traffic that can kill a whole day.

Mae starts cutting back and forth between lanes. She keeps an eye on a taco truck in the middle lane. She gets past it. It passes her. All this fruitless struggle. The gods made LA traffic to train you not to fight back.

Mae fights back. She fights to get ahead one car, three cars. The traffic goes to a total standstill. Mae eyes side streets. South of Sunset it's a maze of loosely connected streets—a bad bet. She's stuck here. She's next to a tour van, a roofless bus sponsored by Truth or Dare that promises celebrity home tours. Instead they're stuck here getting a view of the real LA.

The single chopper up ahead becomes a swarm. Media helicopters join in.

She's ten minutes late. She eyes her phone. Dan said no phones. He said no texts.

She's worried he'll give up on her. She worries he'll decide she can't be trusted.

A Beamer's brake lights flash to her right up ahead—a parking meter opening up. Fuck it. She parks. Two blocks. She walks faster than traffic is moving. She takes off her clogs so she can speed-walk barefoot to the hotel.

Out of the car, the roar of helicopters overhead sounds like a swarm of bees. Sirens rise—police sirens, ambulances, fire trucks. Red lights glimmer in the air.

The intersection in front of the hotel is ground zero. People out of their cars, filming with their phones. A cop in a yellow vest directing traffic, losing the fight. Wind from choppers sets the tall palm trees swaying. Dead fronds spiral down onto the street.

Mae sees a black Tesla half on the road, half on the sidewalk, the driver's door hanging open.

Dan drives a black Tesla.

So does half of Beverly Hills, she tells herself.

She walks faster. She breaks a sweat. There's no second car. There's no collision. There's pebbles of safety glass glittering on the road. Sirens come from every direction.

She's at the intersection now. She sees a spiderweb bullet-hole crack in the windshield. She sees a Jackson Pollock of blood painted against the glass. She sees cops crouching on the sidewalk. Sees a brass casing getting bagged and tagged. She sees a body on a stretcher. A blanket over the body— soaked maroon over the face. She sees black suit-pant legs poking out the bottom of the sheet, leading to battered combat boots. Paramedics load the body into an ambulance. Mae reaches a crowd of looky-loos. Hot wind from the choppers washes down. The blanket covering the body flaps in the gust. She sees wet gray brains blooming from the side of Dan's head. The crowd makes this *uhhhhhhhng* noise. They raise their camera phones to catch the gore.

Chapter Ten

MAE

West Hollywood / Sixth Street

Mae drives home in some hazy dream. She gets stuck on Melrose, regular rush-hour traffic. She drives past the Paul Smith store, the side wall painted this impossible pink. Japanese kids in expensive streetwear line up against it taking selfies, catching that perfect Los Angeles golden-hour light.

She blinks and sees blood soaking through a sheet.

Her phone sits in the center console. She picks up Mandy from doggy daycare—the front desk woman making small talk, Mae nods like she's listening, but it's like there's fingers jammed in her ears so everything the woman says is just *wah-wah-wah-wah*s.

She blinks and sees a cracked windshield wet with bullet-wound splashback.

She sits on her couch—dazed—checks her phone. She turns on the TV. The murder all over Twitter already. TMZ gets it first. FLACK GUNNED DOWN IN BEVERLY HILLS. Truth or Dare a quick second. PUBLICIST MURDERED ON SUNSET. The articles are threadbare so far.

Her clothes constrict on her. She kicks off her pants. She unhooks her bra and pulls it through the armhole of her blouse. She takes a deep breath like the internet tells you to.

Truth or Dare updates the story. This time it has a byline. Should have figured it would be Michelle Weiss—Dan called her a reincarnated dung beetle. Her headline reads: HOLLYWOOD'S SECRETS DIED WITH DAN HENNIGAN. It calls Dan a "black-bag PR wizard"—"Hollywood's crisis manager to the stars"—"the man who knew where the bodies are buried." The article doesn't mention how many stories Dan fed to Michelle, or how many kill fees he arranged for her.

The *LA Times* is late to the game—they wait until the family is notified to publish. They come with hard facts. They picked up details from an unnamed Beverly Hills PD source. A Hispanic male shooter approached the car stuck in traffic. The phrase *possible carjacking* appears.

Mae's phone blows up.

WTF???

I'M SO SORRY.

Sad-face emojis and SORRY FOR YOUR LOSS.

She blinks and sees Dan with his head blown open.

Her phone vibrates in her hand. She yelps—just her phone ringing.

It's Michelle Weiss.

TRUTH OR DARE.

She thinks about not answering.

She clicks it on.

"No comment, Michelle."

"You saw the headline, huh? We were second to the story, we needed a take."

"You wait for Jenny to hear the news?"

"No. You going to take an attitude about it?"

"I don't have anything to say but no comment. Cyrus will speak for the firm, I'm sure."

"Look, chica, I'm sorry for your loss. But a story is a story. You know anything?"

Yeah, I do, she thinks. *I know Dan was working something big and secret. He was planning some sort of epic ratfuck for fuck-you money and he was on his way to cut me in on it when he got killed.*

"I don't know shit, Michelle. What do you know?"

"Shooter's Hispanic, approached on foot. Said he came up shooting. Opened the door—probably wanted to yank Dan out. Witness said he grabbed something from the car before he ran—probably Dan's cell phone."

All these ill-fitting pieces—Mae tries to jam them together. Dan has some get-rich scheme, heavy and illegal. Dan says to Mae *no phones.* And then he's killed and the killer takes his phone and runs.

"Everything we're seeing, looks like it's just some dumb random crime," Weiss says. "I mean, Dan knew a lot of secrets, sure. But nothing that would actually get him killed. Unless you know something I don't."

Everything locks together. Nothing locks together. Mae has a weird impulse to tell Michelle everything—to free herself from this terrible secret. She could let Michelle dig into it, let her find whatever Dan was hiding, whatever it was that surely got him killed.

"No," she says. "I don't know anything."

The conversation ends quick—Michelle is still on the

72

hunt. Mae lets the phone dangle in her hand. She feels something like whales swimming inside her. The world splits up into these colorful diamonds, blurred by kaleidoscopes and prisms. It's not until Mandy pushes her big brick head into Mae's lap that she realizes that she's crying. She gives in to the tears, waves that start somewhere deep in her rolling out as sobs. She cries knowing Dan would laugh at her for it. Call her a girl. She cries knowing she is not soft. She cries with her hands knotted into fists. The tears end. Her fists stay clenched.

Twenty-four ounces of cold brew and a Spam musubi croissant—the breakfast of champions. She drives to work. She parks under the building. Her stomach roils double-time when she sees his empty parking slot. The lot is mostly empty—it's two hours before office time starts. But still his empty spot pokes at her eyes.

She'd talked to Sarah late into the night, told her about Dan—the parts she could tell her about. She told Sarah stories from her crazy life—stories that were safe to whisper. She mourned Dan for real—never mind the lies she told alongside the truth. Never mind the things she left out. Sleep hadn't come for hours. When it had come, it brought along dreams of rooms that must be fled, endless hallways, endless running. Her alarm woke her at 5 a.m., Mandy at her feet, wadding blankets with her kicking paws, dreaming wolf dreams.

The office is blast-chiller cold this early in the day. She walks with purpose down the hallway. She passes her own office. She just wants to look around, clean up anything that might connect her with Dan's death. She wants to wipe up what she can and forget it ever happened. She turns the corner. She walks into Dan's office.

Four men in black stand in a circle. They wear black polo T-shirts over muscle and bulk. The room stinks of body spray and testosterone. They've got blackguard stitched onto their shirts—that weird pyramid logo. A man with a tight brown beard and dead eyes looks at her.

"Who are you?" His voice a flat command.

"Who are you?" she asks back, letting her nerves turn to anger.

"BlackGuard Security, we have a contract with the firm. We're engaging standard protocol for terminated employees with classified client information."

"Did you just fucking say 'terminated'?"

"Please identify yourself."

"Mae Pruitt. I worked with Dan."

"Can we see your ID?"

"No."

"Mae." Cyrus's voice behind her. She turns. He comes toward her with open arms. He doesn't read her body language. He wraps her in a cold hug. A hug of straight lines, no circles. A hug they might teach you in an HR department debriefing.

"In the midst of life we are in death," he says. "Death—especially when it comes for a young man like Dan—is a tragedy. But it's part of the circle of life."

She nods. She says something like *that's so true*. Behind them the BlackGuard men get back to their work packing away Dan's stuff.

"They've just announced a person of interest in the case," Cyrus says.

"Who?"

"A man named John Montez. They aren't saying if he's a suspect yet."

He touches her shoulder—she realizes she's swaying.

"Are you certain you want to take part in work today? I know Dan was a mentor to you. Taking some time to come to grips with your grief is a sensible usage of personal days."

"I want to work," she says. "I need the distraction."

"Very well," he says. "There's work to be done. This Ward Parker story is going to be a challenge. We have to be ready for it."

Behind him, Mae notices Dan's assistant, Tze. Only now does Mae notice the box on her desk—another BlackGuard thickneck standing behind her, watching her pack.

She looks at Cyrus.

"Her severance was generous," Cyrus says.

Tze's eyes are wet but she does not cry.

Mae thinks, *Good girl.*

Mae sits where she usually would, next to Dan's empty seat. She runs her finger around the contours of the live edge of the conference table.

"I'm so sorry," Joss says. "Dan was one of the good ones."

He crinkles an empty water bottle. He doesn't know what to do with it. There are no trash cans anywhere in the office. Cyrus had them all thrown out, put out a press release about the business going green. No more trash cans at desks—the fewer places to put waste, the less waste there will be, at least that was the theory. The single remaining trash can, in the kitchen, filled up at lunch—anybody throwing anything away after that had a fifty-fifty chance of a trash avalanche. But Cyrus got his write-up in *LA Magazine* for his green initiative—and kept a wastebasket in his own office.

"Ward Parker is facing imminent arrest. The timing couldn't be worse—Dan was set to be surfaced on this."

"What do we know?" Helen asks.

"The DA is looking to file charges when the time is right. They're looking for big publicity—and this story is tawdry enough that they might get it."

"I thought Parker was tight with the DA," Joss says.

"He is . . . or was," Mitnick says. "But this accuser is too blatant to ignore. Or maybe Parker's out of favor for reasons we don't know. Unfortunately, Dan was our point man with Parker from the start—I'm afraid he carried a lot of institutional knowledge for this client. Mae—I thought you could be surface in Dan's place, and we put Joss in to handle Parker and dig into the accusation on the legal side."

"Cyrus?"

He looks at her surprised—she didn't know how loud her voice was going to be.

"Here's my pitch: Let me do client relations. I can handle Parker, deal with the accusation. Surface Joss. If we take the homophobia angle—that this is an attack targeted at taking down a gay political figure—it's best to have it come from someone in the LGBTQA community. Dan gave me pointers on how to handle Parker. I'll use Dan's tips to get Parker to trust me. And I'll prep him for an interview, maybe your guy at the *LA Times,* Joss?"

She throws Joss the bone—she needs him to pick it up. Cyrus talked a good game about equality for women—but sometimes he couldn't hear them when they talked.

Joss thinks it over. He stops strangling the water bottle.

"I think it's smart," he says. "Surface me on this one."

Cyrus looks over. He nods to Joss. "Smart," he tells him like it was Joss's idea. For once it doesn't make Mae want to scream.

Nate, this rich-kid intern with a shock of brown hair, walks into the conference room. He's fresh out of Brown, one of their social-media interns who works down in the Bunker. He is the pink-pale of a mole rat.

"There's a car chase on the news," he says.

"Call us when it gets juicy," Joss says.

"Police scanner says it's the suspect who . . . they think it's the man who killed Dan."

The Bunker has this Zoomer tang—energy drinks and natural deodorants. They monitor social media—they create Twitter accounts, Instagram accounts, TikTok accounts. They plant stuff anonymously. They monitor feeds. They work with Indian data farms to write up Twitter bots. Six laptops, two big screens they can throw images to. It's livestream heaven.

The whole staff crams in. They give Cyrus the prime viewing spot. Mae stands next to him. Everybody has their phones out. Everybody's checking different feeds.

The kids in the Bunker look shocked—the gods have

descended en masse. The interns try to hide their lunch trash—with no wastebaskets it's tough. They throw images to the big monitors. Multiple speakers play simultaneously. KNBC has a live feed from a chopper over a winding freeway. This black Dodge Charger swerving across all four lanes.

"That's the Arroyo Secco," Helen says.

The interns pull up feeds from passerby cell phone videos. Rumors and whispers and *fuck-the-police* commentary pepper the speakers. KABC doesn't have a chopper up yet—they throw up images of Dan, images of the murder scene. Mae squints—she can't see herself in the image.

Megan Kang—an intern in selvage denim and an Elvis pompadour—has headphones plugged into her laptop.

"I've got a police scanner feed," she says. Her eyes shine— she's trying to hide how much fun this is. Mae gets it. Her skin tingles. So much information hitting her at once. This feeling like growing extra eyes and ears. She skims her Twitter feed on her phone—she does word searches. People say *go, man, go*. People say *run him off the road*. People say *he's gonna splat*.

"They're saying armed and dangerous," Megan says. "They're saying he's a suspect in a recent homicide."

"Did they say what homicide?" Cyrus asks.

"No, just homicide."

"This could be nothing," Cyrus says. "We've got work to do."

Nobody moves.

"Truth or Dare has a mug shot," Samuel says. He holds up his laptop. This Hispanic kid, shaved head, the letters *WF* inked on one cheek.

78

Joss says, "Looks like a gangbanger."

Samuel pulls the headphones from the speaker jack. The computer's speakers come to life mid-sentence: "—sheriff's department will not confirm that Montez is the suspect in the carjacking-gone-wrong murder of publicist to the stars Daniel Hennigan. Sources in the department say that camera footage from the crime scene has led to a suspect, an arrest was considered to be imminent—but again, they won't confirm if this chase is related."

KNBC's chopper feed goes corrupt—the car smears and bitmaps into digital noise and artifacts. The screen above the crawl goes blank.

Someone says *shit*. Someone says *find a new feed*. The kids click through news sites, search for a livestream.

"Get me Jorge at the sheriff's department public information office," Cyrus says. Behind him his assistant, Taylor, already has his phone out—fifteen seconds later Taylor hands it to him.

"Jorge? Cyrus. Just tell me right now, is this the man?"

Megan's face scrunches. She presses down on her earphones so she can hear over Cyrus barking. Something's happening.

"Jorge, don't you do this to me—this isn't about the favor bank. This is about human decency. Is this the man?"

Megan mouths to Mae: "They've got him. He's stopped."

Cyrus hangs up the phone without saying goodbye, like in a movie. "It's him. It's the son of a bitch who killed Dan."

"Megan," Mae says, prodding with her eyes. "What do you have?"

"I found a livestream on Instagram . . ."

She throws the image up to the main screen. Shaky cell phone footage taken out the window of a pulled-over car on some residential street. Police sirens howling over one another, chopper roars distort everything. It kicks up fresh memories in Mae.

"Goddamn, these motherfuckers rolled up in force," the man holding the camera says. The overtaxed mic distorts his voice. Bitmapped cops pop out of their squad cars, crouch behind their car doors like baby birds. The guy filming it zooms in on a man in a white T-shirt standing next to the Dodge Charger—blurry, but from here it looks like the mug shot. Viewer comments start rolling up the screen—this feed is drawing lots of eyeballs.

"He's got something in his hand," Nate says.

"Fox 11," says some kid in the corner Mae doesn't know. "They've got a chopper right above." The kid throws the image to the other main screen—the same scene with an overhead view. The room watches split-screen live-feed standoff footage.

"Mug shot is for two possession charges—Truth or Dare says he's in the gang registry, he's in some gang called White Fence."

The cell phone live feed has comments scrolling up the side:

GET HIS ASS!!!

FUCK 12

IF HE'S BROWN HE'S GOING DOWN.

The man in the white T-shirt yells something. No noise but cop sirens and chopper wash.

He's got something in his hand. He's moving around. Mae's chest burns—she realizes she stopped breathing.

"They're going to shoot him," Samuel says.

"Oh shit," the man holding the phone says. "Don't give them a reason—"

The man in the white shirt flinches—the metal in his hand glints in the sunlight. The cell phone video lags, freezes—

BANG BANG BANG BANG BANG BANG over a frozen, distorted picture.

The sound redlines the microphone—they come through as blasts of white noise.

The overhead chopper shows the man dropping.

Somebody says *oh my God*.

The cell phone video starts up again—ten seconds in the past. The man is still standing. They watch him—this ghost in the lag. They can't stop what is coming. They watch him die all over again.

Chapter Eleven

MAE

Brentwood

Everyone goes back to their offices. Mae sits with her door closed. She's dizzy heading toward nauseous—three days on a roller coaster.

She trawls the web for reactions. Cyrus surfaces himself for the firm. He makes a statement to the *LA Times,* KNBC, CNN, the *New York Post,* the firm's Instagram page. Helen draws up a statement for the other outlets.

Taylor drops by her office—she's got a three-o'clock appointment tomorrow with Mr. Parker. Mae jots it down. She can't think about it now.

The sheriff makes a statement to a full pressroom. Mae watches a livestream. The sheriff has slicked-back gray hair and a face the color of ham.

"Today at approximately three fifteen there was an officer-involved shooting in the Cypress Park area of Los Angeles. I just want to say there's a lot I don't know yet, and section I-9 of the charter dictates that there will be an independent investigation, so please bear that in mind." Mae's first thought—he's had media training. His voice is strong, the *um*s and pauses edited out of him. "Here's what I can tell you. Sheriff's deputies in East Los Angeles, acting on a

BOLO advisory from Beverly Hills Police Department, attempted to initiate a traffic stop, leading to a pursuit that ended in the Cypress Park area of Los Angeles. As a result of the subsequent pursuit, there was an officer-involved shooting. One hour ago John Montez was pronounced dead at Good Samaritan."

The sheriff answers shooting questions with the standard boilerplate—an investigation will be held, deputies on desk duties. Subtle cues suggest a rapid clearing.

"An investigation will occur that will ensure the constitutional rights of our officers are respected—"

Angry voices from off-camera cut him off.

Someone yells *NO JUSTICE, NO PEACE!*

The sheriff knows to go quiet.

Someone yells *DEFUND THE POLICE!*

Someone yells *ROLL UP YOUR SLEEVES! SHOW US YOUR INK!*

Show us your ink? Mae's never heard that one before.

The voices muffle—the protestors are led away off-camera. The sheriff waits a beat. When he starts again it's like it never happened. He repeats that an investigation is occurring. He says again that he can't comment on an ongoing investigation. He's good—he waits for a question from a friendly before he lays out the case for shooting John Montez.

He explains that Beverly Hills PD pulled security cam footage from the hotel. A man approaching Dan Hennigan at a stoplight in front of the Beverly Hills Hotel in what appeared to be a carjacking. They ID'd Montez—face tattoos make it easy. They released Montez's name to the media. Less than an hour later, the LA Sheriff's Department found him. Mae catches rhythms—she knows the feeling of a story getting nailed down.

Which doesn't mean the story isn't true. She has been on this earth long enough to know that the universe is rude and weird—that sometimes crazy things just happen, things larded with coincidences that mean nothing except that life is insane. And maybe it happened just like they said—maybe Dan and John Montez bounced off each other by random chance. Maybe the fact that Dan was heading toward a meeting with her where he was going to spill some big secret plan was just random chance.

It's possible. And she doesn't believe it at all.

She watches her arms bloom gooseflesh. She can't shake this feeling like someone is standing behind her with a gun pointed at her head.

You're safe—in Dan's voice. *Nobody knows you were there.*

She clicks off the live feed. She tries to prep for her meeting with Parker. One glance at the files kicks the thoughts back up.

What if something in Parker's case was Dan's secret?

The fear comes back. She can feel it like a solid thing in her throat. She tries to swallow it, but it's lodged in fast.

She digs her nails into her arm—she tries to get Montez's ghost out of her head, this guy who was dead already and didn't know it yet.

Chapter Twelve

CHRIS

Calabasas

Leonard DePaulo's backyard is the size of a football field—beyond the marble patio sits a vast orange grove. From De-Paulo's home office, Chris can count six gardeners at work. Beyond the back wall brown scrub dots the bone-dry hills—the orange grove exists as a fuck-you to the gods. The sin of it only makes it more spectacular.

Chris can feel the air on his neck and cheeks. He got a haircut and shave last night. Acker said DePaulo loves cops—he loves to suck up cop energy. He didn't say *you've been looking like lumpy shit lately.* Chris caught the tone anyway. Acker said *dress like a cop-show detective.* Chris dug up his old court suit. The collar scrapes like a knife at his neck—it's a few years old and too tight across his Adam's apple.

Chris's nerves jump inside him—rich people give him the heebie-jeebies. He counts house staff to distract himself. He saw two maids and two assistants, plus the man who introduced himself as DePaulo's majordomo. The muffins on the table in front of them are still warm—add a pastry chef to the staff.

"Gentlemen, thank you for waiting."

Leonard DePaulo is half man / half money. Chris has seen his pre-millionaire news clippings—this doughy nerd with glasses and bad teeth. Then BlackGuard got big and DePaulo got rich. He used his money to reshape himself. He bought himself these weird too-white chompers. PRP injections to fight the hair loss. A trainer and private chef and steroids to get him down to 6 percent body fat. His skin is tanned, microdermabrasion smooth. His head is squat, thickened by years of human growth hormone.

"Chris Tamburro, meet Leonard DePaulo—our benefactor in more ways than one." There's something weird about Acker's voice—it takes Chris a second to nail it. Chris has never seen Acker when he's not the alpha.

Leonard sticks out his hand to Chris—Chris knows he'll try to crush Chris's hand. He's strong; Chris is stronger. His gut tells him *squeeze hard*. DePaulo's eyes flash with pleasure at the crush.

"Hell of a grip," DePaulo says.

"Thank you, sir." Chris knows to give him the *sir*. He only sort of feels like a dog rolling over for a treat.

Acker flashes eyes to Chris like *good boy*.

"Acker speaks highly of you. As does Patrick—thank you for helping him out."

"Glad to do it." Chris makes fists. He lets DePaulo see his scraped-up knuckles. DePaulo grins.

"I understand you have LE experience."

"Ten years in the sheriff's department, mostly out in the shit with the Firearm Trace Task Force. Our job was to get guns out of the hands of people who didn't much want to give them up."

"Chris here was the terror of gangbangers everywhere," Acker says. "You're looking at the OG boogeyman of the San Fernando Valley right here."

There's that geeked-out smile again.

"You've still got contacts at the sheriff's department?"

"Quite a few."

"Chris understands loyalty," Acker says. "And his friends in the department remember that."

DePaulo nods.

"I pride myself on how many services BlackGuard can offer its clients." His voice has changed—now he's the one doing the pitching. Chris passed the audition. Acker picks up on it too—Chris sees him unclench. "But as you know, we can't do it all. We work hand in hand with lawyers like Stephen here, sometimes we go to other firms for cyber-security matters, and of course many of our international jobs require foreign partners. We also sometimes collaborate with PR firms and crisis management firms like Mitnick & Associates," DePaulo says. "I take it you're familiar with them?"

Chris nods—the name kicks up images of Mae. They stop him from making the obvious connection. DePaulo looks at him like he's waiting for him to catch up. Chris puts it together.

"This is about Dan Hennigan."

"Did you know him?"

"We never met directly. I worked with Mae Pruett, his associate, a few times. Solid operator." He leaves the rest out—even Acker doesn't know about his thing with Mae. They kept it secret out of pure instinct.

"But I'm sure you're aware of what happened to him."

"Of course."

"And what's your opinion?"

"Of what?"

The two men trade looks. They want him to be faster on the uptake. He's missing something.

"Of the story as it's being presented to the public so far. That Dan Hennigan was killed in a carjacking gone wrong, and his killer was killed in an officer-involved shooting the next day."

"I haven't seen anything to make me doubt it. Have you?"

"Not exactly," DePaulo says—Chris clocks it as a lie. "It's just that Hennigan was privy to a lot of very sensitive client information. If there's more to the story of his death, we want to know. So we'd like to run our own investigation, parallel to the police."

"You want me to reach out to my department contacts, see what the inside story is?"

"That's right."

DePaulo smiles like *good boy*. Acker smiles like *now you get it*. Chris flashes to them both with broken teeth. He rolls his shoulders to kill the tension.

"Are you the client on this, Mr. DePaulo?"

DePaulo gets this look on his face—not the reaction Chris expected.

"What do you mean?"

"I just wanted to know, are we working this for you, or for Mitnick & Associates?"

"Oh," DePaulo says, recovering—Chris doesn't know why. "Yes, I'm the client."

"We'd like to keep Mitnick & Associates out of the loop on this, Chris," Acker says. Chris nods like *sure*. It had been a routine question—but it jarred DePaulo.

"We'd like you to start with the Montez shooting. Your department contacts and your discretion are what's needed," DePaulo says. "If you find something worth investigating further, bring it to Acker—he'll tell you how to proceed. It's a sensitive assignment—we'll triple your normal rate as a bonus. How does that sound?"

A chance to be more than a fist. A chance to work a case, be something like a cop again. To walk among the living once more. It juices Chris more than the money does.

"I'll do it."

The meeting doesn't last much longer—DePaulo's MMA trainer shows up; he dismisses them quick. He hands them each an orange from his grove. Acker slaps Chris's back on the way back to their cars. He gives him a sotto voce *attaboy*.

A landscaper's truck has parked next to Chris's SUV. The bed of it covered in a tarp. This weird buzzing sound—bees swarm everywhere.

Chris gets curious. He dodges bees to get to the truck. This sick-sweet stench. He pulls back the tarp. Thousands of rotten oranges fill up the truck bed, weeping juice, brown and orange. Chris laughs. Acker gives this sick-scared smile—you never know who is listening.

"They just throw them all away," Chris says through his laughs.

"I guess he just wanted the orange trees. He didn't want the oranges."

Chris tosses his orange into the truck bed. He laughs harder. It's all too perfect. The orange trees look spectacular—you only smell the rot if you get up close.

Chapter Thirteen

MAE

Glendale

Forest Lawn cemetery—tourists wander around, looking for the tomb of Michael Jackson. They shoot side-eyes at Dan's funeral. They wonder if there's someone worth knowing in the coffin. They scan the crowd for famous mourners.

Dan's wife and kids look war-torn. When Mae hugged Jenny, it was like hugging a marionette doll—these hard angles hanging loosely.

Mae stands with the rest of the firm. Mitnick spoke at the funeral. He projected woeful strength. His theme: *He'll be with us always.*

Now, in the cemetery, she looks at his coffin, hears the UNSAID eulogy: *Your secrets go down with you.*

Tze stands at the far edge of the crowd—in a movie it would mean she held a dark secret. But Mae can see how the girl fumbles with her fingers, peeling skin from around her nails—she was just fired; she's hanging back because she feels awkward as hell.

Jenny drops a handful of dirt in Dan's grave. His daughter lets out a sob.

Somebody on the hill yells, "Hey, look, I found Brittany Murphy."

The Dan in Mae's head laughs and laughs.

Tze turns to leave.

Mae waits a beat before she follows.

Tze stands at the side of the parking lot, summoning a rideshare on her phone.

"Hey, Tze."

"Hey . . ." Her voice trails off. Mae guesses maybe medically prescribed benzos. The girl lost her boss and her job, a savage one-two combo.

"Look. I want to buy you lunch. Tomorrow. Are you free?"

A genuine laugh. "Oh, I'm free all right. Like, alarmingly free. But you don't have to do that."

"I want to." She doesn't say *I want to pick your brain about your dead boss.* She doesn't say *I want to know why he was going rogue.* She doesn't say *I want to know if it got him killed.* She doesn't say *I want to know the truth— maybe this time it matters.*

All Dan bequeathed her was this secret. It is hers, and she isn't willing to let it go.

It scares her.

But it juices her more.

PART TWO

Heavier Than a Death
in the Family

Chapter Fourteen

MAE

West Hollywood

West Hollywood City Hall sits catty-corner to the coffee shop. A sheriff's squad car rolls to a stop at the light—see the rainbow flag logo on its door. A big burst of laughter rolls across the street—a drag queen is hosting the weekly bingo game at Hamburger Mary's.

She is here to pitch herself to Parker as the person who will save him from the coming storm. Sublevel one—secure his commitment to the firm. Sublevel two—figure out if Parker was the target of whatever Dan had planned.

Parker comes in, waves to the staff. Shorts and a polo, his skin red-brown from sun. His teeth capped white. Handsome at sixty, not trying too hard to hide his age.

He spots her easy—the only woman customer.

"You must be Mae."

She stands. They do the Hollywood hello hug. He stands back and takes her in.

"Dan's girl Friday. He never said you were so fierce."

Dan in Mae's head: *For Parker, everything sends a message. Whether you understand it or not.* She dressed strategically—she's serving soft-butch supervillain. A black jumpsuit with a slash of emerald at the throat, her bag

Alexander McQueen with a pewter skull on the handle.

"The most important thing about a first impression," she says, "is that you make one."

"Did Dan teach you that?"

She nods. Dan's death still hasn't become a hard fact in her head—it still surprises her each time she remembers. She goes ahead and lets the grief show on her face. The rules say *give the client your trust before you ask for theirs*.

It works. Parker smiles sadly, puts a hand on her arm.

"Oh, my dear girl, I'm so sorry for your loss. He was one of a kind—my punk-rock PR flack. It's just such a tragedy. You have my condolences."

"Thank you."

They sit. A barista brings him an oat-milk cortado without asking. He says, "Thank you, Yonas."

"You're a regular."

"I've lived down the block from here for thirty years. Do you know why?"

"I hear the breakfast at Hugo's is good." The joke lands flat—a test failed.

He nods to city hall.

"I feel safe here. Oh, it's not like the old days—but I still feel safer where I can see that rainbow flag. Do you know why WeHo is the gay mecca of Southern California? Why we banded together here so many years ago?"

Dan in her head: *He has to be the smartest man in the room. Let him be.*

So she says, "Tell me."

"For so many people, the appeal of Los Angeles is that it is a place with no memory—but I've kept mine. I want to remember where we came from. You see, back in the day, the forties and fifties, police made a habit of busting gay bars, arresting everyone, parading queens in front of cameras, putting names in the paper. The LAPD shut down every single gay bar inside LA city limits. The sheriff, however—he loved money more than he hated gays. The men who ran the bars could bribe the sheriff's department to not shut them down. The closest you can get to the heart of Los Angeles and be policed by the sheriff's department is right here in West Hollywood. So the bars here stuck around. It was a place we were safe—because we paid the bribes. We're here because of police corruption—and now the patrol cars in West Hollywood have rainbow flags on them. Funny, isn't it?"

"Is that all true?"

He takes a sip of cortado to cover something.

"I thought you said Dan had trained you well—that's sort of a stupid question for someone in your line of work to ask. Does it matter if it's true?"

Another test failed. The rules say *see the world through their eyes*. Don't ask if what they say is true—figure out *why* they're saying it.

"You're telling me you get what you pay for—and nothing more," she says.

He nods.

"I've raised money for the mayor—West Hollywood and Los Angeles. I've raised money for congressmen and senators and presidents too. That isn't going to change. I might be wounded but I'm not dead. You tell Cyrus that."

"Cyrus knows that—"

"Does he? Cyrus sent you as Dan's replacement—and so far, my dear, you're playing like junior varsity. It makes me think I'm no longer useful. But I promise you, girl, they are wrong. If they think I'm ready for my march out onto the ice floe, they're mistaken."

"Mr. Parker, you're going to be arrested by the end of the week. My associate Joss is working with your attorney to handle statements to the press. But when you are arrested, there is going to be news coverage."

"You're certain you can't kill the story?"

"I could lie to you. I'm a fabulous liar. And then I could spin it later when it all falls apart. But I'd rather tell you what is actually going to happen. The arrest will be public record. You are a public figure. Reza Nuri at the *Times* has fought to cover you before, and Dan managed to kill it. This time he'll get an article. Our job will be to make sure it's as minimal as possible, and that Nuri is out there working the story by himself. We've got friendlies everywhere. We can minimize the coverage. We can keep the story in containment. But we can't kill it."

"Very well. I've come to understand my lifestyle isn't for everyone—maybe even not for you."

"People's sex lives are like their dreams," Mae says. "I only care about them if I'm in them."

He laughs. She's getting her footing. He wants authority. He wants savvy. She gives it: "I suggest a two-pronged approach. For now, we go with search and destroy—keep coverage to a minimum. If it looks like a bigger story is coming—and we'll know, they'll reach out to us for comment—we get ahead of the story. Joss will set you up for an interview with a friendly."

"That sounds correct."

Do it now, Dan says in her head.

"Now, where did you meet the accuser?" She throws the changeup to knock him off-balance. It works. He recognizes the move. He looks at her with more respect.

"You want to talk to him?"

"I need to hear his side of the story. So I can decide how bad it will be when Nuri or another reporter finds him. I need to hear him unfiltered, the way he'll tell it to them. And I need to know what his weaknesses as a witness are. For you."

She feels his eyes digging at her. She holds the gaze.

"Mr. Parker, I don't have much time. This can be the story of a personal arrangement gone wrong—or it can be about a sex-crazed pervert killer who let one get away."

He doesn't react. She can't help but be impressed. Like if you slit his throat nothing would come out.

"Let's be honest, I'm not getting any younger. What I have to offer is money. Maybe it's a crime to pay for sex, but I'm sure it's not a sin. I'm sympathetic to this young man and his wild stories—he may even believe them. Methamphetamine psychosis is a hell of a thing."

"If I talk to him, and there's a way to spin his story to fit with yours, it could lead to charges dropped. But I need to meet him."

"And if he tells you things that could hurt me?"

She draws a zipper-finger across her lips.

"You're my client. Anything he says that doesn't help you, I lock that inside myself. And I'll do what I can to either keep him from the press or poison his story with them."

He smiles—this time it even touches his eyes.

"You'll be my priest, then. The young man's name is Panko—I don't know his real name. He is homeless—I met him on the Santa Monica stroll, but he said he lived in one of the big camps east of there. Over six feet, gorgeous almond eyes, dreadlocks—should look ridiculous on a whiteboy, but they make him look like Heracles. A black circle tattooed on the inside of his wrist. A blotch on his cheek, a birthmark. That's all I know to tell you, I'm afraid."

"It's a start," she says.

He pushes his coffee cup away from him like *meeting's over.*

"Well, then, Sister Mae, go out and absolve me of my sins."

Chapter Fifteen

CHRIS

Koreatown

Chris still has the number in his phone under MAJOR CRIMES.

His thumb hovers over the dial button.

This feeling in his chest—not a phantom heart attack. Something sharper.

He puts the phone down. He looks out the window.

His phone buzzes—a news alert, the Dodgers lost. It breaks his trance. He picks it up again. He unlocks it.

The words MAJOR CRIMES burn into his eyeballs.

He reads them as *you're not a cop anymore*.

He's put off calling the station a full day. He's spent twenty-four hours doing everything he can on public records alone. There are a few things he's ready to be certain about. The hotel released security footage of Hennigan's murder. News sites posted freeze-frames next to Montez's mug shot. You can see the *WF* tat on his face in both. Chris recognized the symbol from his deputy days—*WF* for White Fence, one of LA's oldest gangs. The tattoo made the ID easy. It left no doubt—John Montez pulled the trigger on Dan Hennigan.

The *why* of it still pokes Chris. The working thesis for everybody—a carjacking gone wrong—feels like bullshit.

Gangbangers carjacking people in Beverly Hills is nineties-movie shit.

Witnesses say John grabbed something from Dan's car after killing him—and police on the scene couldn't locate Dan's phone. The phone grab made no sense for a carjacker.

Chris knows better than to expect perfect sense from a crime scene. There are always the details that didn't fit. Maybe the guy wanted a brand-new shiny Tesla and wound up spattering the windshield with a man's brains. Maybe he panicked; maybe he grabbed the first valuable thing he saw.

Maybe.

Maybe not.

A connection between Montez and Hennigan feels far-fetched. A high-end Hollywood publicist and a kid from East Los Angeles might live in the same city, but they exist in different dimensions. If they somehow walked past each other on the street, they wouldn't even see each other.

He thinks about calling Mae, seeing if she has any leads. Or at least offer his condolences. He gets as far as pulling up her name in his texts. He sees he was the one to text last—just a lame HAHAHA to some joke she'd made more than two years ago.

He tells himself reaching out to her is outside of the mission parameters.

He rewatches John Montez snuff footage instead. He watches it slo-mo. The kid has a gun in his hand. Maybe the kid flinched. Maybe he was raising the gun. Maybe he wasn't.

Aerial shots from an overhead chopper reveal nothing. First he's standing, then he's not. First he's alive, then he's dead.

His thumb hovers over the dial button. Pain pops in his chest. It kicks up heart-attack fears. He puts the phone down again. He does the heart-attack checklist the ER doctor taught him.

No nausea—not a heart attack.

The pain isn't in the dead center of his chest—not a heart attack.

His brain dangling a phantom death in front of him. But the real death doesn't come.

Chris looks out the window, phone in hand. Traffic snarls around the strip mall. Electric scooters swerve between cars. He watches it until the pain passes.

He takes a deep breath. He pushes the button. He puts the phone to his ear.

"MCD, Gutierrez."

"Who's captain tonight?" he asks—brusque like a cop would.

"Martinez."

"Get him."

The deputy on the other end doesn't ask questions. Just transfers the call.

"Martinez here." Same throat-slit rasp. Chris is lost for a second in old memories, like when you first plunge into a pool.

Martinez says, "Hello?" It pulls Chris back to the surface.

"Hey, Erwin. It's Tamburro."

"Monster?"

"Often imitated, never duplicated."

"You got that right. Monster Tamburro, back from the dead. How's retirement?"

"Better hours."

"I fucking bet. The streets miss you. These knuckleheads out here don't have the fear anymore. They know big bad Monster Tamburro isn't jumping out a prowler to remind them what asphalt tastes like."

A flash of that invincible feeling—like God had fitted his bulletproof jacket just for him. That old golden glow. He pictures blood smears on the sidewalk. The glow dims.

"I got an ask," he says.

"You've earned one. People don't forget what you did."

"The John Montez shoot. I want the report."

Martinez takes a beat. Chris watches the scene out the window.

"Heard you were working for some defense attorney. You switched teams on me?"

If there's one thing Chris is sure of, it's that there's just one team. But Martinez doesn't want to hear that.

"Man's gotta eat."

"You looking to dry-fuck the department?"

"It's not like that."

"I don't know, Monster. This lawyer you work for, he representing the perp's family? They gonna sue the department on some bullshit? The shoot was in policy."

"No. It's not like that. The client isn't connected to Montez."

"So why you need the report?"

"It's not about the shoot. I'm investigating the kid, not the cops."

"Who's the client?"

"I can't tell you that." Play it as a strength. Don't tell him you don't know.

"Only color I see is blue, man. You still see blue?"

Chris lets the silence speak for him:

Don't make me say *I didn't say your name.*

Don't make me say *I died for your sins as well as mine.*

When it comes, it comes as an anonymous email from an encrypted server. Subject line: REMEMBER WHAT YOU WERE.

It's Friday night—outside Chris's window Koreatown rocks. The strip mall across the street from Chris's apartment window is open-air calamity. Panhandlers work as ad hoc doormen for the 7-Eleven. Crowds mill outside the restaurants—the braised short ribs joint, the knife-cut noodle joint, the spicy pig knuckle joint. The parking lot is jammed—the valets sprint from car to car. They play full-metal Tetris. They swerve, reverse at speed, never clip a bumper.

Chris thumb-scrolls through PDF attachments. He switches to his laptop and starts downloading. He opens up scanned files. He finds Montez's CalGang Database Subject Identification Card. LAPD put him in the database four years ago—John Montez, moniker: Slick. Seventeen years old. Criteria rationale for putting him in the file: riding in a car with known members of the White Fence gang. The Polaroid the cop took at the scene—look at this scared-ass kid.

Chris clicks another file. Form 12.16.05—parental notification of inclusion in the CalGang Database—sent to an address in El Sereno. That's strange—the kid was from El Sereno Rifa turf, but the CalGang file had him as a member of White Fence. He jots the address down. Thoughts of visiting the family give him bad vibes.

These high-pitched squeals outside break his concentration. On the sidewalk below, teenagers eat dragon-breath desserts out of monster-shaped cups. They breathe out plumes of dry-ice vapor. More squeals follow. They hold up phones and livestream it all.

Chris opens more files. Montez only has a few real busts—possession, a drunk and disorderly outside a Hollywood Boulevard nightclub. The mug shot, a transformation, the scared-ass kid now sporting a face tattoo. Only full-tilt doomers fuck with face tattoos—it's strange Montez's jacket is so slight. Somehow he went from this scared-eyed kid to a hard-core gangster without building a rap sheet or doing any time.

He reads Beverly Hills PD reports on the Hennigan shooting. He builds a timeline of the post-murder investigation. Beverly Hills PD yanked video footage from traffic-light cams and hotel security cams—probably had them in hand before Dan got to the morgue. The screen grabs of the footage are blurry—but Montez's face ink would be visible from space. They've got a good ID overnight.

They swear out an arrest warrant by midnight. They hit John's parents' address at 4 a.m. They don't find Montez. The parents don't give them any leads to work off of.

Beverly Hills PD releases John's name as a person of interest at 9:30—less than an hour later, the sheriff's department spots him in East LA.

Why East LA? He has no KAs and no family there.

Chris takes a break, orders fried chicken delivery from a

Korean joint up the street. He digs back into the files while he waits. He pushes past eye blurs. He reads the shooting report, written by a Deputy Marcus Woodcock.

Approximately 1100 hours Deputy Archer and I were patrolling in the area of Floral Drive and N Eastern Avenue when a passerby flagged our unit down and informed us of an armed man sitting in a dodge charger. Deputy Archer advised dispatch of our location en route. Arriving on location of nearby parking lot I identified man sitting in Dodge Charger as fitting description of BOLO subject John Montez. Using loudspeaker we advised man to exit vehicle. The subject refused and instead left the scene. We pursued code 3 while Deputy Archer informed dispatch of our vector. After a pursuit the subject exited his vehicle in an attempt to flee on foot. We both exited vehicle. I observed what appeared to be a firearm in his right hand. I advised subject to drop his weapon and lay facedown on the ground. At this time I became aware of helicopter overhead, making it impossible to hear Montez's verbal responses. I observed the suspect's erratic behavior. The suspect appeared to raise his weapon. Fearing for the safety of ourselves and others Deputy Archer and I opened fire. Once the suspect was down we proceeded to advance and secure control of the suspect, who was unresponsive. At which time I advised dispatch of shots fired. I attempted to render aid to the suspect by applying pressure to the wound . . .

Something in Chris's brain wiggles like a loose tooth. He reads the report again. Chris has an eye for the art of the false report—he's written dozens. He focuses on one phrase:

A PASSERBY FLAGGED OUR UNIT DOWN.

A classic piece of horseshit. In eight years on the street, Chris had been waved down by a random civilian maybe twice—but he'd written it in reports two dozen times. It's a cover story—unfalsifiable by anyone, like saying you smelled pot smoke so you can search a car without a warrant. Chris makes a leap that's barely a leap—there was no passerby. Woodcock got Montez's location from a source he wants to protect.

Maybe it's nothing. Chris has worked enough cases to know the solutions to most mysteries are simple and dumb. That if it looks like some gangster wannabe tried to carjack a man in Beverly Hills at rush hour and ended up killing him, then most of the time that's exactly what happened.

But that tooth keeps wiggling.

A knock at the door breaks his concentration. Dinner. Chris pays—the bag smells like heaven. He thinks he should call it a night on the research—sticky Korean fried chicken doesn't mix with working the laptop.

But that thing in his head goes *wiggle wiggle wiggle.*

He types one-handed. He breaks a full sweat from the spice. He throws the bones back into the delivery bag.

He dives into Deputy Woodcock. He finds a Facebook page—Woodcock is straight from central casting. back the blue images all over his home page. A bland-pretty wife and bland-pretty kids on a Jet Ski in Lake Elsinore. Woodcock posing with guns in both hands, a skull logo on his chest.

Chris does searches. He reads old news articles. Woodcock's name comes up in a lot of news stories. Woodcock is a shooter. Most cops never even pull their gun their whole career. The ones who do tend to do it a lot. Montez is Woodcock's fifth officer-involved shooting. Chris remembers one of them. A seventeen-year-old with seven shots in the back, lots of news coverage, lots of protests. Woodcock cleared the board anyway.

Shooters always cleared the board.

Woodcock's name comes up on some civilian watchdog site. He finds his name in a report on sheriff's department cliques. Woodcock is a Dead Game Boy.

Wiggle wiggle wiggle.

This chorus of horns outside breaks his concentration. This white kid on an electric scooter rolls downhill at high speed. His face is sheer terror. His face is sheer joy. He runs the intersection against a red light. He misses an SUV by inches. The 7-Eleven panhandlers cheer. A valet sprints past the kid—they've got no time for whiteboy shit. The teens drop their phones, bored again—a kill would have gone viral.

Chris wipes his hands off with the towelette the restaurant included. He blinks tired eyes. His burps burn the back of his throat. He summarizes. He rough-drafts a report to Acker.

You have John Montez gunning down Dan Hennigan—a killing that feels random, with no visible connections to the victim. A crime that doesn't make sense. You have a case that breaks quickly—thanks to an alleged hard-core gangster who doesn't know to cover up his face tattoos. You have John's face wind up on the news. An hour later you have cops run into him with a random bullshit story—not just cops, but cliqued-up shooters.

Outside his window Koreatown glows and hums like neon. Chris knows how it feels.

Chapter Sixteen

MAE

Silver Lake

"Like I'm thinking about getting a cat, but all my succulents died, so maybe I ought to take the hint, right?"

Tze sits hunched over, elbows on the table—there are no chairs in the restaurant, only stools. She is not a small girl, but Mae looks at her and sees a baby bird.

Mae picked the place on Silver Lake Boulevard, just down the hill from the reservoir, because it was close to Tze's apartment—and some of the east-side tent cities. She briefed Mitnick, got him to agree that Parker's accuser was job number one.

For his own sake as well as our client's. He'd said it with a straight face.

Mae rolled work calls on her Bluetooth while driving east this morning. She checked with reporters at the dailies, the TV stations, seeing if anybody had wind of the Parker story yet. A few played dumb in a way that let Mae know they were working on something.

She'd stopped by Echo Park on her way over here. First she'd hit the ATM, got five hundred dollars in twenties. She walked around the lake at Echo Park—in the last year or so since she'd been there, it had transformed into a full tent city. Hundreds of tents ringed the lake. Ducks quacked and shat between multi-tent structures connected by tarp hallways. She looked for a tall, pretty man with whiteboy dreads. She asked around. A woman with thick dreads and sad eyes knew Panko, said she'd seen him around. Mae gave her a twenty and a slip of paper with her phone number.

Now, in the artificial air of the restaurant, Tze picks at her avocado hummus with Santa Barbara pistachios. Mae picks at her bowl of ancient grains and bison. It made her jaw tired to eat it.

"Do you come here a lot?" Mae asks.

"A loaf of bread is fourteen dollars here," Tze says, nodding at the front counter. "That seems like an indictable offense."

"I'd just heard it was good," Mae says—she lets a wounded tone seep in. She watches the guilt bloom on the girl's face.

"Oh, it is," Tze says, panic in her voice. She looks over, nods to a table where Beanie Feldstein shares a plate of crudités. "It's really cool."

Her eyes plead *forgive me*.

Mae says a worthless prayer for this girl—someday some man with an eye for weakness is going to get his hooks into her and tear her all apart.

The place is more crowded than Mae would like—she wants Tze to be able to speak freely. The closest table, a man and a woman with a daughter fresh from the reservoir loop. Bicycle-swole calves bulge between shorts and vegan-leather running shoes. The little girl ignores them, watches her phone in a trance. The mom says, "Chrysalis, please, at least try the rock cod."

Mae asks Tze, "How are you holding up?"

"I never knew anybody who died before. I'm still processing it. Sometimes I feel somehow it's my fault."

"It's not your fault." Again Mae thinks about holding a baby bird in her hands. This thing you could crush with one bad squeeze. She quashes her irritation—if she lets Tze see it, the girl will shut down completely.

"I reminded him, he had a last appointment," Tze says. "I kept him a couple minutes signing some checks. What if I hadn't? But that's like latent narcissism, right? Feeling guilty about me and my godlike powers?"

Mae stirs her bowl of food. She hits it with the house-made lacto-fermented hot sauce. She lets Tze tell her story in her own way.

"It's weird," Tze says. "Like, he's still in my phone. Do I delete him? It seems wrong. But like someday my contacts are going to be half dead people and that is weird too, right? Like we're all going to be carrying these little graveyards around with us. Like we're even going to be around that long." She grins, awkward. "Sorry. I'm still processing the trauma."

"It's a sad thing," Mae says. And that's true. But Mae put her own sadness behind a pane of glass, where she can see it but it can't creep in. She wants to tell this girl to do the same.

"Can I ask you something?" Tze asks.

"Sure."

"Is it wrong?" Tze asks.

"Huh?"

"What we did at the firm. Helping these people, our clients. Is it wrong?"

"It's a job," Mae says. "I try to focus on the fun parts. To be on the inside. To have the secrets. I like to fight and I like to win. This job lets me do that."

Tze takes a drink—she wants to hide what she thinks from Mae.

Tze says, "I don't know what I'm going to do. If I don't find something soon, I'll have to go back to Seattle—my parents will start talking about grad school. Or, God save me, med school. I don't know if this is for me anyway. I don't think I was very good at it. I think Dan didn't fire me because he was nice. He was, you know? That was his secret."

"Well, one of them," Mae says. "Dan had a lot of secrets, didn't he?"

Tze fumbles her iced matcha. She flusters so much Mae thinks, *Was she sleeping with Dan?* But no—Dan dug strength. Vulnerable girls wouldn't give him that feeling of victory he craved.

But the girl knows something.

Tze says, "Everything at the firm is a secret. You know how many nondisclosures they had me sign on my way out the door?"

"There's secret, and then there's *secret*. You know what I'm talking about."

Mae does her imitation of Dan talking to a girlfriend, hunched over his desk, hand around his phone. Tze laughs, spraying the air with Santa Barbara pistachio dust. "Oh God, it looks just like him."

Flash to his blood sprayed on a cracked car window.

The little girl at the next table lets loose this primal scream—it knocks Mae from the memory. The girl's parents look at her like she's got a gun—they all but put their hands up in the air. Mae turns back to Tze, focused again. Mae gives her a girls'-club smile. She leans forward. Tze mirrors her.

Got her.

"Dan was the one who taught me, when you're doing dirt, stand tall and smile—the more you look like you're trying to not be noticed, the more you'll look like someone trying not to get caught—but when it came to the women, he couldn't help himself. He couldn't help but act guilty. I think it was because he really did love Jenny—I think it was something he felt guilt about. Not like what he did for the firm. That was just business to him."

Tze laughs. She gets this smile on her face and Mae thinks, *Pay dirt.*

"He had two trainers," Tze says. "Like, he had Thor or whatever—"

"Zeus," Mae says, "he had him for years."

"—and then he has this new one, Katherine."

Two trainers—a classic Dan cover story. He was fit, but it wasn't like he was training to be in a superhero movie. It felt wrong in the right way.

"Katherine? He never mentioned her to me."

"He didn't mention her at all. That's what I mean. He booked those appointments himself. Twice a week." Tze smiles, looking almost relieved. Sometimes a secret can swell up inside you. You have to relieve the pressure. That's why everyone whispers sooner or later.

"Do you have Katherine's last name?"

The little girl behind them fucking *shrieks*. Mae feels her jaw go tight.

The mom says, "Chrysalis, please!"

"I found her on Instagram once," Tze says. "Just lifestyle porn and tummy-tea ads. These thirst-trap yoga poses I can't hardly look at without triggering body issues, you know?"

She hands Mae the phone. Katherine Sparks is mid-twenties, blond, savagely fit, a handstand-splits yoga pose. She has this perfect snub nose. She has this confident smirk. She has these wild eyes.

Dan's type writ large.

At the table behind them, Chrysalis's shit fit goes thermonuclear. The little girl flips her plate. Zhug-smudged rock cod goes flying.

The mom says, "Chrysalis, no!"

Mae catches the waitress's eye. She signs the air like *check, please*. Tze makes a move for her purse—purely ceremonial. Mae waves like *no* and pulls open her purse.

"Thank you."

"My pleasure. It was nice to get to talk. Look, it's none of my business. But you ought to think about going back to Seattle. I don't know if this is the place for you."

"Why?"

"You asked about right and wrong."

Chapter Seventeen

MAE

Silver Lake

Mae takes Silver Lake Boulevard back toward the 101. She tries to scroll Katherine's Instagram feed while driving—horns erupt. She looks up and stomps the brake—tires squeal. She avoids rear-ending a BMW by inches.

She pulls into the parking lot of a Chinese Food & Donuts takeout place. The near crash pours more adrenaline on the fire. Her hands shake. She rests the phone in the cupholder. She browses Katherine's Instagram. See how the mask fits just so. Her smile soft, her eyes hard. Mae scrolls—mirror selfies, shots of gluten-free snack bars, fresh-squeezed beet juices—health-influencer sponcon. Quick videos of her teaching dance classes, teenage girls, teen-actress types doing dancehall moves.

Katherine poses with roommates—a fatless ginger guy with a cocksure face named Kevin, a muscle-bound blond named Loto, a tall and handsome Black man named Tony. Mae scrolls past thirst-trap body shots, trying to look carefree and spontaneous. The living situation screams *wannabe clout house*.

Pictures with celebrities she's trained—there's a Chris, there's a Housewife.

Party shots, reality show stars and former teen actors—there she is with Lydia Lopez, former *As If!* tween star turned minor pop diva. And speaking of *As If!,* here's Katherine with the one and only Hannah Heard, a quick candid in some VIP room. Hannah's grin is pasted on—Mae knows her well enough to see past the twinkle in her eyes to the venom underneath.

Mae keeps scrolling. Vacation shots: Katherine paddle-boarding in Maui, whale watching in Sayulita, yoga stretching at a Bangkok temple, a sunset shot at a Palm Springs luxury spa, surfing in—

Hold up. Scroll back. The Palm Springs spa.

See how the picture is cropped tight? Katherine has cut someone out of the selfie. There at the bottom of the frame, one piece of the other person remains. A slice of a man's arm—thin wrist, dark arm hair.

Just like Dan.

Mae checks the date of the photo—May 23 of last year.

She opens her calendar, scrolls back to last May—a four-day event, color-coded red for Dan—DAN OUT OF OFFICE (PS). *PS* for Palm Springs.

Dan and Katherine in a Palm Springs tryst.

Dan and Katherine—planning some kind of get-fuck-you-rich scheme?

She thinks about how to chase this down. Already this rogue thing she's doing threatens to overwhelm her. She still needs to find Panko, hear his story about Parker—and show him a picture of Dan. That means hitting more tent cities. She also has her day job—and Mitnick is shoveling Dan's workload onto her now that the mourning period has passed. She can't chase this thread, search for Panko, and keep her clients happy all at once.

She thinks it over. She opens her contacts. She calls Tze.

"Hello?" That wary prey-animal voice. The weakness of it makes her want to chew the insides of her mouth.

"Hey, it's Mae. Great to see you today. Look—if you're not heading back to Seattle right away, would you like a job?"

Chapter Eighteen

CHRIS

El Sereno

Scared of a dead kid's mom.

Chickenshit supreme.

The Montez house sits up the hill from Valley Boulevard. A two-story stucco house with painted bars on the windows. The yards dotted with concrete shrines and bougainvillea bracts. He parks behind a 1940s pickup truck, cherry restored. He brushes crumbs off his lap. He grabbed a coffee and a concha at a bakery on Marengo.

He looks at his old badge—a real badge for a fake cop.

He's put it off as long as he can.

He walks up to the house. He makes himself knock soft—years of *fuck-you-I'm-a-cop* make his instinct to pound hard.

The kid who opens the door is maybe fifteen, stretched out and skinny, with the sort of teenage mustache that makes the kid look younger instead of older. He freezes at the sight of Chris. Chris doesn't even bother with flashing his badge. The kid has him pegged as a cop the moment he sees his white ass.

"I'm looking for Gustavo or Marisol Montez."

The kid looks at him—fear and hatred fight behind his

eyes. Chris doesn't blame the kid. The kid pushes the door closed to a crack. Chris hears a muffled call for *Ma*.

Marisol Montez wears business clothes in mourning colors. Chris can see the grief running riot behind her eyes. Sees something else there too, something electric. She's not even five foot—she looks strong but also crushed, like gravity on her world is heavier than on his.

"Can I help you?"

"LA Sheriff's Department, ma'am. I want to talk to you about your son."

"I don't have anything to say to you."

"Ma'am, I'm not investigating your son. I'm with LASD Internal Affairs. I'll be investigating the officer-involved shooting."

"Is that what you're doing? Investigating your own?"

"That's right, ma'am."

"When's the last time a cop got punished for killing someone in LA? Maybe you're not so good at your job. Or maybe you're very good at it."

"Ma'am, I'm trying to be fair. You can help me."

She snorts like *yeah right*. She says, "I have to go to work."

"May I speak to your husband, then?"

"He's sick," she says, after a micro-pause that lets Chris know she's lying.

"Then, please, just a moment of your time."

"And if I say no?"

"Then I'll only have one side of the story to go on."

She opens the door. The look on her face is one he's seen a hundred times. Submitting without breaking, a silent *fuck you*.

"I've got ten minutes before I've got to get to the bank."

He waits for her to say *come in*. He's playing by cop rules. You have to be invited in. Cops are like vampires that way.

Marisol leads him through the living room, where a man he guesses is Gustavo sits on the couch, the morning news traffic report on the television. Chris has been in rooms like this before, seen fathers like this. You either freeze your blood or let it boil and cook you from the inside. Gustavo has chosen the ice. He stares at the wall above the TV, watching some movie projected by his own eyes.

A little girl sits at a kitchen table, eats scrambled eggs and toast in a Dora the Explorer T-shirt. A loaf of Bimbo bread sits on the counter.

"Go eat your breakfast with Papi," Marisol says. The little girl takes in Chris with big eyes. She takes her plate to the next room without words.

Marisol looks at her phone.

"You've got eight minutes," she says.

Chris puts his manila folder on the table. The file is thick with old papers Chris had lying around the house. He pretends to thumb through it, pulls out the CalGang paperwork he printed out this morning.

"There's something that doesn't make a lot of sense," he says. "Looking at your son's file. His CalGang file has him as a member of White Fence—but this is El Sereno turf."

She laughs.

"Turf, is that what this is? That bullshit piece of paper ruined my son's life."

"So you're saying he wasn't a member of a gang?"

She shakes her head, hard—like she could shake loose the truth.

"He was at a street race in Huntington Beach—just watching, driving my Honda Fit, that's no street racer. Police showed up. When the police broke it up, he did what all the kids did, he drove away—he got unlucky, one of the police decided to pull him over. He was a good—Get that look off your face."

"Ma'am?"

"That look like I'm just another mother standing up for her no-good child. I say my son was a good boy and you sit there and you think *they all say that*. Okay, they do. But you know what? Maybe they were. Maybe every single one of them started out a little boy just like you were."

"I didn't mean to have a look."

She fades away, lost in memories.

"He didn't do well with pressure. This cop chasing him, he didn't run, he tried to pull over, but my son, he got confused, he turned the wrong way into a highway exit. He tried to fix it, he backed up and pulled over. But that cop charged him, every single thing he could think of. Three thousand dollars' worth of fines.

"The boy in the car with him, he was already in CalGang, I don't know why, so now the cops think this other boy is a gangster, and since my son was in a car with him, it must make him a gangster too. Like it's a sickness you can catch just by breathing the same air. That policeman, he wrote my son three thousand dollars' worth of tickets and put him in CalGang. That file ruined his life, seventeen years old.

He liked to draw, he liked art. He had a job at a print shop. A trade. Like his father—Gustavo's a butcher. Aren't many trades left in this world that aren't done by a machine, but my boy found one. My son lost his license—he couldn't deliver for the print shop anymore, he lost his job. Once a thing gets put in the files, it can't ever be undone. You can't ever take it away. It becomes the truth, to most people anyway. Once they decided he was with that gang, they never left him alone. They took him in over nothing. Every little thing—he's a teenage boy, you were one, didn't you run wild? Didn't you break some streetlights, maybe get drunk and stupid? But now it was different for him. If everybody thought he was a gangster, he might as well be one. But he never fit in with the real *carnales*. They knew that's not who my son was. They weren't fooled by some database. The cops thought my son was a gangster, but the real gangsters never did.

"So he fell in with some new crowd, people he met in some nightclub. Started getting those tattoos, getting big. He moved west side, got him a job at a bar as security, moved in with some white folk—folk who would believe he was what he pretended to be."

Her voice is getting thick, getting wet with grief now. "And maybe since he found folk who believed him, he could really become that thing. I don't know. He was different these last few months. Started making promises, he was going to pay me back, pay off my car note. He was going to take care of us. But he never lost those eyes. He was my son, this sweet little boy used to draw pictures of lions and tigers for me . . ."

She trails off. Chris takes the moment to fish out his phone. He's got the photo of Dan Hennigan cued up. He shows it to Marisol.

"Did you ever see your son with this man before the shooting?"

"I know who that is. The man. The police say my son shot that man—but that wasn't him. I'm not lying to myself. I saw the tapes. But that wasn't the man my son was supposed to be. They made this mask for him and put it on him and he wore it long enough that it grew onto his face."

Her voice is wet. Chris has that dull panic he felt every time one of their mothers cried.

"They didn't have to shoot him. He wasn't going to shoot. He wasn't what he looked like. He wasn't what he was . . . I know that sounds like crazy talk, but I mean it. He wasn't what he was." The words are coming out of her in clots now. "Did you see his eyes? You saw the tape, did you see his eyes?"

"I saw them," he says. She nods, vindicated.

"A mother knows that look. A mother knows when she's needed. A mother sees that look and all you want to do is run, that look is like a scream, *Mami, Mami . . .* "

She clenches her jaw to keep something inside. Chris sits with her, knowing that if he reached for her she would pull away. That she would be right to do it.

The teenage boy comes to stand in the doorway. He tries to kill Chris with his eyes. Chris stands—his knees are weak.

He says, "If you haven't already, you can talk to a lawyer. Try David Gibson. He's the good kind of bastard. The police will throw a settlement offer at you. Say no to that one. They'll come back with a second offer. That's the one to take."

He shows himself out. On his way out the door, Chris throws one more look toward Gustavo. The man's face is still frozen. His hands in his lap grasp and clench the air like he's trying to find the world's throat and choke it until it's dead.

Chapter Nineteen

MAE

Brentwood

The office is a meat locker. Mae bites the inside of her mouth to kill her shivers—she left her jacket in the car. Thoughts of Katherine loop at the back of her head like a bad song.

She pokes her head into Joss's office. He's eating turmeric couscous, drinking a turmeric latte. He gives her a yellow smile.

"Hey, girl. What's the T?"

"You know, wandering through homeless camps looking for a sex worker. Living that standard-issue Los Angeles dream."

"Oh, she wants glamour," he says, holding up a printout. "She wants prestige. Maybe she'd rather be working on the firm's latest client, Euridyce."

"Sounds like a Swedish pop star."

"Close. It's a 'human tissue procurement company.'"

"Say what now?"

"Human tissue procurement. You know people who donate their organs when they die? You think their parts go to charity? Not even. They go to companies like Euridyce—and, listen, they take your corpse down to the bits and bobs. Organs, sure, of course they take those. But they take your skin too, your tendons, your heart valves—I'm telling you, they turn your bones into paste and put them into dental implants."

He laughs at whatever face she's making.

"I'm feeling really good about this conversation," she says. "These are facts I'm happy to know."

"Who you telling? I'm sitting here reading about how when I die they might cut off my head and sell it to a plastic surgery school—they use your severed head for practice. I mean for real, it doesn't even stop when you're dead, does it?"

"Why'd they hire the firm? I mean, other than the obvious."

"They've got an office right inside the LA coroner's building. And sometimes they get a little eager, they grab the bodies before the coroner okays them. Sometimes it causes problems."

"You got to grab them while they're hot, I reckon," she says.

"Literally. And the *Times* is sniffing around. So here I am. Girl, I don't know if you noticed, but our lives are crazy."

Mae laughs harder than it deserves. She doesn't say *you have no idea*.

She sits down at her desk. She pulls a scarf from a drawer. She wraps it around her head like a mask. She's so cold she can't feel her ears.

First she Venmos Tze some petty cash and two weeks' pay—strictly off the books. When she offered Tze the job, she gave her Panko's description. Tattoos, eyes, the birthmark on his cheek. She gave her a list of places to start—some of the larger tent cities. Just the ones she could think of off the top of her head. The side streets south of Beverly and Vermont. Backstreets south of the Cinerama Dome. The Sunset/Myra overpass. Tze sounded grateful for the work. She sounded scared but she tried to hide it. Mae pitched it as a do-gooder gig—help us find this unhoused person. I'm going to give him money, help him out.

She doesn't say *you'll do my job so I can stalk Katherine Sparks*.

She doesn't say *it's to help a client dodge assault charges*.

She doesn't say *for a bonus, he's maybe the reason that Dan got killed*.

Mae forces herself to do work. She makes some calls on the Bishoi case, orders a report on union organizers for an animation studio. She follows up with some loose ends from Dan's old clients. His voice runs through her head like a bad song.

He tells her, *Do your due diligence.*

Mae makes calls on the landline. She uses her personal phone to cyberstalk Katherine. She turns off Wi-Fi and uses her data plan—she doesn't want the name Katherine Sparks to go across company servers. Katherine teaches a class called Tiger Style—aerobics for Gen X hipster moms, eighties dance tunes, no judgment. Katherine lives in her flesh, rides it comfortably. How her hair curls so effortlessly around her neck—the kind of girl Mae would have said she hated in high school but would obsess over. The way it coughs up memories of Mom watching her dinner plate, judging it with silent eyes as Mae reached for seconds.

Katherine also teaches dance and aerobics to teen girls—she seems to be hooked into the teen-actor ring—they prey on the prettiest girls in their high schools, or just the moms with the fiercest wills, the deepest unlived dreams. They sell them headshots and acting and dance lessons. A few of them make it; most of them stay out for a pilot season or two before moving back poorer and angrier and with disappointed moms.

Katherine does dance classes for ItGirl, the teen-talent casting agency. They are real players in the teen-actress world. They supply basic cable with their tweener stars. This producer named Eric Algar, king of the tweener shows. They find mini pop divas and child actors.

Sometime around noon Mae stops lying to herself. She stops making work calls. She eats a stale salad at her desk. She digs into Katherine's online life.

The ItGirl contact brought in good business. Katherine helped train the second generation of As If! stars. That show had run for years, cast in and out. A lot of famous people started with As If!—ask a girl who was thirteen anytime in the last decade. Lydia Lopez was the most famous—now that Brad was dead—but there were dozens of ex-As-If!ers sprinkled through Hollywood. One hosts a pizza-baking reality competition on Netflix; one caused a mini scandal with her OnlyFans page a few months back.

And then there was Hannah Heard. Mae scrolls back to Katherine's photo with Hannah.

Fuck it.

"What's up, hooker?" Hannah's voice on the phone is cough-syrup thick. Mae can hear Mochi going batshit in the bg.

"Hey, girl. How's your eye?" The thinnest pretext Mae can think of. She scrolls past a muted video of Katherine talking, the words KEEP YA SHITTY COMMENTS TO YOURSELF superimposed over her face.

"It's fine—everybody on-set is scared of Mochi now. They saw my eye and now they know she's a badass." Hannah lies about it so easy—there's no hint that the story is bullshit, even to Mae, who made the story up. Hannah is someone who constantly lives her truth, even if that truth is a lie. She figures maybe that's just what an actress is. "It's ancient history anyway. The production is a shit show. I hate it here. Total nightmare."

Mae remembers a joke Sarah told her once: *How do you make an actor miserable? Hire them.*

"Oh no," Mae says pro forma. She knows she has to let Hannah vent before she'll be able to steer the conversation herself. She scrolls past Katherine doing sponcon for tea-infused beauty collagen powder.

"They've been lighting for three hours—I'm like it's a green-screen box, what's there to light? Anyway, no dialogue in the scene so at least I'm off book."

Mae laughs like she hasn't heard that one before. She says, "So this is totally random, I'm calling for a reference, I'm looking at this new personal trainer—you know a woman named Katherine Sparks?"

Hannah faux-retches. "That clout-sniffing bitch."

"So that's a no on the reference?"

"She's a bottom-feeder. She's plugged in with ItGirl—I used to be with them a million years ago when I was a dumb kid. You saw my picture with her online someplace?"

"Instagram."

"Like, she didn't tell me she was going to use me like that—fucking using me for a billboard, you know? Girl posted that shit everywhere. Tagged me in a picture, used it to sell her dance classes—I never took one of her classes. She's just a three a.m. friend, you know?"

"Actually, no."

"Like, the people who wind their way into the VIP during cocaine hours. Hustlers. Always playing you, everything a game. Always some hustle, some movie pitch, a clothing line, a kilo of coke they're gonna whack up and sell, something something something. Bad news. One of those bitches who never eats and is always hungry, you know?"

Hannah hisses something like *all right* to someone.

"Listen, hooker, I got to run—rumor has it we're filming a movie right now. Short answer is, steer clear of that shark unless you want to get eaten alive."

Chapter Twenty

CHRIS

East LA

Nobody calls it a kill party.

Kill parties are against regulations. Kill parties send the wrong message to the public.

So nobody calls it a kill party.

The air in the tattoo parlor smells like mango vape and testosterone. The mood is scary-festive. The off-duty deputies who crowd the room have sleeve tattoos and cop haircuts. They are Black, white, brown. They kill the tattoo artist's lowrider oldies, commandeer the speakers. They blast frat metal. They laugh louder than they need to, just to mark how they own the place. Like territorial pissing.

The tattoo artist rocks an old-school Chicano style—creased khakis and a white T-shirt under his apron. He's got thick glasses. He's good—his art all over the walls, Aztec warriors and demons and girls in clown makeup. He works in silence—Chris can tell some of his own ink was done behind prison walls. Hosting an after-hours deputy-clique party wasn't his idea.

Deputy cliques share hand signals; they share tattoos—always covered by the uniform. They have names like Little Devils. The Vikings. The Banditos.

But nobody calls them gangs.

Sheriff's department cliques have been outlawed. The sheriff has said their existence is a myth. The sheriff says a few bad apples caused all the problems. The sheriff denies that deputy cliques are gangs at all. Chris has heard the whispers that the sheriff is a member of a clique himself. They say the sheriff has a Bandito—a skeleton with a sombrero and shotgun—riding on his bicep. Sometimes the press asks him about it. Sometimes protestors yell *show us your ink*. The sheriff says it's a lie—and keeps his sleeves rolled down.

But nobody calls them gangs.

Rumor has it the Dead Game Boys require an overt act to get accepted. You have to get some blood on you—a back-alley beatdown, a shoot, plant evidence—or refuse to talk to IA when an investigation comes down. They live by blood in, blood out. You have to do dirt to get initiated. You have to spill blood to earn the red ink. Rumor says the Dead Game Boys run the East Los Angeles station.

But nobody calls them a gang.

Deputy Darvin Archer sits in the tattoo chair, shirtless. Archer already has the snarling pit bull head inked over his heart. Chris knows every Dead Game Boy has the same tattoo inked over their heart, where it would always be covered by a uniform and bulletproof vest. The tattoo gun hums and drools red. The tattoo artist inks red blood on the pit bull's teeth. Archer is dark-skinned—it makes the fresh red ink pop. The rules of the Dead Game Boys say you only get to add the blood after you've killed a man in the line of duty. Archer earned these bloody teeth gunning

down John Montez. The rest of the crew is here to cele-
brate his killer's ink.

But nobody calls it a kill party.

Everyone in the room except the tattoo artist and Chris
is a Dead Game Boy.

Outside the parlor, food trucks crowd Atlantic Boulevard.
The one right across the street features a huge al pastor
trompo of meat roasted by a vertical grill, a pineapple
cooking on top of the rotating pork. The guy working the
trompo is a pro. Chris watches him slice the pork one-
handed, catching the falling meat right on top of the tortilla,
bull's-eye—a quick flick to the pineapple up top, pieces of
roast pineapple falling. Chris makes plans in his head to hit
the stand on his way out the door.

Chris got his introduction from Martinez. Martinez
must have vouched for Chris all the way. Woodcock
invited him to the party. Chris stands next to him now.
Woodcock plays the alpha among alphas. Chris can all
but see how his blood bubbles with horse steroids. He's
cartoonishly jacked and vascular—his arms pop veins
like he's wearing double tourniquets. His shaved head
plays up his wide skull. Chris can see the animal behind
his eyes, kicking its cage door, begging to be let free. He
eyes Chris, wary—he's not used to not being the biggest
man in the room.

"Heard you had a rep back in the day," Woodcock says
to Chris.

Catch how he stresses *back in the day*.

"Martinez said you were crazy."

Catch how he stresses *were*.

Chris holds his eyes. He's already exhausted by the pissing contest. He knows he has to play it just right. Come on too strong and they'll shut him out. Fold too quick and they won't tell him shit.

Play up the old-school. Play up the back-in-the-day. Tell them a story with the moral *I am one of you.*

"One time I was on a raid in Cerritos. Taking down this drug kingpin, they called him the King of Skid Row. This knucklehead had a murdered-out Beamer he'd drive through the heart of Shit City. His people supplied all the homeless drug crews down there. Bargain-basement shit. Crack, H, meth. Heavy stuff and lots of it. We kicked in his door—the stink hit you right off. This awful dry-piss ball-sweat stank-ass smell, the kind you can taste, you know?"

The Dead Game Boys laugh. They lean in.

"The guy comes running at us—I do him a favor and don't blast a hole in him—I just—"

Chris swings an invisible shotgun.

"*Gagoosh.* Turned his nose into a stewed tomato."

Somebody says *hell yeah.*

"So I'm hooking him, and the guy, he's wearing so much cologne you can see the cartoon lines of it coming off him, you know? He's fresh and clean—you know, except his face. But I stand back up and that homeless-guy stank hits me again. Like is this guy running a flophouse out back or what? And I say to my partner, I'm tearing up from the smell, I say we got to figure out what stinks like that."

"So what was it?" Woodcock asks.

"I'll tell you what it was. We open the back bedroom and find the guy's stash—half a million dollars in ones and fives, the whole room full of the greasiest, dirtiest, most crumpled-up cash you ever saw in your life. Think about it—this guy was the kingpin of Skid Row. All this cash had marinated in junkie filth, gray, some of it black. The dirtiest pile of cash you ever saw in your life."

The Dead Game Boys lean forward. They sense a punch line coming.

"I couldn't get the stink out of my wallet for a year."

The Dead Game Boys laugh hard. He can see them unclench. It's an old trick—the little confession to gain trust for a big confession. They let him in the circle—just a little. Someone hands him a drink—a sickly-sweet hard seltzer. He drinks it fast. It helps. It lets him adjust his frequency to theirs.

The deputies drink hard seltzer mixed with vodka. They laugh big, sit splay-legged. They have *nobody-fucks-with-me* eyes. When one of them gets hungry, they run across the street to the al pastor stand. They cut in line. They don't even pretend to go for their wallets. The man who runs the place gives them tacos on the arm.

They tell Chris their own stories. They act out knuckleheads taking headers into concrete. They all use that word—*knucklehead*—Southern California police code for the words they know not to say out loud anymore.

Chris mentions BlackGuard—they all lean in. They all dream of post-retirement second careers as BlackGuard operators. They've all heard of Matt Matilla—they've watched his seminar on the warrior mindset, on how to kill. Because of him they practice shooting targets that look like pregnant women and little kids, because to kill well you must first kill something inside you, destroy anything that might make you hesitate to pull the trigger.

Now they want to impress Chris. They share death-scene selfies—phone snaps of the deputies chucking up Dead Game hand signs in front of car-crash corpses and murder victims. They grade each other on style points. Woodcock is current champion—he was first on scene at a triple murder, put sunglasses on all three corpses, and posed in the middle blasting double birds.

They tell stories—they bitch about pussy-assed DAs who won't try slam-dunk cases. They bitch about brass. Brass and the DAs are the true villains in a cop's life. The knuckle-heads are just the product they trade in.

They sit comfortably—they radiate true power—park where you want, speed if you want, run red lights, and *fuck you* to anyone who has a problem. Food on the arm and badge bunnies lurking at cop bars. This electric life. He knows the brotherhood, the power, it's all a lie. He misses it anyway.

Chris waits until his third drink to bring it up: "Martinez told you why I wanted to talk, right?"

Woodcock talks in air quotes: "The *incident*."

"Two center mass," Archer calls out from the tattoo chair. The cops all laugh. They go *fuck yeah*. But Chris can see how Archer sucks on a pale mixed drink. Like there's something inside him he's trying to drown.

"The shoot was in policy," Woodcock says, fake sincere. He says it loud so some of the other men hear it. "The suspect had a weapon and was brandishing it erratically."

Everybody in the room smiles—they're building up to something.

"Deputy Archer"—all the Dead Game Boys join in a sing-song chorus—"FEARING FOR HIS LIFE / AND THE LIFE OF A FELLOW OFFICER . . ."

The magic words, the words that justify any police shooting—indisputable, unfalsifiable, total justification to kill. As long as you were willing to testify you were scared when you pulled the trigger, the kill was clean.

They smash together cans and chug their drinks. The pure joy of being bulletproof.

Chris lets the scene settle. The other men go back to their own conversations. He talks to Woodcock alone.

"I know the shoot was in policy. That's not the angle I'm chasing. I'm not looking to burn anybody. I just got to know something. I'm investigating Montez, not you. What's your read on him?"

"Just another knucklehead thought he was a genius—'What if I went to where the nice cars are?' He's heard of Beverly Hills, goes there, tries to jack a ride. Murderous shit show ensues. Pure knucklehead logic."

"You wrote the incident report?"

"Yeah—let's see those pussy motherfuckers do something with that. I wrote it tight as white booty."

"I wrote a lot of reports in my day. I wrote a lot of reports starring a random passerby flagging me down. Most of the time, there never was a passerby. There isn't some crowd of good citizens looking to flag us down and help us do our jobs, right? The neighborhoods we work, folk don't flag down shit. But I wrote it a lot anyway. You know what I mean?"

Woodcock's silence is an answer.

Chris says, "I'm not looking to burn you, man. Ask anyone. Ask Martinez. When the time came down I took my lumps. I never talked. You're the one who wrote the paper on the shoot. I just want to know—if it was really a CI who told you where to find John, I want to talk to them. I won't burn you. I won't tell the CI how I found them. Just give me a name is all."

Woodcock looks him over. He shrugs like *fuck it*.

"Kevin Baldassare. Two *s*'s. Deals a little white powder, Hollywood sleazo type. Has this smoke-show girlfriend, a dancer, they live over in the Hollywood Hills. He feeds me busts sometimes."

"How'd you hook up with him?"

"We were sitting on this knucklehead dealer a few years back and this whiteboy in a vintage white Bronco came through to make a buy. Bad luck for him, good luck for me. I flipped him fast as a pancake. He's fed me steady dirt for a few years now. Morning of the shooting, pretty soon after the BOLO on Montez dropped, Baldassare called me up. He said he heard on the news that cops were looking for this guy John Montez, and he could serve him up to me. Said he'd be in this parking lot in East LA in half an hour. And he was."

Chris nods. He connects dots in his head: Montez's mom said he'd started hanging out with west-side whiteboy types. Pieces fit together in Chris's head—this crazy idea.

Woodcock says, "Only thing he asked was keep his name out of it. I don't burn my sources for no reason. So I wrote what I wrote. No harm, no foul."

"He scared of you?"

Woodcock pulls off his shirt. See the snarling dog head—the original Dead Game Boy. See those bloody teeth—read them as *six dead bodies*. Woodcock smiles.

"If he's not," Woodcock says, "he's stupider than he looks."

Somebody pours Chris another drink. Chris takes it down. It burns the right way. Like an engine barking back to life.

Before Chris can ask more, Archer climbs out of the tattoo chair—his tattoo pit bull with bloody jaws weeping little red tears, his blood mixed with the red ink. He gives out a warrior roar. It turns into a pit bull bark. The Dead Game Boys cheer. They bare their teeth. Something in them comes uncapped. The deputies bark in unison, slowly, picking up speed.

It is ludicrous. It is undeniable. Something kicks in Chris's guts—this thing in him he thought was dead. It runs out his mouth in the shape of a growl. Deputies pull guns out of nowhere. They raise them in the air. The barking reaches this mad crescendo.

Archer howls at the moon. He's got these eyes that are half joy and half pain. He points his gun at the storefront glass. GUNSHOTS rip the night. A high-pitched whine fills Chris's ears. The bullets punch spiderwebs into the glass. The food truck crowd runs screaming. The deputies laugh and howl.

The deputies sit in this long silence, in this gunpowder stink. These grins like *holy shit that just happened*.

The tattoo artist shrinks down low in his chair.

Archer has wet eyes. He has this look like he's coming back to reality.

"Okay," Woodcock says. "Somebody call it in and tell dispatch it's—"

The whole glass storefront shatters all at once. This waterfall of glass hits the street.

The deputies' howls run out into the night.

Chapter Twenty-one

MAE

Valley Village

Mae watches Katherine dance through the studio window.

It's taken two days for her to work up the nerve to get here. Two days of cyberstalking. Of working her day job. Of waiting for Tze to find Panko.

Mae nurses a fourteen-dollar juice—beets and kale and apples blurred into maroon muck. She drinks it slow. She doesn't want a lot of liquids—old stakeout tip courtesy of Chris Tamburro. She's wearing yoga pants and a metal band T-shirt. Her yoga mat rides shotgun.

The strip mall has an eyelash salon, an acai bowl shop where Mae bought the juice, a phone store. Mae had to wait twenty minutes before she could get a slot in front of the dance studio.

Mae rolls calls as she watches the class. She checks in with Joss—no word on when Parker will be arrested. She calls Tze to check in. "This is really intense," the girl tells her. No luck finding Panko yet. She says she's hitting downtown tomorrow. Mae thanks her, half listening.

Katherine dances to "Toxic." She's in Day-Glo Lycra aerobics tights, a studded leather belt. The girls look at Katherine like she's a god made flesh. They follow her lead, so much clumsier and reserved. These girls with their hair pulled tight against their skulls in harsh ponytails, sweating and wishing they weren't, hitting their marks, all of them chasing their dreams or maybe someone else's. She's giving these girls something. Mae can see it through the glass—the girls need what Katherine gives them like they need water and air. This way of moving wild and free—she's not teaching technique, not really. She's teaching them how to live unafraid, showing them how to be alive in their bodies. The forever teenager who lives inside Mae wants to pledge allegiance, to crimp her hair to look like Katherine's, to buy her own studded leather belt in an attempt to steal this woman's anima.

The class is all tween actresses and wannabes. The Oakwood apartment complex is on the other side of the Warner Bros. lot. The Oakwood is like a refugee camp for child actors. With their parents or guardians, they take up almost every apartment there. Corey Haim moved back there in his last days. It's where he OD'd. It was the only place he knew to call home.

The girls are divided into invisible tribes. The ones who won't make it. The ones who maybe will. A couple who already have—Mae recognizes a few of the girls from billboards or Netflix preview pages.

At the back of the room momagers whisper and point. They stare at the girls, searching for flaws. They wear Juicy Couture and bleached hair. At the center is a different type of woman—impossible to guess her age, she's had that good plastic surgery, subtle and smooth, not going for miracles—this expensive-looking black suit, rumpled perfection, her hair boy short. Thin like a knife. Every mom in the back of the room looks at her the way the girls up front look at Katherine—like a goddess whose judgment is nigh.

The woman in black watches the girls, the momagers watch her, the girls watch Katherine—all this unspoken power traded through the eyes.

Pregnant women in workout clothes start to line up outside the studio—the next class is prenatal yoga. The bass rumbles stop. Katherine leads the girls in a cooldown.

Mae's heart kicks up a notch. Time to go undercover. Lying, pretending to be another person, she's done it a hundred times for the job. The rules say *know when to be yourself, know when to be someone else.*

The woman in black leaves before the class ends. She doesn't nod or say goodbye to anyone. Mae can see the moms in the back watching her, whispering—they look like they're trying to decode every footstep of the woman. She climbs into a black Genesis parked right next to Mae—up close, she reminds Mae of something—she's seen this woman before.

The class ends. The girls are slow to leave. The girls flock to Katherine, to laugh, reach out and touch her like they could leech some of her life force. The moms push them out—Mae can see how the moms' voices crumple the girls, bring back gravity to their lives.

The moms all wear the same brand of giant sunglasses. The girls follow them—Mae thinks about prisoners filing back into their cellblocks after yard time, these little tastes of freedom.

Something inside Mae says *drive away.* So far she hasn't done anything that can't be taken back. This is an overt act—this is for real. There's this one last chance to let it all go, to let Dan's secret die with him. It's Katherine herself who gives Mae what she needs to get out of the car. That fearless joy—Mae wants to chase it.

Katherine wipes sweat off her face. She hugs the incoming yoga teacher. She picks up her tote bag—NIPSEY HUSSLE RIP stenciled on the side.

Mae picks up her yoga mat and water bottle from the shotgun seat. She gets out of the car—she runs through her simple cover story. She practices a quick smile in the rearview—friendly/ bashful—you give them something to latch onto, vulnerability and the confidence to share that vulnerability. That paradox that leads people to like you, to trust you. Mae knows Katherine would get it, if they could talk about it. It was the way Katherine danced.

Katherine hits the open air. Up close Mae can see the flesh around her rainbow nails is scratched and bloody. Like Katherine has been worrying it the way a caged dog chews its leg. There's some sort of hurricane inside her.

Like maybe her secret boyfriend was just murdered.

Like maybe she knows why.

That's projection, Mae tells herself. *The only way to learn the truth is to ask her.*

Step one—the meet-cute.

The unbreakable moment arrives. Like stepping out of a rocket ship for a spacewalk.

She steps out into outer space.

"Excuse me . . ."

Katherine startles, like being woken from a dream. Mae can smell the post-workout salt of her.

"You need something?"

"You're Katherine Sparks, aren't you?"

"In the flesh."

"I follow you on Instagram—you're a fucking rock star."

"Thanks for noticing." Whatever fear or anxiety Katherine had been living in is gone now, or hidden.

"I had a meeting at Warners," Mae says, "thought I'd catch a class before braving Barham to get back to the city."

The cover story told Katherine that Mae was part of the Industry. It told her that maybe Mae was somebody who could help her. Mae designed it to be vague and tempting. Before Katherine can ask what she does, Mae gestures to the class, the women and their bellies. "Didn't know this was prenatal yoga—that's a yikes from me."

Katherine laughs. "Weirds me out too—like one of them is going to do a downward dog and launch her baby out her cooch like a cannonball."

Mae laughs—genuinely. A woman with a huge belly entering the gym hears this, drops a stink eye on them both—and then they're both laughing.

"I'm Mae."

"Hey, Mae. I'd say my name but you already know it."

"Lookit, I'd love to take a dance class with you sometime."

"That can happen. Come check one out sometime. I do classes all over. Check out my Tiger Style classes."

A horn honk cuts through the air—a restored old-school Bronco, white, modified into a convertible, rolls to a stop in front of the studio. Trap music booming loud from the speakers. The guy in the convertible has red hair and trainer muscles. She recognizes him from Katherine's Instagram—her roommate/maybe-boyfriend Kevin. He has this look on his face Mae has seen on a hundred men with bodies like his—confidence like a cancer.

"That's my ride," Katherine says, nodding to the car like *one second.*

A black modern SUV rolls up behind the white one. A big shape behind the wheel.

"Do you ever do privates?" Mae asks. "Not to be gross, but I have more money than I have free time."

"A common problem," Katherine says. "Yeah, no problem. DM me or something."

"I will," Mae says. She feels Kevin's eyes scanning her, dismissing her.

"You ought to," Katherine says. "Everybody needs a wild rumpus now and then."

She climbs up into the white Bronco. Kevin doesn't look at her—just hits the gas. The exit is spoiled by a big silver Range Rover backing out of a spot in front of him. He slams the brakes. The black SUV rolls up behind him slow. It stops right next to Mae. All these giant vehicles in this tiny-assed lot. Mae thinks she should get the Bronco's license plate.

Something in the back of her mind is humming. Something about that black SUV, the bass notes bleeding through from inside. Mae shoots a glance over to the large shape behind the wheel.

Mae steps to the SUV's window.

It can't be.

Mae's worlds crash together.

The Bronco gets to the mouth of the parking lot. Mae barely glances at it.

The shotgun window of the SUV rolls down. That gangster rap he likes pours out. He kills it.

"Get in," Chris says to her. "I don't want to lose them."

Chapter Twenty-two

CHRIS

Valley Village / Laurel Canyon

"It's good to see you," he says. He means it. Even while he scrambles to make it make sense.

"You too," she says—there's a heavy dose of *what-the-fuck* in her voice.

He keeps one eye on her, one on Kevin's Bronco. She's still got those big witchy eyes.

Mae's voice in his head: *Well, of course I do, dumbass. You thought maybe I'd lose them?*

His heart thuds double-kick-drum fast. This weird detail makes it feel like fate: she's wearing one of his old T-shirts.

"This isn't a coincidence," he says.

"Probably not," Mae says.

"So you going to tell me what it is?"

"You got to give me a second. This is too crazy. 'And then out of nowhere, Chris Tamburro shows up.' "

The Range Rover clears its parking space and pulls away. The parking lot jam unsnarls. The white Bronco turns left onto Colfax. Chris waits a long beat—let some traffic get between them and the car, make it harder to spot the tail.

"You look good."

"Chris . . ."

"I'm just saying. You do."

"I know I do."

He pulls into traffic two cars behind the Bronco. He glances over to Mae. She's got this weird smile on her face.

"You got sheared," she says, miming a beard rub. "You ditched the dirtbag werewolf vibe."

They laugh—he always liked how that sounded, their two laughs in chorus. It gives him that old feeling. Even as he knows she's changing the subject, buying time.

"Acker had me get shined up before I met the BlackGuard boss man last week. He wanted me to look more like a cop."

"So they could put you on a case?"

He tries to figure out a narrative that makes this make sense. Either the Beast is running multiple parallel investigations and Mae is a different angle for them. Or Mae is involved in something deep and dark. Right now her vibe reads like somewhere in the middle—trending toward deep and dark.

"She's the girlfriend?" he asks her.

"Whose girlfriend?"

"Mae. Come on. We gonna play a game with each other, you and me?"

"For now," she says, "let's play *show-me-yours*."

"And if I do?"

She doesn't answer.

"Okay, I'll play," he says. "They've got me investigating Dan's death. I'm sorry, by the way. I know you liked him."

Those big eyes flash pain. She turns away from him like she doesn't want him to see it on her face. He reaches out to touch her shoulder—he pulls it back. He lets the moment pass. After a beat she turns back to face him.

"*They've* got you investigating Dan's death," she says. "Who is *they*?"

The Bronco drives aggressively. It weaves between lanes. Chris drives calm, keeps pace with Kevin easily. LA traffic is like quicksand—struggling just makes you sink faster.

"BlackGuard. After Dan was killed, they brought me in. Leonard DePaulo, the big man himself. The one with the son I always have to clean up for?"

"I remember."

"He brought Acker and me to his place in Calabasas. Said they wanted me to run an investigation into Dan's death, use my contacts at the sheriff's department to look into John Montez. To see if there was any connection, any reason to think it wasn't just a random crime."

They pass under the 101. A mini tent city sits in the concrete wedge under the overpass. They've hung old rugs on the fences like tapestries. A random thought—another homeless camp got firebombed last night. This time down over in Little Bangladesh, just a few scorched tents. The police confirmed that it fit the Bum Bomber signature—they don't say what the signature is. Cops hold back key details on high-publicity cases—it helps disprove false confessions.

"So you're working for BlackGuard specifically? Is there a client?" Mae asks him. "Did Mitnick bring them in?"

"It's not Mitnick, I'm pretty sure. They acted like it was just internal business. Like you said, they're all part of the Beast. They just want to do their due diligence."

"But they didn't give you anything else? They didn't say anything about Dan?"

"No. They just asked me to dig into the shooting, use my LASD contacts."

She nods. Something in her relaxes. A little.

He says, "That's my shirt."

She smiles. She says, "It's a good workout shirt."

"It's a sign."

With the same smile: "There's no such thing as signs. We live in a cold and godless universe."

"There's that good-time girl I remember."

They sit—the only sound inside the SUV the hum of the air conditioner. Traffic clears on the other side of the highway. They speed up. Chris keeps them two car lengths behind the Bronco. The woman leans back, rests her feet by the side-view mirror.

The Bronco takes a right on Moorpark. Chris goes straight.

"They're going—"

"These roads get too small to follow someone without them seeing you. Anyway, I think I know where they're going."

They go deep into the Hills. Looming trees and hills on either side of the road cut the sunlight, this beautiful murk with fingers of light slashing through. He dodges parked Beamers and Mercedes, electric cars with electric cords running in from the house—roads so narrow that when they meet a car coming the other way, one has to pull over to let the other pass.

"So, they asked you to investigate the shooting," Mae says. "And somehow that brought you to a parking lot in Valley Village."

"The deputies who shot John Montez—I saw something in their report didn't feel right to me. I went to talk with them. They told me that they got tipped to Montez's location by a guy, this guy named Kevin Baldassare."

She flinches like he just fired a gun next to her head. She says, "Jesus fucking Christ. *Jesus fucking Christ.* Kevin Baldassare told the cops how to find Montez?"

"So you do know who Kevin is—"

"The ginger in the parking lot just now."

The road is tight and twisty. He can't check her face the way he wants.

"So Kevin is low-level Hollywood sleaze," he says. "He's the first thing I've come across that even suggests a connection between Montez and Dan Hennigan. So I start tailing him. And ten minutes ago I find my one hundred percent, undeniable connection to Dan Hennigan. It goes from Montez to the cops who killed him to Baldassare . . . to you."

They come through Radford Canyon and meet up with Laurel Canyon still on the upslope. They turn south, heading into LA. The traffic is stop-and-go jammed— Chris figures Kevin and the blond woman are five minutes behind them.

"You don't got nothing to say to me, Mae?"

She digs quarter moons into the Lycra of her yoga pants.

"Because I showed you mine," he says. "When I connected Kevin and Montez, it hit you like a Taser. Tell me why."

They turn right onto Mulholland Drive, this patch of wildness on the tall spine of the hills that separate the city from the San Fernando Valley. A sharp drop-off on the north side of the road, dry brush spilling down to Studio City.

She bites her bottom lip. She is wrestling with something big.

They take Laurel Pass Avenue, heading downhill now. They take a right on Wonderland, past the elementary school. They get into the houses from the cocaine-and-Valium seventies heyday of the Hills, the houses descended into shabby chic. Kevin's house is just ahead. Chris sees a gap big enough for the SUV to slip into. He parks the car. He turns to her.

"That's Baldassare's house—rental—him and Katherine live there with three other people. We've got five minutes before they catch up with us. Let's make them count. Connect Montez and you."

He's given her time to make her choice—this time she answers fast.

"I'm not the connection," she says.

"You're wearing workout clothes . . ."

He reaches out, runs a finger down the side of her face. This crazy energy pops behind her eyes when he touches her. Her skin is smooth, hot to the touch.

And dry.

"But you didn't work out."

She nods like *keep going.*

"And watching you with the blonde, I had to guess? It looked like you'd never met before."

"We hadn't," she says like *keep going.*

"I saw you in the parking lot, I figured it was one of two things. Either you were running some kind of investigation for the bosses, same as me . . . or you were a part of the case.

But now I'm thinking there's a third option. You're not in with these people. And you're not working the case for the bosses. You're going rogue," he says. "You're working some angle on your own."

She smiles like *keep going*.

"Mae, I will keep your name out of this. I never saw you. I'll keep your secrets for you."

She says, "Okay." What she tells him after that blows out the back of Chris's head like a book-depository bullet.

Chapter Twenty-three

MAE

Laurel Canyon

He takes it pretty well. He has this shell-shocked look in his eyes. She gets it. She feels fried herself. It's like jamming two pieces of power line together and watching them crackle and spit.

Chris's end of the wire—John Montez as a fake gangster, cops tipped off by Kevin Baldassare, Katherine's boyfriend. Her end of the wire—Dan, his fuck-you-money secret, his affair with Katherine.

She can smell the salt of him—she looks at his big hands on the steering wheel. Memories of those hands everywhere threaten to wash her away.

She knows she needs a partner in this. There's reasons for that partner to be Chris—good and bad. The good is that she can trust him. The bad is, there's still this thing between them. They can't lie to each other. That might hold them together. That might make this all very messy.

She looks up, sees Chris's face—she says this thing she hasn't been able to say to anyone yet. She says, "Chris, I saw his body. I saw . . ."

And she watches her own hands as they try to make the shape of it, the missing scoop of Dan's head. She watches as the hands start to tremble. They go blurry as her eyes fill up.

He doesn't say anything. He knows not to get in the way. He was always good about that. She blinks the tears out of her eyes. She can feel how they roll down her cheeks. She snorts back a little tear snot. She smiles at him like *I'm okay.*

He waits the right amount of time and then asks her, "So you don't know what he was planning?"

"No—but I think it had something to do with that woman. Katherine. I've got some other ideas, some jobs he was working. I'm looking into that too. But now, knowing she's connected to Montez . . . somehow, this is what got him killed."

"So if you're not doing this for the Beast," Chris says, "why are you doing it?"

She looks at Chris like the question doesn't even make sense.

"Dan died," she says. "It doesn't make sense. I want to know why. So I'm going to find out. I mean, have you met me?"

This girl with the warrior eyes. This fighter.

"Yeah," he says. "We've met."

"But lookit. Dan sounded like there was lots of money on the table too. Fuck-you money. And if there is, I'm not going to act like I don't want it. I'm going to find out what Dan was up to with these people. And I'm going to figure out how to use it. Maybe start my own firm."

He doesn't break her eye contact. They hold it long. She knows what he's going to say before he says it.

"I want in. I'll file a dead-end report with Acker. I'll say it's time to sit on it. After all, until I saw you, there wasn't a connection. I can kill the investigation—and when we learn more, we can make a choice about what to do. It's your call. But for now, we're a team."

She says, "Good."

Chapter Twenty-four

CHRIS

Koreatown

Chris gets a pizza and a six-pack. He puts on a nineties action movie. He puts the burner phone in his lap—one of a pair they bought for cash in a Hollywood electronics shop. He opens up his laptop. He checks his notes. He gets back into the practice of writing a false report.

He writes the true one first—the version for himself and Mae. He connects the chain. From John Montez to the cops who killed him to Kevin Baldassare to Katherine Sparks to Dan.

He arranges the moving parts. He rearranges them.

First thing first—the carjacking story is horseshit. John Montez fronted as a big-time gangster—he's a wannabe who fell in with Hollywood bottom-feeders with a connection to Dan Hennigan. Dan's got some kind of big secret—and he's sleeping with Katherine. A small leap: Katherine and her friends are in on the secret.

Somehow things go bad. Dan starts looking for another partner—he picks Mae.

Somehow somebody figures they have to kill Dan. Maybe they know he's looking to double-cross them. Maybe it's something else.

Montez got the job—his big bad gangbanger lie came back to haunt him. He fucked it up big-time—he did it too big, too public. He got his picture taken. He got his face on the morning news. He was dead an hour later.

Chris makes a bigger leap: Montez died *because* he got his face on the morning news. It was a matter of time before he got caught. Figure Kevin Baldassare knows this. He knows if Montez gets picked up, he could point his finger at Kevin and Katherine and God knows who else. He could talk about the real reason Dan Hennigan was killed.

Is Woodcock in on it? Did he kill Montez to keep him silent?

Chris weighs it—he throws it out. If Woodcock knowingly killed Montez for Baldassare, he never would have given Chris his name. No, figure Woodcock is exactly what he appears to be—a natural-born shooter.

They found Montez in East Los Angeles—far from home. Right in Woodcock's turf. So maybe Kevin steers him there—*hey, bro, you're a wanted man, go to East LA and I'll come meet you.* He feeds info to Deputy Woodcock. He knows Woodcock's a shooter. He knows Woodcock is prone to drop bodies. He figures, if the cops are going to find Montez anyway, his best bet is to make sure the cops who find him are likely to not take him alive.

Connecting all the dots: Kevin Baldassare makes a desperate play—he sets up a blind date between John Montez and some trigger-happy cops. The balls of it all.

It works. Woodcock and his partner drop Montez.

His secrets die with him.

All these crazy connections with this black hole at the center of it.

Why?

He copies the report into a new file. The report for Acker. He leaves out Katherine—he leaves the pieces unconnected. He leaves Mae out of it. He writes a tale of no forward motion. He puts forward a milquetoast theory: Montez was a carjacking gangbanger. Baldassare was a drug-dealing rival of Montez. He saw a chance to snitch on him and took it. Chris suggests he stay on Baldassare a few days just to be sure. He pastes the report into an email to Acker.

His finger hovers over the send button. He thinks about Mae. His finger hits send on its own. He's in it now. This fear fills him up, different from the useless fear of the phantom heart attacks. It is terrible but it shines brilliantly. The kind of fear that makes you feel alive, and maybe will keep you that way.

PART THREE

Hollywood Sickos

Chapter Twenty-five

MAE

Laurel Canyon

They click so fast it scares her.

They rent a little gray hatchback—a million of them on the roads of Los Angeles. They get burritos and cold brew. Chris pulls double shifts. He sits there all day. Mae comes when she can, mostly after work. They meet up at the diner on Franklin near the Celebrity Centre. They eat hash browns, tuna melts. They ride back up into the hills together. They watch the house.

The hatchback is too small for Chris. His bad knee aches—sometimes he opens the car door just so he can stretch it out. "Getting old," he says, this look in his eyes like it's something to be ashamed of.

They watch people come and go constantly. The house has a vibe Mae remembers from her early days in LA. When she worked as an agent's assistant, trying to find the good parties, late-night cocaine shivers in cramped bathrooms, some asshole yammering about his development deals—cocaine summons the worst people in the world, and Mae partied with them all when she first got to town.

They sit and watch the house. Chris builds a cop picture of the place. Mae scans their social media—she builds a different picture. They put it all together. They build a picture of all five people in the house.

Katherine the dancer. Kevin the ginger, zero body fat, hollow cheeks and hollow eyes. Loto, short but swollen with muscle, shaggy blond hair, a brawny butterface. Tony, Black, tall, with hot jerk vibes—the kind of guy who wrecked Mae's early twenties. Janice DeWaal, a skin-and-bones fashion girl with straight black hair and raccoon eye makeup. They see Janice the most—always out front with a cigarette and a Diet Coke. Mae can only think of her with her full name, loves to say it over and over again as they watch her, trying different accents, *Janice DEWaal, Janice DeWAAAL*.

Chris follows them during the day. They all have day jobs. Katherine teaches dance classes and works with ItGirl. Kevin does personal training. Loto works at a lifter's gym in Lincoln Heights. Janice DeWaal works at a cosmetics counter. Tony waits tables at a Century City steak house.

Mae goes through their social media. All these people living something like a dream, a facsimile of a dream, fake the way dreams are fake on television.

She figures out their side hustles. They all sell cut-rate sponcon. Katherine sells tummy tea. Kevin sells a pre-workout protein gel. Loto sells phony testosterone supplements. Tony sells an underwear subscription service. Janice DeWaal sells face serum. They all sell filtered versions of themselves.

"It's a wannabe clout house," Mae tells Chris.

"If you say so."

"Heavy on the wannabe."

Chris runs police reports on them. He watches the people who come and go in the late hours. He points out the cage on the front door. The one with the electric buzzer that has to be triggered from the inside. Heavy security for this part of town. The sort of thing that points to illegal businesses. He figures out their side-side hustles.

Katherine and Kevin sell coke and K. Loto sells steroids and HGH. Tony sells pills. Janice DeWaal sells unlicensed Botox injections—Mae and Chris watch women come out of their houses with little poison bumps in lines across their foreheads.

It showed they were hustlers. It showed they played with the law. But none of it was close to rich enough to have interested Dan.

Chris and Mae meet up at night. Mae brings Mandy. She sits in the back seat and farts so bad they have to crack windows—laughing, blinking back tears of laughter and dog farts. Mandy falls in deep love with Chris—these mooning eyes. She leans into him in that way dogs have, like they want to mix their molecules up with yours.

Long hours pass where nothing happens. Chris and Mae talk and talk and talk. They tell stories from the years since they've seen each other. Chris tells her about having to make a pharmacy run for Patrick DePaulo. He'd picked up something in a paper bag from the pharmacist and a single red rose, per Patrick's request. He'd taken both to some woman's apartment in Marina del Rey. He'd given them both to the woman—she looked familiar but he didn't know from where. She'd opened the bag, seen whatever was inside, and thrown the rose in Chris's face. And then she'd stood there and cried, standing in the doorway, staring at Chris, refusing to look away as she sobbed. Making him take her sadness and anger. And he stood there and he took it.

"Sat in my ride for a long time after that one," Chris says. "Like maybe I ought to just start driving. Like I could have made Texas by morning."

"But you stayed," Mae says.

"The purgatory you know, right?" he says like a shrug.

She tells him about this restaurateur who owned a burger bar on Melrose. He got his girlfriend pregnant—and he didn't want his wife to find out. So he asked the girlfriend to get rid of it. She told him she didn't want a thing from him—all she wanted was the baby. He couldn't even let her have that. He bought misoprostol from a dirty pharmacist and ground it up into a powder. He took his girlfriend to dinner. He took her to bed. He dipped his fingers in the misoprostol first. She miscarried the next day. She figured it out. She got proof. She went to the courts. She went to the press. He hired Mitnick & Associates to plant stories smearing the girlfriend. Mae made the calls. She planted the stories. And then she went to the dog shelter and rescued Mandy.

They don't say it out loud: *I wish I could have told you about this when it happened.*

They slip back into this easy way of being with each other. These long electric pauses between them—they both know what they mean. They haven't talked about it yet. They know how messy it will be. At night Mae lies in bed with a toy between her legs, remembering hotel rooms and cars parked on side streets, the furious joy of it all.

A few evenings in, Mae fights traffic on Franklin—the 101 jams solid at rush hour. Mandy stands on the shotgun seat, her head out the window, trying to sniff the whole world. Mae lets her lizard brain drive. The traffic gives Mae the gift of blank time. It lets her obsessions run free.

She thinks about Dan. Everything rotates around this one question: *Why?* She writes down old projects, old clients, people with a secret to hide.

She finds herself scrolling through the clout house's social media at red lights. She's getting obsessed with them, like it's a reality show she's watching.

She thinks about Chris's theory. That a man would send killer cops against his friend, knowing they would probably shoot him. Betting they would shoot first—a fucked-up brain to think up that one.

Her phone buzzes—it breaks her trance. Her phone buzzes again, a string of texts. She must have been in a dead zone.

A missed call. Tze.

A string of text messages. Tze.

I FOUND PANKO

HE'S RIGHT HERE

HE SAYS HE'S MOVING ON

HURRY

Chapter Twenty-six

CHRIS

Laurel Canyon

Mae's phone call is garbled by the hills. She sounds flustered. Something about a homeless guy. Something about some other angle she's working.

"I've got this," he tells her. "Go take care of business."

Chris sits in the hatchback. His back aches. His knee barks. He'd sat on the house hours after Mae left last night. The store stayed open until about three. This steady stream of party girls and fuck boys came and went. They showed up with hungry eyes and left with jitters, their noses red like baboon asses.

The phone rings. ACKER. Shit.

"Hey."

"Hey, champ." He didn't know if Acker ever left the office. Like the spider that lives in a hole.

"What's good, Acker?"

"You tell me."

"I'm sitting on this house right now. I don't see any connections between Hennigan and the shooter. Sometimes the trail goes cold."

"Keep on it," Acker says. "I think I can buy you a few more days at time and a half. But we can't soak them. I do a lot of business with them."

As in, *they're a part of the Beast*. As in, *don't fuck around on this*.

Out front Janice DeWaal smokes. Katherine comes out, sits on the front steps. Watching the road like she's waiting for something. Like maybe a dinner delivery.

The thought makes Chris realize he's hungry too. He thinks about Thai Town. The boat noodles at Sapp's maybe. Or the curry catfish at Pa Ord. He starts the car. A Jeep Wrangler rolls up in front of the house with the top down. Maybe the lunch guy. He waits—he's never seen this Jeep before. He turns on his phone's camera and starts filming. He zooms in on the license plate just in case.

There's this rat-faced guy behind the wheel. There's this tiny girl in the shotgun seat. Katherine and Janice run to the girl's side of the Jeep. The girl looks maybe fourteen. They smile and coo at her. The two women help the girl out of the Jeep. It's not easy for her to climb out. When Chris sees why, he zooms in on his phone. He thinks, *Holy shit, is this it?*

Chapter Twenty-seven

MAE

Atwater Village / LA River

She takes Sunset over to Fountain, through Silver Lake, past the good vegan soft-serve place, past the Trader Joe's where the cops shot that cashier, to the Hyperion Bridge, passing over the 5, the Verdugo Mountains smog-blurred to the north. She glances down to the LA River, this wide concrete canal with a broad, shallow current running through it. From here she can see so many tents in the gravel floes at the center of the river.

She makes her plan of attack. It's complicated—she's working so many angles at once now, she's got to figure out how many different directions the ball can bounce in.

She drives up the hill to Atwater's main strip and parks in front of a restaurant. The customers outside are all hollowed out from the hot-yoga place next door, all eating bowls of wet health: massaged kale, ancient grains, avocado mash. The walls inside are stenciled with sans-serif mantras.

CONSUME TO CREATE

DECOLONIZE YOUR PALATE

WE CANNOT ESCAPE THE VIOLENCE INHERENT IN EATING

Mae walks back down to the river. The women have flat hair and Joni Mitchell hats and handspun peasant blouses that cost eight hundred dollars. The men in dirty jeans and stubble, thin, messy hair, looking like dog shit, and yet these women all cling to them.

She walks past a French bakery, this woman who looks just like Natalie Portman—it is Natalie Portman—eating a chocolate croissant, Zack de la Rocha at the next table. Mae passes some invisible border, the hipness bleeding away just like that, past a Subway, a liquor store, a gas station, panhandlers, down the hill toward the river, passing a woman with her hair formed into a single knotted dread digging for cans in the trash. Mae walks up to the bank of the river, dodging floes of trash. Mandy sniffs and snorts, her tail stump wagging. Tze waits on the broken asphalt path at the top of the riverbank.

Mandy yanks the leash, mouth open to get at Tze.

"Oh, she's so sweet," Tze says as she squats down, sounding so grateful for the love.

"Is he still here?"

"Yeah, he's waiting. I told him you were here to help." Mae can hear the question in Tze's voice.

"We are going to help him."

"He's on that middle island, the one with the clothesline between the tents. He's wearing a purple hoodie." She rubs Mandy's face.

"You did good."

"Is that what I did? 'Cause it sort of feels the other way."

"Do you want to come with me?"

"No. I think I'm going to bail."

"Look, I can try to find you more work, help you keep afloat until you find something solid. I can talk to Mitnick. Say I need an assistant—"

"That's okay, thanks. I don't think this is for me. I think I need something, like you said, something where right and wrong matters. But, like, good luck."

Mae walks across the bridge to the west bank of the river, with its new bike track, wide and smooth and full of intense bike people, all spandex-hugged balls and aerodynamic hairless haunches. She walks pressed against the railing. There are tents everywhere. Below her, large islands in the center of the river, thickets of tents on the islands, more in the grass between the bike path and highway on the other side of the chain-link fence. A raft of ducks floats between little islands of silt and scrub. Dry moss on some of the rocks—drought conditions have reduced the river to a thin scrim of green water. Someone has spray-painted HELL ANGEL CAMP on the concrete slope. Somebody has spray-painted I HATE COPS. Dozens of miniature rubber chickens, grimy with road muck, dot the trail. An old office chair with da big boss inked on the back. A kid with lime–Jell-O hair, rolling on a skateboard as tall as he is, a backpack sprawling with plastic pump shotguns. A black dog with a spiked metal collar sleeps in the dust.

Mae ducks under the guardrails and walks down the concrete slope to the river. Mandy sniffs and snorts—it's a paradise of stink.

A heron walks through the water, maybe a head shorter than Mae, moving on impossible legs. Mandy goes for it, yanking the leash again so Mae feels it in her shoulder joint. The heron takes flight, sails up over the freeway. Mae blinks hard. The traffic and the life and the trash and the beauty all at once are dizzying.

A plywood bridge connects the bank to the tent city island. The island is crowded by structures, tents and shanties linked by blue-tarp hallways. The bridge bows into the water as she walks across it. She worries about her shoes—hates herself for it. She dodges clots of junk. A man works on a half-assembled bike, spokes and gears in the dirt. Next to him, a man in a purple hoodie. The man in the purple hoodie looks up at her—these high cheekbones, this purple blotch on his cheek.

"You're Panko?"

"You must be the cavalry," he says. "Talked to your scout down here before, pretty little girl over her head. Now, you, you're a pretty little girl who isn't over her head at all."

He leans down, his turn to take Mandy's love. "Aye, that's right, we're best friends aren't we?" Mandy flops over and gives him her soft underbelly. He rubs it.

"You're here to talk to me about that man."

"I'm from the *LA Times*," she says. "I'm doing background on a story about Ward Parker. I want to hear your version of it."

"Uh-huh."

"I think it's important to hear what you have to say."

"Uh-huh."

"I can pay you," she says.

"Now, that's really all you had to say."

They cross to the far side of the island, cross another makeshift bridge to the east side of the river, away from the bikes and tents.

"Why do they call you Panko?"

"Can't you guess? I'm always fried."

She hands him an envelope of cash.

"I just want to hear your side of the story."

"You going to record it or something?"

"Not now. I just want to hear your version."

He looks down on the tent city they were just in.

"I can't say nobody warned me. That man is known down on the stroll. The folk who work that stroll told me all about him. That he is party-and-play all the way. Watch out, she said—that's the universal she, understand—watch out for that powder-blue Benz. But that night, I was thirsty—not water thirsty, understand. So when I saw that powder-blue Mercedes roll up to the taco stand, sit there idling with its headlights on me . . . like eyes. He rolled down the window. You know, he had eyes like a cup of ice water poured down your back. I can't say I wasn't warned."

He's in the story now—he's not on the path by the river; he's in a powder-blue Benz—and he's not talking to Mae anymore.

"So he took me to his place. Not his place where he lives and sleeps. The place where he plays. Girl, I've been some places before, believe me, I've been everywhere. But that man's fuck pad was something else. Smelled like lube and cigarette smoke. Ugly wall-to-wall carpeting. A mattress on the floor, purple sheets—hard to see the stains, but they were there all right. And he had the works all set out, the needle and all of it.

"I never shot no tina before—I've smoked it a few times, got spun . . . but I never did no needles. I told the man no. And he just laid out twenties, one after one after one, until I couldn't say no. And I guess maybe you could say that makes it all okay, that I took the money. But one thing life has taught me that I know is true, on God. We got free will, we do. Free will is real. But it's not the only game in town.

"He tied my arm off, talking about it, cooing about my veins, and he put that needle in my arm and it pinched and . . . whole world went supernova. Like I turned into the sun, understand? And I couldn't see shit because I was white-hot burning, hotter than fire, my heart fit to burst. Felt like all my veins got replaced with cosmic beams, I could feel them everywhere in me, the whole wet web inside me sizzling. Feeling like the first three feet of hell, my heart trying to pump this shit in my veins that's not even blood anymore. And the white falls out of my eyes and I breathe for the first time. And he's looking at me and it's like while I was gone he took off his mask and now he's showing me his real face. And I look down and the handcuffs are on me. And he's got another needle in his hand."

After a while he finishes talking. Mae realizes she's bleeding—she's worried the quick of her thumbnail past the point of tearing skin. She wipes the blood away with her fingers. She tries to ignore this seasick feeling at the center of her.

Dan in her head: *This man is a bombshell.*

The man knows how to tell a story. If Dan got to him first—he could be Dan's big secret.

"Have you told this story to anyone except the police?"

He shakes his head like *naw*.

She takes out her phone—she holds it with both hands to hide how it shakes. She's already got the photo of Dan pulled up.

"Have you ever seen this man?"

He squints at the phone.

"No. No, I don't know that man."

She puts the phone away.

"I might need to talk to you again. My assistant said you were leaving here?"

"There's bad folk taking over around here. Call themselves the Hell Angels. Seems like everywhere you go, somehow the bad folk always wind up on top. Even down by the river. Anyhow, I'm taking what I got and I'm heading down to the pinata street, got some folk staying down there."

The heron flies overhead, wings stretched out like Jesus, coming back down to the river. Panko watches it land. When he turns back to Mae there are tears in his eyes.

"I just want to be free and clean," Panko says. "I don't know why it's so hard."

The pain and the openness are too much for her, and she has to look away. There is something she wants to say to him, but it's too big and too scary and anyway she has a job to do so she forces it back down inside her and when she looks at him again her face shows nothing.

"I can bring you money. Every week. I can look for a place for you to live. Just stay out of sight, don't get busted."

"You people, you think money rules everything. And it does too. You come find me down where they sell the pinatas, I won't say no to it. Just next time, don't playact like you're a reporter, huh? Reporters come around all the time wanting to write like they care about us, I've seen plenty. None of them got hair or clothes like you."

She doesn't try to deny it. She just says, "If I need you I'll go to the Pinata District, then. Can I buy you a rideshare downtown?"

"Lady, come on. They won't let me in the car."

She walks back up the hill to Atwater's main strip. Her stomach aches with acid. Her head aches with Panko's words.

I just want to be free and clean.

I don't know why it's so hard.

She thinks about Tze walking away. How the people who leave get forgotten. Margot Danser, who worked at the firm when Mae first started. She'd burned out. She'd quit. Nobody called her weak—not to her face. Mae realizes she hasn't thought about Margot in months. People don't just leave this life—they get disappeared from your mind, so the idea of leaving doesn't even seem real. So that the life feels like the only life that's possible. That thing she wanted to say to Panko floats back up to the surface. A truth that we are told is childish, as if that makes it untrue. A truth that could and should upend everything:

It isn't supposed to be this way.

Her phone buzzes. Chris.

She thinks about not answering. About throwing it all away. Forgetting everything. Forgetting Dan, forgetting secrets.

She answers the phone.

"Hey."

"You free? I've got something to show you."

"Yeah," she says. "I'm free." It strikes her as a bad joke.

She looks up, through the window of the wet health restaurant. All those slogans on the walls.

WE CANNOT ESCAPE THE VIOLENCE INHERENT IN EATING

This time it reads like prophecy.

Chapter Twenty-eight

CHRIS

Hollywood

Something's wrong—he sees it from how she opens the door of the diner. From how she doesn't do her little cocked-eyebrow hello when they make eye contact.

"Everything okay?" he asks as she slides into the booth.

"Everything," she says, "is not okay."

Mae picks up her fork and starts shredding the napkin with it. Before he can ask about it, the waiter comes back to the table. Mae pastes on the smile she always gives to waiters. She orders chamomile. When the waiter leaves, the smile falls again.

"So what happened?"

Chris watches as Mae goes inside herself. She does a little headshake to break out of it.

"Whatever secret Dan was hiding, it wasn't about Panko," she says. "Leave it at that."

"So we'll leave it at that, then."

"What about you?" she asks. "You said it was some-thing big."

Chris hands her his phone. He's already got the video cued up.

"Press play."

"What is it?"

"Press play and then you tell me."

He's trimmed the footage down. He watches her face as she watches it.

It's footage of the front of the clout house. A Jeep Wrangler with the top down. The guy behind the wheel is early twenties. He's got a bad mustache, high-strung and mean. The girl sitting shotgun is still a teenager, no more than fourteen, her brown hair in a high ponytail. Chris fights back a smile. The moment is coming when the girl climbs out of the car. He wants to see her face when the moment comes.

The moment comes.

The teenage girl climbs out of the Jeep. It is not easy for her. Her stomach is huge. She is maybe six months pregnant.

Mae's eyebrow raises like *what the fuck?*

She puts the phone on the table. The video is still playing. Chris watches it upside down. Janice and Katherine hustle the girl into the house.

Chris asks, "So why does this wannabe clout house hang out with a pregnant middle schooler?"

Mae picks up her water glass. She puts it back down— her hand is shaking too much to finish the job.

Her eyes meet Chris's. The look in her eyes jolts him good, jolts him bad.

He expected a reaction. He didn't expect it to be thermonuclear.

Mae says, "You have nieces, right?" like she's quoting someone.

"Huh?"

"Dan asked me that. That day in the Polo Lounge. He asked me about my nieces. He asked me if I was around for my sister's pregnancies."

"No shit?"

"No shit."

The video quits playing. Chris scoops up his phone.

"They came out twenty minutes later," Chris says. "Loaded up with groceries."

"Dan asked me if I was seeing anyone. He asked me if I still had a spare bedroom."

"So the girl . . ."

"The girl. Jesus Christ. Jesus Christ this fucking town." She picks up the shreds of her napkin. She starts tugging at them. Weaving them into this slack rope.

"So this is it, right? This is the secret?"

"It could be."

"So what do we do?" Chris asks.

She holds the paper rope like a garrote.

"We get to fucking work."

Chapter Twenty-nine

MAE

Mid-City

She calls in sick. She doesn't detail her symptoms—that's what liars do. She tells Taylor she'll call Cyrus later about Parker. She doesn't fight the way Panko's face keeps flashing in her head. She doesn't fight the image of the tiny girl with the huge belly. She lets it fuel her.

Dan asked her about pregnancy. The girl was underage and pregnant. It felt wrong in the right way.

Mae does yoga. She sits with what she knows. She tries to focus on how the air feels cool as she draws it in through her nose. She can hold her focus for one breath.

Maybe it's another way. Maybe the guy with the bad mustache was the father—maybe. Maybe the girl is someone's cousin, someone's niece. Some girl who made a mistake trusting the wrong boy and then decided to keep the baby for some reason Mae herself would never understand.

Then there was the other, darker possibility.

Mae forces herself to finish the routine. To hold the position, let the breath come in and out. She counts her breaths in-out up to ten. Once she is done she leaps off the floor.

She gets her laptop out. She gets to work. The girl had the

look of one of Katherine's students: those doe eyes, those cheekbones, that high ponytail. She had the look of a wannabe actress. Maybe even one who could make it. Mae goes back through Katherine's Instagram. She looks at dance-class shots. She doesn't see the girl.

Mandy pads out from the bedroom, knocking Mae from her trance. Mae puts on a sweatshirt over her pajamas and takes her for a walk. There's mist in the morning air. They walk up the block to Mae's favorite tree, a mimosa with puffy pink-and-white flowers. A hummingbird moves in fractured orbit around it. Mandy pays the tree her respect by pissing by the trunk. Mae stares into the mid-distance and thinks about this pregnant girl.

They go back home. She goes through Katherine's pictures again. This time she reads the comments. All these gushing messages, lousy with emojis. She ignores the thirsty replies from men. She clicks on commenters' names. She finds girls from the dance classes. She goes through their feeds. Picture after picture after picture of this alien life of teenage wannabe actresses. Bedroom fashion shoots, selfies at the beach, TikTok dance challenges. Mae scrolls and scrolls and scrolls.

Her eyes are tired. She almost misses it. This picture of dance practice from months back. This girl with wide eyes and a high ponytail leaping in a high split. The caption: GO NEVAEH GO!!!

The photo is six months old. The girl has no pregnant belly.

Chris texts her the video. She watches it again. She pauses it as the girl gets out of the Jeep. She holds it up to the phone. The match is perfect.

Mae looks again at the belly on the video. The undeniability of it.

Dan in her head: *Find an objective correlative.*

She puts together a rough draft of a theory.

The knock on the front door nearly makes her scream.

Chapter Thirty

CHRIS

Sixth Street

Mae's got this look on her face that Chris has only ever seen at crime scenes.

Mae shows him the picture. It's the girl, pre-pregnancy.

He points to the name.

"Nevaeh?"

"It's *heaven* spelled backward. I knew a few Nevaehs back home. White trash ne plus ultra. But it's her, right?"

"Yeah, it's her. So what's it mean?"

"Did you find out anything about the guy driving the Jeep?"

"I ran the plates. Registered to a Jesse Harutyunyan. Couldn't find much about him. I'll keep digging."

"What about an address?"

"Plates are from Minnesota—figure if he's one of these bottom-feeders, he's pretty new, he hasn't been in LA long enough to register the car here."

He waits for her theory—instead she says, "Let's investigate the girl."

Chris runs a search—missing girls named Nevaeh—nothing that matches this girl comes up. Mae works through a web of social media, all these teenage wannabes, all so polished, working on their brand.

"ItGirl," she says out of nowhere.

"Huh?"

"ItGirl—a lot of the girls Katherine teaches are from this one teen talent agency."

She pulls up ItGirl's website. A list of girls—these semi-cheesecake shots of the girls that make Mae look sick.

They go to the "About" page—a photo of a woman, thin and sharp, short dark hair. The caption says she is Carol Goodman, founder and owner of ItGirl.

Mae says, "So that explains the moms' terror."

"Huh?"

"I saw her at the dance class—the moms looked at her like a goddess. I guess to them she is."

She clicks on a page of famous alumni. They see Lydia Lopez. They see Hannah Heard. They see half the cast of *As If!*

She finds a group picture—there's Nevaeh. A caption under the picture. Nevaeh Green.

She puts the name in the search bar.

"Maybe we'll get lucky. Maybe it's her real name."

A picture of this same girl, six years ago, a child actor on a stage in Tulsa. A big orange wig playing Annie.

A quote from her grandmother and guardian. Annabelle Green. Chris runs the name. Finds a landline number in Broken Arrow, Oklahoma. Their eyes lock—they have this UNSAID conversation. She reaches for her phone.

Chapter Thirty-one

MAE

Sixth Street

"Hello?" The Oklahoma accent close enough to her family's Ozark twang to cough up chunks of memories.

"Hello, ma'am." The look on Chris's face tells Mae her long-repressed accent has come out. She leans into it. "Is this Annabelle Green?"

"Last time I checked."

"Well, hello. My name is Courtney Brown. I represent Sixth Street Pictures here in Los Angeles—"

"Must be nice and warm over there."

"Yes, ma'am. We're calling in regard to Nevaeh Green. We were hoping to have her audition for a movie."

"Well now, she'll just be so excited to hear that, won't she? She's so pretty, isn't she? She always was, even as a toddler. I told my daughter, Nevaeh could be one of those grape juice kids. Prettiest girl in Broken Arrow."

"I'm sure she was. Look, it's not a big role, but it's a big movie. Could be a big break for your granddaughter. Ma'am, I'm not supposed to tell you this, but Tom Cruise will be in the film."

"No. Really? Give it to me straight, he really as short as they say?"

"Ma'am we start shooting next week, so we'd really like to get moving on this. We need to set up an audition."

"Well, sure! They got all the permissions and whatnot at that agency. What's its name?"

"ItGirl?"

"That's the one."

"And do you know where she's staying?"

"Well, she's up there in Los Angeles right now. She's a tan little beach bunny."

"You've spoken to her recently?"

"Of course I have, just yesterday. She's my own grand-daughter, and I pretty much raised her, didn't I?"

"And she's available to start work in two weeks?"

The woman laughs.

"Well, of course! It's why she's out there. Only been her dream her whole life to be famous. Of course she's available. Oh, she'll be so excited."

There's no artifice to her voice, no catch, no nervousness.

Her grandmother doesn't know she's pregnant.

"She's my flamingo princess. Like that game she plays. And she made it real, didn't she? She's a flamingo for real."

"Flamingos?"

"That game of hers she's always playing. *The Kingdom of Dreams.*"

"I don't know it. Can you tell me how I can contact her?"

"Well now, she lost her phone about a month ago, hasn't got a new one yet. She's been calling me on borrowed phones. But she's at that place, her and all those other girls. They all live together in one house, all these young girls trying to be actresses and whatnot. There's like a house mother who takes care of them all, but Nevaeh says it's like one big slumber party. Made me nervous, of course, sending her up there all alone, but it's cheaper this way, and they have this house mother, Missy is her name, she stays with the girls. I miss my girl something awful. But she always did have rocket fuel for blood, better out there trying to get to the moon than back here in Broken Arrow burning alive, I always figured. Back here a girl has a way of getting in trouble, you know?"

Mae doesn't say *they have those ways here too.* Instead she says, "Can you tell me how to reach the apartment?"

"Well, it's here somewhere."

She gives Mae a number. Mae writes it on the back of a takeout receipt. A phone number. An address in Burbank.

"Thank you for your time, ma'am."

"You see him, you tell Tom Cruise I don't care if he has to stand on a milk crate, I'm still game."

Mae gets off the call. There's this feeling in her like time is running backward. All these shards of glass on the floor rising out of chaos into a perfect wineglass.

"You believe her?"

"Yeah."

Her phone buzzes. She checks it.

"Oh shit."

"What?"

She shows him the phone: CYRUS.

"I'll call Nevaeh's place," Chris says.

"Have fun."

She walks into her bedroom, clicks on the phone. She hacks some phlegm into her throat, just a touch. Most folk overplay calling in sick.

"Cyrus."

"Mae. How are you doing?"

"Feeling better. I think it's that thing going around."

"I didn't want to disturb you on a personal day—"

"No, I told Taylor, I wanted to talk to you about Parker. I found the accuser."

"Where?"

"This tent city down on the LA River."

"No wonder you're feeling under the weather—they say the tent cities are bringing the bubonic plague back to LA."

"Like it ever left."

He laughs at this.

"Cyrus, I have to tell you. When you hear this story, this guy—it got to me."

"He's convincing?"

"Cyrus—maybe this job—maybe we ought to cut Parker free. Maybe this guy doesn't need us. Maybe what he needs is to go down."

"Mae, you know as well as I do that our responsibility is to our client. Our clients have the right to have their story told. What we do is provide a service. I'm a busy man, I don't have time to explain this to you."

"Cyrus—"

"This is what we do, Mae. You want to go get a job writing press releases for dental products, I'll be happy to write you a recommendation. You might find the compensation less adequate, but life is about making choices."

She sticks a plastic fork into her leg. The tines make cones of pain. She wonders which will break first, the fork or her skin.

"Okay. Forget it. Look, I did my job." "That's all I ever ask of you."

The fork breaks first.

Chapter Thirty-two

CHRIS

Sixth Street

She walks back into the living room—he can see this poison cloud hanging around her.

"Everything okay?"

"Life is a glorious cycle of song. A medley of extemporanea."

"Huh?"

She waves him away like *never mind*.

"I called the place Nevaeh was staying," he says. "The twenty-something in charge, Missy. It sounded like a teenage rampage behind her. That shrieking noise teenage girls do. Anyway, get this. She told me Nevaeh lived there all right. Left about two months ago. To go back home to her grandmother."

"It's the slumber-party trick," Mae says. "You know, you tell your mom you're spending the night with me, I tell my mom I'm spending the night with you. It means the girl is in on it, at least a little."

"Mae—are we gonna talk about this out loud, or you just gonna hold it inside until you pop?"

She gives him this sick smile.

"She's the bloody glove."

He remembers her using that phrase before—but not what it means. She must see it on his face, because she says, "It's the one solid thing that makes a story true. The thing you can point to, something that is undeniable. Nevaeh is fourteen years old. If the father is an adult—"

"She's carrying around DNA evidence of statutory rape in her belly."

"Just call it rape," Mae says. "It's quicker and just as accurate."

He nods like *got it*.

"So the father is an adult," she says. "Somebody with money. Somebody with power. Then the baby in her belly is undeniable proof positive. That girl is walking blackmail."

Something in Mae's voice causes Mandy to pad over to her and lean against her leg. Mae gives her a pat before going on.

"So this girl comes out to LA, fourteen years old, set loose in this place with no parents and no rules. And all these terrible powerful men. And then something awful happens to her. And a little while later Nevaeh realizes she is pregnant. She's scared out of her mind. She can't tell her grandma. She doesn't want to tell the other girls— who knows what's going on in her head? So she goes to Katherine."

"Her dance teacher? That's who she goes to for help?"

"You ought to see how the girls look at her. They worship her—that's exactly who she'd go to," Mae says. "So just follow me here—she goes to Katherine, after class or something. She tells her she's pregnant. My guess is, she tells her everything."

"So what's Katherine do?"

"Well, here's what she didn't do—she didn't go to the authorities. My guess is Katherine sees dollar signs. Her and her roommates put together a plan. And then they bring in Dan, her sometimes boyfriend. Maybe they need bankroll, maybe they need a middleman. Either way, Dan likes what he hears enough to get in."

"That means the man behind it is big-time," Chris says. "Dan had to be thinking this is worth millions, right? That means somebody with deep pockets. Figure the target is rich. Figure he's powerful."

"Or," she says, "figure he's rich but not powerful."

"Aren't they the same thing?"

"Not at a certain level, not all the time," she says. "Real power comes from generating profit for other people. That's the rule, that's what Dan taught me. Nobody really goes down unless the Beast wants him to go down. If they're still generating profit for the Industry, it's a lot harder to take them down. Maybe there's a few days of bad press. Maybe they have to take a year off. But they don't go down all the way if the Beast is behind them."

"The Beast isn't real, Mae. It's just a thing we say."

"Money isn't real either. But here we are."

"So the man who raped her—he's rich, maybe on his way out the door. This girl, she's a wannabe actress, a dance student—"

"Eric." Her voice has this weird tone, like she's imitating someone. "Eric, look what you've done to me."

"Who's Eric?"

She's watching some movie playing behind her eyes.

"Hey, yo." He waves a hand in front of her face. "Where you at?"

She blinks herself back to the world.

"I think I have the who."

Chapter Thirty-three

MAE

Simi Valley

She submarines through clouds of mist on the Ronald Reagan Freeway.

Mae drives in the false dawn—traffic light as it ever gets in LA. She drinks bitter old cold brew she had at the back of her fridge. She checks herself in the mirror—she only looks half-crazy. These weird things wriggling behind her eyes, looking to climb out.

Mae sees a yellow sign stuck to the exit. A black arrow, the word bliss. Mae takes the exit. The mist is thicker here. She drives with her hands at ten and two. Mae follows another yellow sign, another black arrow, into the campus for Brandeis-Bardin University. A bored security guard waves her up the road without stopping her.

The university is dead. Mae passes the main campus, up into the hills. A final black arrow waves her into a parking lot. The lot is mostly full of high-end pickups and luxury sedans. Film crews are made up of union members with good income and no free time. They spend a lot of time driving to locations, so they drive nice cars.

Mae parks next to a group of Teamsters having their morning coffee. A few grips roll a camera rig past her. They wear toolbelts and walkies with their names written on tape, belts studded with clothesline pins.

The line of the horizon is threaded with orange. Hannah has a 6 a.m. call time. They'll run rehearsals, they'll get their marks, and then the DP will take over the set for lighting and camera moves. Hannah will have an hour of downtime. More than enough for what Mae needs to know.

Mae walks past trailers brought in overnight by the Teamsters, full of light rigs and costumes and props and gear.

She follows the crowd toward craft services—steam trays of bacon, eggs, oatmeal. A food truck handing out breakfast burritos. Mae plucks some bacon from a steam tray, pours herself a coffee. Nobody looks at her. She's serving west-side business chic. She wore impractical clothes on purpose—anybody looking will peg her as being from the studio and leave her alone.

Extras in long white robes and shaved heads all in a holding pen. Behind them, at the top of the hill, is the House of the Book, this seventies-futuristic building, Mae's seen it in movies before. She guesses it's going to be the cult headquarters.

She sees a woman with long dark hair all the way down her back, lugging two big binders and her own folding canvas chair. All the telltale signs of a scriptie. Scripties are almost always women—most directors are men, and most men need a mommy. That means she's heading to where the director is, which will soon enough be where Hannah is.

Mae follows the woman to video village. Video monitors—folding chairs—the director, midsixties, a full head of gray hair, a knee brace revealed by his too-short shorts, holds court. Costumes, art direction, the first AD already nervous about the clock. They wear cargo shorts—it'll be hot soon enough. All these folk—the grips, transpo, set dressers, sound, the DP and his camera crew—the DP a wild-haired man with some sort of thick accent—all these sixteen-hour-day people, these people who make the movie, make the show actually happen. All this time spent in the Beast, you forget this is what it is all for.

She posts up behind this nervous-looking woman studying the script—definitely the writer.

There's a safety meeting before call time—the first AD warns about fire hazards.

"What, is there a tent city around here?" somebody asks. Some laughs—the bomber hit a camp off the 101 last night—one woman got third-degree burns.

Behind her at the sound cart, a guy holding a boom mic talks to the guy manning the sound cart. Their tone— clamped-down anger.

"She won't do it."

"This fucking—are you kidding me? Just mic her."

"She won't wear a mic—I said I don't got to be the one to put it on her, if that's the thing. We can get Jasmine to do it—like if it's a man thing. She got fucking tears in her eyes—bro, I can't fuck with tears. We got to boom her."

"It'll sound like shit. She's fucking nutbags."

"You say that like it's not common knowledge."

They're talking about Hannah.

The one with the boom mic spots Mae listening in. He freezes up. They figure they've just been caught badmouthing the talent.

"You need a headset?" the one with the comb-over asks, trying to play it cool.

She shakes her head no. Mae tosses them a smile like *it's our little secret*. They relax a little. They go do the job.

Ryan Gosling walks past Mae—that sort of thing that never stops being surreal, no matter how long you've been here, this face from the movie screens walking past, these faces you know better than the faces of your friends. Mae primps her hair, catches herself doing it, drops her hands to her sides.

A girl with the sides of her head shaved passes, holding a cardboard takeout tray. It takes a second for Mae to recognize her: Shira, Hannah's assistant from the Chateau—the girl now wears the hooded eyes of someone who has been deep in the shit.

"Hey. Shira? Remember me?"

"You're the black bag. Mae, right?"

"That's right. Look, I need a word with Hannah."

"You sure about that?"

"I've handled her at her worst."

"You sure about *that*?"

"It's important."

"She's got hair and makeup in thirty. You could talk to her then."

Hair and makeup artists are megaphones—they act as set therapists for the actors, they know everything, and they whisper louder than anyone. Mae's bribed enough of them to know.

"Nix. I need it to be just me and her. I'll be quick," Mae says. She nods to the tray in the girl's hands. "Done before breakfast."

"Come on, then."

Mae follows Shira to the double-wide trailer, a radar dish on top, Hannah's name on a plastic plaque on the door. A group of crew members—the sound guys Mae saw earlier, alongside a rawboned woman Mae pegs as a second AD—stand outside the trailer, facing it at a safe distance— this image in Mae's head of cops outside a hostage situation. The rawboned woman sees Shira, says, "Can you get her to—"

"No."

"Shira—"

"I do my job, you do yours."

The second AD walks away at speed. Mae turns back to Shira.

"You're born-again badass, you know that?"

"My therapist calls it a maladaptive coping mechanism. But thank you."

The insides of celebrity trailers are never as glamorous as you think they're going to be—the wall-to-wall tan carpet kills the vibe. Every surface of Hannah's trailer is covered with untouched muffin baskets, bottles of wine, flowers—Mae clocks the one from Cyrus, his signature orchid in a pot.

Hannah sits on one of the built-in couches. She looks poisoned and weak—still an improvement from last time.

"Hey, bitch," she says. Shira drops her breakfast tray on the table in front of Hannah.

"How's it going?"

"Thirty-two days until wrap—fuck me with a sticky

dildo. They're trying to mic me up, and this dress I'm wearing is tight as shit and it'll sound bad, I know it, and they won't. Fucking. Listen to me."

"You're a soldier," Mae says. Hannah waves at her like *fuck off.*

"So what's good? You've got like five minutes before that cunt Trisha comes hunting for me."

Mae looks to Shira. Hannah gets it, waves to Shira like *get the fuck out.*

"Guard the door—if you see Trisha coming, brain the bitch and light out for Mexico."

Shira leaves. Hannah pops open the tray—the food limp and healthy and joyless. She pokes at the five cashews next to the gluten-free pancake. Four chunks of dragon fruit sit wetly in their own little tray.

"God, I just want to be fat," Hannah says. "Can you imagine how amazing it would be?"

"I want to talk to you about Eric Algar."

Hannah spits chewed-up cashews back into the tray.

"No, you don't. People like you never want to talk about people like Eric. You want to work for them. You want to get rich off them. But you sure as fuck don't want to talk about them."

"I do this time."

"If you're trying to kill a story, I won't help," Hannah says. "I keep my mouth shut. I don't start shit. But I won't help you help him."

"Is it true?"

"Do you even know what you mean?"

"Then tell me."

203

Hannah laughs. It sounds like drowning. She sits there looking at her hands a long time.

"Tell me."

Hannah keeps her eyes on her hands.

"What is it you say? Everybody whispers? Well, when I was a kid? All anybody whispered was that Eric Algar was my key to the castle."

Her mouth puckers, her jaw moving, like her spit tastes sour.

"When you're a kid, staying at the Oakwood, it was all you talked about—getting to go to one of these pool parties he used to throw—maybe he still does, probably. They called the parties soda pops. How fucking lame is that? All these desperate kid actors wanted to go to a soda pop at Eric's house in the hills. No parents allowed. Soda pop only—that's what they told any parent who gave half a shit, which wasn't many of them. Kids running around in their swimsuits. That horrible woman from ItGirl—"

"Carol Goodman?"

"That rancid bitch. She organized the parties. Made the parents feel like they didn't need to stick around. Everybody knew that's where you got discovered. At the soda pops. All the girls and boys too, they all wanted to go to the soda pops. Eric produced half the shows on the network and Carol cast most of the other half too. I wanted it so fucking bad. I'm in from Chicago, just Dad and me at the Oakwood, and all the sudden I'm running around the pool, the whole house built up against the side of the hills, LA all spilled out below. You're up above it all and you tell yourself it's pretty because it ought to be. But really, when you're up that high you can look down on the smog line, you can see how we all just live in a dirty fucking bowl. But you're up there above it all and it feels so fancy, and there's Brad Cherry—God, he was so cute back then. And there's hot dogs and music and flirting and soda, and then there's the rooms in the back with pills and vodka, don't tell anyone. And then, party number three, when you're used to keeping secrets . . ."

These muscles in her neck spasm, like she's trying to swallow something too big for her throat. Mae flashes to Hannah when she was younger. She can see the ghost of this glowing girl Hannah used to be. The girl who shone, who was meant to shine, and maybe in some other life still does.

"And then you find out there's a different party inside the house. A party for Eric and his buddies. And they just can't wait to meet you."

This terrible long moment. Mae knows she ought to say something but she doesn't know what and it would feel fake anyway.

"Do you think he's still doing it?"

This cruel laugh.

"Why the hell would he ever stop?"

A knock on the door breaks the spell.

"Oh Jesusfuck come on." Fury comes out of Hannah like arterial spray. She throws the champagne bottle against the wall of the trailer. It bounces heavily to the carpet. Hannah looks surprised that it didn't break.

This second AD—the label on her walkie names her the dread Trisha—already bone weary at 6 a.m. One of the sound guys stands sheepishly behind her.

"Hannah. We got to put a mic on you."

"Trisha, no," Hannah says. This desperate sound to her voice. "It won't fit under the costume."

Mae can read the faces. Everybody knows it's a lie. But they can't say it out loud. These people just trying to do their jobs, faced with this person more like a god than a person to them.

"Eddie said I couldn't be mic'ed. He said the way the dress is constructed—"

Mae waves bye to Hannah. Hannah doesn't even see her anymore.

"Hannah," Trish says, "Eddie's right outside the trailer. He says it's fine to mic you."

Mae walks down the trailer steps, past the sound man holding a mic limply in his hands.

"Nobody's going to touch me. Nobody. Nobody."

Mae walks away from the trailer, back to her car. She thinks about the silences.

Hannah screams—it bleeds through the trailer walls.

"Nobody's touching me. Nobody is going to touch me."

Mae walks back to her car. Her impractical shoes dig into the dew-soaked ground. She looks down into the Simi Valley. She looks at the sun rising over the hills, the weird beauty of the House of the Book. She thinks about something Sarah said once.

Everybody talks about how actresses are crazy. Nobody talks about how they got that way.

She sits in her car. All these secrets. All these UNSAID things.

From where she is sitting she can see Shira standing by herself on the hilltop, away from the set. She is motionless, facing the rising sun. The sunrise spills blue-pink over misty green hills. The raw beauty of it seems like it's mocking Mae. *Here is this gorgeous world you were given, you stupid little girl. Look what you all started with.*

She pulls up Sarah's number. That tinny ring again—the call bouncing through space.

"Hey, girl. You're up early. What is it, five there?"

"Something like that. I'm up, figured I'd call. How's Romania?"

"I'm tired. I want a ridiculous margarita with like guava or yuzu in it. I want khao soi. I never want to eat anything wrapped in cabbage again. I want sunshine . . . I want a man with neck tattoos and a blind script deal at Sony to hold me down and pull my hair. I want to pay fifteen dollars for a bottle of beet juice . . . I want to be stuck in traffic . . . I want a pastrami burrito . . . I want dirty air . . . I want Los Angeles."

"Don't worry," Mae says. "That which is dead can never die . . . it'll be here waiting for you."

"You doing okay? With Dan and everything?"

"I'm trying to make sense of it. But lookit, I want to ask you something for work."

Sarah catches the UNSAID part—*we're about to talk dirt.* She casts her voice low down.

"Hold up, I'm going to go over here away from people. Okay, can you hear me?"

"Yeah. I just want your take on someone. He does tween stuff mostly, a producer/writer named Eric Algar."

A long beat before Sarah says, "Eric Algar?"

"Yes."

"You noted the pause there?"

"I did."

"So that's my answer. Is he a client?" Sarah asks.

Mae fights back the urge—she needs to share this with someone, someone who will get the horror of it. Chris got it as much as a man could—but the horror of it doesn't hum in his bones. Sarah would get it. But now isn't the time.

"Just doing due diligence," Mae says.

"God. Your job. Anyway, yes, whatever you heard, I heard it too. As bad as they get."

Nobody talks. But everybody whispers.

Mae says, "The worse they are the better they do."

"Hey, it's a garbage world. Of course the rats are going to thrive."

"What I want to know is, how's his star meter? How much sway does he have these days?"

"Huh. I guess not as much as it used to be. He's on an overall deal with the network, which still has some pull for basic cable. But those tween shows are out of date—three years ago he had maybe six shows on the air—a major powerhouse—these days it's maybe down to one? Is that right? He's probably costing them money at this point—his deal can't be worth what they're paying him, not anymore. He's the past. Kids these days are on YouTube, Twitch, TikTok, shit you or I have never heard of. Those tweener sitcoms are passé. So yeah, he's on his way down. His power level has probably crashed, now that you mention it. He seems ripe for getting taken down, actually. Sort of weird that he hasn't yet."

"That's what I wanted to know. Thanks, girl."

"You know who would know?" Sarah asks. "Hannah Heard. There's got to be some stories from back in the day. He's the creator of *As If !* Her, Lydia Lopez, Brad Cherry— none of them came out of his orbit looking normal. You ought to see if Hannah will come clean."

"Good idea," Mae says. "I'll talk to you soon."

She hangs up. Outside her window, Shira turns back from the rising sun. She wipes tears from her face. She sees Mae in her car. Their eyes lock. There's this perfect moment of understanding between the two of them.

It is not supposed to be this way.

Mae calls Chris's burner with her own. When he answers his voice is froggy with sleep. She'd forgotten the time. He's not awake. She's as awake as she's ever been.

"It's true. Eric Algar and young girls. For years and years. God knows how many. How many wrecked girls there are out there. And nobody cares."

"Mae." The concern in his voice wakes Mae up to what she sounds like, how close she is to the edge of a cliff in her mind.

"I want to take down Eric Algar. I want to stop him. I want to save the girl."

She leaves the part that scares her UNSAID: *If we do it just right, we can save ourselves as well.*

Chapter Thirty-four

CHRIS

Sixth Street

They meet at her place that afternoon after Mae's work. Chris is achy from sitting too long—a fruitless day staking out the Wonderland house. He shakes it off on the walk up to her door.

Mandy greets him feverishly. He lets the dog lean into him. He knows where the name comes from—that there's a part of Mae she's put away, sealed off to become the person she is.

They eat, they talk. She tells him about her day—waiting for Parker's arrest. She talks about it like she's sucking poison from a snakebite. It feels like the old days—only this time the secrets aren't driving them apart. They haven't talked about the two of them yet. Chris doesn't want to talk about it. He just wants to let it happen. The way they sit closer together on the couch, all these old walls slipping down between them.

They put together a biography of Eric. He worked as a teen actor himself—a few family dramas back in the nineties. He aged from cute to awkward. He got behind the camera. He directed kids' shows. He pitched one of his own. He saw a gap in the market, he saw how he could fill it for cheap. The network greenlit it. He had a good idea—not about the content, which was just a tween comedy set at a mall food court. His brainstorm was—all of these out-of-work three-camera sitcom writers needed work. Their jokes were out of touch with the new single-cam sitcoms. Their residuals from the golden age were thinning out—they had Hancock Park houses and alimony to pay. He filled the writers' room with them. They churned out old jokes for kids who had never heard them before.

He had an eye for young talent. He teamed up with Carol Goodman at ItGirl. He discovered Hannah Heard. He discovered Brad Cherry. He discovered Lydia Lopez. He discovered the Two Tylers.

He got more shows on the air. He got so many shows on the air he changed the whole network.

Mae digs up some puff-piece article from ten years ago.

" 'Eric has the mogul's mindset,' an executive raves. 'He knows what it takes to close a deal in Hollywood. Because he doesn't hear the word "no." ' "

As If! led to a massive overall deal. Reading clips, Mae's able to finger the month he hired a publicist—the tone of the articles changes; they get longer. He loses weight, gets an expensive haircut. He gets labeled the King of Tween. He owns the nighttime lineup for the whole channel. He launches teen stars. Some rise. Some crash back down.

Chris and Mae run through the list:

Hannah Heard—lives on the edge of a nervous breakdown.

Brad Cherry—the beautiful dead boy.

Lydia Lopez—pop queen turned junkie turned sober advocate, on the right side of clean for now.

The cute Tyler—a few years back, washed up, he stabbed his landlady to death outside his Los Feliz apartment.

The bad-boy Tyler—mutilated by too much plastic surgery, makes terrible music, the kind of music that goes viral for being so shitty. America's laughingstock.

"It's like they all worked at a nuclear power plant with a bad reactor, and when they get cancer we all just point and laugh at their tumors," Mae says.

Fast-forward to today. Eric's six shows are down to two. Tween shows are passé. His day is done.

Eric's secret is out there—in a limited way.

Nobody talks. But everybody whispers.

They find all these photos—Eric with teenage actresses on-set, these smiles on their mouths, eyes like a rabbit in the shadow of a hawk. She shows him internet threads, amateur detectives, anonymous claims, putting together theories that Eric is a foot freak, a creeper, a perv. Some of it is ludicrous fantasy. Some of it isn't.

Sometimes Mae gets so angry she has to leave the room.

She says, "I wish we had some way to talk to her. To Nevaeh."

"Her grandma said she lost her cell phone."

"That's bullshit—Katherine and them just don't want her reachable."

"So what are we doing here, Mae?"

"Any doubt we're on the right track?"

"Not really. It all adds up."

Mae says, "My guess is, Baldassare and Katherine's plan is straight-up blackmail. Maybe they brought Dan in as a middleman. And then he decided to take over the play. I know Dan. I know what he was thinking—if he did this thing with these amateurs, they'd go down. He knew better than to trust them—and plus, he knew how to do it without them. His idea was to work it with me. And somehow they figured out he was going to double-cross them. And they killed him for it."

"So what are we going to do?"

"We're not going to blackmail him," she says. "We take the girl from Katherine and them. We get the DNA proof that Eric Algar is the father. Undeniable evidence. It's the key. I engineer an eight-figure deal to sell her story—TV interview, book, movie rights. They'll try to stop us. We know what's coming, we know how to avoid it. We find ourselves a lawyer, someone outside the Industry. We work them as a cutout. Look, we both know the shakedowns that work and the ones that don't. I know who will kill a story— that means I know who won't. And here's the main thing. Eric Algar isn't worth much to anyone anymore. He's not worth fighting for. He won't have the full power of the Beast behind him. He's a perfect target. And he fucking deserves it. Just once I want to be a part of someone getting what they deserve." She says it like it's something to be ashamed of. "And if we take our fee off the top, everybody wins."

"These people don't play," he says. "Dan probably died over this. We don't know what these people are capable of."

"They don't know what we're capable of either. You figure out how to find Nevaeh. I'll figure out how to get the story out. Nobody has to get hurt."

PART FOUR

Wonderland

Chapter Thirty-five

MAE

Westwood

The cold of the office like plunging in the ocean. Assistants ask if she's feeling better. She talks about a twenty-four-hour bug. The assistants assume hangovers. They laugh like a wink. She passes Joss's office—he waves like *come in*.

"The story on Parker hits the *LA Times* tomorrow," Joss says. "We got a leaked rough draft passed to us."

"Bad?"

"Headline is DEMOCRATIC FUNDRAISER ACCUSED OF DRUG-DEN ASSAULTS."

"So not good, then."

He waves her over to his computer screen. She scans the story. The paper quotes Panko anonymously. The article goes deep. It tells the whole story. Two dead bodies. Panko's quotes finish him off.

She reads the words *indictment looming*.

All she can think is *good*.

"Mitnick seen this?"

"Haven't talked to him yet. If we're going to stop this, it's going to take a head shot. Mitnick will have to pull heavy shit."

They find Cyrus and Hector in the middle of a conversation.

"We're doing our job," Hector says. "We got positive coverage on two networks and *LA Weekly*. O'Dwyer is still blocking the vote."

"I've never met a city councilman so allergic to progress."

"It's not that," Hector says. "It's O'Dwyer's poll numbers."

"I don't believe that . . . there's a lever somewhere—"

"Hey," Mae says. "Sorry. We need to talk about Parker—"

"No, we don't," Cyrus says. "Parker is no longer a priority at this firm."

Just like that. Two days ago she begged him to drop him. Now he does it without a blink. Somewhere some balance of power shifted.

"I've got the *LA Times* article on Parker, if we're—"

"Ward Parker is not high priority," Mitnick says. "The DA wants a scalp. The amount of social capital we'd have to expend to kill the story simply isn't worth it. Cut him loose."

And it's done. Parker is done. *There's a lesson here,* Mae thinks. See how easily the Beast walks away from a loss when it's the smart play.

Get the girl and Eric goes down.

Chapter Thirty-six

CHRIS

Koreatown / Laurel Canyon

Saturday they take a day of rest. Mae says she's let her life build up—she needs a day to clean and run errands. She says she needs a night on the couch with wine and television.

She doesn't say *before we cross another line*. But he hears it anyway.

Chris wakes up with this clean energy burning inside him—like he's found the right fuel for once. He looks around his place, seeing it through someone else's eyes.

Chris opens up the windows. He picks the clothes up off the floor. The top of the hamper blooms with old laundry. He packs it up. He does all of it. He changes his sheets for the first time in forever. He cleans the bathroom, the fumes of the bleach sawing at his lungs with each breath.

When it is done, it looks like a place another person could walk in. That a woman could visit and not be horrified.

Outside, Koreatown is at full pitch. He catches himself pacing around the apartment. He thinks of animals in small-town zoos, pacing in too-small cages.

He hasn't felt like that for a long time. He chases it. He grabs his keys on the way out the door.

He walks down the street to the parking garage. He leaves Koreatown, heads up Wilshire—past the modern-art KFC, Korean spas, a hot chicken joint with a line around the block—new apartment construction jams traffic just south of Santa Monica—he keeps on into Hollywood, takes a left on Franklin, passes the Scientology Celebrity Centre—he cuts the AC and lets the air in. He takes Franklin up and down the hills, all the way west, cuts down to Hollywood Boulevard, heads toward Laurel Canyon. He hits the Laurel Canyon Country Store for a sandwich and a can of soda. He takes a piss.

He drives with the windows down. This itching feeling. The good kind of itch. Like healing. Like he's climbing out of his old skin. Like there's something new and fresh still inside him.

The little roads up the hill to the house are more jammed than normal, cars parked everywhere. He kills his music as he gets close—instead of silence he hears thumping bass echoing off the hills.

The clout house is a party in full swing. Every light on, door hanging open so the house shouts its music into the hills, garbled by the babble of a hundred voices. All these young pretty people mill about outside. A circle out front passing a blunt. He cruises past slow—he gets an idea. It jolts him—the good kind of jolt. It makes him realize the phantom heart attacks have faded.

Chase this feeling.

He drives past, two blocks before he finds a gap where he can park. He turns on the overhead, checks himself in the rearview. He remembers what Mae said—producers and powerful people don't wear suits anymore. Looking like shit is a power move—it shows you don't have to pretend to care what other people think.

He pulls on his army jacket and clops down the hill to the house. The blunt circle eyeballs him as he walks up the steps. He nods. It works. Act like you belong and you belong.

The house is packed, the air wet with breath and fruity with vape mist, body-heat hot. Chris pops sweat the moment he crosses the threshold. It feels good.

Walking into the house is like walking through a TV screen into the show you've been binging. All these people he's watched through a windshield suddenly all around him. It makes them feel real. Or maybe it's the other way. Maybe Chris is the one who is starting to be real again.

He walks into the crowd. He gets a few eyeballs, nothing more. He's a head taller than most of the crowd. He spots Tony, the tall roommate, with a circle around him. His eyes are cocaine glazed. He's mid-story, says he's got a callback, swears he's going to nail it. Everybody in the circle has that trapped party look, that feeling like you're being held hostage, like maybe the guy who won't stop talking about his Netflix callback has a knife to your throat.

Men with popcorn muscles, hairless chests, swigging champagne from the bottle, weird bright orange cocktails; the constant roar of people makes the pressure of the air more real—a plane during takeoff.

A woman near as tall as him presses against him in the crowd. She's the boring kind of beautiful.

"Who are you with?" she asks him. She's cutting right to the chase. It lets him know his producer pose is working.

"I'm in development," he says, pulling lingo from Mae. "I'm with Nic Cage's pod."

"No shit," the woman says, looking the other way—it's the wrong answer for some reason. He laughs out loud.

Chase this feeling.

He wants a lay of the apartment. He turns the corner to find Janice DeWaal making out with another woman, everybody with their cameras out, everybody chanting *go go go*—it's phony, it's performative lesbian action. Big sloppy kisses, eyes like kids doing a dance number for their family at Christmas.

The kitchen is thick with people. He makes his way to the fridge, snags a beer. He sees Kevin and Katherine drunk-swaying. He sees Loto, his tank top exposing huge muscles—he works at a gym, he juices, he deals steroids. That look in his eye, Chris knows it from juicing. That out-of-control feeling, the joy of running wild and the fear of not being able to control it all at once—the hellfire rush of it. Chris turns to the fridge to grab a—

POP.

The sound makes Chris touch his hip, the ghost of his holster—he just outed himself as an ex-cop if anyone was paying attention. But all eyes are on Kevin, the champagne bottle in his hand spraying foam. Katherine tries to catch the spray. She's way past drunk. Kevin tips champagne into open mouths—a priest with sacrament. Loto tips a tequila bottle, takes big gulps.

Chris has seen this kind of partying before. He's seen it in gangbangers, he's seen it in cops when the hammer is coming down. The frenzy. This joyless, desperate fun.

They're terrified.

They're close to the edge.

Past the kitchen is a hallway, a door that is probably a bathroom, and past that a stairwell leading upstairs. The lights are turned off—off-limits to the partiers. He gets this crazy image: Nevaeh hiding out upstairs while the grown-ups throw a party. It's unlikely in the extreme. It's too crazy not to try. That rocket fuel crackles again.

Chase this feeling.

He weaves through the crowd toward the hallway. A woman waits at the closed door. She is Black, her head is shaved, she is gorgeous.

The door dips back and forth *thud thud thud*, muffled gasps. The woman waiting outside the door smiles, embarrassed.

Chris says, "At that pace we won't be waiting long."

The woman laughs. He joins in—their laughs mixing in with the sex moans. Chris realizes he's half-hard in his pants. Something animal inside him is running at full speed.

Chris looks up the stairs.

"We're not supposed to go up there," the woman says with a posh Brit accent. "But if you—"

The crowd in the kitchen erupts in a roar. The tone is off. It's not a party sound.

TOTAL CHAOS from the kitchen. The woman runs to the sound. Chris follows.

This guy as tall as Chris, bent over, clutching his face. Kevin stands with a new bottle of champagne, foam dripping limply onto his shoes.

"Come on, man, quit playing," Kevin says.

The guy takes his hand away—his left eye this tangle of white and red as blood fills it—the brown of his eye looks like a cracked plate. A woman reaches down, comes back up with the cork in her hand.

"I can't see shit. Motherfucker, I can't see shit."

Screams that sound like laughter. Laughter that sounds like screams.

"Call him an ambulance," somebody says.

"Fuck that noise, call him an Uber, it'll get here faster."

The crowd presses in around the injured guy—the woman who had been at the bathroom doorway a part of it. He turns back to the empty stairwell.

Do it.

He tamps down a howl. He heads up the stairs. He takes them three at a time.

The air has that ticklish quality—it always does when you're somewhere you're not supposed to be. He doesn't bother moving quiet—no one downstairs can hear shit. He's in a hallway with four doors. He's guessing three bedrooms plus a bathroom.

Chris works room to room—the one he pegs as Loto's stinks like sweat marinade, kettlebells everywhere, all these empty energy drinks—there's needles in the trash can, alcohol wipes—Loto's juicer status confirmed. He tosses the place quick, not even sure what he's looking for.

Next he heads all the way down the hallway to what he guesses right is the master bedroom—Kevin and Katherine's room. A bathroom en suite. Chris paws quick through her drawers. He paws through workout clothes, yoga pants, everyday bras—the next drawer over the fancy ones. He catches himself in some sort of horny fantasy starring Mae and Katherine. He pictures what he would look like if someone walked in right now. He shuts the drawer. He switches to the other dresser—Kevin's.

Inside the sock drawer he finds a flat black nine millimeter. It is cold and heavy in his hand. His blood thickens in his veins. He has not held a gun for a long time. He balances it in his hand. He checks the safety—it's not on—he slides it on. He makes a quick call. He tucks it in his waistband.

He hits the hallway and heads toward the stairs. The light coming up the stairwell breaks into shards of shadows—someone's lurching up. Chris clenches his fists, ready to fight his way out. Maybe even wanting to.

Quick thuds roll up the staircase. All these chants of *Puke and rally! Puke and rally!* echo up from the party.

He steps into the door to his left—hopes it's empty—it is.

Katherine shambles past. She's typhoon drunk. She hiccups wetly. She snorts back pre-puke snot. She mumbles something he can't make out as she slams open the door to the master bedroom. The puking starts seconds later. She moans thickly. Chris gets a jolt of instant empathy—you push your body too far and it shows you who is really driving the bus.

"Please," she says. "Please, I'm so fucking sorry. Oh please, oh God, oh no." Chris sneaks down the stairs to the sounds of her begging something invisible, begging it for mercy. Whatever god or demon she prays to doesn't listen and she's retching again.

*

Outside the air is sharp against his skin. The man with the injured eye sits on the curb, a woman holding him, looking over her shoulder to the party like she's dying to get back inside. She tells him the Uber is almost here.

"I can't see," he says.

"They'll fix it."

"A fucking champagne cork. I have a callback tomorrow. My agent's gonna kill me."

They hear Chris coming, turn to look. The man turns to Chris. His shattered eye weeps blood. Like an omen from back when gods were real.

Chapter Thirty-seven

MAE

Sixth Street

"Chris. That was really dumb."

They sit on Mae's couch. Mandy sleeps with her head in Chris's lap. They've sunk into this strange domesticity.

"We need information. The place was packed, I was just another face in the crowd."

"Well, what did you get?"

"They're scared. Fuck that, they're terrified. Whatever they're going to do, they're going to do soon."

"So we have to act sooner."

"Yeah."

Her phone buzzes.

"Parker," she says. She doesn't touch the phone. "He got arrested yesterday."

"And the Beast is done with him?"

"The DA wants him. Somebody somewhere did some calculus and Parker wound up on the wrong side of the equation."

The buzzes stop.

"I searched Kevin and Katherine's bedroom," he says. "I found a gun."

"What did you do with it?"

"I took it."

"We don't need a gun."

"It's stashed," he says. "Better to have and not need. And for sure better that they don't have one."

"So what do we do?" she asks. "What's the next step?"

"I say we talk to one of them."

"Talk?"

"Yeah. Grab one of them, get them talking, and then we flip them."

"You're not a cop anymore, Chris."

This smile on his face she's never seen before. Hellfire joy.

"Well, let's not tell them that. But we need someone on the inside."

"Which one do we start with? Not Katherine. She'll recognize me."

"Not Baldassare either. He's at the center of this. Spook him the wrong way and everything could crash. I say we start at Loto, the bodybuilder. He deals in steroids and shit. We can use that."

She asks him, "So we're really going to do this?"

"We're really going to do this."

The blood in her body moving fast as falling rain.

Chapter Thirty-eight

MAE

Lincoln Heights

A flock of wild parrots fills the trees. The chatter is deafening. The cars in the gym parking lot are carpet-bombed with parrot shit.

Mae welcomes the racket. It drowns out her thoughts.

We're really going to do this.

Across the street is a *carnicería*. Men finish their workouts, head across the street, come out with big plastic bags of raw carne asada, protein, red and striated muscle in a bag. The men so big and cut they look skinned. Mae has to admit, it's hot in a cartoon kind of way.

She drinks a limon soda she bought from the store. She eats dried mango covered in chili.

Loto restacks towels, wipes down benches—sweat everywhere—veins thick as her pinkie. It makes her think of biology class. Beefy men with weight-lifting belts and leather wrist guards.

They wait. They watch men—two or three women in the corner do squat variations, building ass, but the gym is mostly men. The gym used to be a garage—it has these big bay doors, open in the heat, so Mae and Chris can watch everything.

They watch Loto have whispered conversations. Nods back to the changing room. Mae knows drug-deal body language when she sees it.

"What's it like?" she asks Chris. "Taking steroids."

"It's out of this world," he says. "Four lines of coke, mid-cycle with a full pump, strap on a badge and a gun and drive code four—sirens screaming, cherries flashing, flying through red lights through the city at midnight—you figure out pretty quick what kind of god you'd be."

"What kind of god were you?"

"The angry kind."

He shifts around, won't meet her eyes. That mix of shame and hunger—like when she thinks about smoking.

"All you can do now is make up for it."

"Is that what we're doing?"

Loto comes out the front door, a gym bag in his hand, and saves her from having to answer that.

"Okay," he says. "Follow my lead."

Chris says, "After this there's no takebacks."

"No takebacks."

"All right, then," he says. "See you on the other side."

He opens the door—parrot babble cranks to eleven. She watches him move around the car, big strides. Mae can feel all the hairs of her arms individually. She can feel all her veins, how they lace through the flesh of her.

Loto reaches his car. Chris moves fast. He comes up from behind Loto. He bangs Loto's head against the door of his car. Mae vibrates in tune with the sound of it. Chris yanks him backward, pushes him into the back of the SUV.

"Hey, bro, what the fuck?"

"LAPD," Chris says, cuffing the man's wrists. "Get in the back."

Chris yanks the duffel bag from Loto. Loto grasps after it, big hands swinging uselessly.

"Detective Armbruster, LAPD," Chris says. He flashes the badge too quick to read it.

"Man, you need a warrant for this, this is bullshit." The guy's got a hematoma over his right eye.

Chris dumps the bag in the back seat. Hypos, vials, pill bottles, spill out. Chris flips through the bag's contents.

"Stanozolol, Decabol, Oxanabol. Tamoxifen—this stops the juice from growing your tits. HCG, to unshrink balls. You're a real one-stop shop, Loto—you could dump this bag in Echo Park Lake and watch the geese get yoked, am I right?"

Loto looks at Mae—she watches the hematoma inflate over his eye, this crazy blood balloon.

"She's not a cop."

"No shit," Mae says.

Chris takes Loto's jaw in his hand.

"Don't worry about her. Worry about me."

Chris is fully animal in this moment. His voice demanding. *The angry kind of god.*

"Loto, if we wanted to bring you in, I wouldn't have brought my friend here. It's paperwork, Loto, and you're small-time."

Mae's watching a cop show from the shotgun seat. The whole thing thrills her. It makes her sick. The cabin smells like salt and fear. She's turned-on—just another fact at the back of her skull.

This is what power does to you?

Loto blinks—the hematoma threatens to pop and spray blood everywhere. Mae knows how it feels.

"Fuck it, fine," Loto says. "Meacham behind the desk, he's in, he takes me for a cut of the proceeds—I'm not the only one. Half the staff slings it. You got yourself a major-league bust. But I walk."

"If I gave a shit about a gym slinging juice, you'd have a deal. But that's not what we want, Loto. My friend here, you're right, she's not a cop. She's from the Department of Children and Family Services."

Her cue—she knows just how to play it.

"Loto, tell me about Nevaeh Green."

Loto lets out this gut-deep belch—like something he's been holding too long is coming out of him.

"I told them. I told them, it's too fucking big. You got to know your place, on God that's what I said."

"She's pregnant—and you and your friends are going to use her for blackmail."

"It didn't have nothing to do with me, man." Mae doesn't have to look over to Chris to know Loto is lying. "I just do what I do. I told them it was crazy, on God."

"Just tell us we're right, Loto. You're using the girl for blackmail."

"I mean she's fourteen and pregnant, that shit's a sin, you feel me? On God, that shit is wrong. So we take him for some money, so what? He's a sicko, has it coming."

"Do you know the man's name?"

"I don't know, some Hollywood sicko. Eric something."

Chris throws her a millisecond glance. Mae swallows hard.

232

"Eric who?"

"Huh?"

"Eric Algar?"

"Yeah."

"What about Dan Hennigan?"

They talked about it on the drive over—don't press too hard on this. Don't bring up a murder-one conspiracy. Maybe Loto is one of the dumb ones who thinks just because he didn't pull the trigger or have anything to do with the murder, he won't go down for it. Maybe he doesn't know how a criminal conspiracy works.

"I never met him—Kevin figured he was ripping him off. Dan had some other partner he was going to bring in, cut the rest of us out. Kevin figured that's a capital offense, for real."

Chris asks, "This partner have a name?" without glancing over to Mae. Mae holds her breath.

Loto shakes his head.

"Kevin just knew Dan was looking to fuck everybody over, he didn't know with who."

Mae exhales. They don't know her name.

Chris asks, "So he got John to kill him?"

Loto looks to the ceiling like maybe it will rip off and the gods will yank him away. They sit in air thick with salt and fear for this long moment.

"I didn't know until it happened, on God. I don't think Katherine did either. It fucked her up bad."

"So this was all Kevin?"

"There's some folks who do dirt to eat, and there's some folks who eat dirt, you see. Like, yeah, I sling shit, okay? I'm just trying to get bigger by the day, on God. I sell juice to get ahead in this world. But not Kevin. He's straight fucking villainous. He's running the whole show. On God, I'm not even on the inside of it."

"We just want the girl," Chris says. "You're on the fringe, we get that. Tell us where the girl is."

"I don't know where she hangs. That's Jesse's gig. She's safe with him. He don't dig girls of any age, you feel me?"

"Where are they staying?"

"Some hotel down off Venice? I don't know."

Chris touches his ear—the sign that Loto has told them everything he knows. Now it's time to buy his soul. He smiles at Loto.

"Here's the deal—we're your fucking lifeline, Loto. You don't want to go down? You find the name of the hotel they're staying at. Don't press hard. I'd rather hear you don't know than you fucked it up from pressing too hard. You get it? You find out where the girl is, and we take her away—and you never see us again. We got a deal?"

The shift in tone throws Loto. Mae remembers what Chris told her last night: *You want a man's soul, you got to be both God and devil for them.*

"I don't want no more of this. I want to catch me a bus and be done with it all."

"You don't get to run yet, Loto. Not with the girl still out there."

"Please, just let me go."

Loto scrunches his whole face to keep his eyes shut. Tears squeeze out anyway.

"I don't even know how I got here. Some coin flip some-place goes another way and I'm a different man. A better one. On God, I know it."

"One way out. Take it."

Loto opens his eyes.

"All right, then."

Mae hands him the burner phone. He gets out of the car—cool air floods in. They watch him climb in his car. He swerves out of the parking lot. Mae puts her hand on Chris's arm—he's burning up. His eyes are glowing, his eyes are sick.

"Chris?"

Chris gets out of the car. He walks five paces. He pukes at the side of the parking lot. The parrots go batshit. They rise from the trees, this green and red cloud. Their chatter fills Mae's ears. Chris looks up and winks at her. He wipes his mouth and laughs.

Chapter Thirty-nine

CHRIS

Venice

Venice Boulevard is wide here, an endless row of strip malls, Mexican restaurants, Cuban restaurants, Thai restaurants. So many little hotels with beachy names, people rent them not knowing they're still twenty minutes from the ocean. It's Saturday—better make that forty minutes.

They cruise parking lots. They look for Jesse's Jeep.

Chris thinks back to the tattoo parlor with the Dead Game Boys. How he'd joined in with their howling.

He'd felt that same animal inside him with Loto yesterday. How good it felt to hurt the man.

Mae rides shotgun with the windows open. She shifts in the seat. She crosses and uncrosses her legs. He tries not to look.

They cruise through the dusk, all these sleazy hotels.

All these UNSAID thoughts. Glances, smiles. The animal fact of her sitting in the shotgun seat.

All these sleazy hotels.

This thing in him growing. This thing he'd thought was out of him. It had never really left.

He can see it in her too.

It's the joy of breaking free.

But we aren't free yet.

Chapter Forty

MAE

Koreatown

"We need a contingency plan."

They're at one of Chris's favorite places—a noodle joint on Western in a crowded Koreatown strip mall next to a Korean-French bakery and a karaoke bar. A grandma-aged woman runs the place. All these little side dishes, pickled vegetables and sweet little dried fish—Mae's totally lost. She follows his cues. She eats spicy pork, mouthfuls of rice, pickled radish, glass noodles with bits of meat. Soju burns like faraway fires. Vapor rises in her eyes—everything misty.

"Contingency plan?" Chris asks.

"If Loto screws us."

"He won't."

"'Cause who would dare to double-cross the fearsome Mr. Tamburro?"

"Pretty much," he says, and smiles to cover that he isn't joking.

"Humor me. What if he can't help us find her?"

"We could call somebody. I got contacts in the department . . ."

"Chris. You know as well as I do, they've got their own reasons, their own Beasts. If we give her to anyone before

237

we get the story out, then we won't be able to control it. And maybe they run with it. They don't care about women until they're dead—"

"Come on—"

"No. I know what I'm talking about. Death cleans women in the eyes of men."

"There's good cops out there."

"Are there?" she asks. She watches bad movies play behind his eyes. He doesn't answer.

"Maybe you know a cop who would do the right thing. But do you know his boss? Do you know his boss's boss? Chris, I know how these things die. I've been killing them for years."

"So we don't go to the cops."

"The lie we tell ourselves is that anything other than power is power. Good intentions aren't power. Pretty words aren't power. Lies aren't power either—it's how loud you can broadcast them."

"What about the truth? Is the truth power?"

"Dan taught me a long time ago. 'It's not that the truth isn't important. It just doesn't matter.' "

"I don't know why we're talking about Plan B. Plan A is what has me worried. Mae, we're talking about kidnapping a girl, aren't we?"

She stiffens up, looks around—too noisy in the restaurant for anyone to hear. Mostly couples on dates, a group of bored girls on their phones, K-pop ringtones cutting through the din.

"Don't call it a kidnapping," she says.

"It's better," Chris says, "to call something what it is."

*What about things without names? Like this thing
between us?*

"We're not kidnapping her. We're rescuing her."

"You say it like we're doing it for her."

"¿Por qué no los dos?" she asks. "I mean it, why not both? She needs saving, I need out—and I think you do too. And for once we can do it by telling the truth, with actual facts—and we can use it as a weapon, and, hey, maybe we can get rich too. I'm not a hero, I don't want to be. That doesn't make it not the right thing to do."

"I want to do it. That's what scares me, Mae. I want to do it." His eyes so alive.

"So let's do it."

"So say that Loto gives us where Nevaeh is. We find them. Then what? Knock on the door and say, 'Hey, can we borrow the walking blackmail?' "

"You tell me how to do it," she says.

He drains his soju. She picks up the bottle and fills his glass again.

"How would we take her?"

"Like a cop would. We do it in the car," he says. "I get some flashing lights, we rent something that screams under-cover cop—we'll swap out the license plate, just to be safe. I'll badge him, I'll pull the girl out, just say we want to ask her some questions. We leave him sitting at the side of the road."

"That's crazy."

"You got a version that isn't?" And he smiles at her again and Mae realizes that she is going to sleep with Chris tonight and maybe the most dangerous part of all of this is that they might make themselves stupid, drunk on each other.

"Maybe we can find a way to talk to her. Make her a better offer. Ask her to come with us."

"What does that even mean?"

"I think Dan's plan was to have her stay at my place," Mae says. "In the guest room."

"It would be better if we could find another place. If somebody gets onto us, we don't want to make it that easy for them."

"Sarah's place—my friend Sarah, remember? She's in Romania for a month. I've got a key. We could hide out at her place."

"How do we get the girl to not break the window, scream for help?"

"We have to get her on our side—we take her, and then we win her over with money. If she wants to go, we let her go. We're not keeping a girl prisoner, Chris. That's why it's not kidnapping."

"So if she wants, we just let her go?"

"Yes. We offer her a better life. We're going to get her rich. If she doesn't want it, we ask her what she does want, and we get it for her."

"I just want to be honest about what we're doing," he says. "We're going to take a pregnant kid and sell her story, take down a bad person, and make all three of us rich at the same time."

"That's what we're going to do."

"So I can handle how we take her—you handle the rest of it."

Mae shows him the list on her phone—journalists who will take the story. It's a two-step process—first you find a reporter to write up the story, a real reporter, somebody with clout. Then you sell the story to someone else who pays cash—you set up book deals and exclusives and movie rights—you cash out fast—you split the money, sell the rights—she ballparks seven figures, enough to split three ways, no problem.

They'll use a spit-stick paternity test. Mae's dealt with them before. The firm has clients with standard-issue one-night-stand nondisclosure forms. Clients who put padlocks on the trash cans they throw their condoms into.

Chris asks, "How do we get his DNA?"

"Like the paternity lawyers do—follow him around. Everybody eats, everybody drinks. It's only a matter of time."

His phone buzzes. He checks it. He stands.

"Call from the boss man."

She says, "He won't be the boss man for long."

Chapter Forty-one

CHRIS

Koreatown / Laurel Canyon

Valet attendant eyes him, ready to dash. A couple of doumi girls—pancake makeup, clear plastic heels—hustle from a van into the karaoke bar. The driver yells at them; they cut him off with a door slam. He watches them paste on their party faces as they walk into the club. Across the street a fried chicken joint like a cubist castle, boxes rising three stories, the Colonel's head ten feet tall, something religious about it.

He clicks on the phone with a "Hey."

"Talk to me, baby."

"You called me."

"Come in tomorrow. We're going to find work for you. This DePaulo thing is dead. I don't want you to fall idle."

"Don't worry about me."

"Worry's for the weak, champ. Just wanted to check in with you. Everything okay? Your usual taciturn manner is drifting into stoniness."

The soju mist in Chris's head evaporates. Acker doesn't make pleasure calls. He doesn't call to check in on one of his fists.

"I'm out to dinner is all."

"You on a date?"

"Something like that."

He scans the cramped parking lot. He feels exposed—why would anyone be watching?

Acker says, "Glad to hear you're back in the game. Call me tomorrow. I'll find you some work."

"Will do."

"Now, get back in there and seal the deal. Remember that confidence kills."

They finish the meal. They get Chris's SUV from the valet. His burner phone in the center console—one missed call.

The only other person with the number: Loto.

"Call him back," Mae says. Her eyes glitter—she bites her lower lip. He almost grabs her then, kisses her—later on he'll wonder how different their lives would be if he'd done it.

Instead he calls the number. He looks up, sees a bunch of twenty-somethings spilling laughing out of the karaoke bar.

The phone clicks on—no hello, just a dull buzz of the line coming on. He can hear breathing on the other end of the line.

Mae mouths, "What is it?"

"Hey," he says—he roughs up his voice, he doesn't know why. The other end doesn't say anything.

"Hey, you there?" he asks again.

A long nothing. The breath on the other end goes in-out, in-out—breathing fast, like catching their breath.

A voice, far away from the phone, says, "There's nobody—"

The phone call ends.

243

"Was he there?"

"They didn't say anything. And then somebody, not the person holding the phone, started to talk and the phone went dead."

"Weird."

"You think Loto maybe couldn't handle it? Maybe he told them."

He puts the car in drive and heads north on Western.

"Chris?"

He checks his rearview—he doesn't see anyone pulling from a metered spot to follow. He knows it doesn't mean shit. He knows Western is too crowded to spot a tail. He turns right on the next street. He doesn't take it fast. He's trying to spot a tail, not lose it.

"Why would we be followed?" she asks. She's catching his fear.

"Because maybe we're fucked," he says.

Nobody follows. He stays straight.

You're being paranoid.

Seems like the smart thing to be.

"Why would we be fucked?"

"I don't know," he says. "That weird call from Acker—why not just call me tomorrow and tell me to come in?"

"Maybe he was near someone, wasn't sure it was safe to talk."

"Maybe. Let's just do a drive-by," he says. "Just a spot surveillance. We can try Loto's burner again—maybe get him to come out."

"This is too real," she says. "Holy shit, this is too real."

But she smiles as she says it.

244

Something is very wrong.

The porch light of the clout house is unlit. The house sits in total darkness. Somehow even the night is darker than normal. It takes Chris a second to understand.

The streetlight is out.

He squints up at it—maybe a spiderweb of cracks. Like maybe it's been broken.

Drive away.

He pushes the thought down.

"Want to call him?" he asks.

She hits redial on the burner again. It rings for a long time. He can hear the automated voicemail start talking. She clicks off. They trade looks.

Are we going to do this?

I think we have to.

He takes a deep breath.

They walk up slow—he squints in the dark. The metal cage in front of the door hangs open. He goes up the steps— he thinks about the man who wept blood. Just days ago. How loud and bright this place had been then, even at midnight. How the wrecked eye felt like an omen.

"There's blood," she says.

"Maybe from the guy I told you about last week," he says—his whispered voice so loud in his ears. The rush and roar inside him. "He was bleeding, sitting right here."

She shakes her head like *nuh-uh.* She points down.

The spot of blood is black with glints of moonlight. It is still liquid. It is still fresh.

She heads to the door.

245

The porch light is broken—broken glass on the porch.

"Chris . . ."

The front door hangs open a crack. The inside of the house is void-dark.

"We shouldn't be here," he whispers. "We got to get out of here right now."

"I have to see," she says. "I have to see."

"Mae—"

She reaches for the doorknob.

"Hold up," he says. He motions like *use your sleeve*. She tugs her sleeve down over her hand. She swings the door open. Everything inside is black. She turns back to him— those big eyes so full of crackling energy. She walks into the house. The dark swallows her whole. He hears her say *oh my God*.

Chapter Forty-two

MAE

Laurel Canyon

The room is full of dead people.

She blinks the darkness from her eyes—those weird dark lights float in front of her face. She knows the smell of blood well enough to know that it is everywhere. The smell lets her know drops still hang in the air. She's breathing their death. Light creeps in from behind her, illuminates the dead bodies on the couch.

There's another body on the floor next to the knocked-askew coffee table.

There's another body slumped across the kitchen-nook table.

The world darkens—she swallows a scream—it's just Chris shutting the door behind them.

Moonlight comes through the blinds in slashes.

She feels herself sliding down a cliff wall. She takes deep breaths. She can feel Chris behind her. She takes her phone from her purse. She fumbles on the light.

She lights up the two bodies on the couch. Katherine and Janice DeWaal—purple, black, and yellow. Gore paints the wall behind them. Blood in spatter, blood in splashes. Things darker than blood. She can see dents in their heads. Cracks in their heads. Their clothes soaked black. Their hands tied in front of them with plastic cuffs. They're shivering—

Oh God—

—no, they aren't. Mae's hand is shaking. The shuddering light makes the corpses look like they wiggle.

She moves the shaky beam of light to the floor.

Loto lies curled, fetal. His face is dark with burst blood vessels. His tongue droops grossly from his mouth; his eyes bulge out of their sockets. The ties on his wrists are dug into the skin, like he tried with all his muscle to snap them. A deep purple mark around his neck.

She moves the light to Tony, his height crumpled to nothing, facedown at the kitchen table. His brain blooms from his shattered skull. His blood pools around the spilled bowl of oranges and grapefruit.

"We need to leave right now," Chris says behind her.

"Nevaeh," she says. The tone of her own voice scares her. It lets her know how close to the edge she is.

"What about her?"

"What if she is here?"

"We didn't see the Jeep."

She hears the lock *click* as he throws the dead bolt.

"If someone comes to the door, follow me. I know another way out." *How is his voice so calm?* "Get ready. I'm going to turn on the light."

The lights jab her eyes. She squints against the pain. She opens her eyes. The full light makes the tableau obscene. The simple fact of all this death. Blood pools in the folds of the faux-leather couch—fresh and wet. With the light on, she can see how dark Loto's face is. She can see how Tony's blood drips onto the floor. The way the puddle of it quivers with each fat drop.

She shuts her eyes against it all. She forces down the solid scream that wants to launch from her stomach.

"All of the roommates," Chris says. "All of them but Kevin."

Loto's voice rings out in her head: *He's straight fucking villainous, on God.*

He set up Dan's murder.

He set up Montez—murder by cop.

There's another seat at the table, a spilled chair.

A drop of blood halfway to the kitchen.

And a second one.

And a third.

They don't need words. Mae doesn't trust herself to talk. The spots lead one past the next—red stretched ovals pointing the way. Blood drops dot their way up the stairs. She uses her sleeve to trigger the hallway light. Blood spots lead down the hall. Some of them are smeared into the carpet. She glances back—Chris nods. The story is plain.

Someone ran bleeding.

Someone followed.

Too many questions to ask. Her brain shuts them off—only deal with the now, only deal with the facts.

Chris motions like *let me lead*. She steps aside. She follows him into what feels like the master bedroom. Chris flips on the light. She follows him in.

Kevin's body slumps facedown on the bedroom floor. His skull is cracked open. He lies on a pile of spilled socks and underwear. The drawer above him hangs open—he died digging through his sock drawer with plastic-cuffed hands.

Chris says something like *Jesus Christ*. He says something like *fuck me*. He looks like a man who just survived a bombing, still lost in the smoke.

Chapter Forty-three

CHRIS

Sixth Street

Chris can't stop seeing the movie in his head as they drive back to her place.

This brutal massacre.

That open drawer.

Kevin making a mad break for it—bleeding, his friends dead or dying, his hands bound, going for the one thing that could save them. The gun hidden in his sock drawer. Chris couldn't help but think about those crazy last seconds—the insanity Kevin must have felt, feeling for the gun that wasn't there as his killers came up behind him to finish him off.

Chris takes a sharp left like he can leave the thought behind him. It stays with him.

The moon hangs huge overhead, color of bone. Palm trees like flensed hands reach for the sky.

Back at her place they strip down in her living room. Her nakedness just a fact to him now. Mandy sniffs their discarded clothes, curious about the smell of death they've brought with them.

Mae is blank-faced—like she left some part of her back at the massacre. Like maybe there's some part of her that won't ever get to come home.

They throw everything in a trash bag. They take turns showering. Chris lets Mae go first. He stands stupid and naked in her living room, his dick and balls shriveled. The blood in his body has retreated to his core.

He can't stop seeing the movie in his head. Snapshots of gore and dead bodies. He lets the cop images play out. The scene flashes like Polaroids—his mind tints the photos, saturates them with lurid color. He lets the movies play. He puts it together, the way it probably went down. The door wasn't breached. Whoever it was got in on a pretext. Maybe that means the people in the house knew them. Or maybe they posed as a potential customer looking to score. Chris had watched them operate for days. They were sloppy.

Chris figured at least four killers. Once they get in, they take over the house. They sit Kevin and Tony at the table, Katherine and Janice on the couch. They grab Loto—he's the biggest, the scariest. They put something on his neck— Chris flashes to the thick purple band of flesh around Loto's throat—they strangled him in front of the others.

He doesn't let himself speculate on the whys yet. He builds up to the massacre. Loto hadn't been beaten like the others. Maybe they killed him to show they weren't fucking around. Maybe they fucked up torturing Loto, pushing for answers, accidentally pushing too far, pushing until Loto was dead. Maybe the killers make the call right there— they're in for murder one, no reason to leave anyone alive. Or maybe a massacre was the plan from jump. They go to work on Tony and the women with blunt weapons. They don't use guns—the hills amplify sound. They use clubs, pipes, batons, something heavy and cruel. They work quick.

They hit Kevin—he runs bleeding up the stairs. Someone follows. Someone stays downstairs to finish off the rest. Kevin makes it up the stairs. He thinks he's got a chance. He's got enough of a lead on whoever comes after him to get the sock drawer open. Chris figures Kevin has time to wonder who fucked him before someone gets behind him and splits his skull.

Maybe he wouldn't have stopped the massacre even if he'd gotten his gun. But maybe he would have. They were kidnappers, blackmailers—but nobody deserves to die like they did. And maybe Chris helped it happen.

Mae comes out wrapped in a towel, her hair wet and limp. Her skin red like she couldn't stop scrubbing herself.

Chris showers fast. All he has left to wear is old sleepover clothes from when they were together—sweats and a T-shirt. They sit on the couch. They drink vodka from wineglasses. He breaks it down for her, everything he's pieced together.

"Do you think they found Nevaeh?" she asks.

"Maybe it was someone after the drugs. Maybe even somebody at the party, who had the same thought I had—that they were sloppy, that they were begging to get burned. Maybe that's all it was. There's a home invasion crew that has been working the hills—the one who maybe killed that rapper in that Real Housewife's rental house a few months back."

"You really believe that? That it has nothing to do with the girl?"

"Mae, I don't know."

"I think they were looking for Nevaeh. And maybe they found her."

"Maybe. Maybe not."

"What do we do?"

"Do? We fucking hide. We lay low. This is way too big, Mae."

"What about Nevaeh? If she's alive she's in danger."

"We don't know if it has anything to do with her," he says. "We don't know anything."

"We think she's at a hotel somewhere near Venice."

"I'll keep looking, okay?"

"Okay," she says. It eats at him, the way she says it.

"Give me your burner," he says. She does it. She's in another place—some dark and bloody universe. He cracks the phone in half with his hands.

"We should go no-contact for a little while," he says. "Let's meet someplace in two days, regroup."

Her eyes go wide as the real world comes back to her.

"I have to be at work in the morning," she says. "Shit. I can't . . ."

"Go," he says. "We have to act like nothing is going on. Mae, five people are dead over this. Seven including Dan and John Montez. We can't go any deeper."

"What about Nevaeh? What if whoever did this has her?"

"Then," he says, "it's already too late."

Chapter Forty-four

MAE

Brentwood

Blood in spatter.

"We're looking to reimagine *Point Break*," Marcus Brottman says on the phone. "We're looking to diversify the story, bring diverse voices into the writers' room."

Blood in splashes.

"Updating the story for modern audiences with prestige values means confronting prejudices—including my own."

Blood in arcing sprays.

Mae listens to the conference call on her earbuds. Her brain projects a snuff-film loop onto her office wall. Katherine dead, purple hillocks misshaping her face, gore dying her hair.

Nevaeh is out there somewhere. Maybe in a hotel somewhere. Maybe in a ditch.

Death footage in her head ever since they left the clout house. She'd walked Mandy late, after Chris had left. As Mandy panted in the dark, her tongue lolled like Loto's had.

"Can you talk about the character of Warchild?" Marla Orozco, the reporter on the other end of the call, asks.

"Warchild is our opportunity to subvert audience expectations . . ."

Marcus is a showrunner launching a prestige drama. Marla is an unfriendly from a big glossy. Mae is watch-dogging the call, making sure Marla behaves herself. Marla's been warned of the no-fly zones:

—No questions about plagiarism in his last big hit.
—No questions about a Black writer's Twitter thread accusing Marcus of stealing Black stories and stealing credit.
—No questions about a quashed lawsuit from a writers' room assistant.

The conversation is white noise. She struggles to pull herself from the snuff-movie loop. She refreshes the *LA Times* home page. She checks her Twitter list of LA crime reporters. She checks the front page of Truth or Dare.

"We're going to cut through the fog with an aspirational, high-end prestige drama that tells compelling stories about flawed and heroic people while staying true to the source material."

"And how was working with Sandra Bullock?"

Maybe Nevaeh's still out there. Maybe she's still safe. Maybe this doesn't have anything to do with her. Chris said maybe it was about drugs or some other kind of dirt. But it didn't even look like he believed it when he said it.

Mae refreshes Twitter. Truth or Dare tweets a link:

FIVE DEAD IN CLOUT HOUSE HAMMER PARTY

She clicks on the story. It's three sentences long:

LAPD sources report five bodies have been discovered in a house in the Hollywood hills. All five appear to have been beaten to death. No motive known at this time.

The story is tagged DEVELOPING.

Somebody in the comments references Manson. Somebody in the comments references the eighties Wonderland killings, the ones that porn star set up. Someone connected it to the rapper who got shot last month in the Airbnb mansion. The home invasion crew working the hills.

Her heart is a grasping fist in her chest.

Nevaeh is somewhere out there. Or Nevaeh is nothing at all. And maybe there'd been some way to save her, save her all the way, and they hadn't taken it, and Mae had to admit that the girl had only ever been a thing to her. Just a lever.

"What the hell?" Marcus says. It shocks Mae back to the now.

"It's a pretty direct quote," Marla says. "Basically word-for-word. You don't call that plagiarism?"

"Homage . . ." Marcus trails off. Mae clicks off her mute button.

"This interview is over," she says.

"Hey—" Marla manages before Mae kills her line.

"She's gone," Mae says. "Sorry about that—"

"Where the fuck were you?" Marcus switches back into asshole mode. "Wax your snatch on your own time. You made me look like a dick."

The way his voice twists like a knife grits her teeth. The fear she felt moments ago alchemizes into rage.

"You know what, Marcus, I got a line for you to steal for your next script: *fuck you*."

She clicks off the line. The flushing pleasure of fighting back curdles to shame. She stands up, her legs tingling. She sees a hundred more comments about the murders. They'll have to wait. She walks to Cyrus's office. She has to talk to him before Marcus does. Marcus is a run-to-the-manager type—she won't have long.

Cyrus's wing is so cold she swears she can see her breath. She can tell from the coat Taylor has on that Cyrus isn't there. Taylor wouldn't show weakness if he was.

"He's out," Taylor says. He chomps breath mints. "Some emergency meeting in Calabasas."

Calabasas rings bells for Mae—she's not sure why.

"What client?"

"Didn't say. Must be a big one—he had me cancel on Chris Staw, and he runs a network, so I'd say somebody biblical in size. He sort of ran like he was going to impress his boss. But Cyrus doesn't have a boss."

"Just do me a favor—if Marcus Brottman or his reps call, just put them off until I talk to him."

"First one in usually wins," Taylor says in a not-bad Cyrus. "Will do. Might be a while—I mean, Calabasas in this traffic." He thinks for a second. He dares it: "What did you do?"

"Told Marcus Brottman to fuck off."

"Slay, queen," he says. The word *slay* jabs at her. Somehow it makes a connection in her brain.

She asks, "Isn't BlackGuard in Calabasas?"

"So it is."

"Just connect me when you can," she says. "I'm going home. I think I'm coming down with something."

"Like the fuck-off blues? Go, I got you."

She says thanks with a smile plastered on her face, trying to blink the death from her eyes.

Chapter Forty-five

CHRIS

Venice / El Sereno

He cruises hotels all day. He looks for a red Jeep. He badges front desks, playing cop, showing Nevaeh's picture.

He checks for tails all day. He thinks about the thing he never said out loud to Mae. The reason for the forty-eight-hour separation.

Chris double-parks in front of a sensory-deprivation spa. Chris watches looping cars, paranoid—it helps keep his mind off the massacre. It doesn't make sense as a place to stash the girl. But "near Venice" was all Loto had given them. And Loto wasn't giving them anything else ever again.

Five dead—six if you count Dan, seven with John Montez added in.

A man passes Chris dressed like a monk, his face tight from Botox and fillers. Laughing, walking like gravity is different for him.

The pain shoots up Chris's left arm. The fat invisible thing sits on his chest. He runs through the checklist. He tells himself he is not dying. The heart attack ghosts had left for a while. Now the ghosts are back.

He checks his phone—the massacre is just one Horseman of the Apocalypse on the *LA Times* home page. The Bum

Bomber hit Chinatown last night—no casualties, no closer to a suspect. LAPD shot some kid—the "officer-involved shooting" has Leimert Park in chaos. A bartender in Encino killed bad in her apartment—she is pretty and white so it makes the front page. The city council are fighting over the Crenshaw Opportunity Zone—Chris doesn't know what that means, but the safe bet is someone's getting fucked.

He reads what the papers have so far. The massacre is tagged drug related. References to the home invasion crew working the hills. They don't have much. One obvious error—the paper says all five victims were beaten to death. Chris knows better—he saw the purple band around Loto's throat the thickness of a man's belt. He knew Loto had been strangled. Maybe it was a detail they kept back to ID false confessions.

The phone rings—Acker.

Shit. Here it is.

"Champ—how's it hanging?"

"Long and to the left."

Acker doesn't pro forma laugh at the pro forma joke.

Shit.

He says, "Need you to come in for a debrief."

Shit.

"When?"

"End of day tomorrow. BlackGuard main office, Calabasas. Yokoyama and the polygraph."

"I'll be sure to wax my chest."

"Hey. Champ. Maybe don't be cute on this one."

Pain jolts.

It's not a heart attack.

He chews a baby aspirin. The aspirin sour-bitter in his mouth—he slugs water. It half kills the taste.

Maybe it's a standard post-job debrief. Just strap him into the polygraph, ask a few questions. Chris had written the address of the Wonderland house into his reports to Acker. He'd written Kevin Baldassare's name into the reports as well. The Beast can draw a thick line between Chris and the massacre. Maybe they just want to cover their asses. Maybe they want to make sure Chris didn't do it himself.

Or.

The version that scared him the most—the version that was why he'd told Mae to sit tight for forty-eight hours. The version that has Chris checking his rearview for tails. Checking under his car for tracking devices.

Mae's theory was that Eric wasn't worth fighting for. That they'd shelve the investigation. That he was a perfect blackmail target.

What if the theory was wrong?

What if Eric had been worth more than they thought?

Chris assumed that it was BlackGuard itself who hired him to investigate Dan's death, or maybe Mitnick & Associates. The Beast just making sure there was nothing to be worried about.

But he doesn't know that for sure. It's just an assumption.

What if there was a client?

What if the client wasn't satisfied with Chris's dead-end reports? What if they sent someone else to check Chris's work? Someone who played rougher than Chris did?

He thinks of a way to test the theory.

He drives east—a nightmare in rush hour, plenty of time to let the thoughts run wild. He can't shake Kevin from his head—maybe he could have stopped it. Maybe every death was on Chris's head.

Maybe in more ways than one.

You're not having a heart attack.

It would solve a lot of problems if I was.

The traffic is stop-and-go—it's maddening. He lets the GPS take him off the 10 and onto surface streets. It keeps his mind locked into something besides massacres and responsibility. It takes him through side streets, left-right-left, crossing four lanes of jammed traffic with no lights, joining these little GPS caravans.

It gets him toward Mid-Wilshire—not far from Mae's place. He wants to check in with her. He knows he can't. If this is as bad as he thinks, there's still a chance they don't know she's involved. If that's so, the most important thing is to keep her safe.

He makes it to El Sereno at the golden hour—everything's beautiful. He passes a family setting up an al vapor stand near Lincoln Park, setting up the steam trays, laying out the salsas and onions and cilantro. He curves up into the hills off Valley Boulevard. He rolls past the Montez house.

If someone was working off his reports, they'd have come here first.

Did somebody come by here to check my work?

Did they ask you nicely? Or did they get rough?

He sees John's teenage brother roll past on a bike. Chris stops, taps his horn. The kid turns to look at him. Chris squints against the dusk. He sees the kid's neck. The kid has a purple band the size of a man's belt around his throat.

Chris hits the gas. No need to stop. He has his answer now. He squeezes the steering wheel like it's keeping him from falling. This brand-new movie in his mind. The same men who'd choked Loto to death, now in Marisol's house, choking this kid, asking questions as Marisol screams.

Chris had turned in reports to the Beast failing to find a connection between Dan and John Montez. Someone wasn't happy with that. They'd sent a team to check his work. The team followed him from the Montez house to Wonderland. They'd checked his work with violence and fear. He'd led the killers to the Wonderland house.

Put the massacre on him.

Chapter Forty-six

MAE

Sixth Street

She is falling apart. Raw red spots on her fingers where the skin is peeling away. Her hands slick with bag balm. She puts on a sheet mask, cool against her face, sucking out the impurities—she thinks about slapping them all over her body.

She finds Annabelle Green's number in her phone history. She hits redial.

"Hello?" That old-woman late-night wariness.

"Hello, Ms. Green, this is Courtney Brown with Sixth Street Films—" the lies come back as easily as her accent— "and I was just checking in with you about getting hold of Nevaeh."

"You still haven't talked to her?"

"No, ma'am. Have you?"

"Four or five days ago? I told her all about Mr. Tom Cruise and the big movie, thinking she'd be as impressed as me. She sure played it cool, though."

Four or five days ago. Before the massacre.

Breathe in, breathe out.

"You know teenage girls," Mae says.

"Well, I was one, once, if you can believe it."

"Well, maybe I can impress her. Do you have an email address for Nevaeh?"

"Oh, I don't know about that. I have one myself, but I never check it. Only place I know for sure to find that little girl is *The Kingdom of Dreams.*"

It takes a moment for it to click. "That's the video game she likes?"

"She's hooked on it. She's this flamingo princess. She spends hours on it, talking to these electric friends, doesn't know their real names, just their game names."

"Do you know Nevaeh's?"

"She was proud, she got her name, it's Nevaeh05. She told me she loves that place, wishes it was the real world and this one was fake."

The sky is purple in the *Kingdom of Dreams*. Unicorns fly in flocks. Mae has made herself a raccoon in a motorcycle jacket—and now she walks through fields of waving red grass. Her laptop speakers hum with hypnotic synthesizers. She spends the first thirty minutes after making her raccoon avatar just walking around the kingdom, bumping into users, watching them.

Mae drinks white wine from a jelly jar. Her eyes burn. Her raccoon self climbs a mountain.

Another player, a billy goat head inside a hazmat suit, is pushing diamond-like rocks around a field, building something. Mae gets close, sees a username—WAINGRO_RISING—and keeps moving.

"Are you a girl?" The voice through her speakers is that of a teenage boy. "Show me your tits."

Mae googles how to find another player.

Find a mailbox, the internet tells her. The kingdom auto-generates constantly. There is no map. She walks through this imaginary place until the real one disappears.

She sees a mailbox shimmering like a mirage. She walks up to it. It prompts her to press a button. She presses it. She enters in the name that Nevaeh's grandma gave her. She hits the record button. She realizes she doesn't know what she wants to say.

"Nevaeh . . . look, I am a friend, even though you don't know me. I knew Katherine. I know you're probably very scared right now. I want to help you. I want it more than anything."

Mae listens to herself talk. She wonders if she's telling the truth.

She checks her phone—it's 6 a.m. in Bucharest. She calls Sarah—she hopes she has an early call, is being driven to set. She wants to hear about bullshit. She wants to hear about writers too precious to cut a scene, directors not getting coverage because of *aesthetics*. She wants to hear the horrors of Eastern European craft services. She wants to know if Romanian men are circumcised.

She wants to go back to pretending everything is fine.

She gets Sarah's voicemail. She leaves a bland message. She wonders if Sarah will hear the panic underneath.

She walks down the hall to the kitchen—it's a wreck. Bowls caked with yogurt and soup stacked in the sink. The garbage cresting the lip of the can. This smell of rot. She paws through her cabinet, finds an indica cookie. She pours herself a tumbler of pinot grigio—all the wineglasses are lined up used at the edge of the sink.

She has this thought: There is a war being waged inside her and she is losing it.

She has this image of Katherine and Janice dead on the couch—only this time Nevaeh is with them.

She takes the edible—careful with it, it's a multidose cookie; she only needs a chunk. She sits down on the couch, searches for news of the killings. The massacre is getting nationwide coverage. The drug-deal-gone-bad narrative has taken hold. She wonders who set the story in motion. And why.

She chews the cookie—stale, sweet, with that heavy weed aftertaste they can never quite kill. She goes to the Truth or Dare home page. Below Kardashian struggles and D-list bikini selfies—MURDER VICTIM'S BODY PLUNDERED FOR PROFIT.

Sources inside the LA County Morgue have stated that Euridyce—the controversial human tissue procurement company—were given access to murder victim Tyler "Loto" Simpson before his autopsy, harvesting skin and organs that may have been of use in determining the exact cause of death. A spokesperson for Eurydice blamed poor communications for the incident.

That name—Eurydice. Joss told her about it. They strip down dead bodies like a car-theft chop shop.

Loto was the only one to die by strangulation. Chris called it torture. It was a clue that whoever killed him had questions. That maybe it wasn't just a robbery.

Euridyce is a client—a part of the Beast. They just clouded up the investigation into the massacre. Killing questions about what happened to Loto—if someone was torturing him, it meant they were looking for something. Or someone.

Don't go crazy, she thinks. *Sometimes shit just happens.*

She swallows cookie chunks. She looks down.

Shit.

Most of the cookie is gone. She's a lightweight—she's never eaten more than a quarter of a cookie at once before. And now she's overdosed on THC and filled her head with murder.

The panic spreads, *fuck fuck fuck*—just a precursor of what's to come. She draws a bath. The THC puts a thumb on the center of her brain and presses down. It floods her with shame and terror. She strips down for the bath—every stretch mark and rogue hair pops like one of her mother's tongue clucks. She pinches the fat of her belly, wishes she could rip it off like a bandage. The lizard at the base of her brain is screaming—all these caveman fears, these wolves and woolly mammoths and strange men with clubs and spears—and that same brain tries to understand the world. This world we live in, full of invisible monsters, and you can't see them because they're not alive, and she's been a part of them for too long and maybe she's grown into them like an organ, like the organs Euridyce steals from cooling corpses and puts into rich people. The water goes cold around her as she sits there naked in the tub reliving every shame of her life, every time she was cruel at John J. Pershing Junior High, Mary Beth's tears, Kenny the Mormon who nobody liked, all these cruelties that led her here to her trying to scrub herself clean. And this is why she has to be so careful with weed—it takes all the lies away, shows her the world how it really is, and worse, how she really is, the truth about what she is and what she does.

She thinks on how power is like light, how light acts like a particle and a wave at the same time, and power is like that, there is power in a person and the system at the same time, so that if you tear down the person the system remains, and if you tear down the system the person remains. And she realizes that the Beast will regrow from a single cell. Like a tumor made of people.

She is really fucking high.

She opens the drain, sits there as the water drops around her, the groaning gulps of the tub, the cold air chilling her as she's exposed to it inch by inch.

She throws on comfy clothes, moves back into the living room, opens up her laptop. Everything is too much. The colors press against her eyeballs. She opens up *The Kingdom of Dreams*.

She checks her friends list. Nevaeh's not online.

Her raccoon avatar begins to walk. These washes of drones, the colors so pretty—this artificial world. She sits close to it.

Mandy snuggles up against Mae's leg. Mae feels herself falling into the world of the game. The big bright colors more real than the world around her screen. Her little raccoon in her motorcycle jacket. These winged horses in a purple sky. All these avatars walking through these rainbow fields. Chatter of friends laughing, a pig girl and elephant boy tilling an electric flower garden. It's fake and that's why it's beautiful.

When she looks up from the game it is two in the morning.

She sees *The Kingdom of Dreams* in her sleep. The purple clouds fill her dreams—they cover up dead bodies.

Chapter Forty-seven

MAE

Brentwood

Everyone's cars are in the parking lot. Mae woke late, weed residue in her head, so foggy she sat down in the shower and let the water rain down on her. Purple clouds still float behind her eyes—it beats a massacre montage.

She walks past Helen's office—empty. Joss's office, empty. Nate the intern walks by—"I'm doing a coffee run, everyone's in the conference room—you want?"

"Cold brew oat milk, please. What's going on?"

"Big fish just landed in the boat."

The vibe is electric as she enters the conference room. Like a hilltop right before a lightning strike.

"How long 'til it leaks?" Joss asks as Mae walks in.

"At any moment," Helen answers. "Assume it's happening now."

Mae slides next to Megan Kang, busy on a laptop.

"What's up?" Mae asks.

"The LAPD arrested a suspect last night for the homeless camp bombings," Cyrus says from the head of the table. "The suspect is our new client."

"Some guy bombing homeless camps can afford us?"

"The suspect is named Brad O'Dwyer. As in son of."

"Councilman O'Dwyer?"

"It's a radioactive story."

UNSAID: *That means it will glow.*

"This kid is a real piece of work," Joss says. "We've got Megan here wiping his Twitter account right now."

Megan smiles with her mouth, not her eyes.

"Pretty bad," she says. "Lots of oven memes. Lots of *you will not replace us.*"

Joss laughs. Megan doesn't.

"Of course we take a stand against racism," Cyrus says. "Racism is a stain on our national character, and we all need to stand up against it. That's why the firm is a proud member of the Public Relations Committee on Racial Justice. However, in this country we cherish freedom of speech, and we cannot allow someone to be convicted in the court of public opinion not on evidence but simply because they hold views many disagree with."

Joss asks, "What about physical evidence?"

Helen says, "We're getting the police report leaked to us right now—we should get it in time to get our story out—I've got Holmes at the *Times* holding—if we put our statement out before the LAPD, we set the narrative."

Hector leans over to whisper to Cyrus. Cyrus laughs—and something drops into place. Councilman O'Dwyer—the swing vote on the Crenshaw Opportunity Zone bond issue. Councilman Rich O'Dwyer is about to be swallowed by the Beast.

Cyrus grins—Mae can almost see the blood on his chops.

The day goes by fast. Mae pitches in wiping Brad's online presence. She finds some old website he built. Deep-fried memes, old fashwave beats, rare Pepes. A manifesto waiting to be published. They call in BlackGuard's tech department to clean his laptop hard drive. Councilman O'Dwyer comes into the office. Mae gets a glimpse—he looks like the villain in an eighties movie, blow-dried hair and big-shouldered suits, too tan. He shakes hands, he smiles. You'd never know his son just got arrested.

"He's angling for mayor," Joss whispers. "His failson just fucked him up."

They do press triage. They work the *LA Times*. They work blogs, they work Truth or Dare—they kill what they can. They plant doubts. They put out bland statements from the councilman's office.

Mae works the police file—leaked to them by someone in the force. He'd been pulled over for speeding. The cop smelled kerosene. The call came over the radio—someone had just lit up an underpass camp in Reynier Village five minutes away. The cop searched his trunk. They found gas cans and instant cold packs—using the cold-pack accelerant was a detail the cops hid from the public.

Brad O'Dwyer shows up after lunch, fresh from jail. The Bum Bomber himself. Frederick Kim, his lawyer, walks him into the conference room with Cyrus and the councilman. Mae watches from the hall with some of the interns. Brad is handsome; he is scared. Her brain keeps wanting to call him a kid—but he's in his midtwenties. He and his dad hug in the conference room. Their eyes screaming all this UNSAID shit. Mae looks over to Megan—her face screaming all this UNSAID shit.

Joss walks up looking flustered.

"Everything okay?"

"That's the fifth pharmacy I've called today. There is no Lexapro to be found in LA County. Everyone's out."

An intern says, "It's having a real moment."

Chapter Forty-eight

CHRIS

Calabasas

Polygraphs don't detect lies. They detect fear.

Xanax burps scald the back of his throat. Ten milligrams—kiddie dosage—just enough to tamp down the heebie-jeebies. Yokoyama fixes the straps on his chest. He smells like one of those rich-people candles. Chris tries to focus on the way his breath hits cool at the back of his nasal cavity. He lets the Xan do what it does.

Chris checks them both out in the mirror—Yokoyama is antsy. Yokoyama gets the finger cuffs fitted on his third try. He skips the sausage joke.

Eisner keeps his body turned away from the mirror—aiming for casual and missing by miles.

There's someone behind the mirror.

Chris's heart kicks up a notch. It's exactly what he can't have happen.

He's spooked because of the five dead bodies. Because somebody was following his footsteps, shadowing his case. Because he led the killers to the clout house. He's spooked because he cannot let them know he knows.

One easy way to beat a polygraph is to stay nervous the whole time—get your heart revved up, maybe step on a thumbtack hidden in your shoe to give you jolts, give your body these big reactions to mess the charts up. That won't work for Chris. They have six years of charts to compare this one to. If he comes in too hot, they'll notice. If he comes off as too drugged, that will show too. They'll see something's wrong—and they'll want to know why.

He's walking a tightrope. But he's not allowed to get nervous about it.

Chris has one advantage—he's telling them a story they already believe. That he's too stupid to know what he stumbled into. That he's just a tool, a fist.

Chris glances at the mirror, casually, like anybody would. He wipes his eyes. He's running on four hours of sleep. He ran scenarios all night long. He practiced questions they might throw at him, curveballs—he ran through them until his heart didn't double-time when he thought about them asking about Mae, asking about the massacre, surprising him with what they know. He prepped for them to mention Nevaeh. He prepped for them saying *you were there the night of the massacre.*

"Okay," Yokoyama says, taking his seat. "Let's go."

Chris's heart stays steady.

"What's your name?" Eisner is stiff.

"Chris Tamburro."

They get through the baseline questions. Eisner switches to a new sheet of paper, typed-out questions—the questions somebody is feeding him. Chris knows what's coming. He thinks about the question before Eisner asks it.

"Did your work with BlackGuard lead you to investigate the circumstances around the death of Dan Hennigan?"

"Yes."

No flutters. No chest pains. His palms stay dry. His breath goes in. His breath goes out.

"Can you describe your investigation?"

"Dan Hennigan was murdered by a man named John Montez in what appeared to be a carjacking gone wrong. John was then killed in an officer-involved shooting by Los Angeles County sheriff's deputies attempting to apprehend him." He slips into cop-speak so easy. "I was asked by BlackGuard to follow up the investigation, use my contacts at the sheriff's department to probe for any connections between Hennigan and Montez, to make sure that the crime was what it looked like, a tragedy between two unconnected men."

He knows what question is coming next. He doesn't even listen to it. He listens to the in and out of his breath. How his belly rises and falls. When Eisner is done talking Chris delivers his line.

"I ran down many leads and found no connection."

Eisner shuffles papers. Yokoyama makes a note. Chris doesn't let himself read anything into it. He focuses on his breath. He thinks about Mae.

"Did you form an opinion about John Montez?"

"Gangbanger, drug dealer. He had a CalGang card. One hundred percent knucklehead."

It's an easy lie. It's a lie the world was built to make people believe.

"Did your investigation lead you to the house at 2235 Wonderland Avenue?"

He does not think about dead bodies spread everywhere.

"Yes." A smart person under questioning will never answer more than is asked. Chris doesn't want to look smart. "Kevin Baldassare, an informant to deputies with the sheriff's department who dropped a dime on John to them. I sat on Kevin for several days—I learned that the pad was a drug house, they were dealing out of the house, which made the connection to John obvious."

"And you know what happened at that address two nights ago?"

Bodies sprawled in shadows. Kevin dead in front of a sock drawer, reaching for a gun that isn't there.

"Of course. Internet calls it the Clout House Hammer Party."

"Do you have any knowledge of the reason behind the massacre?"

This little girl with a great big belly. Blackmail on two legs.

"No."

Breath goes in. Chris feels the coolness at the back of his nose. The breath comes out warm.

"Do you have any theories?"

I think somebody retraced my steps. Checked my work. I think they followed my trail to that house. I think they tried getting rough to get answers. I think they fucked up. I think Loto was an accident. I think the rest of them were cleanup. I think whoever checked my work probably comes from BlackGuard. I think maybe our bosses are behind it all.

"No. I mean, it was a drug house—I saw they had a steady stream of clients. Somebody tried to rob them and it went bad. One plus one is two, last I checked."

Chris's breath goes in. The breath goes out.

"Do you have anyone not connected to the investigation who might know more about the case?"

He sees Mae in his head—his heart rate jumps. Once it starts it's uncontrollable. He can't stop the hard thud of his heart from being transmitted through the pulse monitors. His fear for her made real. He sees Yokoyama see it. He looks up at Chris.

They have you.

Give them an answer they'll believe.

"Yeah," Chris says, going off the script he practiced all night. "Acker—Stephen Acker, the attorney I work for—I submitted my reports to him. He knows everything I know."

Fear of bosses goosing your heart—these two ought to understand that.

Eisner nods. He jots something down. Maybe they buy it. Maybe they don't.

DePaulo's assistant comes in with a note. Eisner reads it, first to himself, then out loud.

"We would like to remind you that all relevant nondisclosure contracts cover speaking to law enforcement officials. You are to direct any and all questions from law enforcement officials to Stephen Acker."

"I was a cop a long time," Chris says, relaxing, knowing it's over. "You don't got to tell me to lawyer up."

Chris and Yokoyama walk toward the front door together—their usual small talk stuck in their throats. They pass a conference room. There's sliced mangoes and charcuterie on the table. All these middle-aged white men, waiting.

This white-haired guy with pit stains—isn't that Mae's boss? Chris sees Leonard DePaulo and Matt Matilla coming around the corner—from the direction of the room behind the mirror. DePaulo blank-faces Chris on his way into the conference room—his place behind the mirror confirmed. Yokoyama keeps booking it down the hall—he has the sense to get out of the way of the gods.

They get outside—hot air hits them in the face. Chris gets woozy—like stepping into a sauna.

"You want a smoke?" Yokoyama asks, looking like he'd already said it once. Chris shakes himself out of his head.

"Sure."

A buzzing noise in the air.

"That was intense," Yokoyama says.

"Man, the firm doesn't want to even be tangentially linked to something like that killing. That's all."

"Felt strange," Yokoyama says. "Felt like there was a whole crowd behind the mirror."

The buzz gets louder. Chris squints into the sky.

The slow rumble like a storm. The parking lot palm trees shed fronds in the whipping air. They cartwheel through the parking lot. This helicopter comes in low from over the hills—this impossibly red teardrop with a roaring blade above it, this gorgeous work of art churning the air. The roar so loud as it comes in above them, vibrating Chris's clothes against his skin. It blots out the sun, strobe-light shadows from the whirling blades like the chopper can bend light itself. Chris looks up at it as it passes over-head and leaves the sun in its wake so the light of it stabs Chris in the eyes.

"He's here," Yokoyama says as Chris blinks the purple stamp of the sun from his vision. "Oh shit. This thing is really big, isn't it?"

"Why? Who's in the chopper?"

Yokoyama makes a face like *you know*.

"The guy. The big guy."

"What do you mean? We just passed DePaulo."

"Not him. That helicopter pad only ever gets used by the big guy. Kyser. The guy who owns everything."

"Leonard DePaulo owns BlackGuard."

"Yeah—and Kyser owns DePaulo."

Chapter Forty-nine

CHRIS

Downtown

Office-drone morning traffic chokes downtown. It makes Chris think about blocked arteries. Phantom pain runs up his left arm. He crashed within minutes of getting home from BlackGuard. He slept fourteen hours. He woke up feeling like a little boy, scared and confused. He woke up thinking about Matt Matilla and Special Operations. He woke up thinking about a red helicopter.

The downtown library is old and used to be grand, before it was dwarfed by the glass skyscrapers that now block it from the morning sunlight. Chris goes to the information desk. He asks where he can find business periodicals and research. He takes an elevator three floors underground. He looks at himself in the mirrored door. His face a puffy mess. His reflection splits in half as the door opens, replaced by a man with thick dreadlocks and a blanket wrapped like Moses. The man doesn't look at Chris as he croaks, "I'm the man who's burning."

Sublevel three is silent bedlam. True crime and religion and occult phenomenon books draw in the crazies. Men with prophets' eyes, looking like they want to convert you to Satanism or wash you in the blood of the lamb. All these very human smells. So many of the computer stations are camped out, people with everything they own spread out around them, sleeping with their heads on the keyboards.

Chris finds an open computer. He does basic research—Google turns up photos, this smiling man with that rich man's short hair, soft and gray—he doesn't look like a dark god. A few business stories—Lawrence Kyser is a VC owner, with ownership stakes in transnational security firm Clarent and construction conglomerate TAU Construction.

Here's an article in *Vanity Fair* from a decade ago: THE TALENTED MR. KYSER.

> *Kyser gained his reputation as a financier to the stars thanks to his close partnership to the Hart family, majority owners of Hart Conglomerates International. Now his own net worth is rumored to be in the billions.*

Here is Kyser with ex-presidents of both parties.

> *Financial mogul Lawrence Kyser gives generously to politicians—and he hedges his bets with sizable contributions on both sides of the fence.*

Here he is on a private jet. Here he is with a construction hat on, the logo of TAU Construction on top.

> *Kyser, a leading voice for the Crenshaw Opportunity Zone Revitalization Complex.*

Here he is with Hollywood types—Chris recognizes Colson Hart, third-generation Hart heir and sometimes movie star—he was in that *Tarzan* reboot that bombed a few years back.

A Hollywood connection. Chris digs deeper. He runs searches for Kyser and Colson. He looks at red-carpet shots. There's a lot of them—Colson's got a lot of bites at the apple for someone who never had a hit. Kyser's face, the same smile replicated in each one, making it feel less real with each shot, so that Chris hardly sees the photos at all, so that he almost misses the one where Kyser stands arm in arm with Carol Goodman and a young actress.

Tween casting agent Carol Goodman and financier Lawrence Kyser hit the Summer Nights *red carpet with one of Goodman's clients in tow.*

Chris grabs the table—like the hurricane isn't just happening inside him.

"Holy shit."

Somebody laughs. Somebody shushes him.

Mae's theory had been that Eric Algar is small-time. Safe for a shakedown.

But what if his friends aren't? How had that actress put it to Mae?

The soda pop parties had another party inside for Algar. And his buddies.

All these invisible lines like spiderwebs: ItGirl, Hart International, TAU Construction, Mitnick & Associates, BlackGuard, Clarent. Chris and Mae called it the Beast.

They knew the Beast had arms and legs and mouths.

They never thought it had a face.

The view from Patrick DePaulo's penthouse—all the people look like motes of dust. Chris looks down and all he can think about is the glass somehow breaking, him somehow falling. His body twitches at the thought of impact.

What else do you think happens when you fuck with the gods?

He left the library knowing as much about Kyser as the internet could teach him. He needs to know something closer to the bone.

This UNSAID reason for seeing Patrick: *Tell me how scared I should be.*

"They could have waited to catch the Bum Bomber until he'd cleaned up my street," Patrick says from his low-slung leather chair, an IV needle in his arm, a nurse from the infusion-therapy company standing next to him. "You hear it was a councilman's kid?"

Patrick looks bad. Some kind of bad eye job clashing with the hungover face. Overexercised, overindulged. Chris has seen the combo a lot. Call it money poisoning.

Chris steps away from the window. Patrick's place is gorgeous, the penthouse—decorated like he just bought the furniture the real estate agent used to stage the place. All clean lines and white. The penthouse is open, his bed unmade in the corner. Everything else spotless—cleaners three times a week. A gift bag from some red-carpet party on the counter in front of Patrick—earbuds, a teak smartphone case. Chris picks up a chocolate bar wrapped in rough paper, a picture of a Cameroonian farmer on the front of it. All these worlds in this world that he would never know.

"You want it?" Patrick asks. "Sustainable single-origin bean-to-bar, whatever the fuck that means. Take as many as you want. They taste like shit."

He turns to the nurse monitoring the IV bag. Saline and B12 and God knows what else.

"Anastasia, we've got to stop fucking around. Next time you got to bring me some real blood. From Christian college students or whatever."

"We're working on it, Mr. DePaulo."

"So what's up?" Patrick asks Chris. This cold edge under his voice—Chris broke a rule coming here without being summoned.

Chris pats his pocket, as in *I've got something for you.*

The nurse doesn't have to be told—she heads across the vast penthouse to the kitchen area, leans against the counter, gets on her phone. Chris takes out a baggie of pills, tosses it. Patrick catches. He clucks his tongue like *all right all right all right.*

"Adderall thirty milligrams . . . Concerta . . . shit, this is all speedy. More Addy . . . well, hello, Percs. That's what I'm talking about."

He shakes two pills into his hand.

"Grab me some milk, would you? Gotta coat the stomach or I'm gonna hoark."

Chris walks over to the fridge—the nurse doesn't look up from her phone; she knows she's invisible now—and opens the fridge. He brings over a plastic jug of oat milk.

Patrick takes it, says, "Jesus, my head. About the last thing I remember about last night is the nondisclosures coming out and all the phones going in a box. That's when the party gets wild."

Patrick taps the IV bag like it might knock loose the cure.

"Thanks, man, good timing with the hookup." He presses the oat milk jug to his forehead, closes his eyes. It's his way of dismissing Chris. Rage flares—the stupid plain injustice of being subservient to this man-child. Chris imagines bouncing him off the picture window. He stuffs the thought down. He tells himself to stay focused.

"I was at BlackGuard yesterday—just some debrief stuff."

"Oh yeah?" Patrick says in a *who-gives-a-shit* monotone. He opens his eyes, starts classifying and separating the pills.

"I saw this helicopter land on the roof. Race-car red. That belong to your dad?"

Patrick drops the pill he's holding. He picks it up out of his lap, dry-swallows it blind. He laughs, too loud.

"Look, man, thanks for the hookup but I'm only halfway to human, so like . . ."

Chris uses his cop voice: "Shut up, Patrick."

Patrick's eyes flash wide. The leash he has kept Chris on is invisible—if Chris says it's not there, it's not there. Chris takes two steps forward. Patrick presses himself back against his chair. Chris gets in Patrick's face, thinking about hurting him. How good it would feel. He knows Patrick can see it in his eyes. They look at each other while all these UNSAID things crash all around them.

Chris steps back and says, "Tell me about the helicopter."

Patrick breaks the gaze. He looks out the window. When he turns back around, it's like the moment never happened. His voice is almost normal.

"Like Testarossa red? That's not Dad's. That's a Sikorsky, man."

Chris smiles back at him, playing along.

"A Sikorsky? That's wild. Whose is it?"

"Kyser." He says it like it's nothing. But he's holding his phone with both hands. The knuckles popping white.

"Kyser? I've never heard of him."

"Because that's how he likes it. And what Kyser wants, he gets."

Chris looks around the apartment like *what about you?*

"Like the man says, there's levels to this shit. Dad's company is worth maybe fifty mil, tops. That chopper you saw, Kyser's private chopper? That's fifteen mil right there. Get it? Like that helicopter pad was pretty much built for Kyser, and maybe that's the second time he ever used it."

"So Kyser owns part of BlackGuard."

Patrick smiles—this UNSAID plea buried deep in his eyes.

"Man, he owns part of everything. For all I know he owns this building. You know the difference between a million and a billion? A million seconds is eleven days. A billion seconds is thirty-two years. Kyser has billions, man."

"You ever meet him?"

Patrick nods.

"I went to his house one time. He lives on this hill out in Malibu—Dad took me out there once. It's crazy—you pass this gate and head up the hill, and Dad's like *take your phone out*—I look and I've got five bars and then we pull in the main driveway and poof, I've got zero. He's got some sort of setup, you can't make a phone call or get online on his property—not without his permission. Right, so we park and get out of the car, and some dude runs out of the house with a nondisclosure—like before you even set foot inside. And you walk in the door and it's this grand entrance, right? And across the room right as you walk in is a giant fucking Picasso, right? The genuine article. Like even you know what a Picasso looks like, right? And get this—it's got this razor slash"—he slashes the air diagonally—"right across the center of it. Totally fucking ruined. Kyser bought it at an auction, and the day it's delivered, he took it out of its crate and he slashed it with a razor, and then hung it in his foyer. Like the craziest shit in the world. And I asked my dad, what the fuck is that? And he whispered—he whispered like some kid scared of the teacher—he whispered *it's a message*."

"What the hell is the message?" His voice a half whisper.

"That's what I asked my dad, right? Like later, you know. On the way home. And my dad said, what Kyser was saying, right, was—*if I'll do this to a twenty-million-dollar painting for no reason, what the fuck will I do to you if you give me a reason?*"

Chris wanted to know how scared to be.

Now he knows.

Chris walks back to where he left the car. All around him, downtown—this mass of people, gold shops, fast food next to high-end tacos next to dollar-slice pizza. All these people living their lives like the world isn't on fire.

On Chris's way out the door, he and Patrick had done their usual fist bump, their usual smiles. Chris figures it's the last time he'll ever see Patrick. If somehow Chris gets to the other side of all this, Patrick will mention real casually to his dad that they should get him a new fist. He'll have some bullshit reason. He'll never talk about that moment when it all got laid bare.

He checks his phone—time to head back to Mae's house.

He takes Second Street out of downtown, a right onto Glendale into Echo Park. He passes the old puppet theater. He gets this crazy idea. He pulls over in Echo Park just before the 101 overpass, the parking lot of some rich-people bakery. He gets out of his car. He feels around in the wheel wells. He searches carefully. His fingers trail across this lump that shouldn't be there.

He pulls the tracker out from under the bumper.

You always think they're going to look like something. But they don't look like anything at all.

Panic hits hard—*they know everything.*

Mae with a belt around her neck, her eyes filling with blood.

He takes a big breath.

Chris had searched the car right after the massacre. The tracker wasn't on his car then. They must have placed it when he was at BlackGuard. They've only been tracking him since yesterday evening. He left his car parked at the library when he went to see Patrick. They haven't seen anything strange at all. They don't know about Mae.

Pain strobing through his left arm. The world black around the edges. He slumps against the tire. He closes his eyes. His heart double-sized in his chest.

"Are you all right?" A woman carrying a big round loaf covered in seeds looks down at Chris.

He nods. He gets up too fast. He goes light-headed again.

"Just dehydrated," he says.

She nods. He thinks it's not so much that she believes him, more that she wants to believe him, wants to get on with her day. She climbs into her Lexus. He lets himself catch his breath. He comes back to himself.

He puts the tracker back under his bumper. He can't let them know he found it. They'll find other ways of asking questions.

He drives with his hands at ten and two. He drives circular routes. He checks the air for helicopters. He checks the air for drones. Nothing seems crazy anymore.

In his head, he sees Kyser and Carol Goodman. He sees a slashed Picasso. He sees Matilla in all black standing over the Wonderland corpses.

He parks on Third Street, about a mile from Mae's place. A block with lots of restaurants. Nobody tracking his movements would think it strange that he stopped here.

He leaves his phone in the car. He leaves no trace.

He walks to her place. Trying to make sense of it—why his body wants him to think he's dying. He figures maybe the simplest version is the answer.

His body, UNSAID: *Someday you're going to die.*

His body, UNSAID: *So what are you going to do until then?*

The only answer he has is, *Just try to make it until tomorrow*. He knows it's not good enough. But it's going to have to do for now. He can't let Mae wind up like that slashed Picasso. He's got to convince her to run. Leave behind these dreams of exposing Algar, saving the girl. There's no standing in front of the Beast.

Maybe they can run together. Maybe that's good enough anyway.

He knocks on the door with his speech ready. But he's not ready for her eyes—bright with joy.

"We've got to talk—" he starts.

Mae says, "I've found her."

PART FIVE

The Principle of Explosion

Chapter Fifty

MAE

Sixth Street

She drives home from the firm thinking about Brad O'Dwyer's face—this handsome bag of meat and void. These room-temperature eyes. She zombie-walks Mandy. She zombie-eats half a pizza.

Her mind feels like the ground in New Orleans, how you can't bury bodies there because it is too wet and the bodies float up out of the mud. Dan under the sheet, Montez dying on the livestream, all the dead people on Wonderland Avenue painted by her phone's light.

She logs on to *The Kingdom of Dreams* again, wanting escape. She drinks white wine from a coffee mug, feeling too weird and strange to take the time to wash a glass. Fight-or-flight impulses getting gummed up in her brain, nowhere to run and nowhere to hide.

The game, this beautiful lie, this world with rainbow clouds and flying horses. This other, better world, this neon place of birds and unicorns, other people floating and flying around. Sitting by an electric stream, listening to the splash and plop of virtual water, a place of no blood. She learns how to fish, how her controller vibrates when a fish is on the line, and when you pull the fish up it grins at you and winks before jumping back in the water.

Time passes in arterial sprays. All of a sudden it is 3 a.m. again, the glassy hour when things start to slide around, when shapes start to dance at the corners of your eyes. Mae eats saltines from the sleeve, the blandness comforting, all those memories of sick days from school, faked stomach issues—she'd never made herself vomit to lose weight but she'd gagged herself a few times in junior high in a desperate ploy to claim a stomach virus and stay home.

She almost doesn't hear the chirp, almost lets the words pass by her.

NEVAEH_05 WANTS TO CHAT

She hits accept. It goes to close-up mode—this smiling flamingo in a ball gown made out of crystals.

The flamingo says, "Hey?" in a girl's voice.

Mae says, "Hello," before she realizes she doesn't have her headphones in—there's no mic. She fumbles for the cord, everything in her whirring. She fumbles with the dongle.

"Hey, anybody there?" the flamingo asks again.

Mae gets the headphones plugged in.

"Hello?" The silence that follows yawns . . . did Mae lose her?

"Hey."

"Is this Nevaeh?"

The flamingo drops into a curtsy.

"One and only."

"My name's Mae."

"So you really are a lady, huh?" The flamingo's beak moves in time with the voice. "Mostly it's boys pretending, and then it's all show me your feet baby, tits or get the fuck out, you know?"

"I really am a lady. I've been looking for you for a long time."

Another long silence.

"How do you even know me?"

"I know Katherine. Do . . . you know what happened?"

Little pops and hisses, maybe just noise on the microphone. Or maybe the girl is crying.

"They all got got. All of them."

A blue butterfly flaps between them. It turns a quick loop the loop, leaving tracers in the electric sky.

"Nevaeh, I'm sorry."

"It's so messed up." No question the girl is crying now. And maybe Mae is too. The screen blurs, the saturated light splitting into prisms through her tears. "Do you know I have a baby coming?"

"Yeah, Nevaeh, I know."

The flamingo princess smiles as sobs come through the speakers.

"Everything is so messed up. Like I need new vitamins. You got to feed a baby vitamins, but Jesse says we got to stay inside. He says we're on the run."

"Is he hurting you?"

"What? No, he's not . . . I mean, if you met him you wouldn't ask. He's like wet spaghetti. But he says we're on the run. Like the people who got Katherine are going to try to get me. Is that true?"

"Maybe. I think so."

"Well then, I'm fucked AF."

"I can help you, Nevaeh. I can help you and the baby."

"Everybody says that. They think I'm a dumbass—like I don't know everybody wants something. The thing about Jesse is now he's too freaked-out to get it."

"What is he doing?"

"He's making some plan that I don't get. He's talking to somebody in that other language, I don't know what it is. Albanian?"

"Armenian?"

"If you say so. I think he's trying to get rid of me. Pass me on. Everybody does. I'm just this fucking hot potato from Mom to Grandma to, you know. From ItGirl to Katherine to Jesse to who-the-fuck-ever. I'm never gonna do that to my little rider. She's a down little bitch, I know it. Katherine said they're gonna try to take her, that's why we have to hide. She said because Eric wants to take my girl. Is that true?"

"It's probably close to the truth," Mae says, thinking the truth is probably much worse than that. "I have a plan to help you. One that's legal."

"It's all so fucking crazy. I didn't do anything wrong, I don't know why I have to hide. I didn't do anything wrong, Katherine told me."

"Nevaeh, let me help you. Tell me where you are."

She types her phone number into the chat bar.

"That's how you can reach me. Anytime. I'll come get you."

"I don't know you." The helplessness of her voice.

"I'll keep you safe," Mae says—surprised by how much she means it. Looking at the flamingo this girl wants herself to be makes the girl real to her now. "I will help you, and I'll do it in a way that will get money for you and the baby. Nevaeh, I want you to trust me."

This long pause. The flamingo just smiles at her.

Mae says, "I know what you're feeling. I'm scared too."

And the flamingo princess cries these sobs that resonate inside Mae. Like she is a tuning fork that has just been struck. And she closes her eyes against the obscenity of this perfect world on her laptop screen and when she opens them the flamingo is gone. Nevaeh has logged out.

And something breaks in Mae, or maybe something is made whole. Something comes into her, or maybe something leaves. She doesn't know which it is. But she feels clean and light and she falls asleep on the couch sure of something for the first time in a long time.

We can save her.

She wakes up to Mandy barking. She hears Chris coming up the walk. It all comes crashing back to her. She runs to the door.

We can save her.

We can do this one good thing.

One good thing just once.

She opens the door. She can't wait to tell him.

"We've got to talk—" he starts.

Mae says, "I found her."

Only then does she see his face. The terror in his eyes.

Chapter Fifty-one

CHRIS

Sixth Street

Through the kitchen window, Mandy munches dried bougainvillea leaves from the ground of the duplex's backyard. The world is still just the world to her.

Lucky girl.

Mae sits. She stands up seconds later. She's drinking wine out of a coffee cup. All her dishes are dirty. She's wired on fear and anger.

He told her everything. They checked her car for trackers—nothing. And now they dig deeper. She shows him how to sign on to a VPN to hide their online footprints. She shows him open-source corporate trackers.

Everything is out there. They draw these webs of interconnections. They sketch out a skeleton of the Beast. Holding corporations, international registries.

BlackGuard. Mitnick & Associates. Eurydice. TAU Construction. Hart International. The Revitalization Complex. ItGirl. These webs of corporate ownership. Partnerships and percentages.

This beast with many hands. This beast with many eyes. This beast with many heads.

The one at the center—Kyser.

"The Revitalization Complex—this is huge," Mae says. "They're behind that push for the Opportunity Zone in Crenshaw. Billions of dollars at stake. All tied up by Councilman O'Dwyer. They couldn't find a way to crack him—until his son got arrested for being the homeless camp bomber. Now they think they've got him, if they can save his son."

"They'll save him," Chris says. "One way or another."

"He's pretty well fucked," Mae says.

"They'll save him," Chris says again. "Aren't you the one who told me, nobody goes down for real unless somebody wants them to go down?"

"Chris—say what you really want to say."

He gets up—knee pain is a bitch.

"Mae—we've got to talk about this. About how much farther we're going to go."

"Fuck that," she says. "I'm not leaving her out there. I don't care who is after her."

"This is a guy—he paid twenty million dollars for a painting and then slashed it with a knife and hung it in his entryway—"

"I don't know what I'm supposed to make of that."

"That's the point. You think that's something a human being does?"

"So why would Kyser care about Eric Algar?"

"All I know is, we thought we were going up against some has-been TV producer, and nobody would kick. But they're kicking back hard as I've ever seen. And Kyser and Algar are connected, at least through ItGirl. And if we've stumbled into pissing this Kyser guy off, we've got to leave it alone. Maybe even split. I've got cash stashed, I bet you do too. We could run."

Maybe she doesn't get what he's offering. Maybe she doesn't care. Either way she shakes her head *no*.

"That girl is out there, Chris. She's out there and we're the only ones who can help her. We're going to get her back. We're going to help her tell her story. We're going to tell the truth. The truth about all of it."

"You told me the truth didn't matter."

She looks up at him—her eyes make him stop breathing. This anger and joy all wrapped up together in a frenzy. His brain chucks up this phrase from his childhood churchgoing days.

Righteous fury.

"The truth has to matter," she says. "It has to."

"So you want to go to the police?"

She opens her purse. She pulls out the papers she brought from work.

"This is the whole police file from the O'Dwyer case. Somebody at the LAPD passed this directly to Mitnick. We take her to the police, and she's over. We have to get the story out. Chris, come on, you more than anybody ought to know what they're like. You were one."

His teeth grit together.

"Sorry, Chris. It's not like I'm any better. We have to play this game against who we used to be. It's the only advantage we have."

"You don't get it," Chris says. "You want truth? Here's truth. You and me both, we have always been small-time. We're fringe players. This is at another level. And people are dead. I've seen a lot of gang wars pop off. The thing about killing? It's contagious."

"And you think going to the cops blind will stop that? We go to the cops, the Beast will have it in an hour. Before we're out of the building. And we can't protect her anymore."

"What about the internet?" he asks. "Just dump all of this online and try and throw some sunshine on all of it?"

"Viral for a day, maybe—then forgotten. Chris, I know what it takes to make a story actually matter. That's why we've got to play it smart."

"If we do it your way, we won't be able to keep our names out of this," he says. "We'll be targets. And so will she. You put her in the public eye and they'll destroy her."

"We have to use her. She's the proof—we just have to use her to get this done. We have to use her to save her. And us too. We can take our cut. We can use it to start our own firm."

"Our own firm?"

"You and me. We can work for ourselves instead of the Beast."

"Yeah?" As in *me and you*?

"Yeah." As in *me and you*.

This long warm moment passes. He makes his decision.

"We need more info," he says. "We have to figure out why Kyser cares about this."

"I know a man who might know. Who might even tell me."

"Do you trust him?"

"No. Not at all."

A beat, and then she says, "I'm scared."

"I am too."

"Will you help me save her? Even though we're scared?"

"Yeah. Yeah, of course I will."

She kisses him, hard. Before he can really return it, she breaks off. She's got this smile on her face. He'll do anything to keep it there.

Chapter Fifty-two

MAE

West Hollywood

Outside Parker's windows the sky is dark and gray. It's been so long since it's rained Mae had forgotten it was a possibility here.

"Tea?" Parker asks.

"Sure, thanks."

Parker is even thinner now—flesh tanned into redness starting to hang loose over shrinking muscle. His cheekbones, his eyes, everything like it was placed there by a jeweler.

"I've been busy," she says. "I owe you an apology for not reaching out sooner."

He smiles—this glint in his eyes the only clue to how he really feels. He pours from his electric kettle. His jaw pops. He hands her the cup of tea. Panko's face flashes behind her eyes like a blink. She remembers the way his voice got small as he talked.

The tea is delicious.

Parker says, "My excommunication is almost complete. Frederick Kim has fired me as his client. I'm being put on the ice floe. Cast into the wine-dark sea. Societies have their ways of dealing with the newly useless. In ours you simply become invisible. And yet you're here, paying me a visit. I suppose it's our deep friendship that brought you here."

"I wanted to ask you something."

"In other words, you think there's still a drop of usefulness at the bottom of the barrel. Maybe there is. And in return?"

"Maybe I can help you, pro bono PR—you tell me."

"So I can have the best reputation on the cellblock? No, I have another favor in mind. My legal problems are rather my focus these days."

"I don't know how I can help you with that."

"Don't be so sure. First, tell me what you're after."

"I want to talk about Lawrence Kyser."

He blinks. He blinks again.

"Oh, Mae. I rather think you don't."

"I know who he is."

"You've got it wrong already. At a certain point people stop being a *who* and start being a *why*."

"Come on."

"Do you ever think about the sun, how strange it is? This giant fire hanging in the sky, this burning thing that makes the whole world possible, the most powerful thing there is, and the one thing we know, innately, is never look at it. It sits there in plain sight in the sky and your eyes dance around it without you even thinking about it. Because if you look at it directly, it will burn your eyes out of your skull."

The warning in his voice is loud and clear.

"My eyes, my choice," she says. "I want to look."

His own eyes flicker around the room like he is doing some kind of calculation.

"The firm has taken on the case of Councilman O'Dwyer's dreadful son? You're going to try and salvage his reputation? The Bum Bomber himself?"

"He's a client."

"And I suppose they hope to use this to sway Councilman O'Dwyer's vote on the opportunity zone?"

"Of course they do. Are you trying to say it's a frame-up? That the son was set up to pressure O'Dwyer?"

"You've seen the evidence. You tell me."

"No. Brad Dwyer is a horrible little asshole and they caught him dead to rights."

"Fair enough. Sometimes, on top of every other advantage, they get lucky too. The O'Dwyer vote falling into their lap—if they can help his son. Can they help him?"

"It's looking pretty bad. We can spin the story some. Maybe get some sympathy for the kid, minimize jail time. But he's going down, and he's probably taking his dad's political hopes with him."

Parker looks up over her shoulder, thinking about something.

"Your firm has always been accomplished at securing police records—I take it you have all of the evidence they've gathered against the boy? Officer write-ups, evidence lists?"

"I think we have more than his lawyer at this point."

"I want it. All of it. That's my price."

"Brad O'Dwyer's police files? Why?"

"Is 'why?' a question you want us to ask each other? Should I ask why you're interested in Kyser?"

Something in her head says *don't do it*. She ignores it.

"I can get them for you."

Parker puts out his hand.

"Then I'll be your Virgil."

She thinks his hand will be papery and cold. But it is so warm.

"If you tell me what you know, it might help me know where to start."

"I know he's rich. I know he's got some sort of ownership of the firm, and BlackGuard, and TAU Construction. I know about him and Eric Algar. Him and ItGirl. Him and young girls."

"Oh, Eric. That explains it."

"Excuse me?"

"That look on your face. The truth about Eric tends to do that to people. He truly is vile."

"What's Kyser got to do with him?"

"Eric's tastes have led him to cultivate quite the system for harvesting the young and vulnerable."

"Carol Goodman, ItGirl—the soda pop parties."

"I don't know the details. I just know where it leads. Eric passes children to Kyser. Kyser uses them as glue. To bind people."

"Who?"

"These men whose appetites drive them. Men who have had all of their desires fulfilled and don't understand why they don't feel full. They're always looking for something new. For something that no one else has ever had. Along the way Eric turned his hobby into a second career. He and Carol Goodman became farmers for Kyser."

"And then he uses these girls for blackmail?"

"No. I mean, perhaps sometimes. Blackmail is a stupid,

blunt tool. Secrets are more useful kept as secrets. Secrets bind people together. These girls that Eric provides for Kyser, the boys, the men and women too—he creates places, temporary autonomous zones where there is no law but flesh—and when it's over and the plane has landed, there are bonds that can never be broken. Well, almost never."

"This sounds like one of those right-wing conspiracy theories about pizza places."

"Conspiracy theories . . . they fall apart because they imagine this dark room where everything is spoken aloud. But in my experience, it hardly ever works that way. You just do what you're supposed to do. You don't have to be told. Cover-ups happen in glances and silences. In people acting the way they were born to act. Most people who facilitate things like this hate themselves for doing it—and they think that makes it okay. Like it's not really them who is doing it."

Whatever happens to her face makes Parker chuckle.

"Sounds familiar, doesn't it? We all think that the face we show the world is a mask, and the one we carry deep inside ourselves is the real us. But what if it's the other way around? What if you are what you do, not how you feel about it?"

"What if Eric got exposed? What if there was proof?"

"Then Kyser and the rest of them would find another way to do what they do. You can kill an ant, but if you leave the sugar on the floor, more ants will come. Maybe a different type, maybe a different breed. It's the same with people—you can clean out the monsters, but if you leave the money and sex and power on the table, soon enough more monsters will come. And why shouldn't they?"

"What about Kyser?"

"What about him?"

"Could someone take him down? Like, if you put pressure on Eric, he could say everything—"

"Oh, no. Mae, no." The fear in his voice shocks her. "I don't know what you have or what you're thinking. But I promise you, it's quite impossible. Let this go, Mae. I really do quite like you. I'd like to see you stay around. You already know that under all this soft power there is something hard and cold and sharp. Fighting it will only lead to your destruction. Perhaps it already has, and some slow bullet is already heading toward your skull. You have to forget all of this. Best to find your place where you can eat and live and be grateful for it. Be useful to them. And send me those files."

She sits in her car for a long time. She uses her phone to forward the files to Parker that she promised him. She waits for them to upload and go through—they're huge files and West Hollywood's free Wi-Fi is spotty.

She watches men high up in the air, strapped to a palm tree, trimming fronds that spiral down to earth. She triggers the seat-cooling feature of her car. She watches these men work and sweat.

Find your place where you can eat and live and be grateful for it.

The men turn to prisms, dissolve into rainbows. She waits until the tears are done. She wipes her face clean. She tries to fix her makeup in the rearview mirror. But she can't take looking at her face long enough to get it done.

Chapter Fifty-three

CHRIS

Koreatown / The Black Site

Chris drives. He pictures the GPS tracker tracing a red line east on Third Street, some tired-eyed desk jockey at BlackGuard noting the left on Highland, right on Western as Chris heads back into Koreatown. He tries not to think about Kyser. The animal in his brain is pushed to its bolt point, a thing in him threatening to stampede at the next loud sound.

The sky threatens rain—Chris knows the Los Angeles sky is often a liar.

He thinks about dinner, something unhealthy, something soothing. He thinks about tteokbokki, a cheeseburger from Cassell's—he settles on katsu from the curry place. He parks in the red zone, hazard lights flashing. He laughs thinking about the SUV getting towed, the tracking device sketching a red line to Cypress Park, the BlackGuard desk jockey trying to figure out the connection.

Dinner in hand, he drives to the parking garage on Irolo where he rents a space. An Aztec mural on the side wall of a strip mall, fresh enough that no one has tagged it yet. An old man works a fruit stand, slicing mangoes, sprinkling chili on top.

He parks in his spot. He kills the engine. He sits and looks at his hands until they stop shaking. He tries to shove all the thoughts to the back of his head. He hears the voice of his training officer way back in the day:

Never fuck with the gods. It don't end well.

And he never had. Not until now.

He gets out of the car—the sounds of rush hour pour in. Honking horns, music from open windows.

Lost in the movie in his head, Chris doesn't see the men until they are on him.

They wear black hoodies, black dust masks. They pile out of two different cars.

Somebody yells *don't move.*

He throws his dinner like a bomb—takeout curry splats pathetically. Napkins spiral in the breeze of men running toward him.

BlackGuard, he thinks.

The wet-work crew.

Coming to chop off loose ends.

His feet thud hard against concrete. His brain chucks up random facts about professional body disposal.

He barrels toward the staircase.

His brain chucks up images of all these secret graves. Shallow holes scraped in the high desert. Warehouses with industrial drains. Boats at night cruising out past Catalina, where you won't ever wash ashore.

He takes the staircase in a single jump. Pain shoots up his leg. His bad knee buckles. He goes down hard. His face scrapes against pavement grime. A black-masked guy gets on top of him. Chris throws a punch. It crunches into a throat. He hears a *thhpt,* feels a pinch. *Taser,* he thinks in the millisecond before his nervous system explodes—

Chris wakes up surprised to be alive. He's stuffed inside a trunk. The side of his face stings. This hum overhead—it's raining.

His hands cuffed behind his back, tingling into numbness.

He hears muffled voices, men talking. Voices loud, laughing hard. The sound of a victory lap.

He'd been so worried about tails he hadn't thought about traps. He should have known they'd know where he parks his car. He had been sloppy. He hadn't let himself face how real this is, what level they're playing at.

The car bumps. The air gets stale fast. Chris sweats through his clothes. Pain up his left arm.

The trunk door opens. Chris blinks through raindrops.

Deputy Woodcock stands over him.

"You motherfucker," Woodcock says.

It's not BlackGuard who grabbed him—it's the Dead Game Boys.

Chris doesn't know if that's better or worse.

Men yank Chris from the trunk. He looks around. An abandoned office building, stripped-down cars, ancient graffiti, somewhere in the hills. One road in. The building is windowless, a shell.

They put him on his feet. He sees faces from the kill party. They don't bother with masks. That scares him.

The room smells like dried piss. A single wooden chair in the center of the room—they shove him in it. Dried blood speckles the floor. There is a handful of white pebbles under his feet. It takes Chris a beat to understand they are shards of human teeth.

They've taken him to a black site. A place that doesn't exist.

He takes a deep breath. A shape comes up in front of him. Woodcock puts his face close to Chris's. He holds up a rubberized metal baton, showing Chris the tool he is working with.

"What the fuck did you get us into?"

Chris knows the one truth of interrogation—no matter what anyone says, confession can only ever hurt you.

"I don't know what you mean."

The baton thuds into his leg. Chris bites down the scream. It half works.

"I gave you Baldassare's name and a week later him and his whole crew are dead. The fuck kind of shitstorm you put us in?"

"I put what you told me in a report. That's it. That's all."

"Is my name in the file?"

"Yeah."

The baton comes down again. Chris feels the pop at the center of his knee.

"All the sudden I've got Matt Matilla coming by the precinct, asking me questions like he's the goddamn cop and I'm some nobody."

Matilla—checking Chris's work. The hugeness of what it means kills Chris's pain for a beat. Matilla confirmed as a clout-house killer.

Woodcock says, "You said you were with us. You fucking sold us out."

The baton comes down again. The pain comes back in a deluge. His leg is one open nerve.

"Did you do the Wonderland job?"

"No, I didn't, I wouldn't. I just wrote a report," Chris says. "I wrote a report and gave it to my boss."

"So why the hell is Kevin dead?"

"I don't know—a drug heist—"

Woodcock slams the baton into Chris's gut. He pukes air.

"Don't tell me what's in the papers. Tell me the truth."

"I don't know what happened."

"But you got a theory, right?"

Chris's lizard brain pleads with him—*give him the truth, tell him it was the Beast, it was BlackGuard, it was Matilla and his Special Operations Group.* But he keeps it inside. To let it out is to guarantee his death, and probably Mae's too, at the hands of either the Dead Game Boys or Matilla.

"Drug heist—"

"Put the vest on him."

"Woodcock—" The fear in Archer's voice terrifies Chris.

"Put it on him."

He keeps this picture of Mae in his head. From the first night they ever got together. She's got this drink in her hand, and that smile like it's all a joke and God has told her the punch line. He holds on to the picture like a drowning man.

Rough hands grab him. They thread a bulletproof vest over his head. They yank his arms through it. It sits heavy on his chest.

Woodcock holds up a pistol. It is old and battered, the grip wrapped in electrical tape. A gun Woodcock took off the streets. A drop piece, untraceable. Gusts of fear batter Chris.

"The vest is rated to stop .44 Magnum bullets," Woodcock says. "Some of the time."

Chris spits—fresh blood speckles over the dried blood on the floor.

"Please," he says. "Please don't."

"Did you do the Wonderland job?"

"You know they were dealing—"

Woodcock points the gun at Chris's chest. Chris turns his head like if he can't see the bullet it can't kill him.

Please. He can't even say it in words.

Woodcock takes three steps back. There's nothing on his face at all.

"Tell me what I need to know."

"There's nothing, there's nothing to know, I didn't, it's just a coincidence, I swear. Please don't—"

The GUNSHOT rips up the world. Pain rakes his chest. Pain shoots up his arms. He falls from the chair. He lands face-first among the tooth chips. His chest bucks. His lungs don't work. His fingers fumble across the bullet hole in the vest—the hot slug stuck there sizzles his fingertips.

"It was just a job," he says. His voice high-pitched—the child inside him who never left. They laugh at him. His crotch is warm and wet. He comes up off the pavement with his bound hands aimed for Woodcock's throat. Woodcock puts the gun next to Chris's face, the barrel pointed at the floor. The GUNSHOT blinds him—close enough that black powder flecks in his eyes. The world is just white noise and pain.

He comes back to the world small and crumpled.

Woodcock's mouth moves like *fuck this punk*—all Chris can hear is a high white sound.

They get into a circle around him. They stomp. They use batons. Their eyes are wild and free. They are eyes he's seen reflected back at him in cop-car rearview mirrors, going a hundred miles an hour. When he was on the other side of the boot.

So much pain he can't tell what comes from where. Chris curls into a ball. He covers his head as best he can.

So this is what it's like, he thinks as the pain turns from rain into an ocean.

So this is what it's like, he thinks as he drowns.

Chapter Fifty-four

MAE

Los Angeles

The rain scrubs the smog from the skies as Mae drives and drives. Whole mountain ranges that were invisible yesterday rise around the city. How easily these giant things hide from us.

Mae calls Chris. No answer. She drives. She keeps her burner phone on her lap, afraid that Nevaeh will call her and she will miss it.

This poor little girl and all her silly dreams. This girl who pretends she's a flamingo. This girl who pretends she's not a hostage.

Mae drives. The rain slicks the roads. Three months' worth of oil and buildup mix with the rainwater. People drive slow. People crash into each other. Traffic snarls worse than ever.

Mae thinks about herself. This poor woman and all her silly dreams. This woman who pretends she is a bullet. This woman who pretends she could ever do enough good to make amends for everything she has aided and abetted.

Mae drives over the river. The rain has turned it angry. It rushes strong from bank to bank. She thinks of the tent city where she met Panko, underwater now, the citizens even more homeless than before. Panko somewhere in the Pinata District, just wanting to be heard, just wanting someone to say what happened to him was wrong.

She drives across the city, moving with traffic, not paying attention to where she goes. She drifts south on Fairfax, past the Petersen Automotive Museum, where Biggie Smalls was killed, through Little Ethiopia and into West Adams. Fairfax turns into La Cienega before she realizes where she is going.

She tries to fit a man like Kyser into her mind. The simple terror Parker felt for him. The inevitability of him.

She passes the Inglewood oil fields, the wells cranking endlessly. All this money being sucked from the earth. She wonders who owns it. She wonders why she never wondered before.

She drives into Crenshaw.

The opportunity zone.

Here the palm trees have thick beards of dried fronds. She passes Dulan's, a line down the block, this maddening fried-chicken-and-gravy smell drifting out of the door. Nipsey Hussle murals on building after building. The thin face, the big beard, the hooded eyes. Shot dead in front of his strip-mall store in the Crenshaw Opportunity Zone. This place they are going to destroy and rebuild.

She thinks about Parker, telling her about monsters. She thinks about the price she paid—the police files for the O'Dwyer case. What would Parker do with them? He wanted to prove he still had utility. He was looking for a bargain to strike. He'd told her everything about Kyser because he knew it didn't matter.

She pulls into the strip mall where Nipsey Hussle died. This man who thought there was such a thing as escape. A Black kid with braids in his hair and thick glasses stands in front of the parking lot. A white man stands next to a Tesla. He takes pictures of the building, the parking lot. He doesn't look at the people around him having their moment of silence.

She feels something snap clean inside her.

She calls the office. She asks Aneesa to transfer her to Cyrus's office.

"Cyrus Mitnick's office."

"Taylor, it's Mae."

"Oh hey, girl."

"Can I talk to Cyrus?"

"I don't have him right now. Maybe an hour?"

"Can you just take a message?"

"Of course."

"Tell him I'm resigning, effective immediately. You can trash anything in my office."

"Wait, are you serious?"

"Serious as oatmeal. There's a succulent on my window, you can have it if it's not dead yet."

She sits there with her phone in her lap. She feels this weightless *swoosh* in her belly.

Maybe she's flying. Maybe she's falling. It's hard to tell the difference until you hit the ground.

She's halfway home when her phone rings again. She picks it up—but it's the burner that's ringing.

Nevaeh, she thinks.

"Hello?"

This thick, jagged breathing.

"Mae . . ." His voice is mushy.

"Chris?"

"I didn't say nothing," he says. "I didn't say nothing but they hurt me so bad."

Chapter Fifty-five

CHRIS

Sixth Street

His skull feels swollen, a vise on his brain. His pulse throbs all over his body, in the roots of his loose teeth and in the pit of his gut. This dull pain with each heartbeat, like they had replaced his blood with gravel.

"Don't look at me." He can't stand the pity in her eyes.

"Shut up," she says, taking the washcloth to his face. The gentle way she brushes the dirt and blood from him makes the shame grow brighter. "Quit being such a man about it."

"I can do it myself," he says.

"Chris . . ." she says, and the sadness in her voice turns the shame white-hot, and he takes the washcloth too fast from her, and she turns away from him. He hates the weakness in himself so much. And he knows the way he is acting is weaker still but he can't stop himself, and he scrubs his face through the pain. When he is done the washcloth is gray and red. He hands it back to her. Under her glasses her eyes are huge and wet. He turns his head to the wall.

"You have to talk to me, Chris. You have to tell me what happened."

"It was the Dead Game Boys," he says. "BlackGuard came sniffing around them. And Woodcock didn't like it."

"And he wanted to know why," she says. "And they hurt you to find out."

"It's not about that. They hurt me because they were angry and scared," he says. "The questions just gave them the excuse."

"Wow," she says. "It sounds like they're all fucked-up with toxic masculinity. I wonder what that's like."

He laughs even though it hurts.

"Chris," she says. This time with strength. "You got your ass kicked. You have to let me help you."

"Okay," he says, turning back toward her. "Okay."

She helps him out of his clothes. The shoes are the hardest part. The way she has to yank them off sends shockwaves through him.

She leaves. He pisses sitting down. The water in the bowl turns pink.

She comes back in, turns on the shower. Steam fills up the room. She helps him into the tub. The water runs off him pink.

Everything hurts. He runs his tongue from tooth to tooth—nothing comes loose.

When he closes his eyes they are still in the room with him, still stomping.

She puts ointment on the scrapes. She goes all over his body. It's more intimate than anything they ever did in bed. It terrifies him. He lets it happen. She helps him put on sweatpants and a T-shirt. He doesn't tell her about the blood in the toilet bowl. He knows that he should. He's just too weak for now.

She leads him to her bed. It kicks up all these memories. That wild smile she'd get on her way to the bedroom. Her face looking up at him, her face without glasses, this almost unbelieving look in her eyes as she touched his face.

She puts him to bed now so gently. He can feel things scraping together inside him. He tries to hide it.

She takes him by the face. "Quit it," she says. But she smiles as she says it.

It hurts to lift his arm but he does it. He touches her face. He tries to figure out what to say. He drifts off to this yellow place.

"Chris."

He comes back to this world. He feels flattened by the pain. She's holding her burner phone.

"Nevaeh just called me. He's getting rid of her, Chris. He's trading her or something. I have to go get her, now or never."

He sits up. It's like he leaves his brain on the pillow. The world pans and zooms. He breathes in and out. He keeps whatever is in his stomach down.

"Chris—"

He takes a deep breath. He shoves the pain down the best he can.

"I'm coming too."

Chapter Fifty-six

MAE

Thai Town

Signs in three alphabets: English, Thai, Armenian. Bakeries, noodle joints, butcher shops.

There's a cinder-block wall of an Armenian auto shop—a mural on the cinder block, a forearm slashed open from wrist to elbow, the blood spelling out 1915—OUR WOUNDS WILL NEVER BE HEALED.

Mae thinks, *There's dried blood spilled everywhere— once you see it, you'll never stop.*

Nevaeh in her head: *He's taking me to some strip mall in East Hollywood. He told me to pack my stuff—his eyes are gone all dead on me.*

She drives with her hands at ten and two—Chris rides half-zombified in the shotgun seat. He's trying to hide how badly he's hurt—and in how many ways. He stares off into the middle distance, like he's watching a movie of his beating on a loop.

"Who do you think he's taking her to?" she asks to break his trance. His shoulders jump—the guilty look on his face tells her she was right.

"My bet is he knows someone with the Armenian mob. He's washing his hands of her. He's finally figured out this is all too big for him."

"What will they do with her?"

"From their end it's a simple transaction," Chris says. "They'll probably just call Algar and sell her straight up."

A red Jeep up ahead—swerving back and forth, trying to beat the traffic. She pulls herself closer to the windshield. She squints through the haze. She makes out the high ponytail of the girl sitting shotgun.

"Jesus, that's them," she says.

Chris leans over to look. He squints with his good eye. He nods. He unclips his seat belt—the car chimes to scold him.

"Chris. You have to let me take the lead."

"I'm good," he says.

He's not good.

The strip mall's lot is tiny, jammed up with lunch traffic from two Thai restaurants and an Armenian butcher shop. A big black Escalade sits across two handicapped spots in front of a discount smoke shop. Men with drab clothes and shaved heads stand around it. They look like gangsters, too on the nose to be real. *The hands of some other Beast,* Mae thinks. *Like looking in a funhouse mirror.*

"That's got to be them," she says.

The Jeep pulls into the lot, stops in front of the Escalade.

"Don't pull in," Chris says. "We'll be stuck."

She slides into the red zone by the curb. She says, "Stay here." She leaves the car running. She slams the door, killing Chris's *goddamn it.* Leaving the car is like jumping from a plane. The sudden airlock feel of entering the summer Los Angeles air.

Everything ripples in the noonday heat. Car horns and cursing fill the air. One of the men in black sees her coming—she can see his face register "no threat" and turn away.

"Nevaeh," she says. The girl turns to her, blinks, confused. Mae's been living with this girl for so long it's hard to remember the girl has never seen her face.

"Who the fuck are you?" Jesse asks. His voice deeper than she would have guessed. She'd pegged him as adenoidal and whiny. There's steel in him somewhere. That makes this moment worse.

"Nevaeh, it's me," Mae says, letting her accent slip back. Manipulating the girl even now, already. "The red leather raccoon."

Chris comes from behind her. He stands tall—he's good at hiding his wounds. His fucked-up face just makes him feel scarier.

The men in black look to Jesse, uneasy, like they think maybe this is some strange double cross.

"She's coming with us," Mae says.

"The fuck she is."

She holds out her hand to the girl.

The SUV back door swings open—an old man, hair from his ears, looks at them both. His eyes rake over her like Superman beams.

"Have you paid him?" Mae asks the old man. "If you haven't, you're not losing anything."

"Hey—" Jesse snarls.

A cop car rolls past on Sunset. Everyone freezes. This shock of recognition passes around the circle. This sudden moment of being on the same side. Everyone stands frozen until the cops roll out of sight.

"Come with us, Nevaeh," Mae says—loud enough to draw stares.

"Who the fuck are you?" Jesse yells. It's exactly what she wants him to do.

Make a scene.

People watch from a Thai joint, mouths hung open, yellow from khao soi.

"Come on, Nevaeh." Mae tries to pour something into her face, something deep and caring and maybe even true.

"I'm out," Nevaeh tells Jesse. She takes a step toward Mae. Jesse reaches out like he's going to stop her, but his heart isn't in it.

The Armenian mob guys look back to the old man like *what do we do?*

This is the moment.

Mae and the old man have a conversation with their eyes.

The old man leans back into his seat and shuts the door.

Everything unclenches. The men walk back into the smoke shop. Jesse looks around, not sure what just happened. All these different things playing across his face in flashes. Anger, fear, confusion. It locks him up.

"Fuck all the way off," Nevaeh tells him as she walks to Mae's car. Her belly has grown in the time since Mae last saw her, and her shirt is too small for her now.

Jesse stands there staring at them. Like maybe he's still going to make a move. He's still standing there as they drive away. Not even knowing he's free.

Chapter Fifty-seven

CHRIS

Hollywood / Westwood

The girl is in their back seat—real and unreal at the same time. She's lived in his mind for so long. It's the same feeling as meeting a famous person for the first time—your brain can't quite make sense that they are flesh and blood.

Mae takes Santa Monica into Hollywood. Chris twists to glance at the girl—pain pops up all over. The girl has her hand on the door handle. Her face says she's fifty-fifty on the idea of bolting.

"You got me now, y'all might as well tell me if you're really the bad guys." Nevaeh's voice has a heavy shitkicker twang to it.

"We're not with them." A little of Mae's white-trash twang is back in her voice—Chris wonders if she put it there on purpose. The plan says *make her trust us*.

Mae says, "This is Chris, by the way. We both want to help you."

Nevaeh snorts like *yeah right*—but she takes her hand off the handle. "Who fucked you up, anyway?"

"The cops," he says. His tongue too big in his mouth.

"You look like a cop."

"I was one."

"Shit. They turn on their own like everyone, huh?"

They drive past Hollywood High. Students mill around outside—Chris realizes he doesn't know what time it is—it must be afternoon. He'd been in and out of consciousness for fifteen hours.

Nevaeh leans forward.

"My bad little bitch is hungry. Let's hit that In-N-Out." She puts her hand to her swollen belly, flaps it like a puppet mouth and puts on this weird voice to say, "Feed me."

The drive-through line wraps around the building. Nevaeh studies the kids out front, students from Hollywood High—boys with skateboards and shaggy hair and wispy mustaches. She goes into her backpack and pulls out an energy drink. She pops it and chugs. She sees Chris eyeballing her through the rearview—she laughs at him.

"You really are a cop, aren't you?"

"Huh?"

"You're thinking, she's pregnant, she shouldn't be drinking that shit. What's going to happen, Little Miss Ride-or-Die is born with horns or some shit? All right by me. I'll put her horned ass on Instagram, shit. Make her rich and famous."

They get through the line, get their food, everyone hungry enough to eat in the car on the way to Mae's place. Chris drinks a milkshake—his jaw still aches too much for real food. The girl goes to town on her Double-Double animal style.

"So how well did you know Katherine?" she asks out of nowhere, her mouth full of food.

"A little," Mae says.

"Did you go to her funeral?"

"No."

"I wanted to go so bad. I cried and cried. Jesse said no. Jesse's bitch-made, swear to God. Scared of everybody. He said Eric's the reason everybody died. Is that true?"

"It's complicated," Mae says.

"I bet it isn't, really," the girl says. "I bet it's simple as shit. Rich people get what they want or they fuck shit up and then they get what they want. Roll credits."

The girl amazes him. He'd pictured this huddled shell-shocked girl. Even if this bravura is a lie, it's a lie that could become true.

"Katherine was cool," Nevaeh says. "She tried to take care of me. But I knew that guy Kevin was sus from jump. My mom should have named me Hot Potato the way I get passed around. From Mom to Grandma to the dance house to Katherine to Jesse to y'all."

"That's over," Mae says.

The girl cradles her belly with her hands.

"We'll see. What the hell are y'all planning on doing with the two of us?"

The plan says *keep it vague*.

"We're going to make you safe," Mae says. "We're going to make you rich and set you free."

The girl laughs.

"Shit. You sound like Katherine. That seem like a good sign to you?"

Sarah's place in Westwood smells like a fancy hotel—some mix of oils on the air. It has a yoga studio vibe—beige

333

pottery, nubby fabrics, lots of plants. It smells like the lobby of a boutique hotel. They give Nevaeh Sarah's bedroom.

"Guess this beats the Surfrider Inn," she says, flopping onto the bed. She puts her hand to her belly like a mouth again: "Baby love luxury."

Mae takes her stuff into the guest bedroom.

Chris's bad knee aches just looking at the couch.

"We can swap," Mae says.

"No, the couch is fine."

"I've got work to do," she says. "Can you watch her until dinner?"

"What the hell should I do with her?"

"I don't know. Let her watch TV. Don't be scared of her."

"I'm not—"

"She's a teenage girl, Chris. She's had something terrible happen to her. But she's not radioactive."

He thought he'd been hiding it better than that.

The girl falls in love with Mandy right away. She sits on the couch and lets the dog kiss her. She puts her hand to her belly, says in what she calls her bad-bitch voice, "Doggie and bad bitch best friends."

Mandy pads away to go get a drink of water. Nevaeh looks to Chris like *now what?*

The look sets off pure panic. Mae's right. The girl freaks him out. The baby in her belly—the unavoidable truth of what happened. The way her belly rolls and shifts in these earthquake waves as the baby moves. The wrongness of the pregnancy on her teenage frame.

Mae in his head: *Toughen the fuck up.*

He asks her, "Wanna learn how to toss a place?"

"What's that?"

"How to search a place for hidden stuff, the way a cop does."

"Hell yeah I do."

They walk around the apartment. Mandy follows.

"You have to see the world different," he says. "You look at a thing and your brain says *that's a chair*. Don't let it do that. See spaces and shapes. Don't think *chair*, think *object*. See it for what it really is, and you can find hiding places you can't even imagine."

They toss Sarah's bedroom for fun. He keeps Nevaeh away from the bedside table—Mae's friend deserves her privacy.

"Shit, I already looked," she says. "Lady who lives here treats herself right. *Bzzzzzzzz.*"

Chris can't help but laugh.

"You really used to be a cop?" she asks him.

"That a problem?"

"I mean, fuck cops. They just work for rich people or themselves."

She drum-rolls her hands on her belly. The baby inside her kicks or rolls, the belly moving. Chris winces. Nevaeh catches his face. "Boys always think everything's so delicate and they're so strong, but really it's the other way. My little bitch here is a badass. Weren't you a cop? Thought you all saw gross stuff all the time. What's the grossest thing you ever saw?"

Your friends with their skulls bashed in.

He almost says it, catches himself—why does he want to break through this girl's shell?

"Car crash," he says. "This low-slung sports car rear-ended a tractor trailer, took the driver's head clean off."

"No way." Her eyes bright and shining.

"For real," he says. "I was the one who found the head a block away."

"Gag."

Something inside Chris tells him what to say next.

"I dreamed about it. Like every night. And then, after a while, I didn't. After a while it was okay again."

She looks out the window—Westwood glows—it looks like the Los Angeles they put in the movies. She keeps her eyes on the city as she talks.

"Katherine's the only person I ever knew who died. I mean, I met the rest of them, Kevin and them, and their friend John the cops killed. But Katherine, I knew her. Before little bitch here rolled onto the scene, ItGirl had me interview to be Big Little's girlfriend—"

"Big Little?"

"The YouTuber. Come on, catch up."

"You interviewed to be his girlfriend? Like a job interview?"

"It's not that weird. The deal was, I would get my own YouTube channel, and I'd show up on his feed and we'd be all cute and shit, and that would get me a bunch of followers, do sponcon and all that, and Big Little, he'd get a cut of it, you know, for getting me famous. And I went to meet him, and he was so nice to me, but it was only about a half-inch deep, you know, like this front he was putting on, you could break it with a flick of your finger, and it scared me, it scared me bad. And I didn't want it. I didn't want to be his

336

fake girlfriend because I thought it would make me crazy, like living this whole fake life. I'd never had a boyfriend for real, you know? And Katherine was the one who told me I didn't have to do it. She was the only one. That's why I went to her. That's why she was the one I told."

Chris's heart thuds in his chest—Mae's right. He's terrified of this girl. The awfulness she carries in her head. And he wants to change the subject, wait for Mae.

But Mae in his head: *Toughen the fuck up*.

"And she was the one who told me it wasn't okay what Eric did. That there wasn't even a drop of blame on me. I was all fucked-up about it and I guess, real talk, I still am. But she told me I had choices. She told me I could stand up to all of them. And now she's dead."

"You're one tough cookie, anybody ever tell you that?"

She brushes her belly—gently this time.

"Didn't used to be. I got to, for her. I could have maybe gotten rid of her when she was a wad of gum, you know? But now she's a loaf of bread and I love her."

"Of course you do. She's your bad bitch."

Nevaeh smiles. She puts a hand to her belly.

"You're goddamn right."

Chapter Fifty-eight

MAE

Westwood / Studio City

She misses being on the inside. She misses knowing the dirt.
She has to fill in the gaps with her educated guesses.

She reads the papers like a sucker. She can feel the
Beast's fingerprints over every story she reads. She reads
about the Brad O'Dwyer case. A statement from Brad—
"With deep respect for law enforcement, the heroes who
risk everything for our great society, this arrest was made
in error and the facts of the case will totally exonerate
me"—is pure Cyrus verbiage.

Cyrus has done his job—the news stories play ambigu-
ous. It's not going to be enough to save O'Dwyer. Mae can
read the understory—someone in the DA's office is looking
to make a career by taking down a rich-kid firebomber. The
stories say items were recovered during a search of the
vehicle that connect O'Dwyer to the homeless camp bombings. They don't say what. Mae already knows, from the
files she sent Parker—instant ice packs, used to accelerate
the flames—the homeless camp bomber's signature.
Someone from the cops' side leaks Brad's chat room screen
grabs. A deep-fried Hitler meme done up in vaporwave
colors. A photo of brown people tagged THE GREAT

338

REPLACEMENT. Rants about PARASITES and SUCKING OUT THE POISON.

You should have seen what the firm deleted.

A few stories down, an accurate headline for once: POLITICAL ALLIES ABANDON BELEAGUERED WEST HOLLYWOOD POWER BROKER. Parker's story mentions a new lawyer—not Frederick Kim or another of the Beast's lawyers. It mentions an attempt to get a statement—but no one is talking for Parker anymore. He was right—he's been put on the ice floe.

Mae tries to figure the connection between the two cases. Why Parker thought the O'Dwyer police files could be useful to him. How he thought they could save him.

That had been the last deal with the devil, she promises herself. The very last one.

Something in her head: *You've made that promise before.*

She covers the guest bed with notebooks, her laptop, her phone. She sketches out a guerrilla war. She can hear Chris and Nevaeh laughing outside the door. His laugh is good and strong. This weird friendship she never would have guessed at. Mae imagines the pitch for a buddy-cop show, a dirty ex-cop with a fucked-up face and a redneck teen dancer with a powerful man's baby growing in her belly— and together they fight crime.

She gets back to her war plan. One thing makes it easy: she's playing against the ghost of herself. She knows every move the firm will make. She knows every way they've ever lost. She makes a list of every reporter who won't play ball, every publication that won't take a kill fee.

We have to play speed chess. They have a hierarchy—that makes them slow.

Kyser hangs at the back of her head. A billionaire—such a ridiculous idea. That a man could have that much power. Parker in her head: *At a certain point people stop being a* who *and start being a* why.

Mae thinks about the first principles of a cover-up that Dan taught her. She inverts them.

Everything they present is verifiable. The story tells itself.

They have the proof. They have DNA evidence, undeniable.

Dan's voice in her head: *Give them horror or give them heartstrings.*

I'm giving them both.

She can't sleep.

She knows why.

She walks out into the living room. She walks carefully, unsure of this place in the dark. She finds Chris sleeping on the couch. She touches him on the shoulder, gently, not sure if a bruise or scrape is under her hand. He rolls over—his eyes too alert—he hadn't been sleeping.

"I can't let you sleep out here."

"It's fine."

Boys are so dumb, she hears in Nevaeh's voice.

She takes his hand and gently pulls him into sitting. She sits on the couch. The salt of him in her nose. She doesn't shut down the feelings it kicks up. She lets them run riot. She puts her hand on his face.

"I don't want to let you sleep out here."

340

He finally gets it. She can see his smile in the dark.

They undress fast. Everything else they do slow. He is still so bruised.

They are both so bruised.

She wakes up early, thinking about manipulation.

The girl wants to be a star—so give her the star treatment.

Mae walks down the street, buys out a coffee shop's pastry display. Croissants: almond, chocolate, matcha. Kouign-amann and canelés.

She comes back in, walks cat-soft past Chris, still sleeping—she thinks about his hands in the dark.

She sets up breakfast on Sarah's patio. A shadow loops over her—a gull circles hungrily.

Nevaeh doesn't coo about the breakfast spread—she knows the star move is to take it for granted. She grabs a chocolate croissant and starts to scroll Instagram.

Nevaeh shows them a photo—a very famous woman carrying an infant, midriff exposed. Her abs like armor plating. Nevaeh lets out a sigh. "The big downside of my little bitch—my body is going to be weird forever. I gotta figure out how she bounced back from her baby bod so quick. Three weeks after the baby and she looks like this? It's not fair. I mean, I know it's like tummy tucks and all that, but still. That's what I want."

The rules say *give trust to get trust*.

"She's a client of the firm I used to work for," Mae says. "It's not surgery."

"Fuck off. Did you meet her?"

"I met her people. But I know her secret. You want to know it?"

"Hell yeah I want to know." She puts down her phone.

"She faked it."

Nevaeh leans forward. The voice in Mae's head cackles like *got her*.

"Say what, now? Faked what?"

"She was never really pregnant."

"What?"

"She hired a surrogate—a *gestational carrier*. A woman who lived in Mexico City—she had to sign a non-disclosure, diet-restriction clauses—the woman wasn't even able to take aspirin. And someone on her team thought it would be bad for her image, this woman carrying her baby for her, so they decided to fake a pregnancy."

"Nuh-uh," Nevaeh says. "You're lying. I saw her on the red carpet, that big-ass baby bump."

"They got her costume designer to work up some pads like drag queens wear. Foam rubber."

"Nuh-uh. You're lying. It would get out."

"A pap—a photographer—caught her slipping, he got a photo where you could see the foam insert. That's when they brought us in. We set up a kill fee for the pap. Five-figure catch-and-kill."

"That's wild." Mae can see the gleam in her eyes. The thing in Mae's head says *do it now*.

"It's easy if you know how. That's how we're going to help you."

The girl nods like *I'm listening*.

"We don't want to do anything illegal. We don't want to hide in the shadows. What we're going to do is sell your story. Sell it to everyone."

"Would I have to talk about it?"

Don't answer that yet.

"You're the objective correlative—what we call in the biz a bloody glove. Because your baby is DNA-proof—it's undeniable. We can prove what he did. We can stop him from doing it again."

"I don't want everybody to know."

"The papers won't publish your name or picture. We can protect you."

"Kevin and them said these people will hurt me. And look what happened to them. To Katherine."

"Once we have the DNA evidence, you're in the clear. Once it's out in the open, hurting you will only make it worse. This is the way to keep you safe."

The girl nods—neither a yes nor a no.

"We will get you money. First a lawyer. A book deal— We'll come up with a stage name for you. We'll sell the story to the papers, to the publishers, a podcast, movie rights. We'll make you rich, and we'll do it legally."

Mae doesn't say *They'll say horrible things about you. They'll say girls grow up so fast these days. They'll paint you as a Lolita. They'll say it's a cash grab.*

"Money to set you and the little bitch up right—you can skip the day job, work on your dancing or whatever. My early guess is we can get you a couple million all told."

She sees the question on the girl's face. She answers it before the girl can ask it.

343

"Our cut is ten percent. Like an agent."

"But I'd have to talk about it."

Build trust. Then use it.

"Yes."

"A lot?"

"I'll be with you every step of the way."

This long moment, her eyes locked with the girl's. She lets the girl see all of it—the fear and the questions but most of all the fighting.

The girl nods.

The girl says, "Okay."

The thing in Mae's head hoots in victory.

She only hates herself a little.

She's been inside the apartment for so long that Ventura Boulevard feels like a foreign country. Sushi joints and gastro-bistros line the strip.

Assistants from CBS Studios clog the coffee shop line, making the baristas label each oat milk half-caf latte with somebody's name, apologizing for not being able to tip with their bosses' cards.

She gets her cold brew and sits near the front, facing the door. She recognizes Marla from a byline photo—she's wearing denim on denim under an old army jacket. Marla catches her glance and nods like *I see you*. She gets this smile on her face, like Mae's exactly who she guessed she would be. She comes in at speed. She sits down without taking her jacket off.

"Can I get you something?" Mae asks.

"The Marcus Brottman story," Marla says. "My editor

killed it. He called it inflammatory."

"We called in a head shot," Mae says. "When we have to go over a reporter's head to the publisher. Bosses are always amenable to not rocking the boat—bosses understand solidarity. That's why I want to talk to you."

"So what, you going to try and pitch solidarity to me? After fucking up my story?"

"I tendered my resignation from Mitnick & Associates yesterday."

Marla folds her arms like *I'm not giving you a thing yet*.

"That makes sense. You would have kept a better lid on the Hannah Heard story."

"What Hannah Heard story?"

"Wow, you really are out. She got fired off that feature yesterday. She went MIA, came back all sorts of messed up. They cut bait."

This weird pang of guilt—Mae pushes it aside.

"I have a new client," Mae says. "This is off the books. I'm trusting you here. It's okay if you don't trust me back. But my new client is fourteen years old. She is six months pregnant. The father of the child is in his fifties. And he's a power player in the Industry."

Marla's face doesn't move. She can't hide what happens to her eyes, though.

"Tell me more about the man."

"He's been involved with tween television for years."

"You're talking about Eric Algar."

"You've heard."

"Everybody's heard."

"I always say, nobody talks but everybody whispers."

"That's right. Because of people like you."

"I told you, I quit the firm. They don't know I'm doing this."

"They will."

"All I need is a head start. That's where you come in."

"You're trying to play both sides—position yourself as some sort of crusader? But you're still getting paid, right?"

"A lot of people have been hurt by this. It's worse than you can imagine."

"Does this have something to do with Dan Hennigan's death?"

"Yes."

"How?"

"Stay focused on the girl. Stay focused on what you can prove."

"She'll talk?"

"She'll talk. Not exclusively. We do a big interview with someone else—"

"You make your money with the big interview—"

"And then you come in with the deep reporting, the hard facts. There's a lot of people involved. You don't have any idea how big this is. How far back or wide you can take it."

Marla says, "I thought MeToo got rid of all this."

"You're joking."

"Of course I am."

Marla studies her for a beat. Mae can feel the cracks forming. "Why'd you come to me?"

"Because when I was at the firm you were the biggest pain in my ass. Because I think you're a fighter like me. And that's what this girl needs. As many fighters as she can get."

Marla smiles—Mae knows she was right to pick her.

"Meet the girl," Mae says. "Then you'll understand."

"I'll meet her. But if I catch wind that this is a ratfuck, I'll blow up your whole world."

Mae says, "Right back at you."

Chapter Fifty-nine

CHRIS

Westwood

The girl talks like she's been waiting her whole life for someone to listen to her.

They sit in a loose circle. A practice session before the interview with Marla tomorrow. She told Chris, "I need you there. I need her to be able to talk about it in front of anyone."

Chris doesn't want to be there.

He thinks back to when he was the tough one.

The girl talks about dancing. Classes at the Broken Arrow YMCA, learning routines from online videos. She talks about K-pop, these names Chris can't follow, these idols she loves who keep dying.

She talks about dance lessons, feet bleeding, forcing purple bruised toes into dance shoes, never crying, never letting any of it show. The girls who pushed themselves until they puked and the girls who puked to stay thin.

She talks about girls who rose above—the girls she wanted to be, stealing hairs from their scrunchies, eating a strand, knowing it was crazy but needing their magic and not knowing any spells.

She talks about how Katherine was a goddess, a goddess of sweat and stink who didn't shave the hair under her arms. Katherine taught them to love their own stink. It made dancing so much easier when you could welcome the fact that you were an animal.

She talks about the photo shoots, icing moles, plucking stray hairs, some girls getting Botox shots alongside acne pills.

She talks about Carol Goodman, this cosmic force. The one who everyone wanted to please. Who scared even Katherine. This magical person who could pick you up with her red right hand and lift you up among the stars.

She talks about the whispers. The soda pop parties. Eric Algar—a real-life Hollywood producer, who could put you in a show and make you famous for real.

She talks about how he came to dance class. How his eyes set off ancient lizard fears in her. How excited she was when she got the first invitation.

She talks about the soda pop parties. How the kids vied for them—that there would be boys there, boys from the schools, the ones you saw at auditions, the ones you followed online. Everybody knew what Eric could do, what he'd done for Hannah and Brad and so many others. Hot dogs and video games and splashing in the pool. How she was torn. About the boys, who scared her. And the men, who scared her more. She talked about how there were levels. How nothing happened all at once. She talked about how some of the girls couldn't go, the ones who lived with their moms, mostly, the ones whose moms cared about what they did. How those girls hated their moms. How her friend Madison was so angry the first time Nevaeh got to go. Because there wasn't anybody to say no for Nevaeh. How the first time you went it was exactly what you thought it was. But then you went back, and they let you in the house. And how the party inside the house was different. She talked about vodka and little purple pills and how loud a man can laugh.

Mae shows her a picture of Kyser. She nods. She says, "He was there." She says other names too, some of them famous. Men connected by power. Connected by hunger.

Sometimes she doesn't talk at all. The three of them just sit there. Chris holds himself down in his chair. He knows that as awful as this is, of the three of them it is by far the least awful for him. He tries best he can to just bear witness.

She talks about a room with no windows, and she talks about Eric Algar. And when she talks about the worst of it, it is in the third person. Like she wasn't even in the room. Like it knocked her soul clear out of her body.

Chapter Sixty

CHRIS

Westwood

They get up early. They let Nevaeh sleep. She earned it, and she has a hard day coming.

They plan their route to West Adams, where Marla keeps a private office. Chris checks Mae's car for a tracker. He goes outside to check the street. Santa Ana winds hiss. He scans the cars outside the building, looking for possible stakeouts. He sees nothing. It doesn't make him feel better.

He comes back into the apartment to find Mae sitting on the floor in the living room, like maybe she'd fallen. She is holding her phone with both hands.

"What's wrong?"

She does not look up at his question. Her only motion the scrolling of her thumb.

"Mae? Mae, what's wrong?"

"Hannah Heard is dead." Her voice numb.

"What do you mean?"

"It's on Truth or Dare. Hannah is dead. Chris, she's the one . . . she's the one who told me about Algar." She keeps scrolling. "They don't say it outright but they're hinting OD. But of course they would, wouldn't they?"

"You don't think . . ."

"Of course I do. You don't think they would do it?"

"I think they would do anything. That doesn't mean they did."

She puts down her phone so carefully. Everything about her so controlled. He comes to her and crouches down next to her on the floor. She looks at him with wet eyes. He takes her into his arms and lies back, looking up at the ceiling while she lies on his chest.

"Do you remember her?" she asks. "Like whenever the first time you saw her? Do you remember how she shined?"

"Yeah. Some movie where she's a soccer player or something. But she was really good."

"She shined," Mae says. They lie there while something huge passes through her. He holds her through it.

"I can call someone at the sheriff's department," he says. "I know someone in homicide over there who owes me a favor from way back. She'll either help me and I'll get an answer, or she won't and that's our answer."

"You have to do it now. Before the cover-up gels."

"Yeah. I will. You should reschedule with Marla."

She sits up fast.

"No. We've got to get her story on the record. We can't let them stop us. Especially not now." Her voice is strong again. Somebody else might even be fooled by it.

"Okay," Chris says. "You take her to Marla. I'll look into Hannah. Look, I know you knew her. I'm sorry."

She lets out this dark laugh.

"Yeah," Mae says. "So am I."

Chapter Sixty-one

MAE

West Adams

Mae checks her face in the rearview. She can see her throat doing funny little things. She swallows hard. She gets it to stop. Her hands at ten and two. They don't shake.

The rules of the game say *keep your mask on tight.*

Hannah with her face blue and swollen. Hannah on the couch with Katherine and Janice.

She shifts the rearview to check out traffic behind them. She doesn't see any black SUVs.

A wind gust rocks the hatchback—Santa Anas blow hot and heavy.

She says, "If you don't know what to say, don't say anything. They'll use silence as a club sometimes."

Nevaeh says, "You already said that." She gets back to chewing the skin around her nails.

They ran through the story until Nevaeh could do it with a steady voice. Until Mae felt poisoned forever by the girl's words.

Mae says, "Don't lie. You're not on the witness stand. You don't have to say anything you don't want to say."

"I don't want to say anything at all. I don't want people to know what happened. I don't want people to look at me."

"Nobody is going to identify you. It's against the law."

"Yeah, and everybody obeys the law."

Something in Mae's head says *you don't have to do this.*

The phone rings through the car speakers. Chris. She pops in an earphone so Nevaeh can't hear.

"Hey." Keeping her voice sane for the girl.

"Hey. You doing all right?"

"What did you find out?"

"It was suicide. An intentional OD."

"You sure?"

"She left a video on her phone."

"They could have made—"

"I saw it. They didn't."

She can hear it in his voice. She asks anyway.

"Was it bad?"

He hesitates. He says, "Yeah."

"Okay."

"But look, I'm sure. She killed herself."

"Even if she did, she didn't."

She glances over, sees Nevaeh in her own little world. The girl feels eyes on her, looks over and smiles. Mae smiles back.

Keep your mask on tight.

Marla rents a guest house in West Adams for her private office. It's a *getting-to-know-you* meeting. It's a point of no return. You let a secret out into the world and it's not yours anymore.

This close to the West Adams strip, parking is tough. Mae sees a just-barely spot she thinks she can squeeze into.

She tries to parallel park. The spot's too tight or her nerves are too shot. She stomps the brake too hard. Nevaeh looks at her, annoyed.

"You trying to kill me?" Nevaeh curls her lip, a cartoon gesture. Mae almost loses it. She pulls back out, looks behind her—can't see damage on the other car's bumper.

"We're on the run now," Nevaeh says as Mae pulls out and heads down the street.

Something in her head says *just keep going.*

They take a right onto Smiley. Traffic is easier. Mae takes deep breaths, tries to dampen her nerves. She can hear Hannah's sobs through a trailer door. She scans for parking spots—her eyes pass two black SUVs. A man in a black T-shirt and black pants, almost a uniform. His eyes meet hers. This shock of recognition he can't hide.

BlackGuard.

She keeps her hands at ten and two. They do not shake. The man stands there as she cruises by.

Nevaeh says, "There's a spot."

Mae ignores her. She checks the rearview. The man jumps into the SUV. She does not let herself gulp the air. She takes another right as the SUV pulls out a half block behind her.

Her brain screams theories. It coughs up scenarios—men in black grabbing the girl, leaving Mae on the side of the road. Worse images, flashes of guns, flashes of blood.

The hard fact at the center: *They know.*

She pushes the thoughts away. She forces herself into the now.

"Mae, a goddamn elephant could fit there. Mae. Mae!"

She reaches Adams as the light turns yellow. She guns it into a hard left.

"What's going on? What's wrong?"

The fear in Nevaeh's voice jabs Mae—it almost lets the stampede out. She go-kart–dodges lanes. She scans her rearview. The SUV hasn't made it onto Adams yet. She hands Nevaeh her phone.

"Call Marla," she says. She gets into the right lane, inches toward La Cienega.

Nevaeh does as she's told. The phone connects to the car speakers. The call goes straight to voicemail.

"Kill it."

The call goes dead. Mae checks her rearview. A black SUV four cars back, trying to get over into the next lane.

"Try it again."

The SUV gets into the next lane, crawls one car length closer.

Nevaeh hits dial again.

The other lane jams.

The call goes straight to voicemail.

Mae pulls up to the intersection at La Cienega. The black SUV is four car lengths behind and fighting to get back into her lane.

Nevaeh kills the call without being told.

She says, "That's bad. Right? That's bad."

"It isn't good." She thinks she hides the fear well. Her voice doesn't crack at all.

Mae sees a gap in traffic, pulls a fast right onto La Cienega. The entrance to the 10 up ahead. Mae weighs it— she heads toward the freeway. She gets lucky—she cruises straight to the eastbound entrance. She runs the gridlock light. One last glance back—no black SUV.

Please please please don't be jammed.

Nevaeh rocks herself, patting her stomach—good girl, brave girl.

It's not a total standstill. She sees a gap, gets into the flow. She gets lost in the morass.

"Should I call Chris?"

"Yeah. Wait, no. Go to my contacts. Find 'the firm' and call it."

All it will take is three seconds of his voice. I'll know.

The phone rings through the car speakers.

"Mitnick & Associates."

"Cyrus's office, please." Her voice is calm, flawless.

The call transfers. Mae scans the rearview. She can't spot a black SUV.

"Cyrus Mitnick's office."

"Hey, Taylor. It's Mae."

"How you been? Enjoying retirement?"

"Oh, you bet, I've taken up cross-stitch and watching MSNBC and commenting under newspaper articles online, it's really fulfilling." The banter comes out so easy, like inside her head there isn't this thing shrieking *they know they know they know.*

Taylor laughs. He says, "If you can't beat them, join them, I guess."

The forms obeyed, Mae asks him, "Is Cyrus around?"

"Sorry, I don't have him. He's in the conference room with Ward Parker."

She drives in silence.

"Mae. Did I lose you?"

"Sorry, no. You said Ward Parker? He's a client of the firm again?"

"I mean, I guess? He came in yesterday, had a closed-door with Cyrus, and now they've got the whole team in there with him." He cast his voice low like *don't share this part*. "They did a conference call with Mr. DePaulo at BlackGuard. I think they're all helping out with that opportunity zone project somehow?"

She finishes the conversation on autopilot.

Parker helping on the opportunity zone project—he asked for Brad O'Dwyer's police files. Her brain does this brutal math. The connection, so obvious, how had she missed it?

Parker's problem and O'Dwyer's problem—homeless people the common factor. Parker wanted the police files for the homeless camp bomber—he wants the details of the case that the public doesn't know. Panko is in a homeless camp. The homeless camp bomber behind bars—and the Beast wants to clear him. The police hiding details—ice-pack accelerants and bomb parts. It all clicks together—Parker's plan, perfect in its economy, perfect in its sickness.

She gave Parker his lever.

She has Nevaeh call Chris. The phone rings.

"What's up?"

"They know."

"Are you sure?"

"There was a BlackGuard goon parked around the corner. I saw him, he saw us. We're out, we're safe. We have to meet someplace."

"Don't say where. Assume they're listening right now."

"The first place," Mae says. "Do you know what I mean?"

"Of course I do. It will take me a while."

"I need you to do something first. The guy I told you about, Panko?"

"The homeless guy?"

"I need you to find him. He's staying in the Pinata District, in some tent city. Can you just find him, right away, and move him someplace, anyplace? Bring him with you if you have to."

"You going to tell me why?"

"I think we'll be saving his life. The rest will have to wait."

"Okay. Got it."

"I'll text you a description. And thanks."

"You bet."

"We're going to be okay." She's not sure if she means it as a statement or a question.

"Of course we are. See you at the first place."

"Please find him."

Chapter Sixty-two

CHRIS

Pinata District

Downtown traffic snarls at rush hour. The office buildings dump out, mad dashes for the freeways that lock up the streets. Chris cuts south, heading against traffic. The wind roars at his back. Both sides of the streets are lined with wholesale party supply shops. They close early— hundreds of pinatas sit behind cages pulled down over display windows.

Chris passes a guy selling elotes packing up for the day. The tent cities still bustle. Chris scans homeless folk—Mae's description of Panko eliminates most of them. Chris scans for a whiteboy with dreadlocks. In his head he sees Hannah Heard's smartphone video suicide note. This wreck of a woman with a fistful of pills, the other hand a middle finger to the camera, the ghost of the person she was supposed to be trapped behind her eyes.

This litany of anger.

Look what you've done to me.

She doesn't name names. She says it to the whole world.

Look what you've done to me.

He finds a place to park on Olympic. He hits the street— smell that wave of trash and piss. Sweat pops up instantly.

The greedy wind drinks it. He walks past a pot dispensary. A scary smell leaks out: this place cooks shatter—high-grade hash cooked with butane.

He looks around, building a grid in his head. He's going to have to go tent to tent. He starts with a big group of tents, maybe fifty in the parking lot of an abandoned warehouse.

Look what you've done to me.

A guy kneels on the cracked macadam, patching a bike tire. He glances at Chris. Chris takes out his phone.

"Hey," he says. "I'm looking for—"

The flash blinds him. The BLAST a fist of noise knocking him into blackness. When he comes back, the world is on fire. He's on his hands and knees. SCREAMS from the tent city where the blast came from.

Fire splashes the tent city. A gust of wind funnels down Olympic. Clouds of flames splash down the block.

Chris has this nightmare thought: The weed store full of butane tanks. A building-sized bomb ready to go off.

He runs toward the flames.

People run the other way. People trample one another. People help one another up. He looks for Panko. He watches the fire spread faster than he ever could have guessed. Sparks spread through the cages into the pinata stores. Rats spill out in belching waves from the alleys. They pour from holes in the buildings. They come out bleeding from their tails where the rats behind them tried to chew their way out.

A body on the ground. Chris turns it over—the shrapnel wound on the neck hideous red against the ash-blackened skin.

A human candle runs from the flames. Chris sees it fall. Chris moves fast through a swarm of sparks—pinatas burn fast. The stores are tinderboxes. Sirens join the choir of crackles and screams. He reaches the burning body. Fire gobbles up the man's hoodie. He is tall. He has whiteboy dreadlocks. He fits Mae's description. Nothing moves on him but the flames.

Look what you've done to me.

Chris stands over Panko's corpse. The air is full of smoke and sirens and helicopter roars. On Olympic fire trucks roll through in force. The pinata store next to the weed shop is already in full flame. He looks to the alley next to the dispensary. A man with a white buzz cut dressed in combat black watches the flames. It is Matt Matilla, the BlackGuard enforcer—mirrored sunglasses give him eyes of fire.

The facts of what happened come to Chris, simple and plain.

A SCREAM behind Chris. A tent in the heart of the firestorm, its sides bulging from desperate, useless hands inside it struggling to get out.

Chris turns away from Matilla. He moves into the flaming tent city. This guy in a stained army jacket on the ground. This guy slapping flames off his legs. Something explodes behind Chris. The blast shoves him over. He falls on top of the burning guy's legs. It smothers the flames. Chris's shirt smolders against him. He yanks them both up. The man punches Chris in blind panic. Red pain as his nose SNAPS. He shoves the man toward clean air. He says something like *run* but his voice is a useless croak.

He looks behind him. Mattila is gone. He's only a fist on someone else's arm anyway.

Chris moves deeper into the fire. The air like broken glass in his lungs. His foot kicks flesh and bone—a piece of someone torn by the blast. Death is here. All around him, and working itself inside him too. This hellfire smell of burning plastic and trash.

The burning tent rocks and squirms. Someone inside screams a prayer. Chris gets to work. He pulls apart the tent opening. Flames snake up his arms. He puts his hands into the mouth of the flap. Things sizzle. He pulls with all of himself. Things rip.

The woman inside the tent struggles out of the hole as soon as it's big enough. Her lips are blue. She muffles a moan as the fire kisses her. She pushes his burning hands away. He holds them to the sky. Rivulets of melted plastic run across them. He tells them to shut. They don't.

The woman runs. Chris turns to follow. The world pans and zooms. He falls. The air is cleaner on the ground. He crawls on knees and elbows, his burned palms turned up to the sky like a supplicant.

It is so hot the air blurs. A gust of hot wind funnels through the alley—a tornado of flame dances. The fire is inside the dispensary now. The air is full of smoke and sirens and helicopter roars. Chris lies back among the dead. Something *POP-POP-POP*s inside the dispensary. Chris burrows facedown into the trash. The rotten-egg smell of butane floods the alley. Firemen run for their lives.

This crazy long moment of total peace and calm.

EXPLOSION.

PART SIX

The Dead Flag Blues

Chapter Sixty-three

MAE

Pinata District / Dignity Health / Westwood

Time gets chopped up for her now. She bobs in and out between worlds.

She's at the scene, searching for survivors—see a fireman's helmet on the curb, melted.

She's wandering through the trauma ward—see a woman wearing shattered glasses, shards of glass embedded in her eyes.

She's at Sarah's apartment, scrolling the news.

Sources within the LAPD confirmed unmistakable similarities between the fire and the rash of homeless encampment attacks that have plagued Los Angeles through the summer, calling into question the arrest of Brad O'Dwyer, who, according to his Instagram feed, was in Ojai with his family during the attack.

She's at the scene, toxic smoke in her nose, spitting black. See a melted fireman's helmet spilled on the black sidewalk.

She's at the hospital—hear someone ask a victim *do you know who the president is?*

She hears someone yell *yellow-tag her.*

She's at home watching a narrative come together.

Frederick Kim, O'Dwyer's attorney, issued a statement calling for the DA to drop the charges. "These were details known only to LAPD and the attacker, so it's clear that the real assailant is still on the loose," Kim said. "My client should be exonerated immediately."

She's at the scene—see this half-blasted dispensary, looking like it took a rocket hit.

She's in the trauma ward—see a nurse run past with a gleam in her eye—Mae recognizes it instantly. She's seen it in her own eyes enough times. The joy of being where the action is.

She sits on Sarah's couch, scrolling, scrolling. Mae can see Cyrus all over it. She's able to guess which reporters each outlet will use before she sees the stories. The same ones she would have called. The same phrases keep showing up in different reporters' mouths.

Unmistakable similarities.

Calls into question.

She's at the scene, watching ambulances weave around news vans. She's running to her car to follow them. Calling Marla. No answer. She googles her, thinking they'll find her body. Instead she sees Marla's new byline—she spent the day doing a sit-down with a woman who is beyond famous, far beyond the reach of Mitnick and the firm. An exclusive one-on-one. Mae thinks about the kind of strings they'd have to pull to dangle that in front of her. The weight of the powers lining up against them.

She's at the hospital, looking through a window into a dark room. Chris with bandages, Chris with tubes. His hands wrapped in gauze. She opens the door. She goes inside. Some nurse yells behind her. She stands at the foot of the bed. She says his name. His eyes flutter open. They see her. They know her. They have aged a hundred years.

She's on the couch, watching news footage, faces of victims as the dead get names. Panko doesn't make the cut. The channel switches over to its lead story—the tragic end of Hannah Heard. The story comes easy—it's one of their favorites. The beautiful girl eaten by her own demons.

Mae counts the dead. Dan, John, Katherine, Kevin, Loto, Tony, Janice, Hannah, and Panko. All the other people who died in the fire.

All victims of the Beast, one way or another.

Mae's teeth draw blood inside her mouth. She swallows it. She swears on it.

Chapter Sixty-four

MAE

Coldwater Canyon / West Hollywood

She drives up Mulholland into Coldwater. She turns off her phone. She checks for a GPS tracker the way Chris taught her. She doesn't want a record of going there.

Her purse on the shotgun seat yawns—the pistol like a flat black tongue. The cursed gun that Chris stole from Kevin's sock drawer.

I am a bullet.

This cold part of Mae games out the way Parker outplayed her. Parker must have brought the plan to the Beast. It's a twofer. It's good for Parker: Panko dead, his charges dropped. It's good for the Beast: another Bum Bomber attack creates reasonable doubt for Brad O'Dwyer. DA will have to drop the charges now. They can't claim it's a copycat—the evidence they left behind wasn't known to the public.

She guesses they'll announce the okay on the Revitalization Complex in the next week or so. O'Dwyer's vote change will be attributed to new reports or a developing situation on the ground.

She guesses the charges against Parker will be dropped quietly. Maybe Reza Nuri at the *LA Times* will notice, and maybe even his editors will let him write the story: *Ward*

Parker accuser among the dead at the Pinata Street Fire.
The article won't get close to hinting at the truth. Some
people will maybe put two and two together. They'll
whisper. But it won't matter.

The story of poor Hannah Heard will drift into
Hollywood legend. This beautiful girl who wrecked herself.
No one else will take the blame.

*One of their best moves is getting to control what we
call violence and what we don't.*

She drives across the spine of the hills.

The gun is cold. The gun is heavy—they are always
heavier than she remembers.

She doesn't let herself think about what she might or
might not do.

They don't get to win every time. They just don't.

She comes up this curving road that wraps around a
steep hillside covered in dried sage. On the top of the hill, a
fence, and behind it, a massive house. The road winds
around to the front of Algar's house.

The house, the kind that was fancy and new in the
eighties, glass and flat white walls.

Black SUVs in front. Men in black polo shirts. The front
door hangs open. The men are walking an iron cage with a
motor at the bottom into the house.

It's a burn cage—a fast way to destroy things. It's a
BlackGuard cleaning service. They're sanitizing his place of
evidence.

All Mae and Chris have done is shown the Beast a few
weak spots in its armor and given it the tools it needed to
solve a few problems.

She drives by slow. A man in a black polo shirt turns to look at her. She does not stop. She drives down the hills, choking the steering wheel.

"Oh, it's you." Parker is dressed in a purple button-down, the sleeves rolled up. He smells expensive. In her head she comes at him with her chewed-up nails like claws. But in the real she stands there and smiles.

"Expecting someone else?"

Her purse strap digs into her shoulder. The gun growing heavier by the second.

"I'm expecting company. This will have to be brief. There's not much to say, though, is there?"

"You used me."

"Of course I did."

"People are dead."

"Victims of the homeless camp bomber."

"Victims of BlackGuard. And you."

"And you, my dear."

Mae puts her hand into the purse. The gun is even colder now—she must be burning up.

"I didn't know why you wanted those files. I didn't know what you were asking for."

"You only knew it would get you what you wanted. So you did it. I really can sympathize."

It is the golden hour and everything around them glows with a secret light. All this obscene beauty everywhere she looks.

"So everything goes back to the way it was?"

"I hope that Brad O'Dwyer will find a more acceptable means of relieving his tensions. And I suspect that his father will find himself suddenly more amenable to the opportunity zone deal. But other than that, yes."

"They always win."

"That's their defining characteristic, girl."

"Don't call me that." She can't keep the rage out of her voice.

"You have to think about it as a game, Mae. You can't let it get to you like this."

"You don't even know how many people are dead because of you."

"Mae. Why would I ever want to know that?"

She looks away—the setting sun fills her eyes so when she turns back toward him he is bathed in purple.

"How can you live with it?"

"The serenity prayer," Parker says. "You've got to learn what you can change and make peace with what you can't."

He looks over her shoulder. Mae follows the gaze. A man stands on the sidewalk, looking at them, unsure. He is young and his clothes are cheap. He looks at the two of them, then back to his phone, like he's checking something.

"Billy?" Parker asks. The man looks back up. "You're in the right place."

Parker smiles. He steps aside to leave the doorway open.

"He's a monster," Mae says to the man. "He's a killer. Run for your fucking life. I'm not joking."

The man brushes past Mae and goes inside.

Parker says, "That was childish. You know, I do care about them. Love them, even. But I understand if you don't believe me."

She squeezes the grip of the pistol so tightly that the palm of her hand stings. But she knows she's not going to pull it.

"Goodbye, Mae. I hope you keep your head about this. I like you. I didn't tell them that you asked about Kyser. I can see why you were so dear to Dan. You are a fighter. But fighting a battle you can't win will destroy you, one way or another."

Parker steps into the house.

Mae drives back to Sarah's place trying to partition her rage. How much of it is at them. How much of it is aimed at herself.

She counts the dead again. Dan, John, Katherine, Kevin, Loto, Tony, Janice, Hannah, and Panko. All the other people who died in the fire.

All victims of the Beast, one way or another.

All her victims, one way or another.

The apartment is dark. Nevaeh sits mesmerized by *The Kingdom of Dreams,* her face painted blue and purple by the monitor light. She asks, "Is Chris going to be okay?"

"He's beat up pretty bad, but he's going to live. He should be good for visitors tomorrow."

"I want to see him."

"We can't risk taking you out, not now. But I'll tell him you said *hi*."

"What are we going to do?" The girl's voice is thick with old tears. Mandy presses her head against her. Seeing it almost tears down all the beams inside Mae.

She says, "Hide, for now."

Nevaeh puts her hand to her belly like a mouth: "Story of my fucking life."

"You better pack," Mae says. "I found us a hotel over in Sherman Oaks. It's better to keep moving."

Nevaeh asks, "Is this all because of Eric?"

Mae says *no*.

Mae says *yes*.

Mae says *it's complicated*.

She says *it's all connected*.

She doesn't say *it's all connected by me*.

Her phone rings. The firm. She swallows. She answers.

"Hey, girl."

"Hey, Taylor."

"Hope you're living your best life. It's been crazy around here. I'm reaching out to set a lunch with you and Helen— she said you'd know what it was regarding?"

A long beat passes.

"Yeah. Yeah, I do."

"They want to set it ASAP. How is tomorrow looking for you?"

"You know what? Turns out I'm free."

Chapter Sixty-five

MAE

Beverly Hills

The steak house is dark, cold. Primal cuts hang from meat hooks behind the hostess. Helen booked a table upstairs. The upstairs is Beverly Hills' number one high-class call-girl pickup spot—even at lunchtime. Helen sending a message—meeting among the other whores, with a meat-hook backdrop.

The hostess seats her. The area by the bar is full of two-seat tables. Half of them have young women sitting at them, either with a client or waiting by themselves. The ones with clients all wear the same smile, broad and unmoving. This rosewater scent fills the air—they all tend toward the same perfume. She orders a mescal on the rocks to kill jitters. This overwhelming babble. All these laughing men, clinking and laughing and voice over voice over voice. Lips greasy from fat, stained purple from wine, smacking on hunks of meat, bowls of fries, spoons of lobster mac and cheese.

They eat and eat and eat because they've never been hungry.

Helen comes up the stairs sans hostess. It takes her minutes to cross the room, shaking hands with half the tables. She laughs with her mouth wide open—her teeth are so white. She finally reaches Mae's table. She reaches out like she's expecting a hug. When Mae doesn't rise, Helen pivots into sitting without missing a beat.

"It's so good to see you, Mae."

She lets that sit there as the waiter arrives with Mae's drink. Helen orders a pinot noir and a sparkling water.

The waiter leaves.

Helen nods at the girls at their tables.

"So pretty. They've been working girls out of here for forty years."

Mae hears the UNSAID part: *Nothing in this town ever changes.*

Mae says, "I don't know how the men get past knowing it's all a lie."

"I think it's the lie that makes it beautiful for them."

They sit in the babble until Helen's drink arrives.

"This is a business lunch," Helen says as the waitress leaves. "Two business associates. That's what we are, right? Business associates."

"We were."

"And maybe will be again. This is a friendly lunch, Mae, but Cyrus did insist on something at the top. He wants me to remind you that all of the nondisclosures and non-disparagement clauses you agreed to when you signed your contract with the firm are still in effect and will still be enforced."

"I've kept my mouth shut about firm business."

"I know. It's one of the things that gives me hope."

"Hope for what?"

"That we can bring you back in from the cold. The firm has mistreated you. I see now, I've allowed internalized

377

misogyny to color my attitudes toward you. Woman-to-woman, we need to stand together. We want to work with you. We want to bring this girl's story to the world."

"Bullshit."

"Rebels make the best leaders. You put robots in the field, they can't think on their feet. We need people who can show initiative. And your activities since Dan's death show you have that in spades. And the truth is, a rebel is only a rebel until the real payday arrives. And that's what is waiting for you. If you make a show of good faith, then we are prepared to reward you handsomely to come back aboard."

"I can't do this anymore."

"I think you can. When we learned that you were going to sell the story, we knew we could work with you."

"It wasn't about the money—"

"And yet it was there, wasn't it? Isn't that funny? After all, you could have just leaked the story on the internet."

"You know as well as I do, if a story doesn't have muscle behind it, then nothing really happens. Viral for a day and then *poof*, gone. Nobody goes down unless somebody wants them to go down."

"You know, I'm on the board of Women Speaking Out—"

"Do you know how gross that is?"

"What do you want me to say? That the world won't be the world anymore? You got a little bit of leverage, just this one moment. But this is it. You're inside or outside. And you don't want to be outside. You know this is what you want. You don't want to be out in the wilderness. You want your share of money and power, you want control. Come on.

You are selling the girl's story because you're angry. You know that she'll get chewed up and spit out, and you don't care. You know what the media will do—"

"With your help."

"Please. You're one of us. You didn't get where you were by accident. We've known it since Brad Cherry."

Dan in her head: *Nobody needed to tell you what to do. You already had it in you.*

Helen says, "We all understand each other better now. We can get back to work. Dan always said you were a fighter. We'll give you a fight. We'll secure Nevaeh's fortune. This is what winning looks like for you. This is the carrot, dear."

"So what's the stick? I'll be killed?"

"Oh the drama of it all. Mae, the whole point of this lunch is *you aren't someone who has to be killed*. You are one of us. Come home."

Mae looks at Helen and sees herself in ten years, in fifteen years, richer and richer, Botox to keep the mask on tight, yoga-thin, everything clean, everything nice, her teeth whiter and whiter every year, and everything dark or nasty buried someplace deep. Dirtier and dirtier, nastier and nastier, buried deeper and deeper. Her teeth like rows of skulls in her mouth.

Mae asks, "What about Eric Algar? If you're helping sell Nevaeh's story, you can't be helping him anymore. Aren't you scared of what he'll say if he gets taken down?"

The UNSAID part hangs there—until Mae decides, *fuck UNSAID*: "Aren't you worried he'll tell the world about Kyser and his friends?"

This little twitch of one of Helen's eyelids—otherwise

379

the mask stays firm and tight. When she talks her voice is yoga-teacher calm:

"It's probably best if you don't let me know how much you know."

"That's exactly my point, Helen. Eric knows everything. He won't go down quietly."

"He was big in this town once. All those tweener shows, my step-daughter loves them. And the whole time he was using the place as his own little playpen. These poor girls as his little harem. He got nervous yesterday—there's something in the air, isn't there?" Helen lets this hang there. "So he orders some cleaners to his place. I'm not talking about Merry Maids. These cleaners were from BlackGuard. Four lawyers, four BlackGuard security officers, a pyro cage—a portable incinerator—to burn anything they found."

Mae almost says *I saw it*. But there's no reason to give anything away.

Helen says, "There was so much child pornography in his house. They cleaned all day. They found photos, CD-ROMS with girls' names on them. Or men's names. All of it went in the pyro cage. They were so worried about missing something that they put his whole laptop in the cage and burned it up. He had the whole place wired for sound and video. Bedrooms, bathrooms. Pinhole cameras, mics. They pulled it all."

"Why are you telling me this?"

"Eric Algar's friends have come to understand that he may not be worth protecting."

This silent thunderclap between them.

Mae picks up her drink. She's afraid her hand will shake. But it doesn't.

Somebody donkey-laughs a few tables over. The sound of it blooms gooseflesh all over Mae as the waiter walks up.

"Have you made any decisions?" the waiter asks.

Helen looks to Mae.

"Have you?"

Chapter Sixty-six

CHRIS

Dignity Health

He wakes up to find her there.

She says, "They're going to kill him."

He floats weightless, clouds of morphine in his blood. His hands two suns of pain at the end of his arms. The doctors say the pain is good—it means the nerves are still there.

"Hey, Mae."

She says, "They're pulling the plug on Eric Algar. Because of us. We made them realize how sloppy he'd gotten. How many messes he's been making. So they're going to kill him. BlackGuard, probably. Tonight, probably."

"Fine." The word hurts coming out. His voice is cracked and smoke-stained.

"It ought to feel good," Mae says. "But it doesn't. They can stain anything, can't they? Even justice."

"He deserves it."

She waves that away.

"It's just another limited hangout. They just don't want him to talk. He has dirt on all these men. Kyser and his friends. So they will kill him and then they want to work with us to sell Nevaeh's story. Once it can't hurt the Beast. ItGirl will keep on, the parties will keep on. Parker,

Kyser, the firm, BlackGuard, all of it will go on. I will go on."

"I know you will."

"They shouldn't get to always win."

"You can't take on the whole world. And this will stop Eric from hurting another girl. Isn't that enough? Isn't it time to let go?"

"We were going to fight them. We were going to start our own firm and we were going to fight them together."

He coughs so his voice won't sound so torn. He knows he can't begin to tell her the ways the fire has changed him. He lifts his useless wrapped hands as best he can.

"I can't be a fist anymore. I don't want to be one, anyhow. I'm done with all of it. I'll make do on my pension, or I'll find something else. We can just leave, go someplace cheaper. Leave and live a life someplace. Find something good to do. Not fighting bad. Doing something good. Me and you. I'd be happy. Would you?"

He can see the answer in her eyes. But he keeps going anyway.

"I love you," he says. And it's worth it for what it does to her face. Those big eyes.

She says, "Of course you do. And I love you too. You know that, right?"

She doesn't say *but it's not enough.* Instead, she says, "There's this thing I say. To myself. *I am a bullet.* And I am."

"You don't have to be—"

"They didn't change me or corrupt me. They just saw what I was good for and they used it. It's not going to change. But maybe I can point the gun another way."

He searches his brain for the words that could change all this. But he's fuzzy with dope and words don't change the world anyway. She gets up and walks across the room. She kisses him—his burned lips ache. He presses into it anyway, tries to show her, tries to make her understand. She breaks it off. Her big eyes are sad. Underneath the sadness, fire. She looks to his hands.

"Does it hurt?"

"The drugs take care of it. No pain at all."

She buys it—maybe he can lie to her after all. Or maybe she just needs to believe it.

She says, "Goodbye, Chris."

He doesn't say anything at all.

Chapter Sixty-seven

MAE

Sherman Oaks / Glendale / Los Angeles / Beverly Hills / Venice

The next morning at the hotel, Mae gets up early. She checks on Nevaeh sleeping in the next bed and then slips off to the bank. She checks for another tracker, checks the rearview as she drives—she knows she'll be doing it the rest of her life. No matter how this plays out, the invisible walls have fallen down around her, and they'll never come back up.

Once she makes clear what she's trying to do, the teller gets the manager.

They count out fifty thousand dollars. It's bulkier than Mae thought it would be. She barely fits it in the duffel bag. It's heavy on her shoulder—she wears it across her chest like a bandolier.

When she gets back to the hotel, she wakes Nevaeh. She talks soft. She says *get packed*.

"We moving again?"

"Something like that."

She loads Mandy in the back of her car alongside Nevaeh's carry-on. They drive in silence to Glendale. They pass an Armenian judo studio, a vintage video game warehouse. They turn in to the Glendale train station.

Nevaeh reads the sign. She says, "What the shit?"

Mae hands her a printed-out ticket. Nevaeh squints at it. She looks at Mae—the betrayal is written in Day-Glo ink.

"Nuh-uh."

"We aren't going to argue about this."

"I don't want to go back there."

"You have to go where somebody cares about you. That's what you need most of all."

"You said it's not safe for me."

"After tonight, no one is going to care about you or your little rider. No one is going to come after you. You're free."

"My grandma, she can't—"

Mae reaches behind her and pulls out the duffel bag.

"This will help."

Nevaeh looks inside—it knocks the words right out of her.

Mae says, "I'm sorry. I'm sorry about all of this. It's as much as I can give. I'll give more when I can. Your grandma knows you're coming. You're a smart girl. Be smart. Be smart about the money. You have this baby, you do whatever you can for her. You tell anybody you want about what happened to you, or you don't tell anybody if you don't want to. That's not up to me."

"I don't want to go back."

"You want to dance, dance. Just go someplace and be a human being and dance. You use the money to get as safe as you can. You want to dance, just dance. Don't be a bullet. Be a human being."

Nevaeh's sobs come on like a summer storm. Mae chews her lip. Her mask comes off. She reaches for Nevaeh. Nevaeh pushes her hands away.

"You said I was done being a hot potato. You said you'd keep me safe."

"I was using you," Mae says. "I was trying to make you be the hero so I could feel good about myself. You don't have to be the hero."

Nevaeh sobs.

"You're just like them. You say you're not but you are. You're just like them."

"I am. But maybe I can be something else."

Nevaeh flips her the bird as she walks inside the train station. Mae doesn't blame her one bit.

She drives west against traffic. She takes surface streets.

She drives under the train tracks and into Atwater Village, past the wet health restaurant—

WE CANNOT ESCAPE THE VIOLENCE INHERENT IN EATING

—and over the LA River, looking down on the tent city where she first met Panko—

I just want to be free and clean. I don't know why it's so hard.

—and Glendale Boulevard turns into Hyperion, and Mae passes the reservoir, empty and dry now, this big hole, people in yoga pants and shorts jogging, walking, past the dog park and down into Silver Lake, past the restaurant where Tze first told her about Katherine—

I don't know if this is the place for you.

Why?

You asked about right and wrong.

She lets herself forget she's driving and lets herself think. She drives under the 101—dozens of tents built up under the overpass, ash stains on the concrete, one of the first places Brad O'Dwyer firebombed—and into Koreatown. She takes a right on Western, past the noodle shop where she and Chris sat scarfing banchan while up in the hills the BlackGuard wet-work crew murdered Katherine and Loto and the rest of them.

So many dead. She knows their names.

Kyser doesn't, she's sure.

She takes a right on Sixth Street as Koreatown turns to Hancock Park and all its old mansions, past the mayor's mansion, and into Mid-City, past the tar pits, and then she drives past her place, but she doesn't stop, and then Sixth Street ends, and she's in Beverly Hills, on Wilshire, far to the south of the hotel where Dan first shattered her world, and then where the world shattered Dan—

Find your lever.

—and she heads through Beverly Hills, past the lawyer district, where Chris had told her Acker's office is. She drives just south of the steak house where she and Helen met among the working girls—

This is what winning looks like for you.

—and she keeps driving west, driving south, Olympic to Hauser to Venice Boulevard, past Cuban restaurants and In-N-Outs, past the millions of people everywhere, food trucks and minivans, landscapers with tired eyes and truck beds full of lawn mowers.

Her phone buzzes: news alert. A headline on the *LA*

Times app: CITY COUNCIL PASSES OPPORTUNITY ZONE BOND ISSUE 8–7. COUNCILMAN O'DWYER THE SWING VOTE.

They always win.

All these bulletproof people. BlackGuard teams and Dead Game Boys. Parker and Acker and Helen Poirier and Mitnick, and above them all these men with more money than a brain can understand.

At a certain point people stop being a who *and start being a* why.

She cuts into Venice. She rolls down the windows. Mandy sticks her head out to taste the ocean air.

She gets to Venice just in time to watch the Pacific swallow the sun, like it does every night and always will until the end of everything. And she sits there on the dirty sand, grit between her sandal and her foot. She tries to think back to when the ocean changed for her, when coming west got to be too much of a hassle, when the ocean stopped being this rolling infinity and instead became about parking and screaming kids and drunk folks and sand in her shoes. She thinks about Chris; she remembers standing here in the dark with him watching choppers circle and news vans swarm, remembers his hand holding the back of her head as they kissed.

This feeling washes over her, this soul-deep wish to just go back to when she could walk through this burning world without noticing it's on fire. Go back to dinners, go back to drinks. What would have happened if she'd left it alone? If she'd let Dan's death be what everyone wanted it to be—the end of a story. If she'd just gone on with her life. And maybe she would have carried this thing with her the rest of her life, this secret pain, this secret worry, but who doesn't? Who doesn't know their lives are built on top of bones? Who doesn't carry inside them that it's only brutal violence keeping this world afloat? Child slaves making our clothes, factory farms turning animals to slurry, nations of plastic floating in the ocean. Is she supposed to yank all that down too? Just her? She thinks about Parker, how he talked about the secret sun, the thing hanging in the middle of the sky that we cannot look at. And you can keep looking at it all until it burns away everything or you can turn your eyes away.

The ocean lies out in front of her and shows her how small she really is. Less than a flea on the back of the world. She thinks about fleas, how small they are but how much their bites sting.

The idea comes to her fully formed. Like something born from a pit inside her.

It's not Dan's voice in her head anymore. Dan's dead. This voice is pure Mae:

If you want to sell a story, you have to give them heartstrings.

Or give them horror.

She pulls her laptop from its case in the back seat. She opens a file, and she begins to write.

Chapter Sixty-eight

MAE

Coldwater Canyon

The night is perfect. She drives with the windows down. Somewhere below her, coyotes sing desperate love songs.

She takes the last left. The road creeps around a curve up a steep hill—Eric Algar's place twenty feet straight up the scrub-covered hill. She parks her car there below the house. She gets out and walks up the curving road until she stands in front of his house. She finds a place for herself in the shadows in the scrub of a neighbor's yard. She waits a long time. The air is ticklish against her skin. Her purse strap digs into her shoulder. Every breath is a ball of lightning.

She keeps her phone in her hand. She keeps a number cued, ready to dial.

When it happens, it happens so fast.

A black SUV cruises past—Mae can't see shapes through the tinted windows. The doors open before it comes to a full stop. Men unload from the back seat. They wear all black. They wear black masks. Guns and tools strapped all over.

Mae steps out into the night—she thinks about the first person to take a spacewalk. She hits the dial button. The men in black combatglide to Eric's front door. One of them gets to work on the lock.

The phone rings and rings.

Come on, you bastard . . .

They pop the front door open.

The call picks up. This froggy voice says, "Hello?"

"Eric Algar. There are men coming in your house. They are coming to kill you. Go out the back now."

The men go inside, unfastening their guns.

"What the hell—"

"Go out the back now," she says.

"Is this some kind of joke?"

"If you don't listen to me you will die."

"Go to hell." He hangs up. She considers just letting the wet-work team kill him.

But that would be letting them win.

So she needs to convince him they're coming. Dan told her long ago—*It's not that the truth isn't important. It just doesn't matter.* Sometimes you need to paint a picture. Show them a bloody glove.

She reaches into her purse. She raises Kevin Baldassare's pistol in her hand. She aims at the moon. She tries to shoot it out of the sky.

GUNSHOTS fill the air. The echoes bounce off the hills, make her an army.

The shots echo off the hills. The men in the house return fire blindly. Flashes and GUNSHOTS spill through the front door. Mae runs down the hill. She can't hear the slap of her feet through the never-ending BOOM. She starts the engine and pulls a U-turn to face down the hill. She peeks up at the back of Algar's house.

Maybe they'll get him.

This big shadow rises in the night. A shape scrambling over the fence. Algar comes down the hill face-first. He tumbles through dried scrub. He comes out the other side and onto the road. This fear and fury in his eyes.

This monster in her headlights.

Mae's foot thinks about stomping the gas. Flattening him, knocking his life out of his body.

Justice. But not enough of it.

Instead she pulls alongside him. She rolls down her window and looks at him. Just another Hollywood face, puffy with age and excess, you see the type everywhere.

There is so much she wants to say. So much she wants to do.

She says, "It was Kyser. It was Kyser and BlackGuard and all of them."

His eyes narrow. She watches him understand.

She says, "You only have one weapon against them. Your secrets."

She imagines pointing the gun at his head. She saved two bullets just in case. How good it would feel to wipe his face off his skull.

Instead she says, "Now, run, you stupid son of a bitch."

She stomps the gas.

Behind her he picks himself up and begins to run into the dark.

She drives down the hills far enough to get a signal. She links her phone to her laptop. She opens up the Word document she wrote at the ocean. Years of secrets, years of lies.

She makes the email list next. Reporters and gossip columnists and bloggers. She thinks about nondisclosures and non-disparagement clauses. She presses send. She violates them all. She burns herself to the ground.

She shuts the laptop. She drives back up in the hills among the giant houses. She knows now she'll never own one.

All across town, people are opening emails. They're spreading them around. Whispering. Talking.

The Beast slouches all around town. Kyser in his mansion, standing under his slashed Picasso. Parker spreading money and pain around. Mitnick and Helen filling the world with noise so you cannot hear the whispers. All of them will wake tomorrow a little more scared than they are now.

There is a battle coming. She won't win but she will fight.

It scares her.

It juices her more.

Somewhere below her, Eric Algar runs. Now he knows who his enemies are. He can hurt them. In her head he is a torch she has thrown down the hill. All these little sparks spreading through the night. Most won't catch. But maybe one will. She rolls down her windows. Jasmine on the breeze. Under it, smoke. It is still fire season. This city begs to burn.

Acknowledgments

Thanks to Steph Cha, John Covarrubias, Nadine Nettmann, and Ken Woodruff for their thoughts on early drafts of this book. Special thanks to Andrew Bain for his essential aid in shaping the story.